A CRUISE CONTROL NOVEL

the Wedding

SIÂN CEINWEN

ISBN: 978-0-6483621-9-7 (Hardcover)

Front cover image by Mark Reid at authorpackages.com.
Book design by Lorna Reid at authorpackages.com.

This book is dedicated to Ally, for staying with me through the ups and downs of writing it. Thank you for all of the long nights spent in discussion about Harrison and Heather...and mostly, Sebastian. Never say never.

~JUNE~

HARRISON FLETCHER TURNS 30!

Our favorite bass guitarist is turning the big 3-0 on the 6th, and if you can get yourself an invitation to his party, you'll be lucky. Rumor has it that everyone who's anyone is going to be there! Gabriel, Sebastian, and Hayden, the other three members of Cruise Control, are a given, but who else will come to celebrate? We're pretty confident that the guest list will include April Conway, who is a close friend of the band and sang a duet with Gabriel on their last album.

Inside sources tell us that the party will be wildly extravagant, and Harrison's longtime girlfriend, Heather, has gone all out for her man's big day. Who knows how she finds the time, we're pretty sure she's busy preparing Serenity's collection for the fashion line's upcoming debut at New York Fashion Week!

Anyway, happy birthday, Harrison! If you need anyone to come and celebrate with you, we're free!

Chapter 1

GOSSIP, GIRL

Despite herself, Heather York was nervous. She was well and truly used to events like the one she was going to tonight. It would be full of the rich and famous, no doubt. Her boyfriend, Harrison, was turning thirty today, and he happened to be a member of the world's biggest rock band, Cruise Control. Somehow, his management team had convinced them that throwing a massive party would be a brilliant way to celebrate, as well as being good publicity for the band.

Heather loved a good party as much as the next person, but Harrison was very different from her. She'd started out planning something far more low-key for him, but at some point, this whole evening had gotten out of Heather's control. His team had taken over the entire thing, including the guest list, so Heather didn't even really know who would be there now. At least she'd managed to book her favorite stylists, Tristan and Jessica, to do her hair and makeup for tonight, and they were in fine form.

"How do you guys do it?" She asked them, amazed as always at the transformation they were performing on her.

"Lots of practice," Jessica replied with a smile.

"So, I have to ask, Heather, is it true?" Tristan looked

embarrassed about his question.

Heather immediately knew what he was talking about; the news had broken a week ago that Cruise Control's lead singer, Gabriel Knight, had broken up with his girlfriend, Elena Kass, after she was spotted kissing another man at a party.

"Yeah, they've broken up." Heather shrugged.

"She cheated on him? I always thought she was so nice!" Jessica seemed surprised.

Heather was uncomfortable with gossiping. Gabriel was one of her closest friends, and she didn't want to be the one spreading his news.

"No, it was mutual. They broke up a few days before those pictures were taken."

What she didn't tell them was that they'd mostly broken up because Gabriel had been pining after his ex-girlfriend. Heather sighed involuntarily as Ariana Chamberlain came into her memory. Both Tristan and Jessica had met Ariana once before—they'd done her hair and makeup before the 2018 Grammys, where the band had won so many awards that people still joked about it two years later.

The next day, though, Ariana had walked out on them without saying goodbye to anyone but Gabriel and Sebastian. This still hurt Heather. She understood Gabriel, of course, but while she loved Sebastian, it was she who had been Ariana's best friend. Sure, Sebastian was the one who went down to her hotel room to confront her that day, but Heather had called and sent messages for two weeks straight with no reply before Gabriel asked her to stop and give Ariana some space.

It had been so hard for the remainder of that tour. Gabriel could barely function enough to perform, do the interviews they were required to do, or attend any events. Heather had been devastated as well; it had been awful. She hadn't realized how much she'd come to rely on Ariana's presence in her daily life until it was no longer there. Harrison had been an incredible source of support for her, though. He'd been her rock. Eventually, life had returned to some semblance of normality for them all.

That was, of course, until the last night of their most recent tour. As part of his grieving process, Gabriel had written an album called *Heart Wide Open* that was pretty amazing and had garnered the band their second Album of the Year Grammy Award this year. Cruise Control always started and ended their tours in their hometown of Chicago. Everyone had been shocked when Ariana showed up at the meet and greet after the final show of the tour.

None of them were particularly clear on the details of what had happened, but he and Elena had done some counseling. They were still dating for a while after, but everyone in the band could tell it was strained between them. Next thing you know, Elena was out kissing some stranger, and Gabriel was assuring them that he was fine with it because they'd split up, and he was back with Ariana. She supposed that Ariana would be at the party tonight. Perhaps that was a part of her nerves.

Heather wasn't sure she wanted to see Ariana again. She loved Gabriel, but she thought he was making a big mistake by letting her back into his life. Thank goodness the band wasn't touring at the moment—aside from events like tonight, Heather wouldn't have to see Ariana that much.

At that moment, Tristan and Jessica finished up what they were doing and spun Heather to look in the mirror and admire their handiwork. As usual, they had done a fantastic job. Her hair was in a beautiful updo with a braided headband, and her makeup featured smoky eye shadow and bright pink lipstick.

"I love it, darlings. You're absolute miracle workers." Heather smiled at them both.

"Thanks, babe." Tristan grinned.

He gave her a hug, and Jessica followed suit before they exchanged goodbyes and left her home. Heather headed out of the living area and walked into their bedroom to find Harrison relaxing on their bed, his hair wet but wearing only a towel around his waist and looking at his phone. He looked up as she entered the room.

"Hey there, angel," he said, and she could see the desire in his eyes.

"Hi honey, you haven't started getting ready yet?"

He dropped his phone next to him, got up from the bed, came over to her, and slipped his arms around her waist.

"We've got plenty of time before we have to leave," he whispered in her ear before nipping her ear lobe with his teeth.

"Mmmmm," she replied, "except that we don't. We have to leave in about thirty minutes, as much as I would love to stay here and fuck you silly."

He grinned wickedly at her and let her go.

"Okay, we'll go to this party, then I'll come back here, and I'll unwrap my present."

He ran his gaze over her body, and she felt herself getting aroused. Ten years and he still had the ability to make her dizzy with longing. Particularly when she knew that it would be many hours before she would get to scratch this itch.

She stepped forward so that they were close again, reached between them, and slipped her hand under his towel. She looked in his eyes as she did so and heard him groan as she placed her hand over his growing erection. Slowly rubbing it up and down, she felt him become completely hard.

"I promise," she said, continuing to rub him and looking into his eyes, "to give you the best birthday present ever when we get home."

As she continued to stroke him, he reached into her robe to start playing with her breasts. Heather was wet now and thought that it didn't really matter if they were a little bit late, then Harrison's phone alarm started going off.

"Sorry, angel. We'll have to continue this later. That alarm is to let me know that the car will be here in exactly thirty minutes."

He removed his hand from her robe; she sighed and dropped her hand as he pulled her close for a hug and kissed her neck. Harrison was a stickler for timing; he'd never really stand for arriving somewhere late, even if the reason was for them to have sex.

She followed him into their walk-in closet. He dropped his towel in the laundry hamper, and Heather had a chance to approve of his toned ass before he began pulling on underwear and the tuxedo that he was wearing that night. She smirked as she noticed that he was still semi-hard.

Heather pulled off the robe she was wearing to reveal the lingerie that she'd had on underneath it. Harrison caught sight of her, and his eyes went dark appreciatively.

"I know that look, honey, we don't have time."

"Happy birthday to me." He pulled a sad face, and she laughed.

Heather grabbed the glittery, pastel, rainbow dress that she'd designed specifically for tonight. It had taken her hours of drawing and sewing, but she was incredibly pleased with the result. It had a long sleeve on her left arm but was asymmetrically off the shoulder on her right side. It was flared slightly and stopped about two inches above her knee. She unzipped it carefully, stepped into it and pulled it up before walking over to Harrison and turning her back to him.

"Can you zip me up, please?"

"Happily."

He leisurely traced the length of her neck softly with his fingers, and Heather shivered as he continued drawing them down her back to just above where her panties were, and the zip started. He zipped up the dress, kissed her neck softly, and said, "There you go."

"Thanks," she said, breathless with desire.

She grabbed a pair of pale pink heels and slipped them on. Assessing her reflection in the full-length mirror in front of her, she decided to add a shimmering, silver clutch to her ensemble. Happy with her outfit, she turned in time to see Harrison standing up from tying his shoes, looking devastatingly handsome.

Even with heels on, standing at six feet and three inches, he was taller than her. His body was muscular, and he filled out his tuxedo beautifully. He had gorgeous, bronze hair, and his chocolate brown eyes seared into hers. She could tell that he, too, was appreciating the view in front of him.

"I'm the luckiest man in the world." He smiled at her.

"Of course, you are, honey."

He grinned widely at her, came toward her, and took her hand as they walked back into their bedroom and then out into their living room. He got them each a drink from their bar, and they chatted while they waited for their car to arrive.

"Is Gabriel bringing Ariana tonight?" she asked him.

"I'm pretty sure he is."

"Have you seen her yet?"

"No, Gabriel was at the meeting we had on Tuesday, and we all went to lunch afterward, but Ariana was at work, of course."

"I think he's making a huge mistake. There, I said it. Now you have to stop me from saying it to him tonight." She cringed at him.

"Heather, he's happy. Isn't that enough?"

"Come on, Harrison, have you forgotten what it was like for him? For me?" A pang of hurt struck her unexpectedly as she remembered how badly Ariana had hurt them, "Because I haven't. I've still got all the messages I sent to her in my phone. Message after message that she didn't bother replying to. I saw where I stood with her two years ago and, fine, whatever, at least I know my place now."

Harrison put down the glass of whiskey that he was drinking and came over to her, wrapping his arms around her tightly. As usual, the sense of homecoming that it gave her was soothing. This was the place in the world that she fit perfectly. With Harrison.

"I haven't forgotten what it was like, angel. I was sad, too, and I hate to see you upset. I just think that Gabriel is a big boy and he can make his own choices."

Heather sighed and hugged him tighter. It didn't matter that Ariana had ditched their friendship; it didn't matter that Gabriel and Ariana were back together now. All that mattered was that Harrison was here. Through everything in her life, she had him by her side, and that's what counted.

"Okay, I promise to play nicely." She smiled up at him.

"That's all I ask."

Harrison got a message that their car had arrived. He quickly washed their glasses in the sink at the bar, and they went downstairs to get in the sleek, black limousine that was waiting for them. She settled in beside him, and he placed his arm around her shoulders.

They drove to the event in relative silence, enjoying this peaceful time together before arriving at what was surely going to be an eventful night.

Chapter 2

A RED CARPET AFFAIR

When they got to the venue, they were third in a line of limousines waiting to drop people off for the party, with one more at the front that was just now pulling away. In front of the entrance was a red carpet, roped off at the sides, behind which paparazzi waited for pictures and videos of the celebrity guests that were arriving. Within their group, they referred to this as running The Gauntlet.

The limousine two cars in front of them pulled forward in line with the red carpet. The driver got out, walked around, and opened the door, through which Gabriel stepped out. He turned back to the car and held out his hand. Heather could see him ask a question, and then a slim, pale arm appeared through the car door, grabbed his hand, and out of the car stepped Ariana. Heather gasped in surprise and turned to Harrison to check that he was seeing the same thing. His look of shock told her that he was.

"Well, that's something I wasn't expecting," Heather announced.

"I'll be honest, me either."

When Gabriel and Ariana were together, one of her biggest hang-ups was about not wanting to be seen with him in public.

She'd had a real fear of anyone seeing her or getting a photo of them together. Heather had lost count of the number of ways they'd all had to compensate for Ariana's issues. At the time, she hadn't minded doing it because Ariana was her friend, and she cared for her deeply. Looking back at it now, Heather resented it but recognized that her opinion was colored by her feelings about the way Ariana had left.

Gabriel and Ariana were making their way up the red carpet, glacially slowly. The media was going bananas, cameras were constantly flashing, and they were both answering the questions being thrown their way from every different direction. Heather couldn't hear what they were being asked, of course, but she could imagine. It was the first time these two were being seen in public together, and that, combined with Gabriel's very recent breakup, would make for perfect tabloid fodder for who knew how long.

The car in front of theirs was driving away now, and it was their turn to get out. When their driver opened their door, Heather carefully stepped out and onto the red carpet. Harrison did the same, thanking their driver for his service as he did so, and stood next to Heather, putting his arm around her waist.

They walked forward slowly; the cameras were blinding, but Heather posed for the pictures that were being taken of them as they were also asked questions by the media.

"Harrison, happy birthday! How are you feeling?"

"Great, thanks."

"Harrison! What do you think of Gabriel's new girlfriend?" another reporter chimed in.

"She's very nice."

"Have you met her?"

"Yes."

"Heather! Have you met her?"

Heather worked hard to make sure that there was no expression on her face that might betray any of her inner conflict toward Ariana.

"Yes, I have."

"Do you like her?"

Well, fuck, she should've expected that question. She glanced over to where Gabriel and Ariana were standing, barely fifty feet away, and was shocked to meet Ariana's gaze. Heather quickly looked back at the reporter who'd asked her the question.

"He seems very happy," she said, choosing her words carefully.

It would've been easier to just lie to the press, but she'd done so much lying for Ariana in the past, she wasn't going to do it now. At the same time, she also wasn't going to give the press any kind of bullshit drama story to print.

They moved along the red carpet faster than Gabriel and Ariana, due to the intense interest in the new couple. So, it wasn't long before Heather and Harrison caught up to them. Harrison squeezed her waist with his arm for comfort, and Heather took a deep breath.

Okay, so this was going to be it. Their reunion was about to be held in front of the worldwide press, brilliant. Heather pasted a big smile on her face as both couples turned to face each other.

"Hi!" Gabriel said with a massive grin on his face and possibly looking happier than Heather had ever seen him.

He was holding Ariana's hand, and Heather felt guilty for harboring resentment toward Ariana. Harrison was right; Gabriel seemed more at peace now than he did even when they were together before. There was a quality between them that hadn't been there in the past, and she couldn't quite put her finger on what it was.

"Hey, Gabriel." Harrison smiled back at him. "Hey, Ariana."

"Hi, guys."

Ariana seemed nervous. Heather was acutely aware of the camera flashes going off constantly, capturing every millisecond of their interaction. Microphones and video cameras were pointed toward them, trying to ensure that everything they were saying was also recorded.

"Hey, darling," Heather said, stepping forward to give Gabriel an air kiss on his cheek, then turned to her ex-friend, "hello, Ariana."

She gave her a brief hug, and Ariana tensed slightly. Heather knew that it was petty not to call her 'darling' as well; it was the pet name she gave all her friends. They weren't friends anymore, though, and it would be disingenuous to act as though they were.

To the media, nothing strange had happened, but all four people standing in their group knew exactly what had just occurred. Heather had drawn a line in the sand; she would accept that Ariana was Gabriel's girlfriend again. She was even proud of her for making the momentous step of walking The Gauntlet with Gabriel, but she had no personal interest in a friendship with Ariana Chamberlain.

"Can we get a photo of you together?" one of the reporters called.

They dutifully turned and stood next to one another. Heather fought the urge to move as they faced the cameras so that she wouldn't be next to Ariana, but everything that was said or done would be analyzed online worldwide, so it wasn't worth the hassle.

She smiled widely at the cameras and put her arm around behind Ariana and drew her closer. Ariana was standing quite stiffly, but Heather forced herself to relax. In her mind's eye, she could see the picture they were presenting to the world, and no doubt it would look good—two handsome rock stars and two beautiful women, all happy and in love. Ariana's robin-egg blue dress would look lovely next to Heather's rainbow dress, and Gabriel was as dashing as ever with his golden hair and blue eyes, looking as he always did, like a Norse god.

Harrison nodded goodbye to the other couple, who had started answering more questions now, and they started moving toward the venue once again. In Heather's estimation, roughly fifty percent of the questions they were being asked tonight were centered on Gabriel and Ariana. She let Harrison field most of them and gave the same standard answer about Gabriel's happiness when she was asked directly about them.

Eventually, they reached the safety of the venue entrance, and Heather breathed a sigh of relief as they entered. They made their way to a second set of doors that opened into a massive nightclub. As soon as the doors were open, they were assaulted with different sights and sounds. The music was pounding, there was smoke rolling across a packed dance floor, and there was a massive screen scrolling through pictures of Harrison, with huge "HAPPY 30TH BIRTHDAY, HARRISON!" banners throughout the room and balloons with his face on them.

The balloons were so incredibly tacky that Heather loathed knowing that everyone would attribute this to her doing. As expected, the room was full of everyone from politicians to A-list celebrities and many in between. She could feel Harrison tense up as he, too, took in the scene before them. Heather felt guilty that she hadn't been more forceful about throwing the party she'd known he would've wanted. Hopefully, if they just had a few drinks, they'd be able to relax and try to enjoy themselves here.

Heather and Harrison made their way to the bar, amidst greetings from other partygoers and eventually got their hands on some drinks. They headed to a roped-off VIP section up a set of stairs where she could see the remaining two members of Cruise Control, Hayden and Sebastian, were sitting and talking with some other people there.

Sebastian had his arm around a tall, thin, redheaded woman, and she was staring at him with wide eyes, completely enraptured by everything he was saying. He was rarely seen without a woman by his side—he was tall, extremely well-built, and had black hair. That, combined with his fame and magnetic personality, meant that Sebastian often had his pick of women. He was completely unashamed of the way he would sleep with women and never contact them again.

Heather couldn't understand why they would go for it, but she supposed the lure of his celebrity could be very seductive to the women who followed the group around. Hayden was also tall and muscular, with brown hair and eyes, but while he also had plenty of flirtatious interactions with the guys and girls who followed the band, he was much more discerning in his tastes. He liked to flirt and have fun, but he didn't sleep with every person who crossed his path and had just come out of a six-month relationship.

Everyone in the VIP area cheered as Harrison and Heather entered it, wishing him well, and he shook a lot of hands before they managed to make their way to the long banquette where Sebastian and Hayden were sitting.

"Happy birthday, old man!" Sebastian said, grinning widely at Harrison.

"Shut up, dude, it'll be your turn next year." Harrison rolled his eyes at him but smiled as he and Heather sat down on the banquette next to them.

"Ah, yes, but I'll still be eighteen months younger than you when I do."

"Have you had a good day, Harrison?" Hayden asked him.

"Yeah, it's been all right."

"You're looking real good tonight, Heather, if you're ever looking for a younger man, you know where I am." Sebastian drawled at her.

Heather just laughed as she rolled her eyes at him.

"You're going to hit on my girlfriend at my own birthday party?" Harrison laughed. "I'm wounded, Seb."

"Hey, I had to try, she looks banging," he shrugged, and the woman he had his arm around seemed upset that she wasn't the focus of his attention.

Sebastian made jokes like this all the time. Heather knew that he didn't place any importance or value on relationships for himself, and they had a running joke that one day she would leave Harrison for him.

"Any idea when Gabriel will get here?" Hayden asked them.

"Yeah, we saw him and Ariana during The Gauntlet," Harrison told them.

Both Sebastian and Hayden whipped their heads around to stare at Harrison when he imparted this information.

"You saw who doing what?" Sebastian's eyebrows were raised in shock.

"She walked The Gauntlet with him," Heather confirmed. "We had photos with them on the red carpet. That was fun and not awkward at all."

"He's a fucking idiot," Sebastian rolled his eyes.

"Yes! Thank you!" Heather exclaimed, then saw the look Harrison was giving her, "I get it, Harrison, he's happy. Great. It doesn't mean that I have to think this is a good idea."

"Well, I'm personally reserving judgment until I see for myself." Hayden shrugged.

"Speak of the devil," Sebastian said, nodding his head toward the entrance of the big room.

The VIP area was behind some glass, but from their vantage point, it was easy to see Gabriel and Ariana, who had just walked through the door to the main area. They were still holding hands as they searched around the room to find them. Harrison waved as Gabriel's eyes landed on the VIP section; he smiled and gave a quick wave back then leaned over to tell Ariana something before she looked over at them as well and nodded to him. They headed toward the bar to order themselves a drink.

"Do you want to dance, Sebastian?" the redheaded woman purred at him, and he shrugged, then stood up from where he was sitting and led her down the steps to the dance floor.

"I'm not sure he particularly wants to speak to Ariana," Hayden observed, after Sebastian's departure.

"I doubt he'll be able to avoid her forever," Harrison said, "Gabriel will take her with him everywhere he goes now."

"We'll see," Heather said.

She snuggled into Harrison, who put his arm around her shoulders and casually stroked her arm with his hand. He smelled amazing. She lifted her face to his, and he kissed her deeply. The familiarity of his lips on hers was comforting; she loved this man more than anyone else in the world, and he was the best thing in her life.

When their kiss ended, Heather looked out over the dance floor, and she could see Gabriel and Ariana talking to Darius Thompson and a woman she vaguely recognized as his wife. They had their drinks in their hands now, and all four of them were smiling while they talked.

"So, she does The Gauntlet, and she's just totally chill with talking to A-list celebrities now, too?" Heather observed.

"I guess so," Harrison responded.

"Am I the only one who thinks this is totally bizarre?"

"Maybe she's changed, Heather," Hayden said with a shrug.

"Where's Seb when you need him? I know he'd back me up," Heather laughed.

As they were watching the group below, the two couples exchanged hugs and handshakes, then the younger couple turned and made their way toward the VIP area. Heather sighed deeply as security lifted the rope to let them past, and they walked up the stairs toward them. It was less than thirty seconds before Gabriel and Ariana were standing in front of them.

"Hey, Gabriel. Hi, Ariana. It's good to see you again," Hayden said cheerfully as he stood up, gave Ariana a quick hug, and slapped Gabriel on the back.

"Thanks, Hayden. It's great to see you, too. I missed you guys," she gave him a small smile.

Heather snorted involuntarily, and Harrison squeezed her quickly to indicate his disapproval.

"Do you have something you'd like to say, Heather?" Gabriel frowned at her.

"Not particularly."

Heather shrugged back at him, raising her chin in defiance against his cold glare. Nobody said anything, so she finished her drink quickly before standing up and continuing.

"I'm going to get another drink. Does anyone want anything?" She assessed the status of everyone else's drinks and saw that they were all mostly full, "No? Okay, cool. I'll be back."

She caught Harrison's frown as she stood up and felt the disapproval emanating from the group behind her as she walked away. Ariana left them all for two years, and yet, somehow, she was the bad guy for not welcoming her back with open arms.

She walked down the stairs and out of the VIP area to head toward the bar. Sebastian was dancing with his date in a way that was practically indecent. He caught her eye and laughed at her expression as she passed them.

When she reached the bar, Heather ordered a Moscow Mule, then sat on a stool in front of the bar. She turned to watch the party as she waited for it to be made. The music was deafening, and she could see up into the VIP area where everyone was on display for the people below. This was not the venue she would've chosen. Harrison would've been far happier somewhere that they could all talk and laugh together without the pressure of this spectacle.

Heather supposed that in that kind of intimate setting, both she and Sebastian would've had to interact with Ariana. She thanked the bartender for her drink and looked back up at the group in the VIP section as she took a sip. Harrison and Hayden were seated where they had been before she'd left, and Gabriel and Ariana had taken up residence in the spaces that Sebastian and his date had vacated previously. Harrison's family and even her own mom and brother were up in the VIP area now.

Everyone was smiling and laughing, she knew she ought to go back up there and socialize, but she didn't feel like it. Gabriel had his arm around Ariana and was casually playing with her long hair. In Heather's mind, they could easily have been back on tour two years ago. They'd spent hours hanging out together. Not so much at celebrity events like this but always together as a group. How could they possibly spend time with Gabriel now that Ariana was back?

Heather wanted to put Gabriel's happiness first, but she couldn't do it, and she knew that she was being selfish. Ever since the night Ariana had turned up again, she had been reflecting on her feelings toward her. Even more so, since they found out that Gabriel was back together with her—it was still too painful to remember that time when Ariana had left.

She wanted to forgive and forget, but she couldn't. Ariana hadn't even sent a single text. It wouldn't have taken much to just send Heather a simple goodbye, a "sorry for leaving". Heather would've understood the ending of their friendship when Ariana left Gabriel and could've forgiven that if she had at least said goodbye.

Even now, it made Heather feel as though Ariana hadn't valued their friendship, which stung because it had held so much value for Heather. She'd always struggled to find friends, when she was growing up, the girls at school ostracized her. She was tall, thin, and blonde, so the boys at school gave her plenty of attention, and it had led to a reputation that she was easy.

Harrison had moved to Chicago, and they'd met during their junior year of high school. He was the new kid and incredibly handsome, talented with music, and joined the school band. They became friends, but she hadn't thought he could ever possibly want her. Between junior and senior years, Harrison went to a summer music program that was highly competitive and met Gabriel, Sebastian, and Hayden, officially becoming Cruise Control before they entered their senior year.

Heather had been there on the sidelines right from the start of their meteoric rise to fame. She'd officially started dating Harrison shortly after they drunkenly hooked up during her twentieth birthday party, and they had been inseparable ever since.

This had made it even harder for Heather to make new friends. Fans of the band knew exactly who she was, and she had gotten really good at assessing people. Within a minute, she would be able to tell if they were using her. Nine times out of ten, they were. As Cruise Control had gotten more fame, it had gotten worse, to the point that Heather got quite jaded about people in general.

Then, along came Ariana Chamberlain. Gabriel's new girlfriend, so sweet and kind, and terrified of their lifestyle. In a way, Heather had fallen in love with her as well. Ariana never judged her for anything she said or did, and she didn't want anything from Heather but her company. They had a lot of free time together and would talk and laugh together for hours. It was the friendship that Heather had longed for her whole life. Finally, she was able to let her guard down and be free.

She'd tried her hardest to help Ariana get over her fear of Gabriel's celebrity, but it was always there. She had basically been phobic about it, and Heather had never understood it. Sure, this life wasn't easy, but it certainly wasn't as hard as Ariana had seemed to think it was. A lot of the difficulties they'd had seemed to be borne purely out of Ariana's fear.

When she left, the loss was deep for everyone in the band. On some level, it had triggered those feelings in Heather from long ago that nobody wanted to be her friend. Her walls were firmly put back up in place, and when Gabriel later started dating Elena, Heather hadn't made any effort to become more than a friendly acquaintance. Considering they only ended up dating for a few months before he hooked back up with Ariana, that was probably for the best.

Heather was distracted from her thoughts as Sebastian headed over toward her. She couldn't see any trace of the redheaded woman whose name she still didn't know and would probably never learn.

"Yo, Heather, wanna dance?" He grinned at her.

"Let's see, dance with you or go upstairs and make small talk with Ariana? Hmmmmm, it's a tough choice."

"Oof, you'd actually rather talk to her than dance with me?" He raised an eyebrow at her, then clutched his chest in mock agony, and she laughed.

"Okay, come on, let's dance then. I just need to finish my drink first. I figure if I get completely trashed, maybe I can forget these awful balloons ever existed!"

Sebastian laughed, "What? They don't meet your elevated taste in design?"

"Just looking at them is burning holes in my corneas!" she announced dramatically.

She finished the last of her cocktail, then followed him out on to the dance floor, and they danced together. It wasn't at all like the way he'd been dancing with the other woman. He took her hand and spun her in a circle as she laughed, her dress flaring out around her.

They'd been dancing together for a song or two when Harrison joined them on the dance floor, taking Heather's hand and spinning her around as well. All three were laughing and dancing together in a circle when the song changed to a slower song.

Harrison wrapped his arms around Heather from behind, and she melted into him, her senses flaring up with his nearness.

"Have fun, lovebirds!" Sebastian said with a laugh and a wave, then headed back to the bar.

Heather's back was to Harrison's chest, and he had his arms crossed over her shoulders, she tilted her head to the side, giving him access to her neck and he took the cue, immediately leaning down to kiss her there. Her skin seared where his lips had touched her; he lifted his head slightly to say, "I love you, Heather" in her ear, and she just smiled.

She turned her face up so he could kiss her fully on the mouth, and their tongues intertwined as they kissed. When their kiss ended, Heather was breathless. Harrison spun her around so she was facing him and dropped his hands to her waist to hold her tightly against him. She looked up into his brown eyes and could read the lust in them. She tilted her head up to his, and they kissed again, Heather wound her arms around his neck as he held her tightly to him.

Her attention was brought back to their surroundings as Heather realized that there was now an empty space around them, they were suddenly standing alone together in the middle of the dance floor and spotlights were shining down on them. She broke their kiss, and they both looked around in a lust-filled daze.

"Happy thirtieth birthday, Harrison!" Cooper Powell, Cruise Control's manager, was announcing into a microphone as he walked toward them. Heather dropped her hands from around Harrison's neck, and instinctively, she reached for and found his hand, linking it with her own.

Everyone cheered, and Heather saw that the rest of the band, Harrison's parents, and her own family were following in Cooper's wake. Heather felt guilty that she hadn't sought them out to say hello sooner this evening. Harrison's mom gave her a big smile when she saw her, and Heather returned it. His parents were like family to her, and his mom particularly seemed to view Heather as the daughter she'd never had.

Cooper's wife, Helen, and Madeline Turner, one of Cooper's assistants, were pushing a table toward them. Sitting on it was a massive cake in the shape of Harrison's signature, custom Fender bass guitar. The detailing was so intricate that it genuinely looked like Harrison could pick it up and play it. It even had the Cruise

Control symbol near the bridge, a perfect replica of the one Harrison used on stage.

She looked at his face and saw how pleased he was, and Heather was happy that Cooper's team had managed to get something right for his big day. There was someone with a video camera near them, streaming the footage to the big screen above the crowd so everyone could see. The partygoers all cheered, and there was a rousing chorus of "Happy Birthday To You" before Harrison cut the cake.

As quickly as it had arrived, the cake was wheeled away again so that the staff could cut it into slices for their guests, and Cooper turned to Harrison, speaking into the microphone once again.

"I think it's time for a speech, Harrison!"

The crowd cheered their approval, and Heather was surprised when Harrison took the mic from Cooper. She'd expected him to refuse; it wasn't like him. He had gone white all over now and was looking incredibly nervous.

"Thanks so much for coming out tonight, everyone!"

Another cheer from the party guests.

"It means so much to me that everyone wanted to come and help us celebrate my thirtieth birthday. Thank you so much for this wonderful evening. This last decade has been pretty crazy." He smiled over at his bandmates and parents. "I am so lucky to be where I am. Mom and Dad, you supported my dreams, and I love you for that. Seb, Hayden, and Gabriel, you guys are like my brothers."

He turned to Heather, and his eyes met hers. He was perspiring slightly now, and she was surprised that he was so nervous. He didn't like giving speeches, but he'd given so many interviews and even accepted awards with his speeches being streamed live worldwide that it seemed odd that he was so on edge tonight.

"Heather," his voice softened the way it always did when he

said her name, "you're my angel. I love you so much. You've been by my side for ten years now, and I couldn't ask for a better person to be my life partner. I can't imagine my life without you in it."

He reached into his pocket and pulled out a small box, before dropping to one knee in front of her. There was a collective gasp from the vast majority of the crowd around them, and Heather's mouth dropped open.

"Most importantly, I don't *want* to imagine my life without you in it. Heather Lillian York, will you marry me?" he said into the microphone.

Time seemed to stop as Heather took everything in. The camera was still on them; she could see them both on the massive screen behind Harrison. Everyone was waiting for her answer. She looked down at Harrison, their eyes met, and her entire body shook as one word flashed through her brain. *Mine.*

"Yes," she finally managed to respond. "Of course!"

She wasn't sure if the microphone had caught her words, but the entire venue seemed to erupt, as Harrison stood up and slipped the engagement ring on her left hand. She looked down at it and was amazed; Heather had never seen anything like it before. There was a massive, oval diamond set in the center, with a pink diamond either side and a split band set with diamonds down it. It was stunning.

She looked up at Harrison with tears in her eyes, and he leaned down to kiss her before they were enveloped by people wanting to wish them well. Harrison's parents were first, followed by her mom, and then her brother. Next were the other members of Cruise Control.

"You know, Heather, there's still time to change your mind and run away with me!" Sebastian winked at her as he hugged her.

"I'll think about it, Seb." She laughed at him.

"I fucking hope not!" Harrison said with a wry grin.

"Hey, if Heather's happy to have mediocre sex with you for

the rest of her life, that's on her."

Sebastian hugged him, as they both laughed. He moved aside, and then Gabriel and Ariana were there, both were smiling widely at them. In her current mood, Heather couldn't muster up any anger; she was a bundle of pure joy. So, she accepted their congratulations and a hug from each of them without any incident.

The rest of the evening flew by in a whirl of congratulations, music, dancing, and drinking. Heather kept staring at her hand, disbelieving of the ring sitting there. Harrison had actually proposed. She hadn't needed this; she was happy with their life together. Yet, she loved that he was her fiancé now and couldn't wait for their wedding.

It was nearly four in the morning when she and Harrison finally got into a limousine to head home. It felt like thousands of pictures had been taken just on the walk from the venue entrance to their limo. Knowing that the news would be out before the morning, Heather had posted a picture of her engagement ring to Instagram hours ago, so she just posed for pictures with Harrison and happily showed off her ring. Finally, it was just them again.

"Are you happy, angel?" He smiled down at her.

"More than ever. How did you know?" she asked him.

"How did I know what?"

"The ring," she held her hand up and stared at it, mesmerized, "it's more perfect and beautiful than I could ever have imagined."

"It was the only design I found that came even close to matching your beauty."

Her heart skipped a beat, and she looked up at him.

"You're my fiancé."

"I'm your fiancé," he confirmed.

"We should probably find out if engaged sex is as good as dating sex, then." She grinned wickedly at him and moved closer so he could kiss her.

He didn't need any further invitation, and he crashed his lips down on hers. Heather opened her mouth to his as she moved around, so she was sitting on his lap and facing him. They continued their kiss, and she felt him getting hard beneath her.

"I love you, Harrison Fletcher," she said, and leaned down to kiss his neck.

"I need you so badly, Heather," Harrison groaned.

As she began to kiss him on the lips again, he reached under her dress and slipped his hand into her underwear. She moaned his name loudly as he began to rub her clit, she was so wet, and she desperately needed him inside of her. She moved off him and slipped off her underwear, keeping eye contact with him as she did so.

"You're so fucking sexy, angel."

She unbuttoned his trousers, and he lifted his ass as she pulled them down to his feet. He looked amazing, still wearing his tuxedo shirt but with his massive erection and muscled legs exposed. She moved back, so she was straddling him again and lowered herself onto his cock.

He filled her so completely, and she slid up and down on him, loving the feeling of him filling her again each time she slid back down. He brought his mouth to hers, and they continued to move in rhythm. She felt herself approaching orgasm and wanted to hold off to keep this feeling going forever, but she couldn't stop it from crashing over her. He continued to fuck her, and the intensity of it brought tears to her eyes. Her body was so sensitive that she didn't think she could handle it, and soon she felt a second orgasm rock her body as he spasmed inside of her and let himself go.

She stayed there on top of him for a good five minutes before she could move again. When she did, it was exquisitely painful as he slid out of her. He reached over for some tissues, and they cleaned up as best they could.

"Engaged sex is definitely better than dating sex!" she declared as the car turned into their street. Harrison just laughed and kissed her again.

~JULY~

THIS CRUISE CONTROL FAN THEORY WILL BLOW YOUR MIND!

We've all seen the pictures of Gabriel Knight looking super in love with his new girlfriend, Ariana Chamberlain. Everyone is so happy for the couple, but Reddit user, cruisefanforever, thinks that Ariana might not be such a new girlfriend after all!

They suggested that Ariana might just be the infamous 'Ariel,' the mysterious girl who broke Gabriel's heart in the past and led to him writing 'Heart Wide Open.' It didn't take long for the internet to agree and #ArianaIsAriel has already started trending on social media.

Pictures have begun to surface of Gabriel on the 'Cards Have Been Dealt' tour with a brunette girl that does look suspiciously like Ariana. It's hard to say for sure.

Meanwhile, Harrison's proposal to Heather last month might just have been the cutest thing we've ever seen. Those two are 100% #couplegoals. Will Heather design her own wedding gown? Maybe Ariana can be a bridesmaid? Otherwise, we know plenty of people who would love to be a part of your special day, Heather! Inside sources tell us they're looking at a May wedding, so we'll keep our calendars open.

More to come.

Chapter 3

NOT EVEN YOKO

Heather was exhausted. It was five in the evening, and she'd been up since roughly five this morning, sketching designs for her New York Fashion Week collection. She was in her large studio space, surrounded by mannequins, fabrics, and different types of sewing machines, overlockers, and more.

She was pleased with the work she'd completed today, though, and her collection was coming together nicely. In some ways, she could thank Ariana for Serenity's success. It had been through opening up to Ariana about Heather's desire to become a fashion designer that she had pursued it at all.

After Ariana left, when Gabriel had thrown himself into making music to get through his grief, she had turned to designing clothes. A large part of Heather worried that her designs were only popular due to the Cruise Control fans, and their desire to have any kind of connection to the band. Slowly, though, she had started getting positive reviews from critics as well.

She'd been making everything herself in the beginning, but now had a small group of women working for her doing most of the day to day work, leaving her to focus on the big picture for the line. Initially, she had sold her designs online but had started to be stocked in some high-end boutiques throughout the country now.

Still, everyone had been surprised when Heather had been given an invitation to show at New York Fashion Week this year. She'd had two small showings in Chicago when she was launching Serenity, but it was absolutely terrifying to be putting on her first big show, and she was so worried that she would completely bomb in New York.

She had a very real concern that the fashion world might write her off as just the girlfriend of a famous rock star, playing at being a fashion designer. There had already been more than a few nasty articles when she'd been invited to Fashion Week, implying that she was only invited because of Harrison, and saying that they thought she would bomb. Heather tried not to let them get to her; all she could do was focus on making her show the best it could possibly be.

Her focus for this collection was on flowing, free styles. No constraints; as much as possible, she was avoiding zippers and buttons. Everything felt fluid, and the color palette was bright and airy. She was trying to capture the essence behind the name she'd chosen for her label—Serenity. It had come to her early on because that's how she felt when designing—serene. Everything else in the world could be blocked out while she focused on what she was trying to create.

Her phone buzzed and lit up; Harrison's name and picture were displayed on the screen.

"Hi, honey." She answered it.

"Hey, angel, are you leaving any time soon?"

Heather stood up and stretched her muscles; she hadn't realized how much they had been aching until she moved.

"Yeah, I'll leave in about half an hour or so, I guess. Why?"

"Sebastian wants us all to come around to his place tonight."

"Who is 'us all'?" Heather's eyes narrowed as she asked the question.

"Yes, Gabriel and Ariana are invited, too."

"Why would Sebastian invite her?" She pursed her lips.

"He invited Gabriel, and that meant inviting Ariana. Heather, we haven't all been together since my birthday, can't we just get along?"

They'd argued off and on over the last month about this. Heather had dodged a couple of Cruise Control events, using the excuse of needing to work on her collection. Heather didn't know if he'd done it on purpose, but he'd caught her out tonight by asking her plans first.

"You're kidding yourself if you think Seb's going to play nicely," Heather warned him.

"Sebastian isn't my concern, Heather. Gabriel told me that Ariana is really upset by the fact that you haven't spoken to her since they got back together."

A wave of anger flooded over her. Once again, she was being made out to be the bad guy. Did Ariana really think that she could just come back and everything would be as if the last two years had never happened? She was an idiot if she thought that.

"I'm not going to dignify that with an answer, Harrison. All I will say is that I have made my position perfectly clear to you. I do not want to be friends with her, but okay, for your sake and *only* for your sake, I promise to be civil."

"So, you will come tonight, then?"

"Yes, I'll come. I'll leave now. Are we eating there?"

"I'm pretty sure Seb's ordering food. We're just going to hang out and play pool, drink some alcohol; it'll be like old times."

Heather seethed internally, but took a deep breath and let it slide without comment. It wasn't worth the argument. Clearly, she had a very different view on 'old times' than Harrison did. Every memory of those days was upsetting for her. She wished that Gabriel had never met Ariana at all.

"Right. Well, I'll see you soon. Love you, honey."

"Love you, angel." He paused. "So much. You know that, right?"

Just like that, her bad mood cleared, and she smiled at his words. He was her constant.

"I do. I can't wait to see you. Bye."

They hung up, and Heather started clearing away her workspace. She didn't need to; nobody would come in before she was back here tomorrow to do some more work, but she needed this time to clear her head before driving home.

After carefully making sure that the lights were off and the doors were locked, Heather headed down to the parking garage underneath the building. As she approached her red Tesla, the door handles popped out, and she opened the door to slide into the driver's seat. She pressed the button for the car to direct her home and pulled out into the street.

She relied on the car to drive her home probably more than she should have, her mind distracted with thoughts about the coming evening. She found that she wanted to talk to Sebastian, so she pulled up his number from her contacts on the big screen in the middle of the car and dialed him.

"Yo, what's up, sexy lady?" Sebastian answered her call.

"Sebastian, darling, what the fuck? We're *all* coming to your place tonight?"

"Yeah." She could almost hear him roll his eyes as he said it.

"Why?"

"We haven't all hung out in ages, and I wanted to see your sexy body, of course!"

Now Heather was the one rolling her eyes.

"Seb, be serious."

"I was, but okay. Also, I just really fucking miss everyone and thought it would be fun to hang out."

It was often easy to forget that Sebastian had any emotions at all, but the love he did have was reserved almost entirely for the band. He closed himself off to women and relationships, but loved them all and was incredibly loyal. That was probably part of why he'd refused to forgive Ariana for her departure.

"Can't you give me some warning next time?"

"What? So you have an opportunity to make some excuse and avoid us? I doubt it." He laughed. "Plus, if I have to make small talk with Ariana Chamberlain just to get to spend time with Gabriel, then so do you, friend."

"You suck."

"Yeah, I do, but I'll still see you tonight."

He hung up their call, and Heather laughed at his audacity. She had missed hanging out with them over the last month. Maybe tonight wouldn't be too bad, after all. She pulled into the garage under the apartment building that she and Harrison lived in, leaving her car next to Harrison's own black Tesla. She headed upstairs to their apartment and called out to Harrison.

"Honey, I'm home!"

"Hey, there, angel." A look of concern crossed his face. "You look wrecked."

She felt wrecked. She realized that she hadn't eaten since breakfast; she'd been so focused on her designs. Harrison walked over to her and enveloped her in a hug.

"I think I just need something to eat."

"Did you have lunch?" His voice had a worried note to it.

"No, I forgot. When do we have to leave?"

"Probably another hour or so"—Harrison checked his watch—"do you want to go shower? I'll get you something to tide you over until we have dinner if you want."

"That would be great, honey, thank you."

She lifted her arms to pull his head down to hers so she could kiss him. Their tongues intertwined as they kissed deeply, and he cupped her ass with his hands. She could feel her body's reaction to him and felt herself becoming overcome with desire, despite her tiredness. Heather broke the kiss, grabbed his hand, and began to pull him toward their bedroom.

"I thought you were tired, angel." He smiled at her.

"I am, damn you. You'll have to do most of the work, I guess." She gave him a cheeky grin as they reached the bed.

She unbuttoned his jeans and pulled them down as she dropped to her knees in front of him. He groaned as she took him in her mouth. One of her favorite things in the world was feeling him get bigger in her mouth as she sucked him to a full-blown erection. He put his hand on the back of her head as she moved it back and forth on him, looking into his eyes.

After a few minutes, she stood up, and they both quickly removed their clothes. Heather lay back with her head on the pillows, and Harrison took a moment to let his gaze roam over her from head to toe.

"You're so goddamn sexy. How did I get so lucky?"

She looked at him, all tanned, smooth skin and bulging muscles, with his impressive erection jutting out in front of him.

"I'm wondering the same thing," she told him. "Now, come here and make me forget how tired I am."

He climbed onto the bed and parted her legs in front of him. She bit her lip as he looked into her eyes before he dropped his head, kissing her inner thighs first on the right side and then the left.

"Is this what you want, angel?" He placed his head in the center of her legs as he said it, and she felt his breath on her, so incredibly erotic and arousing.

"Yes, please, Harrison. Please," she begged, needing him to satisfy her.

"Well, since you asked so nicely." He smiled.

He gave her what she wanted, then, and she moaned in ecstasy. He used his tongue expertly while his fingers were inside her, not taking long at all to bring her to the brink of orgasm, and she moaned his name as she came.

He positioned himself over her and pushed himself inside agonizingly slowly. She bucked her hips toward him, trying to get him to move faster, and he laughed.

"What's wrong, angel?"

"I need you, Harrison. Now."

He lowered his mouth to hers and kissed her as he pushed himself the rest of the way inside. She would never tire of this feeling, he fit her so perfectly, and they moved in a synchronized rhythm together. He braced himself with one hand and used the other to play with her breasts before reaching between them to rub her clit as they continued fucking.

She moaned loudly as her ecstasy grew to the point that she could feel herself coming around his cock. He leaned back down to kiss her again, and it wasn't long before he was coming inside her, and it felt so good that it led Heather to come again.

They lay there, panting together before Harrison kissed her lips gently, climbed off her, and went into the bathroom to clean himself up and shower. Heather felt the tiredness begin to creep back as soon as her post-orgasm adrenalin started seeping away. She was still lying where he'd left her when Harrison came back into the bedroom, his hair wet, and picked up their clothes from where they'd left them to take them with him into the wardrobe.

"Have a shower, angel. I'll get you food," he said as he came back into the room, fully dressed now.

She nodded, and he left the room. Heading into the bathroom, it was still warm and steamy from Harrison's shower. The water didn't take long to heat up, and she pulled her hair into a bun before stepping into the spray. The hot water soothed her aching muscles, and she spent longer in the shower than she usually would.

She stepped out onto the marble tiles and grabbed a towel off the rack to dry herself. She hung it back up and made her way to the walk-in closet, where she got out a matching set of underwear and put them on.

Pulling out a pair of tight, black jeans, she pulled them on before getting a loose, blue, collared shirt that hung to her mid-thigh to go with it. She found some low-heeled light blue boots and put them and a pair of socks on. She got a brush, pulled her hair out of its bun, and stood in front of the mirror as she brushed it out.

She decided not to do any more with her hair but put on some mascara and red lipstick. Happy with her look, she headed to the kitchen to find Harrison. He was sitting on a stool at their kitchen bench, looking through his phone. Heather slid onto the seat beside Harrison, in front of a plate with some crackers, different cheeses, and a small selection of deli meats. There was a glass of ice water sitting next to it.

"Thanks, honey." She leaned over to give him a kiss on the cheek.

"Any time, angel. I worry about you. You're working too hard."

"I know," she admitted. "It's just until Fashion Week is done; I need everything to be perfect."

"I'm worried you're going to collapse from exhaustion before then."

She finished her mouthful of food and took a sip of water.

"I'll take care of myself, Harrison, I promise."

They chatted about general topics after that while Heather finished her plate of food. Harrison took it and rinsed it and the glass in the sink before putting them in the dishwasher, and they headed out. They took an Uber to Sebastian's high-rise apartment building, which was only about ten minutes from theirs. They entered the lobby of the building and waited for the elevator. When they got in it, Harrison swiped a key tag Sebastian had given them so they could take it up to his penthouse.

When the doors opened, they were in his entry hall. They could hear music playing from a sound system near a massive entertainment set-up as they walked into his living area. Sebastian was sitting on the sofa with his head leaning against the back of it. His eyes were closed, and he had a drink of amber liquid in his hand. He looked up as they entered and smiled at them.

"Hey, guys."

"Hey, Seb," Harrison said as he dropped onto the sofa.

"Hi, darling," Heather said, leaning over to give him a hug before she sat down between Harrison and Sebastian.

"You guys want anything to drink?"

"I'll have whatever you're drinking."

"Sure, Heather?"

"Same, I'm not picky."

Sebastian put his glass down on the coffee table, stood up, walked over to his bar, and poured their drinks. He handed them each a drink and sat down again.

"Oh, this is good," Harrison said. "What is it?"

"Forty-year-old Glenfiddich."

"Ah, makes sense. Tasty."

The whisky was smooth, and Heather felt it warm her stomach as she drank it. She was feeling unreasonably nervous now that they were here.

"You all right, Heather? You look like someone just told you that you have to walk over hot coals."

"Oh, that's not what I have to do? What a relief!" She cringed at Sebastian. "I don't know why I'm so nervous."

"You'll be fine, angel; it's only a big deal because you've been putting it off."

Harrison put his arm around her shoulders and drew her closer to him.

"Yeah, I suppose."

"Harrison's right, I'll keep you safe from the big, bad Ariana, even though you've left me to fend for myself for the last month!" Sebastian grinned at her.

"As if you need my help dealing with her."

"I could say the same to you. Come on, where's the Heather I know and love that gives zero fucks what anyone thinks of her?" Sebastian nudged her, and she smiled back at him before relaxing into Harrison's embrace again.

"You're right. I'm being stupid. So, no girl tonight, Seb?"

"Are you ready to leave Harrison for me yet?"

"Nope, not today, darling. Try again tomorrow." She winked at him.

"Well, then, no. I can get laid anytime. Apparently, us all hanging out is a rare occurrence these days." He shrugged.

This was part of what she and Harrison had argued about. He felt as though Gabriel was happy and they should accept Ariana back, but she couldn't forgive her for leaving the way she did. Heather felt guilty about that, though. She didn't want this rift between her and Ariana to cause problems with the guys. She knew that she could talk Sebastian around if she was so inclined…but she wasn't.

Just then, the elevator made a sound as it opened, and Hayden, Gabriel, and Ariana all stepped out together.

"Look who we found in the lobby!" Gabriel announced, jerking his head in Hayden's direction.

Heather could see that Ariana was gripping his hand tightly. She caught Heather's eye, and Heather looked away quickly. The new arrivals sat down on the sofa—Hayden next to Sebastian, while Gabriel and Ariana sat next to Hayden.

"Would you guys like anything to drink? We're drinking Glenfiddich whisky."

Heather noted that Sebastian had waited until they were seated to ask this, meaning that Ariana wouldn't have a chance to sit next to Heather on the sofa, and she appreciated the effort.

"Sounds fine to me, Ari?"

"Yeah, that sounds nice, thanks."

Gabriel frowned slightly when she said this but didn't say anything. Heather knew that Ariana usually drank vodka, so she was obviously trying not to make a fuss.

"Sounds good to me, too," Hayden added.

Sebastian got their drinks before sitting down again. There was a strange silence as everyone sipped their drinks. It had never been like this between them, ever.

"Food should be here in about thirty minutes," Sebastian informed them. "I got Chinese; I hope that's okay."

"Sounds good, Seb," Gabriel replied.

The odd silence fell again, and Heather looked up into Harrison's face. He looked strained, and she could tell he disliked the apparent tension in the room. Heather sighed mentally; she hated being a part of something that was causing him any distress. She still wasn't interested in friendship with Ariana, but she had promised to be civil, so she mentally buckled in and put a smile on her face.

"So. Who's going to play me at pool?" she asked the group in general.

Sebastian raised an eyebrow at her in surprise, but it was Hayden who replied.

"I will. Do you think you've got what it takes to beat me?"

"You? Yes. Sebastian? No." Heather laughed at him.

They got up and walked over to the pool table. It was custom made from heavy, white stone with black cloth and the Cruise Control symbol in the middle of it. It sat near the floor-to-ceiling windows that provided a fantastic view of Chicago at night, lights glittering in the distance. Heather picked a cue from the rack on the wall, and Hayden did the same.

"Who's going to break?" he asked her.

"Paper, scissors, rock?" she suggested with a laugh.

"Sure, why not."

They played the game, and Heather beat Hayden's paper with her scissors.

"I'll break," she told him.

Sebastian had gotten up from the sofa and set up the table for them while they'd been picking their cues and deciding who would start. Heather took her shot, breaking the triangle of balls at the other end of the table, and the purple number-four ball dropped into the corner pocket.

"Solids. Interesting."

She assessed the status of the balls on the table and aimed for the yellow number-one ball near the middle pocket and was pleased when she sunk the ball.

"Way to go, Heather!" Harrison called from his spot on the sofa where he and the other couple were sitting and chatting.

"Thanks, honey," she replied.

She took her next turn but failed to sink the ball this time. Hayden got three balls down before Heather managed to drop her next one in the pocket. The game stayed relatively close, with them trading balls back and forth until Heather managed to sink the black eight ball in the corner pocket to win the game.

She stood up from taking her shot and backed into Harrison, who was standing right behind her. He wrapped his arm around her waist and dropped his head to kiss her neck.

"Well done, angel."

"Thanks. Who's next?"

"I'll play you," Gabriel announced from the sofa.

He and Ariana stood up together and came over to where everyone else was now standing. Gabriel took the cue off Hayden as Heather started racking up the balls.

"You can break if you'd like," Gabriel told her with a friendly smile.

"Sure."

She hit the white ball hard, and it smacked into the triangle at the other end of the table, sending the balls scattering, and the red eleven ball fell into one pocket while its counterpart, the red three ball, fell into another.

"Stripes or solids?" Gabriel asked her.

Heather looked at the status of the balls left on the table. She couldn't see that there was much advantage to one over the other, and she'd just played solids.

"Stripes, I guess."

She aimed for and missed getting the orange number-thirteen ball into the middle pocket, and Gabriel took his shot, successfully sinking the brown number-seven ball.

"Way to go, Gabe!"

Ariana smiled at Gabriel, and as he looked at her, Heather saw that he really was happy now. She hadn't seen him this at ease, well, since the last time they were together, to be honest. He took his next shot and sank the blue number-two ball before missing the purple number four.

"Your turn," Gabriel informed Heather, stepping away from the table, putting his arms around Ariana, then dropping his head to kiss her.

Heather was frustrated by this; it did remind her of 'old times.' They'd spent so many hours playing pool while they were on tour together. It felt like Gabriel was trying to force them to get used to Ariana's presence in their lives again, and she didn't want to. She didn't want this; Ariana hadn't even apologized since she came back, either.

Heather was off her game and failed to sink the orange thirteen ball, but she did knock down Gabriel's green six ball instead.

"Two shots to me, sorry, Heather!"

She frowned at him. So, he could apologize for her own shitty pool playing, but Ariana couldn't apologize for ditching her for two years. Heather looked over at Ariana as Gabriel took his shots and found Ariana looking back at her. Ariana smiled and gave a small wave, but Heather just looked back at the pool table.

She'd lost interest in the game and was glad when their food arrived near the end. She only sunk one more ball before Gabriel won the game, and Heather was relieved that she wouldn't need to play again.

They all sat at the dining table to eat, Heather tried to keep her tone light and airy, but she felt strained. That bone tiredness was sinking in on her again, and she just wanted to go home. After they'd finished eating and had a second round of drinks, Gabriel pushed his chair back from the table.

"Who's going to play me, then?"

"I will," Harrison volunteered.

They headed over to the pool table to start their game, and the rest of them remained seated.

"Are you looking forward to Fashion Week?" Ariana asked her.

"Do you care, Ariana?" Heather raised an eyebrow at her and Ariana looked hurt.

"Of course, I care. Look, we haven't really talked since—"

"Sebastian, do you need some help cleaning this up?" She turned to look at him.

"Brutal." Sebastian raised his eyebrows at Heather. "Yeah, sure."

He pushed his chair back and stood up to start cleaning the table. Ariana stood as well and walked away from them without saying anything more; Heather thought that she might be crying. Hayden followed her slowly but not before frowning and sending some parting words in her direction.

"You're being pretty unfair, Heather."

She followed Sebastian into the kitchen, their hands full of plates, cups, and half-empty food containers. They put their loads on the marble benchtop, and Heather started rinsing the dishware before handing it to Sebastian to put in the dishwasher.

"You're stone cold," he told her with a laugh. "I didn't know you could be like that; I'm impressed!"

"Come on, darling. You don't feel any more kindly toward her than I do."

"Yeah, but if we're not careful, we won't get to see Gabriel anymore."

Heather sighed. She knew that was a possible risk.

"I just keep remembering what it was like when she left. She never even fucking said goodbye to me. I don't think I'll ever forgive her for that."

They'd finished with the dishes and were putting the leftover food in the fridge now.

"Trust me, I got a goodbye, and you didn't miss out on much. I told her how upset Gabriel was and she didn't give a shit, she just walked out after giving me some pathetic apology."

He spat this out with venom. Heather had never asked him what their final conversation had actually entailed, and she was surprised by this new information.

"I don't understand why *he* has forgiven her. How could he? She ruined him."

"Me either. I'm glad you came tonight, though, Heather. I thought you wouldn't as soon as you knew Yoko Ono was coming." He laughed.

"Not even Yo—"

She was cut off by a cold, angry voice at the entrance to the kitchen.

"Are you sure that you want to finish that sentence, Heather?"

Gabriel was furious, his entire body was tensed, and his fists were clenched at his sides.

"Good, you two are together. I've got something to say to both of you. Ariana is my girlfriend; do you hear me? We will be together for the rest of our lives if I have anything to say about it, and I will *not* have you two treating her like shit."

"But will you have a say in it, Gabriel?" Sebastian asked in a cool tone. "Did you have a say in it the last time she left?"

Gabriel strode toward them, and Heather thought wildly that he was going to punch Sebastian, but he didn't. He got right in his face before replying, though.

"How fucking dare you, Seb. You don't have a single goddamn clue what you're talking about."

"Don't I? You don't think that *we*"—he indicated to himself and Heather—"have any clue? We were there, Gabriel. Who the fuck do you think covered for you in fucking interviews about the Grammys? Who do you think carried the load at those first few concerts? Heather wouldn't fucking speak to anyone, either. Who do you think was there comforting Harrison when he was terrified for Heather's wellbeing because she wasn't eating anything? Who was it that was watching their friends fall the fuck apart and couldn't do any goddamn thing about it because *she* wouldn't talk to any of us?"

Heather was shocked by this. She remembered being utterly numb at the time but had no idea how much she had worried Harrison. Gabriel looked stunned, then recomposed himself.

"Well, if you hadn't brought that bitch to the Grammys, none of it would have happened."

"Oh, fuck off, Gabriel," Heather interjected. "That's bullshit, and you know it. If it hadn't been Sebastian's bitchy date, it would've been something else. Ariana was just looking for a reason to leave, I don't know what her fucking problem was but she sure as shit had one."

"I'd like to go home now." Their conversation was interrupted by a quiet, sad voice behind Gabriel, and they all turned to look at Ariana, with Hayden and Harrison standing behind her. "Thank you for your hospitality, Sebastian."

"Ari. I'm sorry." Gabriel rushed to follow her as she walked to the elevator, obviously crying.

"You two couldn't just be nice to her for one evening?" Harrison's voice was cold, and he was looking directly at Heather.

"Clearly not, Captain Obvious," Sebastian replied.

Heather's mind was whirling. She was full of pent-up rage and sadness, but Ariana's face was burned into her brain. She'd looked truly hurt by their conversation. Heather hadn't meant to take it that far, but nothing that she'd said was untrue.

There was no valid reason for Ariana to leave them the way she did; Heather couldn't imagine anything that Ariana could tell her that would change her mind. Still, as angry as she was at Ariana, Heather had made a promise to Harrison, and he was glaring at her right now.

"I'm sorry, honey. I tried."

"Aww, Heather, don't ruin your badass bitch persona by apologizing for it." Sebastian grinned at her, and she had to hold back a smile.

"Shut your fucking mouth, Seb. This isn't the time." Harrison was angrier than Heather had seen him in a long time. "Both of you owe Gabriel and Ariana an apology."

"Perhaps, you're right. I'd say she fucking owes us one, too." Heather met his steely gaze with her own.

"Sometimes, you have to take the high road, Heather," Hayden joined in.

"This isn't about you, Hayden. This is about the fact that Ariana Chamberlain stopped talking to me for two years and now wants me to act like I'm her best friend again. Well, I'm not."

"Like fuck, it's not about me. Do you and Sebastian have any idea what you've done? If Gabriel refuses to be around you, that's one thing. If he refuses to be around Sebastian, what the hell do you think will happen to Cruise Control, Heather?"

With shock, Heather realized that he was right. It was all well and good to take the moral high ground, but Gabriel and Sebastian needed, at the very least, to work together or everything would go to shit. Heather looked at Sebastian but saw no such fear on his face.

"Hell will freeze over before I ever forgive Ariana for what she did," he said with a casual shrug of his shoulders as he stalked out of the room.

"We should probably leave," Harrison said, and both Heather and Hayden followed him to the elevator as he pulled out his phone to call them an Uber.

They said goodbye to Hayden, made their way outside, and got into their Uber when it arrived. Sebastian had disappeared somewhere in the apartment and didn't come out to say goodbye to them when they left. It was an ominous end to the evening.

They didn't talk at all in the Uber on the ride home, and by the time they got into their apartment, Heather was waiting for the inevitable argument.

"I didn't think that I was asking much of you when I asked you to not argue with Gabriel and Ariana tonight." Harrison glared at her.

"Hey, Gabriel is the one who came in and started an argument." Heather shrugged.

"Yes, because you and Seb were off bitching about his girlfriend, together."

"It feels as though you care more about Gabriel's happiness than you do about mine," Heather frowned.

Harrison raised his eyebrows at her. "Does it, angel? Well, it feels as though you don't care about my happiness, or the band, at all. You could talk sense into Sebastian, instead of turning this into some kind of turf war."

"Did Ariana give a fuck about the band when she left, Harrison? Did she give a fuck about me? Because if we're talking about feelings, I still feel like she didn't." She glared at Harrison.

“I was tired before we went out, and I’m utterly exhausted now. I’m going to bed.”

She spun on her heel and walked to their bedroom. The evening had taken a lot out of her. Sebastian’s last words were ringing in Heather’s ears. Surely, he didn’t mean it. Yet, somehow, she knew that he did.

Chapter 4

HAVE YOU EVER TRIED TO ORGANIZE A WEDDING?

Heather and Harrison were seated at the table in his parents' house. Across from them were both her mom and Harrison's mom, Sarah. There were lists of names in front of them; they were trying to cull the guestlist for their engagement party. The goal was to get it down to under two hundred of their nearest and dearest friends and family. This was the maximum capacity for the venue they'd chosen, and it was more difficult than they'd expected to narrow their list down.

"It's crazy that we have this many people on the list," Harrison said.

"There were twice that many people at your birthday party, honey," she told him.

"I know, but who organized that? Does Cooper's entire management team really have to come to our engagement party?"

"Probably not. Helen can come, though," Heather said, striking four names off the list under their names.

"What about Sierra Capitol Music executives?" Harrison's mom asked him, looking at about ten names under that heading on their list.

"Unless there's any record label execs that you're particularly attached to, Harrison, they can come to the wedding but not the engagement party?" She looked at him.

"New plan. Let's just elope." He smiled at her.

"Solid idea. Mom? Sarah? Thoughts?"

Both women looked up from the lists in front of them and laughed.

"I never thought I'd say this," Sarah said, "but yes, you should absolutely elope."

"We'll just cancel everything. I'm sure all the services we've booked will be fine with that!" her mom added with a grin.

"Oh, sure, none of them seemed at all excited to be involved in the wedding of a member of Cruise Control when we booked them." Heather laughed.

"They probably think if they do a good job, they can do more Cruise Control weddings in the future," her mom added.

"Maybe Gabriel and Ariana," Sarah suggested.

Heather cringed, their moms knew a little bit about Gabriel and Ariana's history, but they weren't fully versed on what had happened in the past. Being on tour was a strange thing; you were oddly cut off from your family and friends. Nobody but the closest inner circle of Cruise Control had seen the devastation when Ariana left.

"Yeah, maybe," Heather said with a tight smile, and Harrison frowned at her.

"Do you not like her, Heather?" Sarah asked with open curiosity.

"It's complicated. Let's just say that I'm not her biggest fan."

"What about you, Harrison?" her mom asked him.

"I'm neutral. I think Gabriel is happy, and I'd like it to stay that way."

"Yeah, well, he was happy before, wasn't he?" Heather sighed. "He was happy until he wasn't."

"We've talked about this, Heather. They're together, and being angry about that isn't going to change it." He shrugged at her, but there was a hard note to his voice.

They had talked about it, frequently, over the last week since they'd played pool at Sebastian's. In the end, they'd come to a cold truce where they basically no longer discussed it. Their mothers looked uncomfortable with the tone of their conversation, and Heather knew this wasn't the time or the place to have this conversation.

"Fine." She took a deep breath and exhaled slowly. "I'm sorry, everyone. It's been…an adjustment with her suddenly being back."

Harrison leaned over and put his arm around her. He pulled her tightly to him, and she put her arms around him before burying her face in his chest. She smelled the scent of him, masculine and warm. Her senses were filled with him, and for a second, she forgot where they were, she forgot about everyone else and their party and the guest list, and it was just her and Harrison in the world. She lifted her face to his and kissed him softly on the lips.

"I love you, honey."

He smiled at her, and the tension in the room dissipated. Heather looked back at the list in front of her.

"So, record executives, Harrison? Where did we land?" She smiled at him.

They spent the rest of the afternoon whittling down the guest list to two hundred and five people and taking a chance that at least five people wouldn't be able to make it. They ran through the decorations that had been organized already and looked through invitation designs before settling on one that fit their black-and-white theme perfectly.

"Well, I'll get those sent to the printer tomorrow, and they should send them off this week. Do you need any help with dinner, Sarah?" Heather asked her future mother-in-law as they were cleaning up the table from all the engagement party paperwork.

"Sure, thanks, Heather. Robert should be home soon, and we can eat."

Heather loved Harrison's parents; she'd spent so much time here in their home back when she was in high school. They'd spent hours studying together in Harrison's room, and even though nothing had happened at the time, both sets of parents had been glad when they'd finally gotten together later on.

Everyone was ecstatic to have a wedding to plan now, and it was exciting, but with even just organizing the engagement party, Heather was amazed by how much work it was. She was still working day and night on Serenity's collection for Fashion Week, and all of her limited spare time had been taken up with organizing this party. She'd be glad when it and the wedding were over, and she could just go back to living her life with Harrison.

She followed Sarah into their kitchen. Even after Harrison had gotten a lot of money from being in Cruise Control and could afford to buy them a new house, his parents had wanted to stay in their family home. He had convinced them to allow him to pay for an upgrade to their kitchen, however, and it was pretty spectacular.

They'd had dark cupboards, exposed brick, and a linoleum floor, before. It had been very seventies, but the new wood flooring, white cabinets with gray accents throughout the room, marble benchtops, built-in sink, and all new appliances had brought it into the two thousands.

Heather opened the fridge and pulled out the things she needed to make a salad while Sarah pulled a dish of apricot chicken out of the oven and set it on the stovetop before covering it with tin foil. It was her specialty and one of Heather's favorite meals.

"Is everything okay with you and Harry?" Sarah asked her as she removed her oven mitts and turned to Heather.

"Yeah, we're fine. Why do you ask?" Heather focused intently on chopping some cherry tomatoes for the salad but thought she could guess where this conversation was going.

"It just seemed tense for a bit there. I've never seen you and Harry like that before."

Sarah began getting out plates and cutlery for their dinner, and Heather sighed.

"Everything's fine with Harrison and me, Sarah. You don't need to worry."

"What about with Gabriel?" Sarah asked her.

Gabriel, Hayden, and Sebastian were like second sons to Sarah and Robert. They often shared Christmas and Thanksgiving with all the families; she knew their moms even had their own group chat on WhatsApp. Heather wondered what would happen this year, given how strained it was between everyone at the moment.

"Well, yeah, it's been a bit tense there." Heather stopped chopping vegetables and turned to Sarah. "I don't know how much Harrison has told you."

"Not much. A little bit, just that they were together once before, and now they're back together again."

"And what has Josie told you?" Heather asked with a smile, knowing that Gabriel's mom had to have told them something.

"To be honest? I really don't think she knows much more than I do. Heather, what happened? She said she'd met Ariana, and she's lovely, but you seem to dislike her, and Bianca said Sebastian had some very unkind words to say about Ariana, but he didn't give her much information, either."

Heather threw some pine nuts and chopped feta into the salad bowl, covered it, and put it into the fridge before sitting down on a stool at the kitchen bench, and Sarah sat down next to her.

"Okay, well, Gabriel met Ariana just before the *Cards Have Been Dealt* tour started and invited her to come on tour with them. I thought she was really nice; we became really good friends. Then the day after the Grammys, Ariana left without talking to anyone, and we never heard from her again."

"So, she was the 'Ariel' girl that none of you would talk to us about?" Sarah looked like she was having a lot of questions answered, and Heather was certain she would be rushing to tell the other moms the first chance she got.

"That's the one."

"Why did she leave? Just the drama from that girl?"

"Nobody really knows. Well, maybe Gabriel does, I guess. She didn't tell any of us, Sarah, she literally just left with no contact, not even a text." Heather's face fell as she remembered it.

"Oh dear, that must have been awful for you. I know you haven't had many friends." Sarah was sympathetic and gave her a hug.

"Yeah, it was. So, then she just shows up again on the last night of the *Heart Wide Open* tour, and now she and Gabriel are back together, and everyone thinks I'm being a massive bitch because I don't want to be friends with her. I'm happy for Gabriel, I really am, but how do we know she won't just leave us again?"

"Leave Gabriel? Or leave you?"

That was the crux of the matter. Heather didn't feel that she could trust Ariana anymore. Maybe everyone was right, and she had changed; Ariana was undoubtedly doing things she would never have done before, but she'd broken Heather's faith in her, and Heather didn't know if their friendship could ever be repaired.

"Both," Heather replied. "I'm still really hurt by the way she left. I tried calling her and texting her, and she didn't reply at all. I'm just scared that it'll happen again."

"I guess time will tell," Sarah said. "How are you looking for Fashion Week?"

"I think it's going well. I'm flying to New York next week for model castings. It's completely insane; invitations have started going out, and it's all getting too real. April's already agreed to come, so at least there will be one celebrity there."

Heather was glad that April had agreed to come. She knew that celebrity attendance at a fashion show was crucial. Harrison would be there, too, of course, and probably Sebastian and Hayden, as well. She wasn't sure about Gabriel, now. She still worried that people would think that she wasn't really good enough to show at Fashion Week and that she'd only gotten the opportunity through being Harrison's girlfriend, though.

"Oh, she's so lovely! I'm sure plenty of people will want to come to your show, though." Sarah smiled at her.

Heather had no idea when she'd been invited to show at Fashion Week, exactly what it would entail. It was so incredibly competitive. First, she'd just been hoping to get a good show time. Now her publicist had started trying to woo celebrities to come to her show. Next, they would be casting models, but even if they liked someone, there was no guarantee that one of the major fashion houses wouldn't want them as well.

Then, there was the exorbitant cost. Most new designers had to seek finance or sponsors for their shows, but Heather counted herself incredibly lucky to have Harrison in her life. He was totally supportive of her dreams, but she had been horrified to find out how much they would be out of pocket for her show. Harrison hadn't blinked an eye, however, vowing to pay whatever the total was at the end of the day.

It was added pressure, though, part of why she was pushing herself to strive for perfection. Harrison had so much faith in her abilities; she couldn't let him down. If her show were successful, they would be able to scale up the production of her designs. If it wasn't, she didn't dare think of how many thousands of dollars would be wasted and how many outfits she would have to sell to recoup that cost.

Harrison had assured her that it didn't matter because his money was her money as well, but Heather had it in her mind that it was a loan from them to her label and was set on Serenity paying them back in full as soon as it could manage.

Heather's thoughts were interrupted as Robert Fletcher

walked into the room. Harrison's father was an older version of him, tall and good looking with graying bronze hair.

"Hello, sweetheart," he said to Sarah, kissing her cheek. "Heather, lovely to see you!"

He gave Heather a hug as she stood up to greet him.

"Well, shall we get this dinner on the table, then?" Sarah turned to look at Heather.

"Sure."

"Can I help carry anything?" Robert asked, and Sarah indicated to the dish of apricot chicken sitting on the stove.

They took everything they needed for dinner out to the table, where Harrison was still sitting and chatting to her mom. Heather took a seat next to Harrison, and immediately, he leaned over to kiss her cheek and squeezed her leg with his hand. His nearness was the thing that soothed her the most in the world.

Heather got herself some rice and topped it with a healthy serving of apricot chicken before adding some salad on the side, and began to eat it. It was absolutely delicious, as always.

"Harrison, how's the next album coming?" her mom asked him.

"Nothing really, yet. Gabriel wrote some stuff during the tour, but we're all going out to Galena in October for a songwriting retreat at Sebastian's place."

About a year ago, Sebastian had bought a massive property in Galena. There had been an old house on the property, but he'd had it gutted, renovated, expanded, and built a music studio with the intention of them recording their next album there.

"That should be nice," Sarah said.

"Yeah, it'll be great to be in our own studio. Not having to stick to someone else's schedule. We're really excited to have the freedom to experiment and hopefully make something great."

"*Heart Wide Open* was pretty great!" her mom protested.

"Thanks, Lillian. You're right; it was, but we've grown and

changed, and it's so exciting to see how that reflects in our music."

Harrison's face was alight with enthusiasm. It changed his features and brought a smile to Heather's face. She loved how passionate he got about the music he made with the band and found herself excited to see what they produced as well.

"Are you going to Galena?" Robert asked Heather.

"Oh, I'm not sure if I'm invited." Heather shrugged.

"As if Sebastian would ever say no to you!" Harrison laughed.

Heather bit her tongue, not wanting to clarify that she was specifically referring to Gabriel's presence and whether or not he would want her there.

"We'll see what happens. It probably depends on how Fashion Week goes."

"Okay, well, I'm not going a month without seeing you, so you're either coming out to Galena, or I'm driving back to Chicago, I guess."

"A month?" his father asked him.

"Well, we don't know for sure, but we've all blocked out October to work on the album. No interviews, no business, just being out there and seeing what happens. It might take longer; it might take less time. The important thing is that we're not tied to any timeframe."

"It sounds very exciting, Harry," Sarah said with a proud smile on her face.

"Thanks, Mom."

The conversation moved on, and Heather checked out. Maybe she'd be able to time her visits to Galena so she wouldn't have to see Ariana. Sebastian would probably help her do that, almost certainly not without bitching at her about it, of course. It was just better for everyone if Heather stayed away from Ariana, though, especially while they were all concentrating on the new album.

On some level, Heather knew that there was a conversation

between herself and Ariana that was long overdue, but she also felt that the time for that conversation had well passed. It should have happened over two years ago, and the only reason it hadn't was through Ariana's choice not to have it at the time.

This was the thing; the band was so close-knit that Heather had no idea how long she could possibly continue like this. Gabriel clearly wanted Ariana in his life, and that meant Ariana being in their lives. It was so unfair that Heather had no choice in the matter. Not without ruining the one thing in Harrison's life that was perhaps even more important to him than she was. If he didn't have his music, didn't have Cruise Control, Heather didn't know how he would survive. She needed to do everything she could to make sure that she didn't ruin it for him.

After dinner was finished, Heather and Harrison both helped to clean up the dishes. It was something they'd done so many times before; they fell into a comfortable routine.

"You've been quiet tonight, angel," Harrison commented.

"I've just got a lot on my mind," she replied.

"Anything you want to share with your fiancé?" He gave her a good-natured smile.

"Just stressing about Fashion Week and money and the like."

Harrison set the dish he'd been about to rinse down in the sink and walked over to Heather, putting his arms around her and hugging her tightly to him. She could feel his chest moving up and down as he breathed, and she sank into his warm embrace.

"I've told you not to worry about the money, angel," he said.

"I know you have. It doesn't stop me worrying, though," she whispered around a lump that was forming in her throat.

Keeping one arm around her, he put his other hand under her chin and turned her face up to his so he could look into her eyes.

"You're going to be my wife soon. Even if you weren't, I would still have invested in you. I believe in you, angel; you're talented, and I'm proud to be the man who gets to place his bets on you."

With that, he lowered his mouth to hers and kissed her passionately. Her heart raced, and she felt an ache between her thighs; they were in his parents' house, however, so they couldn't exactly have sex right now. She broke the kiss, and they were both breathless.

"Remind me to show you how grateful I am for your support when we get home," she said to him, her voice husky.

"Don't think I won't." He grinned at her wickedly.

They finished cleaning up, then went to say goodbye to their parents, and it wasn't long before they were sitting in Harrison's car as he drove them home. He had his right hand casually on her thigh and was stroking it lightly. Heather felt a steady thrum of arousal echoing throughout her body. She played with the ring on her left hand as she looked out the window and watched the city lights of Chicago passing by them.

She really was incredibly lucky to have Harrison in her life. With everything else that had happened over the last ten years—the change from renting shithole apartments and taking public transport to driving around in expensive cars and flying in private planes—Harrison had remained the same. Their relationship was as strong as it had ever been, and soon, he would be her husband. She closed her eyes and let the familiar tiredness that she felt so frequently these days wash over her. Harrison had begun singing one of her favorite Cruise Control songs, and she smiled as she drifted off to sleep.

~AUGUST~

LOVE IS IN THE AIR!

Harrison Fletcher and his longtime girlfriend, Heather York, are having their engagement party this month. From what we've heard, it's being held at an exclusive Chicago location with only their closest family and friends in attendance.

Everyone is eager for more details, but our sources tell us that they're being very tight-lipped on the arrangements. If Heather is involved, it's bound to be classy. Her clothing designs are to die for, and we are eagerly awaiting her debut at New York Fashion Week next month!

Meanwhile, Gabriel Knight and his new girlfriend, Ariana, were spotted having lunch at a café in the city this week. They looked very loved up from the pictures we saw. Elena who?

We also caught Hayden and Sebastian having a night out on the town, looking pretty drunk and enjoying the company of some very beautiful ladies. The two eligible bachelors of Cruise Control sure know how to have a good time! Hands up, anyone who volunteers as tribute to be one of their girlfriends!

I think the question we all want to know the answer to, though, is when can we expect a new album?

Chapter 5

A DIAMOND IN THE ROUGH

Heather and the fashion show director she'd hired, Ally Morrison, were sitting behind a table in a conference room they'd booked at her hotel in New York City. In the hallway, models were lined up, waiting to come inside. The room was filled with racks of clothes that Heather and her employees had carefully prepared for the lucky models to try on during callbacks tomorrow. Heather was stunned by how many models Ally had successfully organized to come to the casting call.

"Is this normal? There's so many!" Heather exclaimed as Ally's assistant, Emma, opened the door to let some models into the room.

"The response was phenomenal," Ally told her, "I never get these many options for a debut designer; it's crazy. No offense."

"None taken." Heather smiled at her.

Heather wondered how many of the models happened to be Cruise Control fans. She pushed that thought to the back of her brain, though. She would be paying these women to model her designs; Harrison's day job had nothing to do with this. She was officially a designer who would be showing her collection at Fashion Week.

As Emma let the models in five at a time, she would take a

headshot of each of them with a Polaroid camera. Heather and Ally would then attach that picture to their notes about the model. Heather wanted to talk to the models and get more of a feeling for what they were like, but Ally kept pressing her to move through them quickly.

"I want to ask them more questions!" Heather protested after the third group of models left the room, while Emma took the pictures of the next group.

"I know you do, but I want to go to bed before midnight. Trust me. That's what callbacks are for. You'll see." Ally smiled at her knowingly.

Heather did see. She quickly lost count of the number of models they'd seen. They started to all blend into one another for Heather. They generally fell into the same tall, thin template. Occasionally, though, one of them would spark hers or Ally's interest. Something unique would sparkle through, and Heather now looked forward to seeing it.

She marked these women down carefully on her notes, hoping against hope that she would have succeeded in getting them for a callback tomorrow. All in all, Heather was planning on having forty looks for her show. They were hoping to find this many models, but Ally had warned her that she might struggle. In that case, their plan was to get as many models as they could and figure out who they would have do a quick-change backstage once they had their final models booked.

Ally had been right about how long it would take; they didn't finish seeing the last group of models until seven in the evening, having started at ten in the morning. A hotel staff member had brought them lunch, but that was many hours ago, and Heather was starving now, and her stomach started rumbling uncomfortably.

"Are you a bit hungry, Heather?" Ally laughed.

"Just a bit. Don't be concerned if I suddenly keel over; I'll just be dying of starvation." She smiled back at her.

"Emma, can you order us some food? I could go some Pad Thai while we sort through these." Ally gestured to the piles of photographs and notes on the table in front of them.

"Pad Thai sounds amazing," Heather agreed.

They couldn't leave until they'd decided which models Ally would contact for callbacks, and then she would send the emails to the relevant agencies today so they could see the models again tomorrow afternoon. The women started the process as they waited for Emma to come back with their food.

"Jess is a must-have," Heather said, pushing across the notes she'd taken on a tall, dark-skinned woman who'd had stunning braids and a brilliant smile.

"Agreed. Also, Carrie." Ally put a picture of a thin, red-headed woman, whose curly hair had really stuck out in the crowd, on top of the photograph Heather had put between them, starting a pile of possible callback models.

Heather was excited now; she dug through the notes she'd made to find her special models, putting them all on the pile. Ally did the same for the models that she'd liked as well, and they came up with twenty-five models that were their favorites before Emma arrived with their food. She'd also thought ahead and brought them each a much-needed coffee. They sat back in their chairs, holding their containers of food in front of them as they discussed the day.

"Okay, so we have our top picks. Time to find some second choices, I guess?" Heather asked Ally.

"Exactly, sometimes a girl will come back and just lights up the room on the second go-see, so it's worth getting anyone you even slightly liked to come back if you can."

It was astounding how much knowledge Ally had about how this all worked; Heather was incredibly grateful that she'd agreed to work with her even though she was a debut designer.

"How the hell would I do this without you?" She grinned at Ally.

"Lucky for you, you don't have to!"

"Ally is the best fashion show director I've ever worked with," Emma added.

Ally Morrison wasn't the most famous fashion show director, but Heather had appreciated her candor when she'd been looking for someone to work with on her show. She was only a few years older than Heather; she had beautiful, caramel-colored skin, her hair was cut into a shoulder-length bob, and she was short and curvy. They'd clicked almost immediately, and it was great to have someone to guide her through the process. Ally was so down to earth and had been completely realistic about what Heather could expect.

"Same here," Heather said to Emma, even though Ally was the only fashion show director she'd ever worked with, and they all laughed.

Emma collected up their containers, so Ally and Heather could continue their work. Ultimately, they decided on seventy women they'd like to see again.

"So many!" Heather exclaimed.

"We'll invite that many, but it's unlikely they'll all show up," Ally told her. "Most of these girls will have gone on anywhere from five to ten go-sees today. They'll have more tomorrow, and if our callback is in conflict with one of those and they want that job more, they'll skip us."

"What if nobody shows tomorrow?" Heather suddenly felt worried that she would end up with no models at all, and Ally laughed.

"Trust me, Heather, you will have plenty of models to choose from. If nobody shows tomorrow at all, I will happily refund you my fee and quit the business entirely."

"What do we do with these?"

Heather indicated to the pile of paperwork with the rejected models. She felt terrible for them, knowing they weren't going to receive a callback. All of the models had been lovely; it couldn't be pleasant facing the constant possibility of rejection at every casting you attended.

"We keep them; I'll keep them all. I'll send the emails tonight to the agencies about the ones we want for callbacks. We'll see how those go, and then if we still find ourselves short of models, we'll revisit these or do another casting call," Ally told her.

"Have you ever had to do that?" Heather wondered.

"I could count on one hand the number of times we've had to do a second casting call. We almost always get what we need from the first one," Ally said with a reassuring smile.

It was close to nine o'clock by the time they'd cleared the room up and said their farewells. Heather was exhausted and was incredibly glad that she'd made the decision to stay in the same hotel where they were doing their business.

Heather took the lift up to the twelfth floor, and headed to her suite, swiping her room key to get inside. She made her way to the bedroom and collapsed on the king-sized bed, her phone in her hand. She was so tired that she just wanted to sleep, but she needed to call Harrison.

Unlocking her phone, she went to her favorite contacts and clicked his name at the top of the list. It was only eight in Chicago, so she wasn't surprised when he answered the phone and she could hear noise in the background.

"Hey, honey," she greeted him.

"Hi angel, how did it go today?" he asked her.

She smiled at the sound of his voice. She'd missed him today; it would be so much better if he were here in bed with her, and she longed to have his arms around her.

"Really well, actually. We've got seventy models that we're asking for callbacks."

"Seventy? That seems like a lot!" He echoed her previous surprise.

"I thought so, too. Ally said they probably wouldn't all come, though."

"How many do you need?"

"Forty. There were twenty-five that we loved, so I'm just hoping they all come back, at least."

"I'm sure they will," he told her reassuringly.

She really hoped he was right. Even if she only managed to get those twenty-five, she would be happy with fifteen of them doing changes behind the scenes. Heather knew it was unlikely that she would manage to get all of her favorites, however, so she tried to keep her optimism in check.

"What are you up to this evening?" she asked him.

She thought that it sounded as though he might be at a restaurant from the general chatter and clinking of plates in the background.

"I'm out at dinner with Gabriel and Ariana."

Heather didn't quite know what to say to this. She hadn't forgotten their argument the night that they'd been at Sebastian's, and she didn't have the energy for one right now.

"How is it?" she asked him carefully.

"It's good. We're at Giovanni's."

It was one of their favorite Italian restaurants. This wasn't something Ariana would've done in the past, either. They generally had eaten in private or at secluded, out of the way restaurants to minimize the people who might see them. Considering Gabriel and Ariana were on almost every gossip magazine and website now, it probably didn't matter. Though, Heather knew from experience that whenever there were more than one of the band members out together, the public interest was exponentially multiplied and was mildly curious how Ariana was coping with that.

"Nice, are Hayden and Seb there, too?" She was very

interested in this, particularly if Sebastian had joined them for dinner or not.

"Nah, Hayden had a date and Sebastian…" he trailed off.

"Is Sebastian." She finished his sentence with a laugh.

"Pretty much," he said as he laughed, too.

She missed him so much. It had only been a day, but she hated to be separated from him. Heather had thought she'd get used to it on the *Heart Wide Open* tour, but she never really had. It was generally fine when she was busy working, in meetings etc., but it was always this time of night when she was ready to go to bed that she yearned to have him with her.

"I miss you, honey. I wish you were here with me."

"Me too. I can catch a plane tomorrow if you want?"

A smile crossed her lips. That was Harrison, always willing to do everything for others. As much as she would love to have him here with her, this was something that she felt as though she needed to do on her own. It was important to her that her design career wasn't entangled with Cruise Control, plus, she'd already dealt with the paparazzi when she had first arrived here yesterday. They would almost certainly double down on their attention if Harrison were in town with her.

"No, I'm fine. It's just the weekend, and then I'll be home. I love you."

"I love you, too, angel. Call me tomorrow when you're free."

"I will."

Heather hung up their call and thought vaguely about texting Sebastian to see what was up but couldn't be bothered. The exhaustion had hit her in full force now, and she couldn't even muster up the energy to gossip with him about Gabriel and Ariana tonight.

She fell asleep exactly where she was lying, fully clothed, and with a head full of models strutting back and forth on a runway wearing her designs.

♥

The next morning, Heather was woken by her alarm at seven. She was meeting the DJ and lighting technician in the conference room at eight-thirty. She called room service and ordered breakfast before heading to the bathroom to shower and change.

As she toweled herself dry after her shower, Heather caught sight of herself in the mirror and was shocked by her reflection. She looked too thin, there were dark circles under her eyes, and she almost didn't recognize herself. No wonder Harrison had been worried about her lately.

There was still so much to do before Fashion Week, though. It was six weeks away, which should be a lot of time, but Heather knew it would pass in what felt like an instant. She quickly pulled her makeup bag out from a drawer and covered her face in foundation, immediately looking a lot better. Once Heather had finished doing her makeup, the difference was astonishing. She looked fresh and ready to work, nothing at all like the tired woman she'd seen less than fifteen minutes ago.

She went to the wardrobe and pulled out a pair of black jeans, which she paired with an oversized, pink, knitted sweater and pulled on black ankle boots to go with it. As she was zipping them up, there was a knock on the door, and she went to answer it to find room service there with her breakfast.

Thanking the hotel employee, and tipping him generously after he set her breakfast up on the table, she sat down to eat. The food was delicious; it was a hot breakfast of scrambled eggs and bacon on sourdough toast. She devoured it all and drank her orange juice.

Heather grabbed her sketchbook. She'd been sketching out ideas for her wedding dress and bridesmaid dresses. She had no idea who she would have as bridesmaids, which made that more difficult, but she was so pleased with her wedding dress. Most of all, it was the knowledge that this dress would be the one she was going to be wearing when she married Harrison that made it special for her.

Heather glanced at the clock, then put her sketchbook away. She headed down to the conference room, arriving just after eight. She began looking through the outfits that were so carefully hung up on racks. As she did, Heather pulled out her phone and saw a message from Sebastian that he'd sent to her last night.

Hey sexy legs, how's NYC?

She laughed and sent him a reply.

Good. Callbacks today. You didn't go to dinner last night?

It was only seven in Chicago, so she didn't expect a reply from him any time soon. She wanted to call Harrison and speak to him but knew it was probably too early for that as well. Heather opened the photo app on her phone and started looking through the pictures she'd taken of the notes from their favorite models. She began to match models to outfits in her mind. She was probably getting ahead of herself, but she felt that some of the designs so perfectly matched a few of the models that she was terrified they wouldn't be able to book them. Heather's show was starting to come together in her head, and she was excited to turn it into a reality.

It wasn't long before there was a knock on the door to the conference room, and she called out for the person to enter. Russell Cross walked into the room. He was in his late forties, medium height and build, and was one of the best lighting technicians in the business. He'd worked on both of the Cruise Control tours, and aside from the money Harrison was lending her, this was one of the few favors she'd pulled in for her show. He was the only person she would trust to organize the lighting and was so pleased when he'd agreed to work for her.

"Heather! So good to see you." He gave her a massive smile as he walked over to her and gave her a hug.

"Hi, darling, it's so lovely to see you again. I can't thank you enough for doing this for me."

"It's not a problem; I'm honored you wanted me to do it." He smiled at her. "Are you excited?"

"I'm shitting bricks," she confessed to him, and he laughed.

"Well, if I recall correctly, I know four guys who were shitting bricks before their first live concert, and they seem to have done well for themselves," he reminded her with a wink.

He was right; she'd been there the first night of Cruise Control's *Cards Have Been Dealt* tour, and they truly had been shitting bricks. Even Sebastian, probably the single most confident person she knew, had been terrified. It had all been fine as soon as they were on stage and in their element, but for Heather, it was different.

Heather had to do all the work in the lead-up to the big day. Then, she just had to hope and pray that it all came together flawlessly. There were so many moving parts in a fashion show that it could fall apart easily at many different points. She took a deep breath and exhaled slowly; she was doing everything she could and hiring the best people possible to make it a success. Heather just needed to trust that they would perform as well as she knew they could.

Damien Hudson walked through the door to the conference room. He was younger than Heather, only twenty-two years old. Tall, slim and dressed casually in jeans and a T-shirt. He was carrying a backpack, which she knew would have his laptop in it. He was relatively unknown, going by DJ Atmos online.

"Hi, Heather," he said, holding his hand out to shake hers, "it's great to finally meet you in person!"

She'd found him on SoundCloud when she was looking for someone to DJ the show and had loved his work, so she'd approached him through his direct messages to see if he was interested in working with her. They'd talked on the phone a few times since, and he'd been ecstatic to be given this opportunity, and Heather had faith that he could pull it off.

"Damien, thank you so much for coming and working with us."

"No, thank you for asking me! I can't believe I'm going to DJ a Fashion Week show; this is insane." He gave her a shy smile as he opened his bag and began to set up his laptop.

"I feel pretty similar! I still can't believe there's a show for you to even DJ." She grinned at him.

"You're both going to do great," Russell told them.

"Oh, I'm so sorry. Where are my manners? Damien, this is Russell Cross, probably one of the best lighting technicians in the United States. Russell, this is Damien Hudson, our DJ."

The two men shook hands.

"Have you lit fashion shows before?" Damien asked.

"Yeah, quite a few. I mostly work on concert tours now, though." He smiled at Heather.

"He did the two Cruise Control tours," Heather informed Damien, and he looked impressed.

"Oh, I went to the *Heart Wide Open* tour. It was amazing!"

Heather smiled at Damien's evident enthusiasm and felt a glow of pride at the effect that Cruise Control had on people. The guys had worked hard and earned this reaction from their fans.

"It really was." She smiled at him. "Okay, where do we start?"

Damien had been working on possible music for her show over the last few months, and Heather loved what he'd done. She'd told him about her inspiration for the collection and had sent him pictures of some of the designs as she'd finished them so that he could get a feel for what she wanted.

Russell closed his eyes as he listened, Heather imagined that he was envisioning the lighting needed to complete the show. The music was soft and lilting; it fit her goals beautifully. It took you away to some kind of fairy tale world where life was perfect and easy. She gave him some feedback on a few songs that she thought could probably be switched around to match the designs better, and he wrote a note on his computer so he could move them around in the playlist.

Russell described his ideas for lighting, wanting to go with soft, colored lighting between outfits but explaining that they would need full-spectrum white lights as the models walked the runway to allow the clothes to really shine and to make for the best photographs.

"It's a lot different than lighting the stage for a concert," he explained, "we want to make sure that your designs look as good as they possibly can, Heather. So, we need some ambient lighting for mood mixed with medium temperature white lighting so that the colors in the clothes stand out when they're on the runway."

"I'll take your word for it," Heather said with a laugh.

"I won't let you down," he reassured her.

Heather appreciated his confidence. It was comforting to know that he was so sure of himself. This morning's work had helped her to feel better about the show. It was coming together exactly as she'd planned, and it was a huge relief. She'd been so worried about this show for so long that having some things set in stone now eased her mind.

"Thank you so much for coming today, gentlemen," she said to them as they were leaving the room.

"No worries, Heather." Russell smiled at her.

"Yeah, I was happy to. It was great to meet you," Damien said.

"Well, I guess the next time I see you two, it'll be at the dress rehearsal!"

They said their goodbyes, and as the men walked off to the lobby of the hotel, Heather headed back upstairs to her room. She was planning to order room service for lunch before coming back down in time for their one o'clock callback time. It was only ten-thirty now, so she had a couple of hours to decompress in her room before she had to come back down.

As the elevator traveled up to her floor, she pulled out her phone and looked at it, seeing Sebastian's reply to her text from this morning displayed on the screen.

You're surprised? Got any models' numbers for me yet?

Ah, Sebastian, he could always be counted on to be on the prowl.

Not really. Were you invited, though? Sorry, darling, I need all the models I can get. None for you.

Heather wondered if Sebastian had been invited to dinner last night and declined to go or if he hadn't been invited at all. She thought it would be the former and was unsurprised when his reply came through.

Yeah. They asked me. Why would I go if you're not there, anyway? No Heather and no models. My life sucks.

He was deflecting, and she knew it. Sebastian had some deep issues, that was for sure. She opened the door to her hotel suite and flopped down on the bed before writing her reply to him.

I'm sure you'll survive. Ariana went out in public with him. Maybe Hayden's right. Has she changed?

No, Heather. You need to stay on Team Sebastian. Forever. Team Gabriel and Ariana sucks.

She laughed out loud; he was so dramatic.

Hey, I haven't changed my position. I was just wondering. I'll talk to you later. I have to call Harrison and eat lunch before callbacks.

Okay. Don't forget to get me those phone numbers, though!

Heather rolled her eyes as she dialed Harrison's number.

"Hey, angel."

Her heart skipped a beat, hearing his smooth voice in her ear.

"Hey, honey. How's it going?"

"Not bad. I'm lying in bed, wishing you were here with me."

Her heart raced; he slept naked, and she knew precisely what they would be doing if she was there with him.

"I'll be home tomorrow; I can't wait to get my mouth around your cock," she said wickedly.

"Is that a promise?" She could hear the arousal and amusement in his voice.

"Absolutely. If I don't have some kind of carpet burn by tomorrow evening, I'll be sorely disappointed."

"Fuck, Heather, do you know what you're doing to me?"

She knew exactly what she was doing, of course, and she loved doing it. Calls like this were the only way she'd been able to survive their long stretches of separation during the last tour.

"You bet your sexy ass, I do. If I'm right, you should be stroking a pretty impressive erection right now. Am I right, Harrison?"

She dropped her hand to her waist and slipped it underneath her jeans and underwear. She was already wet, and her breathing quickened as he answered her question, and she began to finger herself.

"You're right, angel. I can't wait until it's your hand stroking me instead of mine. I want you on your knees in front of me so I can fuck your face before I fuck your pussy."

Heather thought she might come immediately from that. She loved when strait-laced Harrison talked dirty to her, but he knew this, too. He knew just what to say to drive her wild, and she began to moan his name.

"Come for me, sexy. I want to hear your orgasm."

She gave way, then. Not holding back, even though she knew she was being too loud, given she was in a hotel. She fingered herself until she came loudly, and her satisfaction doubled as she heard him come on the other end of the line.

"I love you, Harrison," she breathed into the phone.

"I love you, too," he replied, and his voice sounded further away from the phone. "Hang on. I'm just cleaning up."

Heather laughed at the sudden silence on the other end of the phone and thought that this probably made her love him even more.

"Okay, I'm back," he announced a minute later.

"God, I love you. Mr. Neat Freak!" She laughed.

"I love you, too, Future Mrs. Neat Freak." She could hear his smile. "So, I meant to ask before someone so rudely interrupted me, how did the meeting go this morning?"

"It went brilliantly," she told him proudly. "Damien's mix is absolutely perfect, and you know Russell is a genius. I don't want to jinx it, but I think the show might actually end up being amazing."

"I don't think it will. I know it will," he assured her. "What time are your callbacks today?"

"One o'clock."

"What time is your flight tomorrow morning?"

She had decided to fly back on Monday morning instead of tonight just in case they hadn't finished the callbacks in time.

"Eleven. I wish I was coming home tonight, though."

"Me too, angel. I'll be waiting for you."

They had given up on airport meetups long ago. It was always crazy between fans and the media. They instead preferred to reunite in the privacy of their own home, and Heather longed to be there with him.

"I'm going to go now, honey, I need to order some lunch and eat it before I go back down for the callbacks."

"Okay, love you."

She hung up and then used the room phone to call down and order some sandwiches and a soda for her lunch. After she finished eating, she made her way back downstairs for hopefully the last time this weekend to do the callbacks, and it wasn't long before Ally and Emma joined her.

"Hi, darlings!" Heather gave them each a hug as they arrived. "Did you get a good response for today?"

"Overwhelmingly positive. Only two of our favorites can't make it. Plenty of others can, and I've got between fifty-five to sixty confirmed as coming today."

Heather was mildly disappointed by this. Even though she'd been telling herself that she wouldn't get all of her favorites back, there was part of her that had hoped she would. Ally could see the disappointment in her face and laughed.

"You don't have to look like someone kicked your cat, Heather! I've been in this business for a long time. Please trust me when I say that this kind of response is unusual for a debut designer. Normally, I'd be telling you that you managed to get back fifteen out of the twenty-five girls you wanted."

"Really? Do you think it's just because of Harrison?" Heather chewed her lip and voiced the concern that still crept around in the back of her brain.

Sometimes she wondered who she was, outside of Cruise Control. She was working hard on Serenity, but a part of her felt as though she only had the success that she had because of Harrison. Heather wondered if anyone would ever see her as her own person.

"Do you want my honest opinion? Or do you want some fluffy bullshit?" Ally gave her a wry smile, and Heather laughed.

"Honest opinion. Never, ever do I want fluffy bullshit!"

"Okay, well, yes. I think part of the buzz around you is because of who you are. Cruise Control are gods, and you're from that world, making you a demi-god, I guess. What you create, though? That's all you. The only benefit it's given you is the ability to get noticed. If what you'd designed was anything less than amazing, no amount of public intrigue in the world would help make up for it."

"You're too kind, darling." Heather smiled at her.

"It's the honest truth. I think you're going to be big. You're talented, and when it's combined with an ability to get noticed, that can lead to something that's next level. I'm pretty excited to be getting in on the ground floor."

Their conversation ended as Emma started bringing the models in. They saw them one at a time now, and Heather did get to ask more questions. They would try on one or sometimes two of her designs that Heather felt might suit them and then would go on their way again.

Ally was right. There were only one or two of their previous favorite models that didn't blow Heather away today. However, there were quite a few models that she'd been lukewarm about yesterday, that sparkled like diamonds once they were given a chance to wear her clothes and show them more of their personality.

At the end of the day, they had a list of forty-seven models that they would be more than happy to have in her show.

"So, now we have too many? I really didn't think this would be our problem!" Heather laughed.

"Me, either," Ally replied.

There were three piles of photographs in front of Ally. One had the forty models they were going to hire; another had the seven models whose agencies they were going to keep on notice in case of a no-show on the day and a final pile with the rest of the models.

It had been another long day. Heather said goodbye to Ally and Emma, then slowly started moving around the room to carefully pack up the clothes hanging on the racks. She had photos of all the models they were hiring and began to pin these to the outfits she wanted them to wear whenever she came across one that she knew would be perfect for them.

Once everything was packed away, she left the carefully boxed up clothes where they were. The hotel staff would hand them off to the courier company tomorrow so they could make their way back to Chicago. It was late when she made her way back up to her suite. It had been a long and very productive weekend, but she was tired and was more than ready to go home.

Chapter 6

RAISE A GLASS

Harrison had Heather's hand in his as they walked into the room where their engagement party was being held. They had been delayed during The Gauntlet, so they were arriving later than expected. Fashion Week was a little over two weeks away, and people were desperate to know what she had planned.

The room looked stunning, and Heather was pleased. The whole place was filled with guests wearing either black or white outfits. All of the decorations were in the same theme; the stark black against the white meant all of the embellishments in them stood out. The venue had even managed to find black plates and cutlery for the event.

People cheered as they entered the room, and their DJ for the evening lowered the volume of the music to announce their arrival. There were twenty round tables, spaced evenly around the outside of the room to create a dance floor in the middle, all with white tablecloths and centerpieces of black candles carved with intricate floral patterns. People were already dancing; Heather could see Sebastian and Hayden dancing amongst them. Hayden was dancing with Tristan, and she gave them both a wave. Tristan was so awesome; it would be great if they got together. Sebastian was dancing with her cousin, Nikki, and Heather cringed. Dammit, he would eat her alive, and she liked her cousin. She'd talk to him later.

Heather and Harrison greeted guests as they crossed the large room before stopping at the table next to their own. Harrison's parents and her mom were sitting at this table, along with their grandparents, and they greeted them all before continuing to their table. Heather sought out the seat that had her name on a place card; she was going to be sitting in between Harrison and Sebastian. There was an empty chair next to Sebastian's seat, and Heather frowned. It had been intended for Sebastian's theoretical date, who didn't seem to be in attendance.

Next to the empty chair was a woman with a friendly smile and long, brown hair. Hayden's sister, Vanessa, had come with him tonight. Heather was pleased to see her, and she stood up to give Heather a hug.

"Vanessa, I'm so glad you could come! Alex is at home with the kids, I guess?"

"Yup, Mama needs a night out." She laughed. "Congratulations, guys."

"Thanks, oh, don't get up!"

Heather turned to her brother Jake's wife, Chloe, who was sitting next to Vanessa and had started to stand to give Heather a hug. Heather leaned down to hug her instead, as Chloe was heavily pregnant.

"Congratulations, Heather! I'm so sorry I missed your birthday, Harrison."

"Not a problem, Chloe. I completely understood." He gave her a warm smile.

Chloe had been at home, sick, during his birthday party. Her morning sickness had continued well into the second trimester.

"I was bummed I couldn't come; Jake told me it was awesome.

I'm so sad I missed the proposal, too!"

Heather had moved on to hug her brother now; he was sitting next to his wife and gave Heather a huge grin.

"Congratulations, sis! I'm so happy for you guys."

"Thanks, Jake, I'm pretty happy, too!"

Then she'd reached them. Ariana was sitting next to her brother, and Gabriel was seated next to Harrison tonight. She hadn't seen them since they'd been at Sebastian's. Harrison had caught up with them on multiple occasions, and even Sebastian had seen them several times, often keeping Heather updated via text and always complaining to her that she should be there, too.

It had caused some strain between her and Harrison when they had been organizing the seating plan for tonight. They had to be at the same table, that was without question, but Heather had been adamant that there was no scenario where she wanted Ariana to be seated next to her. She had also insisted that Ariana wasn't to be seated next to Sebastian, either, because she wanted tonight to be a good night with little to no drama if she could help it.

"Hello Gabriel and Ariana, I'm glad you two could come." She forced a smile onto her face.

There was an obvious tension between them, and Gabriel frowned at Heather before opening his mouth to say something, but Ariana spoke before he could.

"Thank you for inviting us, Heather," Ariana said politely. "We're happy to be here to celebrate with you. Aren't we, Gabriel?"

Ariana and Gabriel looked at each other, and Heather saw something pass between them. It was some kind of unspoken message that caused Gabriel's posture to relax, and Heather hadn't even noticed how tense he had been until this happened.

"Yes, of course, we are." He smiled now.

"Well, we're stoked that you guys came." Harrison gave them a friendly smile and leaned down to hug Ariana.

Heather moved over to her seat, and Harrison took his place

next to her. They chatted with the guests at the table, and Heather started to relax. Harrison had his arm resting casually on the back of her chair and was softly stroking the exposed skin of her back. She found it incredibly arousing and, for a second, lost track of the conversation at the table as she focused on the feeling of his hand tracing a pattern back and forth on her.

"Your dress looks amazing, Heather!" Vanessa complimented her.

Heather blinked for a second while her brain caught up and processed the comment, then she smiled her appreciation at Vanessa. She had worn one of her own designs tonight, something she had made specifically for this evening. It was made from soft, white satin and was fitted tightly at the top with a plunging back and hugged the curves over her ass before flaring out from her upper thighs. Heather had hand sewn the black, floral embellishments onto the dress herself. She'd felt guilty spending so much time on it this close to Fashion Week, but tonight was important to her, and she wanted it to be just as perfect as she wanted her show to be.

"I wish I could pull off wearing something like that!" Chloe laughed.

"You're pregnant, darling. In a few weeks, you'll have the baby, and you can wear anything you want," Heather assured her.

"Ignore Heather," Vanessa interjected, "she doesn't know anything, I didn't get back to my pre-baby weight for over a year, just in time to get pregnant with baby number two!"

"Is it really like that?" Heather asked, laughing. "I always thought that once the baby was out, you just went back to normal!"

"Maybe for some women, but definitely not for me! As for wearing whatever you want, well sure, as long as you're fine with it getting puked or pooped on by the tiny human that you've just pushed out of your chacha."

"What have I done?!" Chloe looked absolutely horrified, and

everyone at the table laughed.

"I'm sure you'll be fine, though, of course." Vanessa gave her a reassuring smile. "I take it back; ignore me and listen to Heather!"

The DJ changed the music to something quiet and classical, announcing that their entrées would be served soon and asked the dancers to return to their tables.

Hayden and Sebastian appeared shortly after that. They both looked mildly out of breath and had obviously been enjoying themselves on the dance floor.

"Hi, guys," Harrison said as they approached.

"Hey, Harrison, hey, Heather! Congratulations, again," Hayden said, giving them each a quick hug before sitting down next to his sister.

"Thanks." Heather smiled at him.

"Hi, Harrison," Sebastian said, throwing an arm around his shoulders.

"Hey, Seb. Having fun?" Harrison asked him.

"Heaps, I was dancing with the hottest chick I've seen in a while!" he announced.

"Yes, about that, could you try not to break my cousin's heart, please?" Heather told him in a mock stern tone.

Sebastian looked at her for a second, then threw back his head and laughed as he pulled her up from her seat to hug her.

"Those fucking York genes must be pretty amazing," he announced to them all, still laughing as he and Heather took their seats. "I should've known someone that hot would be related to you."

The waiter arrived at their table, so they could all pick what they wanted for their appetizers from the options on the menu.

"Sebastian, I can't help but notice the empty seat next to you. What happened there?" Heather raised her eyebrow at him as she asked this.

"Well, I was going to bring someone, but then I didn't want

her to get the wrong idea, you know? I mean, if I start bringing girls to engagement parties and weddings, they're going to start thinking those things are a good life choice."

Heather had a look around the table and saw zero surprise at his announcement; everyone here had been exposed to this lecture from Sebastian at one point or another. She was mildly annoyed that he'd wasted an invite, though.

"So, we spent hours working out who to invite and cutting people from the list, but left you a plus-one for absolutely no reason?" She rolled her eyes at him.

"Not 'no reason,' Heather. Your cousin can sit with me now! Or we can leave it empty, so there's no one to compete with you for my affection." He winked at her, a cheeky smile on his face.

"You do know that my sister is getting married to someone else, don't you?" Jake said from across the table, with a slightly frosty tone to his voice.

He'd told Heather in the past when he'd heard Sebastian make comments like this to her, that it made him uncomfortable. Objectively, she did understand that for normal people, they were inappropriate. It was something that Sebastian had been doing for so long, though, that it had kind of just become one of their running in-jokes in the band. She'd tried to explain to Jake that Sebastian didn't mean anything by it, but he still didn't get it.

"She is?" Sebastian raised his eyes in faux surprise and turned to look at her. "Heather, you're marrying someone that isn't me? How could you? I'm heartbroken."

"Yes, she's marrying me, Sebastian. I'm sorry," Harrison said as he faked regret, "we didn't mean it to happen. We just fell in love; we never meant to hurt you!"

"Heather? Tell me this isn't true!" Sebastian looked back and forth from Harrison to her, dramatically. "It can't be true."

"I'm sorry, darling. It is true." She held her left hand up to show him her ring, as though he'd never seen it before. "I love

Harrison, and he loves me. Can't you just be happy for us?"

"No! You're the only woman for me. I will never get over this betrayal!" He stood up, pushing his chair back so violently as he did so that it fell over and stormed away from their table toward the bar.

Heather, Harrison, Hayden, and even Gabriel and Ariana all burst into laughter at his theatrics. Guests at other tables were looking over at them quizzically, trying to understand what the fuss was about.

"You guys are assholes," Jake said to them with a roll of his eyes.

"Aww, sweetie." Chloe had an amused grin on her face. "Come on. It was pretty funny."

"Traitor," Jake said, but was smiling now and leaned over to give his wife a kiss.

Sebastian arrived back at their table with a tumbler of amber liquid as the waiters brought the entrées out to the tables. He picked his chair up off the floor in a fluid motion as he passed it and sat down on it next to Heather again.

"I'm sorry for my outburst, everyone. It's just hard for me to accept that mine and Heather's love story is over, you know," he told the table as he raised his glass to them. "I've got alcohol now, though, so I'll be okay. To Harrison and Heather!"

The rest of the table raised their glasses to the happy couple as well, and all of them took a drink. Heather leaned over to kiss Sebastian on the cheek.

"Now, now, Heather. That kind of behavior is unbecoming of an engaged woman," he told her, sternly, as he took a bite of his food. "Don't go giving me ideas that you're ready to call off the engagement to be with me."

"My bad." She leaned over to kiss Harrison thoroughly on the lips, winding her arms around his neck and deepening their kiss as she did so. "Better?" She turned her head to ask Sebastian this when the kiss ended but left her arms around Harrison's neck.

"Much. I think I get the hint now." Sebastian laughed, and Heather turned back to the table to start eating her food.

Heather had ordered herself a bruschetta, and the flavors exploded in her mouth when she took a bite. Bruschetta was one of her favorite appetizers, and she loved it when it was done well, as this one was.

"So, Heather, how are the plans for the wedding going?" Chloe asked her.

"I have barely done anything," Heather cringed, "we've got the major vendors booked, but I've been so flat-out with getting ready for Fashion Week and this party that I haven't even had a second to think about the wedding."

"Harrison should be helping you." Hayden shook his finger at Harrison.

"Hey, if you think I haven't tried, you'd be wrong." He laughed.

"He is helping," Heather confirmed, "I just haven't had time to focus on the wedding itself, yet."

"What about the bridal party?" Vanessa asked her.

That was an aspect of the wedding that Heather had been mentally avoiding. She had no clue who the hell she would have in her bridal party. Harrison knew. They hadn't discussed it, but it would one hundred percent consist of Hayden, Gabriel, and Sebastian. She didn't know which of them he would ask to be the best man, but she was sure it would be one of the three of them. He was an only child, and they were the closest thing he had to brothers.

Heather had no one, and it made her feel awful. She did think she might ask Chloe but was unsure if it would be too hard with a new baby. Other than that, there was no one, and the part of her brain that obsessed over aesthetics needed three bridesmaids to match the number of groomsmen.

"We haven't really discussed it." Heather shrugged as nonchalantly as she could.

"You'll want to organize it soon," Chloe warned her. "You'll need time to organize the bridesmaids' dresses. The bridal shops usually want months of advance notice."

"Are you not going to design the dresses yourself, Heather?"

Heather was surprised when Ariana finally joined the conversation. She felt, more than saw, the immediate tension from Gabriel, Harrison, and Hayden as they waited for her reply. For fuck's sake, it's not like she couldn't be civilized with the woman. Of course, Heather hadn't really proved that in recent times. Well, watch this, boys!

"Thank you for asking, Ariana," she said while smiling politely at her, "yes, I was thinking of making the bridesmaid dresses myself and definitely my wedding dress. I've actually already started designing it."

Heather's eyes went slightly out of focus as she envisaged what she was planning for the dresses. Her wedding dress would take the most time to create, but if she pulled it off, it would be amazing.

It would have a tight bodice, full skirt, and intricate detailing. It was the dress she had been fantasizing about wearing on her wedding day since she was a little girl, and she had some ideas about ways to take that childhood dream and turn it into a modern reality. The sketches that she'd started in New York were turning into something amazing, and she would start work on the actual dress, soon.

"I'm sure it'll be amazing," Ariana assured her, "your designs are absolutely beautiful."

Heather wondered how many of her designs Ariana had seen. She was curious how closely she had followed them in the two years since she'd seen her. A frown crossed Heather's face as this thought came to her. Everything came rushing back to her—Ariana had left them for two years.

Dammit, she'd almost forgotten it for a moment. Tonight, they had effortlessly slipped back into their old rapport. The joking with Sebastian, the random chitchat. No. She needed to remember that Ariana Chamberlain wasn't her friend anymore.

"Yes, they are. Thank you."

Heather hadn't been able to keep the cold tone from creeping into her voice as she said it. She saw a look of disappointment cross Ariana's face, and she looked away from Heather's frown to talk to Jake instead. Heather saw her grab Gabriel's hand and squeeze it as she did, and felt a tiny pang of guilt at hurting her. She looked away from Ariana and saw Sebastian watching her. He, too, was frowning.

"Heather, do you want to dance with me?" Sebastian asked her.

Most people had finished their appetizers now, and the DJ had recently started up the party music again in between the courses.

"I thought you had a cousin to be dancing with?" Hayden asked him.

"Why have the pale imitation when you can have the original and the best?" Sebastian smirked.

"I don't know whether I should be flattered at the compliment or outraged on Nikki's behalf." Heather laughed and pretended to look confused.

"You can be both, just come dance."

He grabbed her hand and dragged her to the dance floor. There was a fairly slow song playing, so he put his arms around her waist, and she put her arms on his shoulders. They had been dancing for less than a minute when he finally spoke.

"Team Sebastian, Heather. You're fraternizing with the enemy."

"I'm being polite. Something you could probably work on." She stuck her tongue out at him.

"I thought you were defecting for a minute, there." He raised an eyebrow at her.

"Me, too." She admitted to him. "I almost forgot...until I didn't. That being said, I don't want a scene at my engagement party, Seb. Please be nice, just for tonight."

"Hey, I'm getting good at it. *Some* of us don't have the luxury of avoiding practically every event she's at," he said and gave her a pointed look.

Heather was beginning to see why she had avoided these events, though. She felt as though she might easily fall back into friendship with Ariana, and she didn't want that. She couldn't risk the possibility of being hurt that way again. Heather felt a strange longing for friendship with her and for wanting to go back to what they'd had two years ago, though.

She imagined how it all could've been so different if Ariana had never left. Tonight would've been less stressful; they could've sat next to each other at the table, gossiping together all night, getting excited while making plans for Heather's wedding and Fashion Week. It brought a sense of sorrow to Heather, and she sighed deeply.

"Don't worry; I'm Team Sebastian and Heather. Forever." She grinned at him. "I'm pretty sure it's actually Team Gabriel, Ariana, Hayden, and Harrison, though."

They looked over at their table. Sure enough, everyone was laughing and chatting together as if nothing had ever changed within their group from the time they first met Ariana until now. Heather became acutely aware that she and Sebastian were the cause of the tension now. Ariana really had been nothing but polite and friendly since her return to their group. Would their inability to forgive Ariana be the thing that tore the group apart at the seams?

"Seb, why do you hate Ariana so much?"

"You really want to do this now?"

He frowned at her, and she looked around. People were dancing around them; they were at her engagement party. She was dancing with a man who wasn't her fiancé and talking about bloody Ariana. Not how she thought this evening would go. She felt bad about being part of the source of conflict in their group, and she needed to know the answer to her question.

"Yes, I do. Follow me."

He followed her off the dance floor and out of the room. She found a small, empty room off the hallway and entered it.

"I'm worried, Seb. I think if we don't forgive her, things are going to go to shit soon."

"That is not a good reason to forgive someone."

"Then what is?"

"Nothing. I've told you that I won't forgive her." He shrugged. "Didn't you tell me less than five minutes ago that you wouldn't, either?"

Heather frowned and rubbed her face with her hands. She had basically said that.

"Tell me why you hate her so much."

"The same reason you do. I love Gabriel. I love you, Harrison, and Hayden. I fucking loved her, too. I don't think any of you understand what it was like for me. It was supposed to be the best moment of our lives. We'd won the Grammys, swept the fucking things. Fulfilled a literal lifelong dream, and that moment was stolen from us. Instead of getting to enjoy it, everything was falling apart."

He crossed his arms across his chest, protectively. Heather could see the disappointment and hurt written all over his face.

"What else? I know there's more to it than that."

She stared at him, waiting for an answer. He could be selfish sometimes, but even he wouldn't refuse to forgive Ariana over something like that.

"I was so scared." His voice had dropped to a whisper now, as he admitted it. "Gabriel…I didn't know what he would do. I was terrified to leave him alone. Then, Harrison told me that you weren't eating, and he was so worried about you. You were like a zombie, Heather."

She felt guilty for the concern that she had caused everyone. Heather had opened herself up to Ariana, and the rejection that came from having her best friend ditch her without a word had been brutally painful.

"I couldn't fix the people I loved; you were both going through some kind of hell, and I couldn't get through to either of you. I don't understand how Hayden or Harrison can have forgiven her. They saw it, too. I know Gabriel's happy, and I want that for him, but I also know how much power she has over us. If she ever decided to leave again…"

He trailed off, unable to continue and obviously lost in the terrible possibilities that could entail. Heather's mind was whirling; Sebastian had given a powerful voice to the fears she'd been carrying about what might happen if Ariana decided to up and leave them again. It reaffirmed why she could not open herself up to friendship with her again.

They both looked up as the door to the room opened, and Harrison appeared in the doorway.

"There you guys are, they want us to order our main courses. What the fuck are you doing in here?"

"Sorry, honey, we were just talking. We'll come now, Seb, are you coming?"

She looked at Sebastian, and for a second, she really thought he might ditch the rest of the party until his expression cleared and he nodded. Heather walked over to Harrison with Sebastian following behind her. She took Harrison's hand in hers as they walked back into the main room for the party.

Heather found it hard to focus on the party after that. Sebastian's words were echoing around her brain, coloring their interactions with the others. Ariana had changed, Heather could see that, but had she changed enough to be trusted again? That was a question to which Heather didn't know the answer. They'd all trusted Ariana once before, and she threw it back in their faces. It was pretty hard to forget that.

After dinner, the DJ invited Heather and Harrison onto the dance floor so they could dance together. The song they'd chosen for this moment was a Cruise Control song called "If I Were You." Harrison had written it with Gabriel, and it was 'their' song. Soft and soothing, she relaxed into Harrison's embrace as they danced.

As she looked into his chocolate brown eyes, all of her stresses melted away. Nothing else mattered when she was with him, all of the drama with Ariana and Sebastian meant nothing. The terrible time when Ariana had left them all was long gone, but Harrison, he was here, and he was hers.

Heather couldn't believe that she had wasted most of their engagement party feeling bitter, stressed, and indulging in the drama when she could have been just enjoying her time with Harrison—celebrating their love.

"I'm sorry, Harrison," she said as she looked up at him.

"For what, angel?" He smiled at her.

There were so many things to be sorry about. Not being capable of forgiving Ariana. Not being one hundred percent present with him all evening. For siding with Sebastian instead of him. For being the cause of conflict at a time in their lives when they should be nothing but blissfully happy.

"For everything."

He leaned down and kissed her, which caused quite a few of their guests to cheer, bringing Heather back to reality with a powerful force. As the song ended, they made their way back to their seats, her hand in his and her heart feeling slightly less bruised than it had been earlier.

"It's time for speeches!" the DJ announced.

Her mom gave a beautiful, heartfelt speech about how Heather's dad would be so proud of them and that he'd loved Harrison as much as he had loved his own son. Robert gave a similar speech about Heather and how he and Sarah had considered her their daughter many years ago but would be glad to have it be official. Her brother gave a speech about how proud he was of her for what she was doing with her design career, and for Harrison supporting her dreams, then the microphone was handed to Hayden.

"Harrison and Heather, you are two of my favorite people in the world. Getting to watch you two fall in love and grow together as a couple has been a true honor. You have the kind of once-in-a-lifetime love that people write songs about, in fact, we actually did..." he paused until the laughter that was echoing around the room died down, "...but at the end of the day, I know that you two will be incredibly happy together. Congratulations!"

The room exploded into applause as Hayden finished his speech, and passed the microphone to Sebastian, who stood up to give his toast.

"Heather, when the wedding day arrives, I'll be up there and already wearing a suit, so if you change your mind, I can easily step right in."

Both Harrison and Heather laughed at this, which seemed to be the cue for others to laugh since a lot of their guests didn't quite know how to take this comment.

"But, seriously, as Hayden said, you two are pretty damn great together. I know I joke a lot, but everyone can see how Harrison lights up as soon as Heather comes into a room and vice versa. It's kind of gross, but if Harrison's happy sleeping with one person for the rest of his life, I guess he's just leaving more women for me!"

He looked around the room and found her cousin in the crowd of guests.

"What's up, Nikki?" He raised his eyebrows at her

suggestively, and she turned pink at the attention as other guests looked at her, too. Sebastian laughed and raised his glass in the air. "to Freedom!"

Their guests didn't seem to know exactly how to respond to Sebastian's speech, and there was some confused clapping as he handed the microphone over to Gabriel.

"Harrison. Heather. I've known you since we were teenagers. We always knew you two would get together. Heather, you have no idea how much shit we gave him for how madly in love with you he was before you hooked up! At the end of the day, it's obvious to the world that you two are meant to be together, and we're all so happy that you're finally getting married." He raised his glass in the air, "Congratulations, guys. To Harrison and Heather!"

Their guests all dutifully repeated the phrase as they took a sip of their drinks. Gabriel smiled widely at them, and Heather returned his smile, even smiling over at Ariana, who was also beaming at them.

Gabriel gave the microphone to Harrison, who held it out to Heather.

"Do you want a turn, angel?"

"Sure, why not."

She took the microphone from him and stood up.

"I want to thank everyone for coming tonight to celebrate with us. We really appreciate it. Harrison Fletcher"—she looked down at him, and her heart felt as though it might explode with the love she felt for him right now—"you are my everything. I can't wait to spend the rest of my life with you. Our lives are pretty crazy, sometimes, but whatever comes our way, I always know that I can handle it because I have you by my side. When I've been too weak to stand, you've held me up, and I can't thank you enough for that. I love you, honey."

He stood up and kissed her deeply, drawing more cheers from

their guests, then took the microphone from her hand as she sat down.

"Like Heather, I want to thank everyone who came tonight. It's been a great night, and part of that has been having you all here with us. Heather," he said as he looked down at her now, "you are the brightest star in the sky. You bring light to my world, and I consider myself so grateful to have you in it. I look forward to every day of our future together. I know that there will be ups and downs, challenges to overcome, but I also know that we will be facing them together, which is all that matters to me."

The DJ took the microphone back off Harrison, and he sat down, wrapping his arms around Heather and pulling her close to him. She could smell his scent, feel his warmth, and his strong arms enveloping her. She was safe. She was home.

The evening wound down and, eventually, they said goodbye to their guests and headed out to their waiting limousine amidst camera flashes from those paparazzi that had stayed around, waiting for them to leave. She sat next to Harrison, his arm around her as the car headed home. It had been a good evening. Not perfect, but good.

"Are you going to tell me now what you and Sebastian were talking about? Or should I guess?" Harrison asked her.

"You can probably guess," she said with a wry grin at him.

"Just tell me you were having crazy sex with him and weren't off in another room, bitching about Ariana."

She laughed at him.

"Yes, crazy sex, that was it." A serious look crossed her face as she remembered what Sebastian had told her. "What was it like for you when Ariana left?"

"I don't want to talk about it, Heather." A pained look crossed his face.

"Well, I need to talk about it. Tell me, Harrison."

"Yes, what Sebastian said the other night was true. You

stopped eating, and I was so, so worried about you. He and Hayden did pick up a lot of the slack at the time. Gabriel was out of commission, and most of my time was spent with you or worried about you."

"How have you and Hayden forgiven her?" she asked him, echoing Sebastian's thoughts from earlier.

"I can't speak for Hayden," he said solemnly, "as for me, I want Gabriel to be happy, and she makes him happy. I have to trust that she won't hurt us all again, but if she does, we survived it once before, and we'll survive it again. If she doesn't, then I get to see my friend happy and in love, which is all I've ever wanted for him.

Heather thought about this for a while as they drove along in silence. Tonight had given her a lot to think about. She still didn't know if she could forgive Ariana and get over her fear of being hurt again. What she'd said in her speech tonight was true, though. With Harrison by her side, she knew that she could face anything, was there any reason that one of those things wouldn't be the possibility of Ariana leaving again?

~SEPTEMBER~

THIS CRUISE CONTROL GOSSIP IS TOO HOT TO HANDLE!

Longtime couple, Harrison Fletcher and Heather York's engagement party was last weekend, and the gossip coming out of it is insane. A close friend of the band told us that super sexy Sebastian Fox was apparently upset by something early in the evening, enough to leave the table that Cruise Control was sitting at in quite a mood!

Later in the night, Sebastian and Heather disappeared together for a clandestine rendezvous somewhere outside and didn't come back until Harrison went looking for them. Is there trouble in paradise? Have Sebastian and Heather been having a secret love affair? We wouldn't blame her, who wouldn't want to break off a piece of that, but we thought she and Harrison were meant to be!

Meanwhile, New York Fashion Week is upon us, and WE ARE NOT CALM. Heather is making her debut with her collection for her fashion line, Serenity, and we can't wait. Inside sources tell us that her show is going to be spectacular, but we just want to know if any or all of our favorite boys will be front row! Who gets to be front and center, though? Sebastian or Harrison…

Chapter 7

FASHION IS AN ISLAND

Heather groaned as she rolled over in the bed in her hotel suite and looked at the clock. She'd slept in; it was already nine. It was Thursday, and she had been in New York all week. Ally had been amazing, organizing all of the different facets of the show that Heather didn't need to have a direct hand in organizing. She and her team had liaised with Heather's PR firm, the models' agencies, security, and even catering for the event.

They'd spent hours going over possible seating charts, coming up with multiple iterations depending on who actually showed up on the day. Heather felt like they'd done hundreds of options, but it was probably closer to twenty, all of which had the flexibility to be switched around if need be. In between that, there had been model fittings and time spent with Tristan and Jessica to work out what hair and makeup she wanted for the show.

Each of them would have a team of makeup artists and hairstylists working under them to ensure the models all featured the same look, and everyone got ready in time. Ally had thought she was crazy, not choosing a lead makeup artist and hairstylist with experience doing fashion shows, but she trusted them and wanted to give them a chance to prove themselves.

All in all, Heather was utterly exhausted, but the finish line was in sight. Now, she had a constant ball of nerves in her stomach, though, suffering permanent anxiety and spending roughly fifty percent of her time running through worst-case scenarios in her head.

She couldn't figure out which would be worse—nobody showing up to be in the audience or no models turning up to work. Her nightmares were split between the two options and sometimes would feature both possibilities at once. When she wasn't obsessing about apocalyptically bad outcomes, she was hyper-focused on ensuring that everything was absolutely perfect for her show.

Two of her employees, Rachel and Louise, had come out to New York to assist her with any last-minute alterations they needed to make to her designs. She was meeting up with Ally today to run through the designs a final time and ensure they were all organized in the correct order and assigned to each model for the dress rehearsal tomorrow morning.

Most importantly, Harrison would be arriving this afternoon. She needed him; his presence would help soothe her frayed nerves. He'd be traveling with Sebastian and Hayden, while Gabriel and Ariana would be staying in Chicago. Apparently, one of Ariana's friends was turning twenty-five, and she was organizing the birthday party for her.

On some level, Heather was hurt by this. It wasn't so much the fact that Gabriel and Ariana wouldn't be attending her show—Heather had told herself and it had been proven multiple times that Ariana wasn't her friend anymore. It was more that Ariana had friends, ones she organized birthday parties for, and Heather didn't have that. She loved Harrison and the guys, but the longing for the friendship she'd once had with Ariana hit her, and it stung.

Heather wanted to talk to Ariana; their long-overdue conversation needed to be had. She'd been thinking about it a lot since her engagement party. What Sebastian had told her had certainly provided a compelling reason for staying clear of the situation, but what Harrison had told her also stuck with her. They had survived it last time, and it couldn't be any worse now. Heather just needed to get through Fashion Week, and then she'd try and figure out what to do about Ariana.

Her phone buzzed on the table next to the bed, and she picked it up and looked at the screen.

Hey, angel. I can't wait to see you.

A smile came to her lips. She couldn't wait to see him, as well.

Me, either. Room 606. Not a moment too soon.

Everything okay?

She could read the concern coming through from his text.

Yeah. I just need you.

Her phone started ringing, and Heather wasn't surprised to see that it was Harrison calling her.

"Hey, honey."

"Are you okay, angel?"

It hit her unexpectedly. All the tiredness and stress, combined with Harrison's concern about her, and she suddenly felt like crying. Heather felt like she was unraveling, and this was literally the one day that she couldn't do that.

"I'm not coping, Harrison," she admitted to him quietly.

"I wish I was there with you. You can do this."

"I have to do this. I don't have another choice. I know I can do it, but it just"—she paused, and took a deep breath, then exhaled slowly—"it's been a lot. I'll feel better when you're here. Tomorrow's the day, and then it'll be done, and we'll know how it went."

"It's going to go brilliantly, Heather," he assured her, "I know it will. Your designs are amazing, and from what you've told me, everything there is going according to plan."

"You're right; my brain is just being a scumbag and making

me think bad things. I've got this."

She tried to sound confident and almost hit the mark, but just missed.

"I'll be there before you know it."

"I know. Thank you, honey."

"Have you eaten?" he asked her, the concerned tone creeping back into his voice.

"Not yet, I only just woke up. I'm going to get room service before I go meet Ally."

"Make sure you do. You don't want to get distracted and forget to eat."

"I promise I will. I love you; I'll see you this afternoon." She smiled at the thought as she said it.

"I love you, too, angel. See you then."

They hung up, and Heather followed through with her promise, immediately calling room service to order a large, hot breakfast. Harrison was right; she'd be so slammed today that she might not get a chance to eat.

As she waited for her food to arrive, she showered and dressed, ready for the day. She was seated at the table, eating her room service and scrolling through her emails when a text from Sebastian popped up on the screen.

Hey there, lover. Wanna screw later?

She laughed out loud. They'd all thought it was hysterical when the media had started printing articles about her and Sebastian having an affair. He'd gone so far as to rename her in his phone to 'My Lover.'

Sure. What is a secret love affair with no sex?

A pretty crappy one, that's for sure. How come we haven't fucked yet?

I'm not sure. We should get on that, I guess.

She finished eating her meal and stood up from the table as her phone pinged again with another text from Sebastian.

Tomorrow is going to be just as awesome as you are.

Of course, he and Harrison were together. Either Sebastian had overheard the conversation she'd had with him, or Harrison had told him about it. Either way, it was nice to feel so loved and supported. Being here on her own had really been messing with her head, it would be so good to have her support system around her.

Her mom was flying in with Robert and Sarah tomorrow morning, hoping to avoid the craziness that occurred when the guys were traveling together. The more of her family that was here in this city with her, the stronger she would feel, she knew it.

Heather checked her watch and realized that, in the meantime, she really needed to get going if she was hoping to meet Ally on time. She grabbed her hotel key and headed out of her room. She took an elevator to the ground floor, ordering an Uber on the way down, and arrived out the front of the hotel about a minute before her Uber was due to arrive.

As soon as she'd stepped outside of the sanctuary of her hotel, she was accosted by people taking her picture, shoving cameras and microphones in her face, and asking her questions. She ignored them and tried to walk past, but somebody grabbed her arm and tried to pull her back. Heather panicked and she felt a bolt of fear run through her. She was surrounded, but she managed to pull her arm out of their grasp and make her way to the safety of her Uber just as it arrived. She instructed her driver, Paul, to leave quickly as soon as she'd opened the door to slide inside.

She locked the car door behind her and tried to calm her breathing. That had been terrifying; she was already on edge with nerves, and being attacked by the paparazzi was unexpected. It had never been like this before; she'd always managed to exist safely on the edges of the Cruise Control world. When she was with the guys, she experienced it, but they were the focus of everyone's attention. Since Harrison had proposed, though, the attention had reached the next level. It was intense and scary. It felt like everyone wanted a piece of her, and now she often found herself being followed around, even when she wasn't with anyone from the band.

Paul drove to the address she'd put into the app, and as she got out of the car, she thanked him and apologized for the drama at the start of the trip. Heather was relieved that no one seemed to have followed them here and took the lift in the building up to the fifth floor. Ally shared office space with an interior designer friend that she had. They both spent so much time out with clients that, apparently, they rarely clashed over the need for actual office space. At the moment, though, Heather's collection had very much taken over their office.

"Hi, darling," Heather greeted Ally as she walked into the big room.

"Hi, Heather." Ally smiled at her from where she sat in front of a big desk stacked high with paperwork for Heather's show.

"I hope your office roommate doesn't hate me too much." Heather cringed, looking around at the clutter.

"Claire is probably my oldest friend; we met in elementary school. Besides, I almost drowned in curtain fabrics two months ago, so she owes me one."

Heather laughed but wondered what it must be like to have such a long-lasting and close friendship. She was envious of them. It must be nice to have someone to rely on like that. She reminded herself that Hayden, Sebastian, and Gabriel were as much her friends as Harrison's. Even though she did have those friendships, it had never been like those six months she'd spent being friends with Ariana. Sebastian wasn't interested in going to the nail salon together, and Hayden didn't particularly enjoy spending the day with Heather while she tried on clothes at whatever local boutique she'd recently found.

Heather had spent so long pushing down the memories of the

time she'd spent with Ariana that she'd almost forgotten how much fun they'd had together. She was hit by a tidal wave of memories. She could practically hear Ariana's laugh as they joked together one day long ago. They had spent the day window shopping, then sat at a café in Philadelphia where they served s'mores to your table.

"Are you serious?" Ariana seemed incredulous and laughed.

"Deadly." Heather grinned at her.

"Sebastian really used to hate Gabriel?"

"Oh, yes. 'Perfect Gabriel' is what he used to call him, and Gabriel was also very *artistic when we met him. Tragically so. He wore these turtlenecks all the time and carried around a notebook with him everywhere. He was always writing away in it." Heather speared a marshmallow on the toasting fork and held it in the flame, "Of course, a lot of the stuff he wrote in that notebook eventually became* Cards Have Been Dealt, *so I probably shouldn't mock him."*

"No, you should definitely *mock him. That's hilarious!" Ariana's green eyes were alight with mischief as Heather put the biscuit, chocolate, and marshmallow together before stuffing it in her mouth. "Oh my god, Heather, we should go buy turtlenecks and wear them to dinner tonight!"*

They both doubled over in hysterical laughter, and Heather covered her mouth to stop herself from spitting her food everywhere.

"Fuck, Ariana, that's brilliant! Yes. I am in."

"Heather?" She realized that Ally was trying to get her attention and shook her head as she came back to the present.

"Sorry, darling, I missed what you said." She looked over to see Ally had a frown on her face.

"Are you okay? You seem distracted, and you don't look"—Ally paused and searched for the word she wanted—"well, there's no nice way to put this, but you don't look great. You normally look great!"

Heather hadn't spent a massive amount of time on her

appearance today, to be fair. She'd rushed getting ready, hadn't gone with a full face of makeup, and if she looked half as frazzled as she felt, she must look like shit. Damn, the paparazzi were probably loving the opportunity she had given them to rake her over the coals for not looking amazing this morning—especially so close to her show.

"I'm so fucking stressed. I think I might snap," Heather wrinkled her nose at Ally. "I got attacked by paparazzi on the way here. It's getting beyond a joke."

"Don't you have a bodyguard?" Ally asked her.

"Nope. We've never really needed them, certainly not me, that's for sure. There's security on tour, anyway, and it's only recently that it's started getting this crazy."

"You should really consider it. I'm surprised the guys don't have them, at the very least. I've seen some of the mobs that celebrities deal with at events in the past. I'm shocked to hear that Cruise Control doesn't have personal bodyguards!"

"We'll probably have to soon if it keeps going like this. I feel like such a prat wanting personal security." Heather rolled her eyes.

"Your safety is absolutely the most important thing, though."

"You're right. I might talk to Harrison and see what he says." She smiled at Ally, then sobered as she remembered this morning, "It was truly terrifying. I'll be so glad when Harrison's here with me, even though that will probably make them crazier. At least I won't be alone, you know?"

"That makes sense. When's he getting in?"

"This afternoon, he'll probably be at the hotel by the time I'm back." She smiled and felt a sense of calm wash over her just knowing that she'd be seeing Harrison soon.

"You two are disgustingly cute together." Ally laughed.

"You've never even seen us together, though!"

"Oh please, Heather, everyone's seen you two together at some point or another! Besides, you just get this look about you when you talk about him. Like I said, disgustingly cute."

"Well, thanks, I guess?"

"How is the wedding planning coming along?" Ally asked her.

"It's going okay. I'm completely slammed with the show, of course, but both our moms are helping to organize it. We're going to lock in all the vendors by the end of the month. Harrison will be out at Galena on a songwriting retreat with the guys for all of October, so we kind of have to."

"What about the dress? I assume you're making it yourself?" Ally smiled.

"Of course. Oh my god, Ally. If I can pull off what's in my head, it's going to be epic. I can't believe I'm actually getting married!" Heather shook her head.

They moved on to the work they needed to complete. Reviewing all of the outfits, running through the results from the last model fittings, and double-checking the alterations that Heather, Louise, and Rachel had made to the outfits.

Ally had a minute-by-minute itinerary prepared for the show tomorrow, and they ran through it.

"I've left plenty of buffers for anything that might come up, but this needs to be followed as if our lives depend on it."

"Mine kind of does!" Heather cringed at her.

"Well, I didn't want to be the one to say it"—Ally laughed—"we will be fine, though. Don't get me wrong, I've been in better positions before a show in the past, but I've been in a lot of worse ones that still led to a brilliant show."

"So, we're middling?" Heather raised an eyebrow at her.

"More than middling, and for a debut show, we are *well* ahead of the curve."

"That's a relief!" Heather laughed.

Once again, Heather found herself so glad that she had Ally to guide her through this. She couldn't even bear to think about how hard it would've been to get this all done if she'd had to work with someone who knew less or who she had clashed with. Aside from the incredible amount of stress, mostly caused by the pressure of trying to meet her own expectations for tomorrow, Ally had made it a fairly pain-free process.

Her phone buzzed in her pocket, and she pulled it out to look at the screen.

Hey, angel. Just landed. See you soon.

"Harrison?" Ally asked her, and Heather looked up.

"Yeah, how did you guess?"

"Your face"—Ally faked a gag, and Heather laughed—"is he here already?"

"Yup, he is." Heather tried unsuccessfully to wipe the smile off her face.

Harrison was finally here in this city with her, and she'd be seeing him soon.

"Okay, well, let's get this finished as quickly as we can, so you can go see your sexy man." Ally grinned at her.

It was another hour and a half before they were satisfied with everything they had achieved. Confident that everything was in order for the next day, Heather gave Ally a hug.

"Thank you so much, darling. I don't think I'll ever be able to thank you enough."

"My fee is all the thanks I need," she said, and Heather laughed.

"I would pay double, and you would still be worth every cent."

"Good, because there's something I've been meaning to tell you"—Ally paused as though trying to find the right words and Heather wondered for a second if she really did want more money—"if my calculations are correct, you should have one fiancé waiting for you at your hotel by now."

Heather glanced at her watch, "Oh my goodness, you're right! Time flies when you're having fun!"

"Please be careful on your way back to the hotel, Heather,"

Ally said seriously, "and please talk to Harrison about security. You guys need it."

"I will. Thanks, darling."

They exchanged hugs, and Heather took the elevator downstairs. This time, she stood in the lobby of the building to wait for her Uber. Thank god they would be using a car service for tomorrow. Heather didn't think her nerves could handle any more scenes like this morning. There was something safe and secure about limousine travel. She didn't mind taking Ubers or even taxis when needed, but they didn't offer that added level of protection that the blacked-out windows of a limousine did.

While she was waiting, she pulled out her phone and texted Harrison.

On my way! Took longer than I expected. You at the hotel?

It was about a minute before his reply came through.

Yup. Chilling with Hayden and Seb. I'll meet you in room 606. Love you, angel.

Her Uber arrived a couple of minutes after that, and Heather made her way out and got into it. Her driver, this time, was named David, and she warned him that it would likely be a bit hectic at her hotel. He offered to drop her off a block away but backtracked quickly at Heather's reaction to that idea. No way could she make her way to the hotel on foot, someone would spot her, and it would be just that much further that she would have to fend them off.

As they pulled up to her hotel, David looked awkward, as though he wanted to say something but wasn't sure if he could. Heather placed where she'd seen this look on people's faces before just as he said his next words.

"Could I, um, possibly get your autograph?" he said quickly.

"What? Why?" she asked him in confusion, and he just shrugged in response.

He held out a pen, along with a random gas station receipt

that he'd obviously grabbed from next to him on the front seat. Feeling as though this was some kind of weird out-of-body experience, Heather took the items from him and quickly signed her first name on the slip of paper before handing the items back to him.

"Thanks, Cruise Control is awesome!" He grinned widely at her.

In some ways, this confirmed for her that the world saw her as nothing more than Harrison Fletcher's girlfriend. Heather wasn't a part of Cruise Control, but people saw her as that connection to the band. She was working hard on her fashion line, but there were definitely people in the fashion world who were questioning her validity as a designer. She didn't know if she could ever truly step out of the shadow of Cruise Control.

She smiled at him and quickly got out of the car. "Uh, you're welcome."

She'd been so thrown by the interaction with her Uber driver that she had completely forgotten that the paparazzi who had been waiting for her that morning would still be there. Even worse, the guys had arrived in her absence, so the number of people there had, at the very least, tripled, if not quadrupled. There were fans there now as well, all wearing Cruise Control T-shirts and quite a few were holding signs proclaiming their commitment to the band.

Chapter 8

KEEP YOUR VOICE DOWN

Fuck. There was a split second of intense clarity for Heather as she took in the scene in front of her before everyone descended upon her.

"Heather! Why didn't Gabriel come?"

"Heather, what's the show going to be like, tomorrow?"

She began to make her way through the crowd, pushing microphones to the side to get past them, but they kept pressing in on her. Video cameras were in her face as well, and she held her hand up in front of her face to block them.

"Heather! Tell Sebastian I want to marry him!"

"Are you having an affair with Sebastian? Do you have any quote on the claims that you're calling off the wedding to be with him?"

"Is it true that Anna Wintour is coming tomorrow?"

Fuck, she hoped not. She hadn't heard that rumor before, but Heather didn't think she could handle the editor-in-chief of Vogue assessing her show. Great, another thing to stress about, she could just add it to the growing list. They had invited her, of course, but Ally said it was beyond unlikely that she would show up. If Vogue sent anyone at all, it would be some lowly fashion assistant. You couldn't not invite, Anna, though. That would be fashion suicide.

"Heather! If you're with Sebastian, does that mean I can date Harrison?"

Heather didn't even look in the direction of the fan who asked this. She had regained her composure now as she neared the hotel doors, and she knew that, as always, everything she said or did right now would be judged by people online.

She was nearing the front of the crowd and was about to break through it to the clear space in front of the entryway, when the hotel manager rushed out to assist her, having noticed what was happening.

"I'm *so* sorry, Miss York!" he exclaimed deferentially as he took her hand and rushed her inside.

"It's fine"—she smiled at him, checking his name badge as she did—"I'm fine, Jared."

"We've been trying to get rid of them all day, but it's gotten worse since…" he didn't finish his sentence.

"Since some of my favorite people in the world rocked up to ruin your day?" she asked with a grin.

"Well, that's not how I would have put it, Ma'am." He was clearly trying to contain a smile.

"Thank you so much for your help. I appreciate it."

"Anytime, Miss York. If you need anything at all during your stay, please do not hesitate to ask, and again, I'm sorry for the inconvenience outside."

"Not a concern"—she gave him a smile—"I'm getting used to it."

With that, she gave him a wave goodbye and practically skipped to the elevators. Harrison was here. After everything that had happened today and over the last week, she needed to see him more than ever.

As soon as the elevator doors opened, she began running toward her suite. It was at the end of the hallway, and it had never felt further away than it did right now. She swiped her card and pushed open the door, rushed into the room, and stopped just inside. She swung her head around to scan the room, and there he was.

Harrison was sitting on the sofa, reading a book. His back was against the end of the sofa, and his long legs stretched out along its length. She drank in the sight of him. Harrison's face was more than handsome; it was beautiful—high cheekbones, square jaw, and full, kissable lips. His brown hair was casually messy from his time spent traveling. He was wearing blue jeans and a tight, white T-shirt with the *Heart Wide Open* album cover on it, emphasizing his well-built upper body. Her heart raced at the sight of him, or maybe it was just from the rush she'd been in to get here, to be with him.

Harrison looked up, saw her, and his face broke into a massive smile. He put his book down on the coffee table as she ran over to him and climbed on top of him. She lowered her face to his and began to kiss him. He wrapped his arms around her, and she sighed against his mouth.

"Did you miss me, angel?" he asked her with a smile, looking into her eyes.

"More than you will ever be able to imagine," she said dramatically as she leaned down and kissed his neck, feeling his laugh reverberate against her lips.

"I can imagine quite a bit. You know us creative types." He winked at her.

"And what are you imagining right now, Harrison Fletcher?"

She could feel his physical reaction to her and was pleased by it. Her body was craving his; she needed him to satisfy the ache she was feeling between her thighs right now.

"Nothing. There is nothing better than you, here, on top of me. Why would I bother imagining anything else?"

"Good fucking god, man! You sure know how to get a girl wet."

"Hmmm, I'd better check if that's true. You know, just to see if my skills are up to par."

His hand slid down her side to find her hip bone before he slipped it between their bodies and pushed it further down until his hand was cupping the place between her legs, and she groaned. There were too many layers of fabric between her and his hand; she wanted his flesh on hers, and she told him so.

"Oh, I'm getting there, angel."

Her head was raised as she ground her hips on his hand, and he lifted his head to lick and kiss her neck while he used his other hand to pull her dress up over her hips. He slipped his fingers under the band of her underwear, and she moaned loudly as he found her wet slit. He pushed two fingers inside of her, easily sliding them in and out.

"You're so wet," he told her as she bucked her hips back and forth on his hand.

She couldn't stop herself; she needed an orgasm so badly right now, and she would take it from him if she had to. Harrison didn't seem to mind at all; he kept finger-fucking her and started playing with her breasts as well. Heather felt her orgasm approaching as Harrison tweaked her nipple. He pulled his fingers out of her and began to quickly rub them back and forth over her clit. That did her in. She screamed as her orgasm overtook her, unable to hold it back. Heather collapsed on Harrison, breathing heavily.

"God, you're so beautiful when you come," he said into her hair.

After a few seconds, he kissed her again, slowly and leisurely. She enjoyed it; he was rubbing his hands all over her body, touching her everywhere he could get to. He was so hard beneath her, and she ached to have him inside her.

She broke their kiss, climbed off him and knelt on the floor next to his crotch, inadvertently licking her lips as she did so. He unzipped his jeans and pulled them down, along with his boxers, to release his erection for her pleasure.

As she stroked, sucked, and licked him, he groaned, and his breathing became ragged. She watched him as she continued what she was doing; he had his head back, and his eyes closed, clearly enjoying her efforts. Heather loved giving him head and hearing the reactions she could elicit from him. Harrison was such a reserved person in general, but that all fell by the wayside when they were having sex, and she loved that about him.

"Fuck me, angel. I need to be inside you."

He groaned again, and she slowly removed her mouth from his cock. She stood up and peeled off her dress before throwing it to the side. She unclipped her bra and let her breasts fall free as she pulled it off and dropped it beside her, before sliding her underwear to the floor as well. She straddled him right there on the sofa and eased herself down on his erection. They groaned in unison as he filled her completely.

"I missed you, honey."

He reached up and cupped a breast in each of his hands, rubbing her nipples with his thumbs as she rode him. He twisted one of her nipples with his right hand, and she felt a shock rush straight to her sex. Harrison pulled her down to kiss her again as he used his left hand to twist her other nipple and the multiple sensations that she was feeling all at once sent Heather over the edge again.

"Harrison!"

She screamed his name even louder this time as she came. He watched her coming, a smug grin on his face. After her orgasm ended, Harrison dropped both hands to her hips and held her steady as he pumped in and out of her, seeking his own orgasm now. She could barely hold on; all her nerve endings were on fire, but she could tell that it wouldn't be long for him now. His eyes squeezed tightly, and she felt his cock jerk inside her as he came, and she smiled. She really had missed him, missed this.

"All my tension this week, I probably just needed a good fucking." She collapsed on him, feeling utterly relaxed, as though every muscle in her body had turned to goo.

"Damn. I should've been here," Harrison said, "I would happily fuck you every day of the week. Just to help keep your stress levels down, of course. I'm nice like that."

"Best fiancé I've ever had, that's for sure!"

Heather climbed carefully off him, grabbed her underwear, and put it on to try and minimize the mess as she headed to the bathroom. She turned on the shower and got in to clean herself off. Harrison joined her after she'd been in there for a few minutes.

He kissed her and held her in his arms. She loved this feeling, the feeling of being home that she got whenever he held her. Heather didn't think she would ever tire of it. They stayed there for quite some time, Harrison just holding her to his chest under the warm spray. It was incredibly soothing, and Heather felt herself unwinding. Her stress was draining away like the water around her.

"What's the plan now?" Heather asked after they'd finally finished their shower and gotten dressed again.

"I thought we could go to Seb's room, and we'll decide what we want to do from there."

"Sounds like a plan."

She took his hand in hers as he led her out of their room into the hallway. He turned right and walked to the next door along the hall, stopping in front of it.

"Seb's next to us?" Heather laughed as Harrison knocked on the door.

"Yup, we figured it'll make it easier for you two to have whatever crazy fuckfest it is that you're planning now."

"Makes sense." Heather nodded, putting a very serious look on her face as she said it, and Hayden opened the door to the room so he could let them in.

They walked into Sebastian's sitting room, and he started

applauding as he stood up from where he was seated in an armchair. Hayden joined in as well, and both of them were grinning wickedly.

"Great performance, guys!" Sebastian announced.

"Thoroughly enjoyable," Hayden agreed as he followed Heather and Harrison over to where Sebastian was.

"Oh, fuck."

Heather said this as she looked from Sebastian's laughing face in front of her, over to the wall to her right—the one that was shared with the living area of their own suite. She had the horrifying realization that the guys would've been able to hear everything they'd just done as Harrison followed her gaze, put two and two together as well, and burst out laughing.

"Did you enjoy the show, then?"

"Well, I mean, Heather seems to have forgotten how to say my name mid-orgasm, but other than that, yes. Very entertaining, guys. You should take it to Broadway!"

"Stop laughing," she chided Harrison but started laughing herself as well, "fucking hell. How embarrassing. Hi, darlings."

She managed to compose herself as she gave Sebastian and Hayden each a hug. Sebastian dropped back into the armchair he'd been sitting in previously, and Hayden sat on the other one, leaving the sofa free for Heather and Harrison.

"How was the flight?" she asked them.

"Not bad," Hayden replied, "the press was insane, though."

"I swear to god, somebody grabbed my junk when we were trying to get in here. It was fucking crazy." Sebastian frowned.

"Not everybody is after your junk, Seb. It was probably an accident," Harrison said with a laugh.

"You don't think everybody is after my junk? Tell that to my lover!" Sebastian winked at Heather, and she laughed.

"But seriously, though. If that really did happen, Seb, that's not okay." Heather was concerned that the situation with them going out in public seemed to be escalating rapidly, "It was pretty bad for me, too. Ally thinks that we should get some kind of permanent security."

All three of them frowned. Heather could tell they were having the same gut reaction that she'd had. It felt as though they were trying to be more important than they were. Heather knew that Cruise Control was famous and that their lifestyle was no longer normal; she also felt like they were totally normal, though. They'd been together so long and had really only exploded almost four years ago.

The idea of being the focus of enough attention to warrant bodyguards was extremely odd to her. It highlighted the fact that their lives really weren't normal anymore, even if they still were.

"Are we sure that it's not going to die down, though?" Hayden asked them. "I mean, it's not that bad at home; maybe it's just because we're here for Heather's show and everyone knows where we are?"

"I don't know that you're right about that, Hayden," Harrison said slowly, "Gabriel and Ariana have been followed around a bit, lately. Someone even had Ariana showing them houses; she'd seen them three or four times before she realized that they kept asking too many personal questions and figured out it was a reporter."

"That's disgusting!" Heather exclaimed. "Poor, Ariana. That must have been awful."

She, Sebastian, and Hayden were all wearing equal expressions of disgust. To have someone infiltrate your life like that was so intrusive. It made her feel squeamish to think about.

"How come none of us know about this?" Hayden asked him.

"She only figured it out the other day. I don't think you've seen them since, Hayden, and Sebastian and Heather..."

He didn't need to finish the sentence; they all knew that lines had been drawn in the sand.

"I may not be her biggest fan," Sebastian said, "but I would never wish that on her. That's fucked up."

A somber silence fell over the group, then. They had accepted this would be a part of their lives as they'd gotten more fame. The being photographed in public, the being talked about online by both the media and the fans, it was all to be expected. This kind of intrusion felt different, though, it was calculated and cruel. Ariana had been one of the sweetest people Heather had ever met, back when she knew her.

Maybe she had been right to be as scared of their lifestyle as she was. Heather hadn't been able to see it at the time, but Ariana was apparently being proven right now. She distinctly remembered discussing this exact topic one day as she and Ariana were in Gabriel's dressing room backstage while the guys were doing a soundcheck.

"I still don't get it, Ariana. What is the absolute worst thing that could happen if someone found out about you and Gabriel? Spades are trumps."

They were sitting at the table in Gabriel's dressing room, playing Euchre. Heather picked up the black jack card from the top of the pile and put the nine of diamonds down on the deck, face down, so Ariana couldn't see what she'd thrown out.

"I know you don't get it. Everyone knows about you. There's no harm in anyone seeing you with Harrison." Ariana shrugged as she put the ace of hearts down on the table.

"Exactly. No harm has come to me, even though the world knows who I am." Heather cringed as she put the king of hearts on top of the ace, and Ariana took the trick and placed it in front of her.

Ariana looked through the cards in her hand, then put the king of clubs down on the table as she said, "It could, though. You have to be so careful, Heather. People get crazy. They get desperate. They do insane stuff; they'll dig through your trash and do all sorts of things to try and get close to you."

It was odd seeing Ariana so subdued. She had a haunted look about her as she said it, looking so sorrowful that Heather wondered where this was coming from.

"How do you know all that?" Heather frowned, putting the queen of clubs down, and was frustrated as Ariana picked up the second trick to put it on top of the first one that she'd won.

"I can just imagine," her voice was quiet, and that haunted look was still in place as she raised her eyes to meet Heather's, "and the idea of it is scary as fuck, Heather."

Ariana put the king of diamonds on the table, but Heather couldn't even muster up any exhilaration as she put the ace on top of it and picked up her first trick of the hand.

"You have to get over this fear of celebrity," Heather told her, as she put the jack of spades down, hoping that the card she was still holding would be able to win her the third and final trick that she needed. "It's really not as dangerous as you think it is."

"It's not a fear of celebrity, as such," Ariana put the ten of spades on top of Heather's jack, "it's all the stuff that comes with it. I'm scared of that, Heather, fucking terrified. I don't want people digging through my trash to see if they can find a pregnancy test because they're trying to figure out if I'm pregnant or not."

"Just because it could theoretically happen, doesn't mean it will," Heather told her, as she picked up the trick and put it on her first one.

"Just because you don't think it will happen, doesn't mean it won't," Ariana warned her.

"I love you, darling, but you're really worrying about nothing." Heather smiled and put the ace of spades on the table between them.

"I'm really not," Ariana said as she placed the jack of clubs on top of Heather's ace, "and you're Euchred. Two points to me."

Heather hadn't placed a huge amount of importance on the conversation at the time. It had been one of many they'd had on the topic, amongst too many conversations to count about other things. Something about that day struck her now, though. It was the memory of Ariana's haunted look—the naked fear on her face as she spoke.

Had there been more to her fear than Heather had been able to get out of her at the time? Why wouldn't she have shared it with her if there was? They had been best friends. Heather had held nothing back from Ariana in their friendship, so if there really had been a reason behind her all-consuming fear of the life of a celebrity, what would that have been?

These thoughts whirled around Heather's mind all evening. They had dinner, but the group's mood was strained after hearing about what had happened to Ariana, and Heather's stress was coming back. Her show was tomorrow; it was the biggest day of her life, something she'd been working toward and dreaming about for a long time. She made her excuses to the guys shortly after dinner that she needed to go to bed early, but she was still lying awake when Harrison joined her in bed and wrapped his arms around her.

She dreamed about Anna Wintour screaming at her that her designs were awful, as they stood in trash that had been strewn everywhere, and Ariana told her with that haunted look on her face, "See, Heather? I told you it would be like this."

Chapter 9

LIGHTS, CAMERA, WHY THE HELL DID I DO THIS?

The phone on the table next to Heather wouldn't stop ringing. She picked it up and heard a far too cheerful voice announcing to her that it was six-thirty and that they were providing the wakeup call she'd requested. She felt awful; she'd woken up from that nightmare about Anna Wintour and Ariana sometime around two, but she'd struggled to get back to sleep.

The more she'd realized that time was ticking away and that she *really* needed to get some sleep, the less she'd been able to actually get any. She last remembered looking at the clock somewhere around four-thirty this morning. Now, she had to face the most important day of her fashion career so far, on less than four hours of total sleep. Brilliant.

Harrison moved closer to her in the bed and wrapped his arms around her, kissing her lips gently.

"Good morning, angel. I missed you. So much. It was so good to sleep in a bed with you last night. Did you sleep okay?"

"I barely slept a wink," she said and then cringed.

"You only have to be strong enough to get through today. I promise that you can be completely and utterly non-functional as soon as we get back here tonight. Just hold it together until then."

"There's so much to do! What if it all goes terribly?" she moaned.

"It won't, but if it does, I'll be there. So will Ally, Seb and Hayden. We will work it out."

Heather relaxed into his embrace. She needed to get up and get the day started, but she wanted just ten more minutes of bliss before then. She began running through the day in her head; there was a set order in which things needed to happen today.

She would freak out if she thought too hard about what was happening, so she decided to focus entirely on the first thing on her list—getting up and ready to leave. Taking on each task as its own thing, instead of looking at the day as a whole, was the only way she would manage to survive.

Step one, get the fuck out of bed. Heather kissed Harrison one last time, squeezed him tightly, and then made her way to the shower for step two. Two things down now, only about five hundred and eighty-three to go.

She put on the carefully considered outfit that she had chosen to wear this morning. She was saving her show outfit for later but knew that she would appear in plenty of photographs before the show, wanting to make sure that she looked stylish but not like she was trying too hard. She had decided to go with tight, black pants, red ankle boots, and a red, silk button-up shirt. Not that anyone would see the shirt, as it would be hidden under a soft, woolen red coat that hung mid-thigh.

Harrison had ordered breakfast for them while she was showering, and they sat in the living area to eat it together.

"Gabriel and Ariana said to wish you good luck," Harrison said, tentatively, seemingly unsure of how she would react to their well wishes.

"Oh, that's early for them, isn't it?" Heather stalled for time.

"I was speaking to Gabriel last night after you'd gone to bed."

"That makes more sense," she measured her next words carefully, "well, let them know I said thank you."

"I will."

They slipped back into silence, again, as they finished their food, but Harrison looked pleased with her reaction. For the first time in a long while, Heather thought that it could be possible for them all to get back to an easy friendship sometime in the future. She'd felt practically on the verge of a breakdown with the stress she'd been under lately, and it had become obvious to her that she needed all the support she could get.

Holding on to this emotional burden from two years ago might kill her if she didn't let it go soon. With so much external pressure coming at them, Heather knew that Cruise Control didn't need to be dealing with petty in-fighting, as well. The fact was that Ariana must have changed; it was without question because the Ariana of old would never be in the position she'd been put in with that reporter.

"I'm going to shower, angel; I'll be ready to leave in half an hour."

He stood up as he said it, coming over to give her a soft kiss before making his way to the bathroom. The topic of Ariana was something that Heather would need to discuss with Harrison later; she simply didn't have the emotional or mental reserves to broach that issue right now.

She made her way to the bedroom to do her makeup. She used just enough to look human but added her signature red lipstick. She didn't want to make too much work for Jessica, who would have to remove it all and do her makeup again, later.

Heather sat on the sofa to wait for Harrison and tried to check her social media feeds, but there were so many mentions of her that she was overwhelmed. Instead of replying to any of them, she took a selfie, relaxed on the sofa, with the big, glass windows behind her providing an amazing background with an excellent view of the city. She captioned it 'The calm before the storm.', and it had been up for less than ten seconds when her phone started blowing up with notifications of replies.

She quit the app and started checking her emails, responding to a question from Ally about the jewelry the models would be wearing. There were quite a few press queries that she flicked on to her PR firm. Eventually, she locked her phone and rested her head against the back of the couch, then closed her eyes and focused on her breathing.

She was still sitting there, in quiet mindfulness, when Harrison came out to the living area, fully dressed and ready to leave. She beamed at him as he walked toward her; he looked incredibly handsome and stylish. He had black jeans and boots on, with a grey T-shirt and an open, black blazer. His hair was slicked back from his face, and she couldn't resist going over to kiss him.

"You look great, honey. Shall we go?"

"Yup, I've called the car company. They should be here and ready when we are."

"Well, I guess there's no sense in delaying, is there."

Harrison took her hand in his after they left their room and headed toward the elevators. Sebastian and Hayden would be coming to the show together, later, with Heather and Harrison's family. Harrison had opted to go early with her to support her with the dress rehearsal, and she couldn't be more grateful for that.

They arrived in the lobby, and as soon as the doors of the elevator opened, they could see the crowd that had already gathered at the entrance of the hotel. Harrison squeezed her hand, and she felt comforted. She had him here with her; this was far less scary than it was yesterday. Their limousine was visible behind the crowd that was waiting for them.

As they walked across the lobby, the hotel's morning manager approached them.

"Good morning, Mr. Fletcher. Miss York."

"Morning." Harrison smiled brightly at him.

"We have prepared some security personnel to assist with yourself and our other guests getting to and from their transport today."

"Thank you, Daniel. We really appreciate it," Heather could see the men in black suits standing by the doors to the hotel.

"No worries, have a great day, and good luck today, Miss York!"

They had almost reached the doors now, so she thanked him politely as the security guards walked through the hotel doors ahead of them, clearing space in the crowd as they made their way through. It was an explosion of camera flashes and questions, the same as yesterday, but it was over much quicker, and it was much less scary than before. Once they were in their limousine, Heather wasn't shaking and terrified like she'd been yesterday. The idea of getting some kind of personal security might not be such a bad one, after all.

"That wasn't too bad," Harrison voiced her own thoughts aloud.

"No, it really wasn't. Maybe Ally is right."

"It's possible. We'll see what happens; I might talk to Cooper and see what he says."

Heather nodded, then they drifted into silence. Her brain was running a million miles a minute right now. She pushed the media and security issue to the back of her brain and began focusing on what needed to be done. Next up on her list, run The Gauntlet to get into the venue, and once she was inside, there would be a lot to get done.

Harrison put his arm around her shoulders and pulled her to him so that her head was resting on his chest, and she physically relaxed. She hadn't even realized she'd been as tense as she was. His thumb stroked her skin softly, and she put her arm around him, closing her eyes and simply focused on the sound of his heart beating in his chest. The world was reduced to nothing but that comforting sound and the feeling of his arms holding her safe against him.

It was entirely too quickly that they arrived at the venue for the show. Heather saw the group of people gathered out the front of the venue and steeled herself for the walk inside. It wasn't even eight-thirty in the morning yet, so she was surprised that so many people had already made it here; there were even several eager fans.

Their driver opened their door and smiled at them. Heather thanked him and stepped out; she was getting used to this feeling, the racing heartbeat and butterflies in her stomach as her senses of sight and sound were assaulted.

"Heather! Good luck for today!"

"Harrison, where's the rest of Cruise Control?"

They answered a few questions this time, also posing for some photos. These reporters had done the right thing by coming to her show rather than waiting at their hotel, and Heather felt they should be rewarded for that.

Harrison made his way over to the group of ten or so Cruise Control fans who were calling out to him and signed some of their T-shirts and albums. He posed for a few selfies with them and chatted politely as Heather answered more questions from the media.

"Heather, what was the inspiration for your collection?"

"I'm focusing on the feelings of serenity and freedom, so I'm hoping that others who look at it can see and embrace those feelings. No restraints."

"Why isn't Gabriel here today?" someone else asked her a few minutes later.

"He had commitments in Chicago, and unfortunately couldn't make it today."

"What do you have to say about rumors of a rift in the band?"

Heather tensed slightly, then forced herself to relax so that she wouldn't show it. She did worry that it might cause some issues between them when they were trying to record the new album next month. She heard Harrison's voice as he answered the question for her.

"We say that's insane." He'd returned to Heather's side and laughed as he continued, "But I'll certainly text Gabriel and let him know we're apparently splitting up!"

Even the person who'd asked the question laughed at his response.

"Thanks for coming, guys," Harrison said to the group as he took her hand in his, "I'd better get my gorgeous fiancée inside, though. No doubt, there's plenty to be done in there."

Harrison waved goodbye to the fans and smiled at them in particular as they walked away from the group of people outside, and into the venue. Heather loved how sweet and kind he was. As much as she would have liked to have him by her side for every second of those interactions, Harrison didn't have it in him to ignore the fans who had gone to the effort of coming out this early to see him.

Heather's mouth fell into a silent 'O' as they walked into the venue. It looked like a real fashion show; it was nothing like the tiny showings she'd held in Chicago. She knew that it was a real fashion show, of course, but she was still stunned. Heather only had a moment or two to take in the stage, the lights shining on it, the backdrop with the word "Serenity" on it in her stylized logo, and the chairs that would later be filled with guests before Ally rushed over to her.

She was looking more stressed than Heather had ever seen her. She was wearing a tight blue dress that accentuated her curves and was carrying a clipboard with the itinerary on it and had a headset on that had a mic near her mouth.

"You're here! Great, right on time! We have so much to do, let's go. Hi Harrison, nice to meet you."

Ally held out her hand and shook Harrison's before turning and heading backstage. Heather and Harrison followed her dutifully. Harrison caught Heather's eye and mouthed, 'I like her.' Heather smiled and mouthed back, 'me too.'

The backstage area was a hive of activity. To the side of one of the entrances to the runway, there was a big board that had pictures of all of the models wearing their outfits for the show, in the order that they would appear on the runway.

There were people everywhere, some were carrying items around, but most were models. A few were standing near the craft services table with food on it and chatting, but a lot were in various stages of dress, getting either their hair or makeup done. Heather could see Tristan working on one of her favorite models, and he gave her a quick wave before going back to his work.

"Okay, the dress rehearsal is at ten," Ally told them, "as you can see, not all of the models will be fully ready for that, but it's okay, they never are. It's just to give us an idea and decide on any last-minute changes we want to make. I've already had word that two models won't be able to make the dress rehearsal, but can make the show. We need to decide if we're okay with that."

"Which models?" Heather asked her, with a sinking feeling in the pit of her stomach.

"Liia and Carrie."

Heather cringed, Carrie had been one of her absolute favorites and was set to literally open the show.

"I know. Look, it isn't a huge deal. Carrie is *good*, she'll be fine, and Liia was okay; she's mid-show, so not a lot to screw up there. I say we run with them and have them do a run-through backstage."

"I trust you," Heather decided to take a leap of faith, "if you think it'll be okay, let's go with that."

"Awesome, I'll let the agencies know. I'll also let them know I'm pissed. Harrison, you sit your gorgeous butt over there and relax"—she pointed to a cream, leather sofa at the edge of the room near the craft services table—"I'm going to get your wonderful fiancée to come and give her approval of the accessories. All we need from you is to sit there and look pretty!"

"I'll do my best," and Harrison laughed as Ally winked at him.

He gave Heather a quick kiss and a hug before he headed over to the sofa as instructed. As soon as he sat down, quite a few of the models who had been eating before rushed over to talk to him, and Ally rolled her eyes.

"I thought that might happen. I'll save him in a few minutes if you're okay with that?"

"I'm fine. If Harrison wanted to leave me for a model, he would've done it long before now!"

They walked over to the racks of clothing at the back of the room. Each one was carefully hung up with an outfit, with the matching shoes and accessories sitting underneath them along with a picture of the associated model attached to the hanger.

"Okay, so as I said in my email, we weren't able to source enough of the purple bracelets you wanted, so we got some of these pink ones as well. We went with half and half of each"—Ally indicated to a pile of purple and pink bracelets that were sitting on a table near the racks of clothing—"I just need you to decide which outfits you want to have purple, and which should have pink. We could just alternate them, but I didn't want to make that call if you felt some suited one better than the other. If I can leave you to that, I'll call those agencies, and you come get me when you're done, okay?"

Heather nodded her approval and released a breath as Ally walked away from her. She could feel herself getting overwhelmed, but Ally was so cool, calm, and collected, that she felt safe in the knowledge that everything really was under control.

She found herself glad that they hadn't made this decision for her. As she looked at each outfit, she got a feeling for which bracelet worked best in her mind, and while the alternating of them would probably have been fine, Heather knew she would've hated it.

It took her about ten to twenty minutes to get everything sorted. As she did it, she moved around a few of the other accessories as well. Heather didn't think she'd ever be one hundred percent happy with everything, but time was rapidly ticking by, and soon there would be no chance to make any further changes, anyway.

She left the clothing area and went and found Ally, who was talking to one of the hairstylists, ensuring that they had perfectly fulfilled the brief for the model they were working on. Heather had gone with soft, gentle makeup, and the models' hair was to fall in loose waves, barring one of her favorite models, Jess, whose braids would remain in but also be left loose.

"Perfect. Great work, Anthony. Ah, there you are, Heather! All sorted?"

"Yup, I changed some of the other accessories around, too"—Ally cringed as Heather said this—"oh no, did I do the wrong thing? I can change them all back if you want!"

"No, it's fine. You're the creative!" Ally gave her a reassuring smile as she called her assistant over to them, "Emma! Heather's changed a few of the accessories around, can you take a fresh set of pictures to ensure we get them all right for the show?"

"Not a problem."

"I'm *so* sorry for being a hassle!" Heather bit her lip as she said it, feeling very much like she'd fucked up.

"No, it really isn't an issue," Emma smiled at her, "I don't mind at all. We're just here to present your vision."

With that, she quickly headed off to the area Heather had just left.

"Fuck, I'm so sorry!" Heather said to Ally again.

"Stop apologizing. I'm just glad you told me; it would've caused hell if you hadn't. Now we know, and we'll get it fixed. As

Emma said, we're here to do what *you* want. Trust me; it's not the worst thing a client has ever done to me on show day, not by a long shot. Ladies!" She strode over to the sofa where several models were still talking to Harrison, "You are not here to fangirl over the client's fiancé; you are here to work, and if you ever want me to book you again, I suggest you do that!"

Ally was scary when she was in full-on fashion show director mode, and the girls quickly scattered to the winds.

"You're mean," Harrison laughed.

"And you're far more distracting than I expected you'd be," Ally quipped.

"Just be glad Sebastian isn't here"—he looked at Heather—"can you imagine?"

"I'd rather not! Trust us, Ally, it would be a nightmare."

"Oh, I can certainly imagine how Mr. Sex-On-Legs would love it here"—Ally looked at Heather—"do you promise to never bring him backstage to one of your shows if I'm directing it?"

"You say that as if I'm ever going to do another show! How about I promise never to do another show, instead?" She wrinkled her nose, and both Ally and Harrison laughed.

"Okay, obviously, you're suffering from some nerves right now. If you still feel that way after the show is done, though, I'll personally help you to set fire to all your designs"—she laughed again, owing to the horrified look on Heather's face at the thought of setting her designs on fire—"and that look is why I know that you'll be booking my services again before you know it. Now, if your delicious, but troublesome fiancé could try to cause less of a commotion from now on, we still have plenty to get done. Look a little *less* pretty, would you?"

She directed this comment at Harrison, who laughed and saluted her, "Yes, ma'am!" He pulled out his phone and looked down at the screen as Ally led Heather away from him.

"You're one lucky girl." She sighed dramatically.

"Tell me about it, darling. We had crazy, hot sex yesterday!" Heather winked at her.

"Well now, bragging is just rude," Ally scolded her, "some of us have practically forgotten what crazy, hot sex is even like!"

They both laughed and toned down the conversation as they neared the area where the models were getting ready. Heather went from model to model, chatting to them as they had their hair and makeup done, talking about what she wanted from the show, and answering any questions they had for her.

She got the impression from the models that this wasn't normal behavior for a designer, but she didn't care, Heather wanted to be involved and connect with everyone working on the show. She wanted to be sure that everyone involved was invested in the end result being amazing, and she hoped that she had chosen people to participate that would be as invested as she was.

Around nine-thirty, Damien arrived, and she was thrilled to see him again. Ally directed him out to set up for the dress rehearsal, and that was when Heather discovered Russell had been there for some time already, setting up the lighting.

"Darling! How did I not know you were here?" she asked him.

"You literally walked under me on your way in," he laughed, "I don't normally climb up and rig lights myself, but on occasion, a man's gotta do what a man's gotta do!"

"Well, I definitely appreciate the effort."

As ten o'clock rolled around, Ally, Heather, and Harrison were all sat in some of the front row seats when the dress rehearsal began. The show was spectacular; Heather could scarcely believe that this was *her* show. It felt too good like it must be from some "proper" designer, but those were her designs. Everything flowed beautifully, exactly as she'd wanted it.

She felt exhilarated when the dress rehearsal was complete and the models stood in their places. Heather joined them on the catwalk to practice her walk down the runway for the end of the show. Harrison and Ally cheered and clapped for her, pretending to be the audience, and she laughed.

Even though the dress rehearsal went well, Heather was definitely worried about the missing models. The two designs that weren't in the rehearsal were the only sticking points for her—particularly the one for the middle, as it interrupted the flow of the show because it was the link between the designs before and after it.

Ally reassured her that she'd received confirmation from both agencies that the girls would definitely be able to make it, and they should be here in less than half an hour. They headed backstage, and Harrison insisted that Heather sit with him on the cream sofa as he got them both a plate of food, since this was probably their last chance for some downtime before the actual show.

Heather flopped onto the sofa and pulled out her phone. Gabriel had texted her.

Good luck, H. You don't need it!

She smiled. Amidst all of this drama lately, she'd almost forgotten that he was her friend. It really meant so much to her that he'd texted her today. Despite everything that had happened between them lately, she loved him dearly, so she replied.

Thanks. I think I do, so I'll take all the luck I can get.

She saw a text from Sebastian as well and opened it.

What's happening, lover? We'll be heading over soon. Wanna pick out a model and we can have a threesome?

Heather laughed and showed her phone to Harrison as he sat down next to her with their food.

"You'd better not let Seb backstage!" he warned her with a grin as he handed her plate over.

She set her plate on her lap and replied to Sebastian while still laughing.

Nobody is letting you near any models until the show is over. Just FYI.

Why do you have to ruin all my fun?

My show > your fun. Just saying.

Heather picked up a sandwich off her plate and took a bite as Sebastian's reply popped up.

You = my fun. Also, just saying.

Harrison had a wicked gleam in his eye as he read the message on her screen, "Seb's such a fucker, give me your phone for a sec?" Heather handed her phone to him.

Heather = mine. Am too, just saying. – Harrison

Heather leaned over and kissed him, as he gave her phone back to her.

Tell your old man that he wouldn't feel the need to stake a claim if he didn't feel threatened.

Heather burst into laughter at this as she showed Harrison her phone again, and he laughed with her. She put her phone away and talked with him as they ate the rest of their food. This was comforting—the food was delicious, and it was nice to spend this time with him. It wasn't long before Ally came to get her, though.

"Sorry to interrupt, guys, but we need Heather into hair and makeup now. Harrison, we didn't talk about this, but are you planning on doing any of the press outside with Sebastian and Hayden when they arrive, or are you going straight to your seat?"

"Is it better for me to do press again? We did some when we got here," Harrison asked her.

"It really couldn't hurt if you're willing. Emma will liaise with Sebastian and Hayden on their arrival, and we'll get you to where you need to be."

"Well, since I've been nothing but trouble back here, I guess it's the least I could do," he winked at Ally.

"Great. Okay, Heather! Let's go."

Heather stood and followed Ally over to the area the models had been getting ready in earlier. She hadn't even noticed, but most of them were done now, there were only a few left here. Looking at her watch, Heather realized that it wasn't long at all until showtime, and her stomach became a ball of nerves.

She sat in a seat in front of a mirror, and it was incredibly soothing to have Jessica working on her. It felt familiar and put her at ease. When Jessica was almost done, Tristan became free and joined them to start on her hair.

"Can you even believe this is happening, guys?" he asked them.

"I really and truly can't," Heather answered honestly, "I'm so glad you guys are here. You've done an amazing job on the models, by the way."

"I was so nervous when you asked me to do the makeup," Jessica confessed. "I was Googling all of the procedures and what to do. You're insane to hire me!"

"I won't lie, that's what Ally said at the time, but I knew I was right. You guys get me, and you get my style. I didn't want to work with anyone else."

Jessica gave her a quick hug before continuing to work on her face. It wasn't long at all until they were done, and by the time they were finished, she felt like she might throw up but looked as though she was glowing.

"Thank fuck, I don't look anything like how I feel!" she told them.

"The show is amazing," Tristan said, "we had a peek during the dress rehearsal. You have nothing to worry about."

"You really don't," Ally arrived, and interrupted their conversation.

She spirited Heather away quickly, to the area with the clothes so that Heather could change into the outfit she'd be wearing for the show.

"Now, I have some information for you, and I don't want you to freak out." Ally said carefully.

"Well, now I'm definitely going to freak out! Carrie didn't show up?!"

"No, nothing bad! Okay…Vogue sent Nicole Spencer."

"What the hell? You said we'd get a fashion assistant or intern. Not, the bloody fashion director! I think I'm going to be sick."

Heather breathed deeply in through her nose, before releasing it through her mouth. This was too much pressure; she couldn't handle it. If Vogue slammed her collection, that would be the end of her short-lived fashion career.

"This is a good thing, Heather. It means that they're already skewed toward liking you if they've gone to the effort of sending her. They wouldn't waste her time with anything they thought was sub-par. Needless to say, this could truly make your career, and your show is worthy of it."

"I'm definitely going to be sick." Heather put her head in her hands.

"No, you're not. I'm not going to let you wallow in self-pity for having designs so amazing that Vogue warranted sending their fashion director to your show. So, suck it up, princess. Go get dressed and let's get this show on the road!"

Ally pushed her over to where her outfit was hanging on a rack. It fit right in with the rest of her collection. In fact, it could really have been worn by one of the models, but she had made it for herself.

It had long sleeves and was fitted at the top before flaring out from her waist. It had flowing, interlocking patterns of different pastel colors, and it might possibly be the best thing she'd ever designed. Of all the outfits in her collection, this was her favorite.

She carefully removed it from its hanger and slipped it over her head, knowing she'd need Tristan to fix her hair again. Dammit, she hadn't thought of this when she'd designed it. Adding in the jewelry that was there, and the shoes, she caught her reflection in a mirror and was amazed by what she saw.

Aside from the fact that her hair was out of place from pulling the dress on, she looked like any of the other models in this area.

Damn. She wouldn't stand out as the designer; this dress was a mistake. Heather considered removing it and just wearing what she'd been wearing earlier when Emma came over to get her and gasped.

"Heather, you look phenomenal! I've never seen anything like that dress!"

"It's too much, darling. I was just thinking about taking it off."

"No, you can't, it's perfect! Ally sent me to get you, anyway; we need to go"—she frowned at Heather's hair—"okay, we need to get you to Tristan ASAP, but the show is going to start any minute."

Emma rushed her over to Tristan, who had her hair looking perfect again in less than five minutes' time, and then it was happening. The models were all lined up, Carrie at the front and looking phenomenal, all the way back to Jess at the end. It felt like forever ago that she and Ally had picked these two women out as their frontrunners for callbacks.

So much had happened to get to this point, and soon it would be done. They heard the music start and Ally signaled for Carrie to go, then it was all on. Time passed by in a blur as each model walked the runway and made their way backstage with a huge smile on their face.

Every timing change was met in what Heather considered to be a complete miracle but knew was entirely down to Ally's skill at organizing fashion shows. Then it was her turn to walk the runway. She followed Jess up the stairs, then stood at the end of the catwalk as Jess made her way to her spot to the side. There was a gap in the middle of the models for Heather to walk through.

She was absolutely terrified that she would fall flat on her face as she walked down the middle of the runway. The models lined up on either side of her were all clapping for her, as was the audience. She saw Sebastian stand to applaud her as she passed them, and then everyone else was standing, including Nicole

Spencer, who had been front and center across from Harrison, Sebastian, and Hayden.

She stood at the end of the runway, posed for photos, and then made a small bow, as Ally had instructed her to do, before turning to walk back up the runway, with the models falling into line behind her as she did.

Suddenly, it was over. Heather had never before felt such an intense mixture of exhilaration, relief, and pure joy. She was ecstatic, and everyone backstage was laughing and clapping for her. After a moment or two, Harrison appeared, and somebody popped a bottle of champagne as she kissed him deeply.

They cheered and toasted one another. Ally invited Nicole Spencer backstage to meet her and Heather discovered that she was actually quite lovely. She didn't give much away, though she did appear to be a big fan of Cruise Control. Heather felt like the review was going to be a positive one, at least. If she could bottle the way she was feeling right now and sell it, Heather thought she could probably make a fortune.

She went out that night to a club with Harrison, Sebastian, and Hayden. Heather invited Ally, Emma, Damien, and Russell along to celebrate with them. Without them, the show couldn't have been the success it was. April Conway said that she'd be happy to come out with them as well when Heather asked her, and she was thrilled when April told her that she'd loved the show and wanted her to design a gown for an upcoming awards night she was attending. Some early reviews were already coming through online for the show, and not one of them had anything bad to say.

"Will you direct my next fashion show, too?" Heather asked Ally, much later in the evening, when they were all three sheets to the wind.

"So, I guess we're not setting fire to your designs, then?" Ally laughed at her.

Heather looked down at the stunning dress that she was still wearing and grinned back at her, "No, I guess we're not."

~OCTOBER~

WHERE IN THE WORLD IS CRUISE CONTROL?

This is not a drill. We repeat: this is not a drill! After the amazing, critical success of Heather York's debut at Fashion Week last month for her fashion line, Serenity, Cruise Control appears to have gone underground.

We saw them back in Chicago after the show, but they've been MIA for over a week now. Nobody has seen any of the band members in public. Heather was spotted having lunch in the city, while Gabriel's girlfriend, Ariana Chamberlain, was also seen at a popular Chicago nightclub with friends, but none of the guys seem to be around.

Rumors have been rife of a rift forming within the band. While we're used to seeing them together all the time, they've been spotted out and about with different people much more often, lately, than they have in the past.

Is it possible that Cruise Control really is on the verge of breaking up? Tell us it isn't true!

Chapter 10

THANK FUCK IT'S FRIDAY!

It was late on Friday afternoon, and Heather was excited. She was making the drive to Sebastian's place in Galena; it had been over a week since she'd seen Harrison, and it was far too long. They'd agreed that she wouldn't visit the first weekend they were out there so that the guys could really focus on making music.

She'd almost given in earlier in the week and driven up there, but she had some really important business meetings that she couldn't blow off. Heather was now signed to Cooper's management team as one of his clients, and she was going to be doing a cameo for Saturday Night Live on Halloween, which she thought was completely insane.

April Conway was going to be the host as well as the musical guest. It was a big honor for her to be pulling double duty, and they'd been talking about it when Heather was designing her gown last month. April joked about Heather making a cameo in a sketch about Cruise Control, where she was singing at Heather's wedding, and they'd thought it was a funny idea. Later, April had mentioned it to one of the producers, and they had jumped at the idea of having her on the show.

Her fashion line had also really taken off in the last month, they were planning a soft launch in some high-end department stores soon and had secured some factory space in the industrial area of Chicago. Heather had kept the employees she'd had from the beginning and given them promotions, each had a team of other women working under them now, and she trusted them implicitly. She was devoted to the idea of keeping production here in Chicago, and absolutely counted herself lucky to have Harrison as her financial backer because if she'd had any other investor, they almost certainly would've been pressuring her to move production off-shore for larger profit margins.

It did affect the price point of her clothing, though, which was why her PR firm had encouraged her to take the outstanding critical response to her show and use it to make her way in with the high-end stores. Targeting customers that were already willing to pay a premium meant that the extra cost of staying in the USA for production only came out of Heather's bottom line, and that was a price she was willing to pay. As it was, she was hopeful that Serenity would be able to pay back the loan from Harrison within its first year of trading, or two at the latest.

She tried to ensure that she was hiring people who needed jobs, as well. It was something of a passion for her. While she certainly wanted and needed talented people in her organization, if she could do some good with it by finding people who actually needed a job, that was a bonus. She'd partnered with a not-for-profit job agency that specialized in assisting people who had been out of work to get themselves gainful employment.

It often made Heather acutely aware of exactly how lucky she and her friends were. They had so much money now that they didn't know what to do with it all. She was literally on her way to Sebastian's estate; she hadn't been there before, but she had no doubt that he would've had it completed to an extravagant level of luxury.

Heather knew that there were so many people in the world

who were suffering and needed help, but she also wasn't arrogant enough to think that just handing them money would be appreciated by everyone. Approaching it this way helped her to feel better when she went to sleep at night in a bed with expensive silk sheets and her rock star fiancé by her side.

When she reached Galena, she drove through the small town, following the directions her car gave until she reached a road on the other side of it. This road wound away from the town into a secluded area, and eventually, she reached her destination. She pulled her car into Sebastian's driveway and up to the ornate, iron gates barring access to his property with its name emblazoned across it in massive gold script.

Maison De L'amour Et De La Musique

Heather pressed the button on the intercom and waited patiently for a minute before pressing the button again. Still nothing. She reached over to the screen in her car, pulled up Sebastian's name from her contacts, and called him.

"Hey there, lover. What's happening?"

"I'm sitting at your gates and waiting *very* impatiently to come in and fuck your brains out, that's what's happening." She laughed.

"What are you waiting for, Seb?" she heard Harrison's voice in the background. Clearly, she was on speakerphone, "You should probably let her in and get some!"

Her entire body melted at the sound of his voice. They might be joking about her having sex with Sebastian, but she was aching to have Harrison between her thighs right now. The sooner Sebastian opened these fucking gates, the better. It had been a long week and a half without Harrison in bed beside her.

"All right, in you come then, sexy," Sebastian announced to her, "see you soon!"

The call ended as the gates in front of her slowly started to swing open. This place was insane. There were rolling fields of green grass that must take somebody days to mow, the driveway was lined with neatly trimmed green hedges and had trees behind them, providing a lovely canopy for the driveway.

When she reached the building, she was even more astounded. She had thought of it as driving toward Sebastian's house, but it was nothing short of a mansion, maybe closer to a bloody castle.

It was massive and imposing. She felt like royalty could easily make themselves at home here. It looked nothing like the building Sebastian had shown them on the sales listing when he'd originally bought this property. Heather parked her car under the porte-cochère at the front of the building, unsure where else she might need to park it.

She grabbed her luggage out of the trunk and wheeled it toward the front door. It opened before she even reached it, and Harrison was standing there, smiling at her. She squealed, left her suitcase where it was, and ran to him, jumping into his arms and wrapping her legs around his waist. He laughed as he caught her, then he kissed her. She could feel the ache between her thighs that had been there from the moment she'd heard his voice on the phone.

"I missed you," she smiled at him.

"I missed you, too, angel," he told her as she dropped her legs to the ground, and he let go of her.

"Can we go fuck now, or do we have to be social first?" she asked him, wickedly.

"We're literally in the middle of recording a song, I'm afraid, so being social it is."

"Well, damn…couldn't we just be quick, though?" She poked her tongue out at him.

He dropped his head to hers, pulled her to him and kissed her deeply, exploring her mouth expertly with his tongue, and she was panting when he ended the kiss.

"I don't want to be quick," his voice was husky, and his eyes were hooded, "I want you long, slow, and over many, *many* hours. Now, let me get your suitcase."

Heather could feel how wet she was getting, and she groaned as he walked away from her to get her luggage from where she'd dropped it so that he could bring it inside.

"You suck!" She pouted at him dramatically.

"No, *you* suck. Me. Really, fucking well and to completion. Just not right now."

She narrowed her eyes at him and said slowly, "You're doing this on purpose."

He set her suitcase to the side of the front door, came back over to her and put his arms around her waist, holding her tightly against him. She could feel the bulge in his pants and bit her lip. He dropped his head to kiss her neck softly before drawing his tongue over her skin from her neck up to her ear, where he nipped her ear lobe with his teeth.

"Now, what makes you think that, angel?" he whispered into her ear, and she thought that she might just melt into a puddle right where they were.

"Harrison James Fletcher, if you don't want me to throw you down on the floor right where we are and fuck you immediately, then you should stop what you're doing right now!"

He gave her an evil grin but pulled back from her to allow some space between them. She still ached for him, and Heather had no idea how she would manage to last until they could get somewhere private, together. As it stood, she might have to take herself off and relieve this tension on her own if he didn't ease up on her. He took his hand in hers and led her down a corridor off the entry hall, but she was so wound up right now, that even that small touch felt erotic to her.

"Wait until you see the studio," Harrison's voice was still husky, and she could tell he was trying to get control of his own arousal, "it's amazing."

"How has the process been, now that you have the freedom to do whatever you want?"

"It's been pretty epic," he turned and smiled at her as he said it, she didn't think his face had ever looked so kissable, she was so fucking horny right now, "the other night, Gabriel woke up at two and went into the studio and wrote the most amazing song. We could never have gotten it the same without that flexibility to act on it in the moment."

They reached the end of the hallway, and there was a door that Harrison held open for her to walk through so she could head down the set of stairs that was behind it.

"Wait? Were you all up at two in the morning?" she asked him with a laugh.

They reached the bottom of the stairs and continued down another corridor, lit with recessed lights in the ceiling above them and with promotional photos of Cruise Control hanging on the walls. She could see another door on their right, about halfway down the corridor.

"Yeah, Seb wasn't thrilled when Gabriel went to wake him, but once we started working, he was just as excited as the rest of us."

"You guys are crazy!"

"Because I've never woken up in the middle of the night to see you sketching whatever design came to you at the time?" He raised an eyebrow at her, and she poked her tongue out at him, as he pushed open the door they'd just reached and let her walk through it in front of him.

Hayden was in this room in front of what appeared to be a rocket ship's control panel, but which Heather knew was almost certainly just recording equipment. Through a glass window, Heather could see Gabriel and Sebastian sitting at a piano, side on to them. They were laughing as Gabriel played the same four bars of music over and over, each time singing an alternate line for the song, but every option was more ridiculous than the last, and Sebastian was laughing at him.

Hayden looked up as she and Harrison entered the room. He

came over and gave her a hug, "Hey, Heather."

"Hi, darling. How have you been?"

"Great. You found the place okay, then?" Hayden asked her.

"It's a bit hard to miss, isn't it?" she asked with a wry grin at him.

"No kidding," he laughed before he leaned over to press a button in front of him and announced, "they're here, guys!"

Both the men in the booth looked up, smiled at them all, and headed out of the studio, into the control room.

"My lover is here!" Sebastian announced with a grin, coming over to give her a hug. "So glad to see your face, sexy."

"Thanks, Seb." She smiled, genuinely happy to see him. "How come nobody told me you'd built a fucking castle out here?"

"Only the best for you, princess. Ooh, is that better than 'lover'?" he wondered aloud.

"You could just go with 'Heather'," Hayden suggested.

"Blasphemy!" Sebastian said dramatically.

He walked away, and Gabriel came toward Heather. She was nervous to see him; they'd texted here and there since her show, but she hadn't seen him since her engagement party. He was smiling at her, though; this was a good sign.

"Hi, *Heather*," he directed this at Sebastian, and everyone laughed.

"Hey, darling. It's so good to see you." She stepped forward and hugged him tightly.

There was a lot that they needed to say, she still wanted to talk to Ariana, but she'd been so busy since Fashion Week that they hadn't crossed paths yet. Heather had thought about sending her a text as well, but it didn't feel right. They needed to talk face to face.

She wasn't fully ready to forgive her yet; it would really depend on what Ariana told her when they finally did talk. Heather was hoping that they'd get a chance to talk while she was out here, but it didn't seem like Ariana was here. Now wasn't the time to ask Gabriel about it, though. There would be plenty of time to talk later.

"So, what are you guys working on?" she asked them as she took a seat next to Sebastian on a black leather sofa against the wall that backed on to the corridor behind them.

"Would you believe me if I said 'music'?" Sebastian asked her dryly.

"No? 'Music,' you say?" She turned to him, a pensive look on her face, "Tell me more. Is this something you've just discovered?"

"Oh, yes," he nodded at her, seriously, "so, it turns out there are these things called 'instruments', and they make different sounds."

"Wow, how fascinating. I'm surprised no one's ever thought of this before."

"Look, we were shocked, too. It's pretty new and different, but we think it could be *big*." His eyes widened at his apparent discovery and wonder at the possibilities it entailed.

"Well, I wish you the very best of luck with that. I'm sure it'll catch on."

"If you two are finished," Hayden interrupted their ridiculous conversation, and they finally broke character to burst into laughter, "maybe if we finish this song, we could take a break."

"You want me to take a break, don't you, Heather?" Harrison raised an eyebrow at her, meaningfully, and immediately a rush of lust hit her.

"Yes, yes, I do. Go forth, my music men! Discover new worlds and let me fuck my fiancé!"

They all laughed, and Harrison, Sebastian, and Gabriel headed back into the studio, leaving her sitting on the couch behind Hayden to watch them. She'd seen them making music in the past, but this felt different. It was obvious that they were enjoying the control they now had over the whole process.

The guys were back on the song that Gabriel had been singing previously, with more appropriate lyrics now, though. There were moments of brilliance when one of them would hit on the perfect melody or lyrics, and she felt so honored to be allowed to witness it. It was crazy to think that, sometime next year, people worldwide would probably be listening to music that was created here, today, in this place.

She lost track of time as she watched them; occasionally, they would ask for her thoughts to solve some difference of opinion. It was nice to get to be involved in this. In the past, Heather had been in the studio with them, but there had always been some music executive or someone else from the label hovering over them.

They were free, now, to explore what they wanted to do with the song, and she could see that, for the most part, the guys collaborated really well and agreed on what the song needed. Hayden spent some time showing her how to use the bare minimum of the control panel so that he could stop running back and forth between the two rooms as much as he was. It was nice to actually be helpful.

By the time Heather pressed the button that played back the song in its entirety, they were all thrilled with how it sounded. She was sitting on the chair in front of the controls, Harrison was behind her, his arms around her, and resting his head on hers as they listened to it. The song was amazing; she couldn't believe that she got to be a part of making it, as small a part as that was.

"First single?" she asked the room when the song ended.

"You haven't even heard any of the other songs we've recorded," Gabriel grinned at her.

"I know a hit when I record one." She flipped her hair and gave him a haughty look.

"Just how many songs have you got under your recording belt, then, Heather?" Hayden asked her.

"Well, just the one, but it was a good one. You should hear it sometime! Probably, when it becomes the first single off the new album for this awesome band that I know."

She heard Harrison's laughter above her, and he spun the chair around so that she was facing him. He dropped his lips to hers and kissed her softly. She wound her arms around his neck and leaned back in the chair, pulling him further toward her to deepen their kiss as she did so. He stepped closer to her chair, and she crossed her legs behind him, trapping him in between them, as they continued their kiss.

"You guys are aware that I have more rooms in this house than the one we're currently in, right?" Sebastian drawled at them.

Heather had completely forgotten where they were for a second, and she blushed as she registered Sebastian's words.

"Good point, Seb," Harrison broke their kiss to say this, "I think I'll just help Heather take her luggage to our room. It's currently in the entryway, and I'd hate for someone to trip over it or something."

"Sounds like a real safety hazard," Gabriel grinned at him, "you should definitely get right on that."

Harrison took her hand in his, and she waved goodbye to them as he led her out of the room. Safety hazard, indeed. Heather was worried that she might self-combust if she didn't get sexual relief soon. They grabbed her suitcase, and Harrison took her up a sweeping staircase that came off the entry hall. It led to an upper level of the house, and she walked along the plush carpet to a door a short way down a corridor. He opened it to reveal a room that would've been suitable in any number of the ludicrously expensive hotels they'd stayed in previously.

She was going to make a comment along these lines to Harrison, but she turned and saw his face. All of her previous thoughts flew out of her head, and the world was reduced to the two of them, as he set her suitcase down in the walk-in closet and came back out toward her.

"I believe I promised you long, slow, and over many, *many* hours?" He raised an eyebrow at her.

"I think I also recall you requesting to be sucked really fucking well and to completion..." she trailed off as she licked her lips, and her eyes flickered to his crotch where she could see a telltale bulge already forming.

"On your knees, angel," he instructed her.

She dropped to her knees right where she was. Harrison strode over to her, unbuttoning his jeans as he did. He stopped in front of her and freed his erection, which she swiftly took in her mouth. He placed a hand on the back of her head, his fingers clutching her hair in their grasp, and watched her with lust-filled eyes. She took to her task with vigor and kept sucking him much longer than she usually would. Heather normally got too frustrated and eager, so she would jump on him to fuck him long before he could ever come in her mouth. She was determined to finish him with her mouth today, though, and was pleased when she got to swallow his offering.

He took her over to the bed, instructing her to stand still as he stripped her clothes off her, slowly. His hands seemed to need to touch every inch of her exposed skin as he did it. With each item that he removed, he gained more and more access to her body. When she was completely naked, he walked around her in a circle, touching her and occasionally kissing some random part of her exposed flesh.

"Harrison." She could barely manage a whisper, her voice full of lust and longing.

"On the bed, on your back, angel."

She climbed onto the bed to lay down with her head on the pillows. He parted her thighs and buried his face between them. It wasn't long at all before Heather finally got the orgasm she'd been craving for hours.

"So soon?" He raised an eyebrow, and she laughed.

"I'm not sure what you expected, honey, you've had me wound tighter than a spring since I got here."

"What I expect," he bent his head and softly bit her inner thigh, before kissing the flesh he'd bitten and then moving his tongue closer to her sweet spot, "is to hear you scream my name multiple times before I even consider actually fucking you."

Heather loved this man like crazy. He knew exactly how to torment her in just the right way, and they spent hours in bed together, as he had promised her. They had sex, but not until he'd driven her wild by teasing her and bringing her to orgasm several times, first. They also spent a long chunk of time just lying there together in each other's arms before finally showering and getting dressed to head downstairs and socialize with the others.

"Finally decided that we're worthy of your company?" Hayden grinned at them as they walked into one of the rooms downstairs, where the other three guys were playing pool.

"We figured we weren't missing much; we've seen Seb whoop your ass at pool plenty of times before," Heather smirked at him.

"Ouch! You know how to cut deep, lady. Today's the day I'll finally beat him; I can feel it."

Heather looked at the pool table, where Hayden had about twice as many balls left as Sebastian did. She laughed and patted him on the back as she walked past him, "You keep telling yourself that, darling."

Heather sat down on a stool next to Gabriel at the side of the room, and Harrison went over to the bar that was in the corner of the room to pour them some drinks.

"By the way, you don't need to worry, Heather," Sebastian spoke up, as he was chalking his pool cue before lining up his next shot, "I made sure that all the rooms in this house were soundproofed before I moved in. We couldn't hear a thing."

She, Harrison, and Hayden all laughed, while Gabriel looked confused.

"Seb had the room next to us in New York," Harrison told him, by way of an explanation.

Gabriel continued to look confused for a second until his expression cleared, and he laughed out loud, "Well, that doesn't seem like it would be too awkward at all."

"They gave us *quite* the show," Sebastian nodded at Gabriel, "honestly, it seemed kind of deliberate, to me. I think Heather just wanted to make sure she had a permanent place in my spank bank."

"Shut up, asshole," she said. "You know that's not true!"

"Are you sure, Heather?" Harrison frowned at her. "I mean, you were *very* loud that day. I just thought it was because I was a sex god, but the more I think about it..." he trailed off and raised his eyebrows at her.

"Don't you start." She laughed. "You know that I didn't know Sebastian was staying next to us until afterward!"

"What I'm hearing," Gabriel said with a wicked grin, "is that your inner exhibitionist doesn't care *who* is in the next room, as long as *someone* hears you. It just happened to be Sebastian on this occasion."

"You guys suck balls," she growled at them.

"Wait, isn't that what *you* were doing in New York?" Hayden laughed at her glare.

"I'm not discussing this further. Yes, honey, you're a fucking sex god. These guys are just jealous that they're not as good in bed as you are."

She blew him a kiss to emphasize her point and laughed as the other guys tried to defend their sexual prowess to her.

"Just shut up and play pool," she said and stuck her tongue out at Sebastian.

He laughed and took his next shot. Harrison brought her over a vodka and orange juice, and she thanked him with a kiss on his cheek as she took it off him. It reminded her of Ariana, and she thought that now was as good a time as any to have a conversation with Gabriel about her.

"How is Ariana?" she asked him.

"She's good, really good." His voice and expression softened as he was obviously thinking of her. It was nice to see him happy.

"Is she coming up this weekend?"

"Unfortunately, not. She's working as a real estate agent now, so she has to do open houses pretty much every weekend. She's worked out with her boss to take a couple of days off each week this month to come up here, but they have to be mid-week to have the least effect on her work." He shrugged.

It was an interesting career choice for Ariana. When Heather had known her, she was generally pretty shy. It was hard to imagine Ariana as a salesperson, convincing people to purchase things took a certain quality that she hadn't known Ariana had.

"That's really nice"—Heather hesitated but decided to continue—"I heard what happened with that reporter. I'm really sorry, that would have been awful for her."

Gabriel's expression clouded over, and she could tell that he was furious just from thinking about it.

"I don't think I've ever been angrier in my life," Gabriel's voice was rough with anger mixed with concern for Ariana, "I'm lucky that I didn't find out until after, to be honest. I would've fucking killed him."

"It's so predatory and awful. My fashion show director thinks that we should all get personal security."

"Ally?" Gabriel asked Heather, much to her surprise.

"Yeah…wait…how did you know?" she raised her eyebrows at him.

"Ask Hayden." He nodded over to him, and Heather's mouth dropped open.

"They didn't!"

"You'll have to ask him, but I think she's planning to come out here sometime while we're here," Gabriel informed her.

"Wow! That's awesome, she's amazing."

Ally and Hayden, Heather liked it. They were both so cool, and she just wanted the people in her life to be happy. Obviously, you didn't have to be in a relationship to be happy, but in their world, it was so hard to find someone genuine, that wasn't after them for their fame and money, so the idea of Hayden hooking up with Ally was a relief to Heather. She trusted her.

Gabriel was watching the pool game now; he was so relaxed and at ease. Heather hadn't forgotten what it was like when Ariana had left them, but she also couldn't deny that he was a different person when he was with her. At peace with the world, and she couldn't resent him for wanting that again.

"I'm sorry for being such a bitch the night that we were at Sebastian's place," Heather said, causing Gabriel to turn and look at her.

He took a moment before replying, "You've been one of my best friends for a long, long time, Heather. That night really hurt me, though. I've had time to think about it since, and I think I kind of understand. You were hurt and lashing out, Ariana knows that, as well."

"I'm still hurt, Gabriel." Heather was surprised to find herself fighting back tears that were threatening to fall. "She was my best friend, and she left. I still don't know why. I can't imagine why she would ever have done that to us."

Gabriel put his arm and her shoulders and pulled her into a hug. "It's not my place to tell you. Ariana wants to talk to you sometime soon, whenever you guys can organize it and when you both feel ready. Just know that she has been your biggest champion since we got back together. She talked me out of quitting the band, the night we were at Sebastian's place."

Heather was shocked to hear that he had considered quitting the band, and that must have been reflected on her face.

"It would've been a dumb move, very irrational." He laughed at her expression. "I was very angry. She told me to give you and

Sebastian time. She's"—he paused, searching for the right word—"different now. I know that what she did wasn't right, Heather. You have every right to be hurt, but please give her a chance and just hear her out when the time comes."

Heather swallowed back the bitter words that she still wanted to say and nodded at him. This wound was deep, but she was willing to at least hear what Ariana had to tell her. Gabriel squeezed her shoulders, then let go of her.

Reading between the lines to try and figure out what he wasn't telling her, Heather came to the conclusion that there was clearly some sort of reason that Ariana had for leaving. She still couldn't think of any reason that would make sense, but the haunted look on Ariana's face the day they'd played Euchre had been playing on her mind ever since she had remembered it.

Ariana had been well and truly initiated into their world, now. When she'd been a part of their lives previously, she'd always been slightly apart from them, owing to the fact that no one knew about her existence and importance in their lives. Now, though, Ariana was as much a part of "the band," in the public's opinion, as Heather was.

Ever since Fashion Week, though, the media spotlight on Heather had intensified dramatically. She realized that at some point, she had been catapulted into the next echelon of stardom and was now becoming a celebrity in her own right. These days, she was frequently referred to in online articles specifically for her fashion line, and not simply in context as Harrison's fiancé.

It was nice to feel like her own person, but the flip side of that was that now people seemed to feel that same kind of ownership over her that they did over the band. She had been asked for her autograph several times, and she could no longer go out in public without being followed, photographed, and asked a thousand and one questions.

People also felt free to give her their honest opinion on

everything from her designs, down to what she'd chosen to wear that day. One day, she'd been flat out at the new workspace and left with her hair all over the place, barely any makeup on and wearing an old, comfortable sweatshirt with jeans.

Unfortunately, she'd had to stop for milk on the way home and had been rewarded with no fewer than three different strangers telling her how bad she looked in person when compared with what they had seen in magazines and online. It was bizarre that people seemed to not realize that she was a real human being with feelings like anyone else.

They still hadn't really made any decisions about personal security. Nothing overly bad had happened since they'd returned to Chicago, though, and now the guys were safely ensconced here in Galena where nobody could bother them. Perhaps that was part of why people were hassling her so much more lately.

"Penny for your thoughts?" Hayden sat on the seat to her right.

"Just thinking about the whole security issue," Heather said honestly.

"We need to talk to Cooper about it," Gabriel told them.

"I'm still hoping that it'll just die down," Hayden shrugged his shoulders.

"Cool. Meanwhile, my girlfriend is being harassed at her place of work," Gabriel said with a frosty voice.

"Whoa, Gabriel. No. I didn't mean it like that." Hayden looked abashed. "I don't want Ariana being followed around. We should definitely talk to Cooper."

"I got what you meant, Hayden." Heather came to his rescue. "It would be good if we didn't need to consider getting personal security. I didn't like the idea at first, either, but you guys have been out here, and I don't know about Ariana, but it's gotten much worse for me since you left."

Harrison and Sebastian walked over to where they were sitting to join the conversation.

"They're still going on with that dumbass rumor that you guys are splitting up, plus no one knows where you are, so they're following me around to try and see where I go, or if I'm meeting up with any of you." Heather cringed.

"It's pretty much the same for Ariana," Gabriel confirmed, "they're constantly bombarding her with questions about us breaking up."

Sebastian had a frown on his face. "So what do we do? Do Heather and Ariana need security now? Or do we wait until we're all back from Galena?"

"Fuck Cooper, I'm calling it," Gabriel said in a firm voice. "I'm getting Ariana a bodyguard, and I think Heather needs one, too. We can worry about ourselves after we get back to Chicago. Nobody is hassling us out here, so we're safe."

"I agree," Harrison said, and Heather looked up into his warm, brown eyes that were full of love and concern for her. "What do you think, angel?"

Heather thought that she might burst into tears right there and then. She hadn't realized how stressed she'd been about the paparazzi. Now that she was faced with the prospect of having a bodyguard to assist with those interactions, it seemed absolutely crazy that she'd been handling this without one.

"Please do it sooner rather than later." Her voice was croaky.

Harrison embraced her in a hug, and she melted into him. Feeling so secure, so safe, and so very glad that they'd come to this decision.

Chapter 11

SREĆAN TRIDESETI ROĐENDAN, HAIDEN

Heather closed her laptop and breathed a sigh of relief. She'd just been double-checking her itinerary for her trip to New York next week. She would be flying out on Thursday, in time for the Saturday Night Live rehearsals, and she was incredibly nervous. She had no idea why she'd ever agreed to do it—she wasn't a performer; she was a designer.

Cruise Control had to attend a massive Halloween charity function in Los Angeles, along with Cooper and his team. Now that she was one of Cooper's clients herself, it was interesting to see how his management style differed with her.

He gave Cruise Control a *lot* of attention in comparison. She wondered if his other clients ever got bitter about the fact that he would consistently drop everything to ensure the guys were taken care of. Then again, Cruise Control almost certainly earned him more than all of his other clients put together, so maybe he didn't care about what his other clients thought that much, anyway.

Heather put her laptop in its bag, grabbed her phone, and headed out of her office, turning the light off on her way out. She went out to check the main sewing floor and make sure that everything was switched off out there, but couldn't resist walking past her wedding dress on the way out. It was already looking so beautiful. There was still so much to do, lots of hand-embroidery, but it was coming together wonderfully.

Everyone else at Serenity had left over an hour ago, and she'd stayed back longer than she'd intended to. She wouldn't get out to Galena until almost nine now; it was Friday night, and they were celebrating Hayden's thirtieth birthday in a much more low-key manner than they had for Harrison's, but she felt guilty that she'd be arriving so late tonight.

"Are you ready to leave, Miss York?" Callum Archer asked her as she approached him near the entry of the building.

"I sure am, I can't wait to see Harrison." She smiled widely at him.

"I'm sure."

He was tall, well-built, and was wearing a black, fitted suit. Callum had been her personal bodyguard for over a week now, and they'd gotten into a fairly steady rhythm. He arrived at her apartment each morning to collect her and drove her around in a big, black Range Rover with blacked-out windows whenever she had meetings or appointments. She had driven her Tesla out to Galena herself last weekend, though, leaving him behind. They'd agreed that unless they started to have any problems out there, it was pointless to have him hanging around for no reason.

All in all, it was working well and had been an incredible relief for Heather. Saturday Night Live had announced last week that she would be a guest on the show, and the reaction had been intense. She didn't think she would have been able to handle it without Callum's help. She didn't mind signing autographs for people—and did it often—but as soon as people started to get too close or too handsy, he shut them down in an instant.

There was a small group of people waiting at the front of the building today. Heather could tell they were mostly fans. Only one person had a heavy camera hanging around his neck. Callum opened the door and stepped through it, holding everyone off as Heather locked up the building. Once she'd done that, she turned and moved over to where the fans were standing.

"Hi Heather, can you sign this?" The fan held out a Sharpie and a picture of her standing at the end of the runway at Fashion Week.

"Sure, what's your name?" Heather smiled at her; she looked like she was only about sixteen.

"Megan." She grinned at her, as Heather signed her photo.

To Megan,

Stay awesome!

Heather

Heather struggled for what to write when signing things. Sometimes she just signed her name, but when the person wanting her autograph was someone young like this, she wanted to do more than just the bare minimum. They were so young and impressionable. The world was a harsh place, so if she were able to bring some light to people's lives with something as simple as this, she would do it.

"There you go, Megan," Heather said as she handed the photo back.

"Can I get a selfie?" Megan asked nervously.

"Sure."

Heather posed for the photo, then signed the other things that were handed to her by the other fans, who were definitely adults. She also posed for photos with them, and all the while, the photographer was snapping pics of them all. She'd started to walk to the Range Rover, which wasn't far away, but something was bothering her, so she stopped and turned back to the group.

"Megan?"

"Yeah?" The young girl smiled at her as Heather walked back to her.

"Are you here alone?"

"Yeah, I am."

"Do you live nearby?" Heather asked her with a frown.

"Yup, I live in an apartment near here." Megan was still smiling.

"How far away?"

"About a fifteen-minute walk." Megan shrugged.

There was no way that Heather could let her walk home on her own. She would probably be fine. Clearly, she wasn't bothered by it, but Heather's conscience wouldn't let her just leave her there on her own.

"Come with us"—Heather jerked her head toward the nearby car—"we'll give you a lift."

"Are you sure?" Megan's mouth dropped open.

"Absolutely. It can't be far out of our way if it's only a fifteen-minute walk, and I'd rather see you home safe and sound than leave you here."

"Wow, thank you so much!"

Megan followed her into the Range Rover, a stunned look on her face. Callum asked for her address, and Megan told him as she was strapping herself in.

"You're *so* nice. I can't believe this." Megan was looking all around the car, trying to take everything in.

Heather gave her a reassuring smile, "it's fine, darling. It's really no trouble at all."

Megan was still clutching the picture that Heather had signed for her earlier. The people who had asked for her autograph so far had come to her with a mixture of her designs or pictures of her, more frequently than not though, they had her sign some kind of Cruise Control merchandise. It was really bizarre to sign the guys' CD and have the person be as thrilled as if it was Gabriel or Sebastian signing it for them.

"So, are you a Cruise Control fan?" Heather asked Megan.

"Yup, they're the best!" she had a massive grin on her face as she said it. "That's how I found out about you. Your designs are *amazing*! I love them so much; I can't believe I'm here with you. This is crazy! I've been following you on Instagram for, like, *ever*!"

"Okay, take a breath, darling." Heather laughed.

"Sorry, I talk a lot when I'm nervous. I'm dumb." Megan cringed at her.

"Don't say that. You're not dumb, you're just excited," Heather gave her a warm smile, "and I was your age, once, so I get it. Do you want to know a secret?"

"Yes! Of course!" Megan's eyes were wide.

"Celebrities are just people, darling. We're no different to you; people just pay more attention to what we do, but we're not special. There are plenty of people more talented than Cruise Control, more talented designers than me. It just happened that with talent, hard work, and an extreme amount of luck, we got to be successful."

"I don't think anyone is more talented than Cruise Control!" Megan shook her head, and Heather laughed.

"Sure, they're very good at making music, but Hayden loses practically every game of pool that he plays, Sebastian can't cook for shit, Harrison pretty much can't draw anything more difficult than a stick figure, and Gabriel once played a game of golf so badly that he broke a record for most shots over par at that golf club." Heather laughed at the memory; she didn't think she should tell Megan that Gabriel had been drunk as a skunk at the time, though.

Callum pulled the car into a parking spot, outside of an apartment building that Heather assumed must be where Megan lived.

"My point is, everyone has their strengths and their weaknesses, and we're all human. Even celebrities." Heather smiled at her, "Is this your building?"

"Yeah, it is. Thank you so much for driving me home, you're so nice!"

"You're welcome. Will you be okay to get inside?" Heather wondered where her parents were and why they weren't concerned that their daughter wasn't home yet.

"Yeah, I'll be fine. Thanks again!" Megan opened the door, jumped out of the car, and headed into the building with a wave.

Heather waved back, as Callum pulled the car back into traffic and headed toward her own apartment building. Luckily, Megan's home had been pretty much on their way, anyway, so she hadn't lost much time in leaving for Galena. They had almost reached their destination when her phone lit up with a tag on Instagram from @meggggzy2005. She opened the app and saw the selfie Megan had taken with her and the caption:

OMGGGGG I met @officialheatheryork today and she is the nicest person ever!!!! #lifegoals #CruiseControl #sheLITERALLYdrovemehome

Heather laughed; Megan was sweet. She didn't think that her lecture about celebrity had gotten through to her at all, but she knew that at that age, she probably wouldn't have listened, either. It was only through experiencing celebrity and life in the spotlight, that Heather had ever been able to understand. She commented on the photo:

It was great to meet you, @meggggzy2005. I hope you have a great night! Xox

Heather clicked the follow button on Megan's profile as comments started popping up on the thread underneath hers. She ignored them and closed the app as Callum pulled the car into the underground garage for her building. She'd have to leave pretty much immediately for Galena, and she'd still be driving most of the way there in the dark.

She thanked Callum for his help this week, then headed upstairs and grabbed the weekend bag she'd already packed that morning. Morning Heather had been optimistic about getting home early and being able to head off to see Harrison sometime this afternoon. Evening Heather was just glad that she didn't have to pack a bag now, and could leave straight away.

As she took the elevator back downstairs, she shot Harrison a text.

On my way! Can't wait to see you.

She jumped into her car and threw the bag on the passenger seat beside her, entered Sebastian's address into the car's satellite navigation system, and headed off as Harrison's reply came through.

I was wondering where you were. Ally's here for Hayden's birthday. Love you.

It was a three-hour drive, and she stopped in Rockford to get a burger and chips on the way, choosing to go through the drive-thru and eat on the way to save time. She could imagine the horrified look Harrison would have if he knew, and she laughed. He never ate in his car at all, for any reason. Heather tried not to unless it was something like this where she just didn't want to stop, and she was aching to be with Harrison.

This was what it was like whenever they were apart. Everything felt wrong until she was with him again. Maybe it was just because they'd been together for so long now, but the *Heart Wide Open* tour had been a special kind of hell for her. She knew that as her career was taking off, separations like this would become more frequent, and she hated that knowledge.

When she arrived at Galena, she used a remote that Sebastian had given her to open the gates. She drove up to the house and pulled around to the garage, which she opened with the same remote. There were several sports cars in here, along with an SUV and some sedans. She recognized Harrison's black Tesla and Gabriel's Aston Martin; she saw Hayden's Lamborghini as well, and maybe Ally had driven a rental here if she didn't come with Hayden, but the rest would be Sebastian's.

Heather pulled into one of the spare bays. There was practically enough room in here for an entire showroom's worth of cars, and she rolled her eyes. It was so ostentatious, then again, everything about this place was over the top. She'd gotten used to their lifestyle, but occasionally, something would happen, and it would remind her that their lives weren't normal, and their wealth was obscene. Usually, that something was done by Sebastian. He had no problem with spending his money, where she and Harrison certainly made use of it but nowhere near to the same extent that Seb did.

She made her way into the house, took her bag up to the room that she'd be staying in with Harrison, then headed back downstairs and followed the sound of voices to a room near the back of the house. They were all seated around a large, oval table with felt on top of it, and were playing poker. Like most things that Sebastian got custom made, it had the Cruise Control symbol in the center.

Heather stood there, just observing for a while. Sebastian was closest and had his back to her, next to him was Gabriel, and both men were still in the current hand. Harrison was sitting at the end of the table, his face in profile to her, and she was just so happy to see him that she couldn't stop the grin that came over her face. He folded his cards and took a sip from a drink that she was sure would be whisky, before picking up the deck of cards in front of him to put another card on the table.

On the side of the table that was facing her, Ally and Hayden were sitting together. They were flirting terribly, as they ate some chips from a packet that was sitting between them. Both had folded their cards already, and Sebastian and Gabriel continued on the hand. Being here was soothing; these were the people in the world that meant the most to her. She was so lucky to have them in her life.

"Heather!" Hayden yelled as he looked up and saw her standing in the doorway.

"My lover!" Sebastian added, turning to grin at her.

Heather realized that they were all pretty drunk right now and laughed, "Clearly, I'm about four drinks behind you guys. Happy birthday, Hayden!"

Harrison put his drink down in the cup holder that was built into the table and handed the deck of cards and dealer chip to Gabriel, "Here."

He strode over to her, swiftly, put his arms around her, and claimed her lips with his. His hands roamed over her body, landing on her ass and pulling her hard against him. The group at the table cheered and catcalled them. Yup, they were drunk.

When Harrison ended the kiss, they were both breathless, and he put his forehead to hers, looking intensely into her eyes.

"I want to fuck you, Heather York."

"I can tell," she laughed, his arousal was blatantly obvious when she was pressed up against him like this, "we should probably be social first, though."

He groaned at her, and she laughed, "Payback's a bitch, and so am I! Go sit down, I'll get myself liquored up and then you can have your wicked way with me, I promise."

Harrison headed back to the table to sit down as Heather made her way to the side of the room where there were bottles of alcohol sitting out, and a fridge which she was hoping would have some mixers in it. She was pleased when she discovered that it did, so she poured herself a heavy-handed rum and Coke since she had some catching up to do.

"Do you want us to deal you in?" Sebastian asked her as she walked back toward the table with her drink.

"Nah, I'll just watch." She smiled at him.

"You can be my good luck charm, angel." Harrison winked at her.

Heather set her drink in the cup holder next to his but didn't take a seat, choosing instead to sit on Harrison's lap, and he wrapped his arms around her waist at once, resting his chin on her shoulder to watch the rest of the hand, which he had once again folded on.

He turned his head to kiss her cheek before going back to watching the game. Heather took a sip of her drink to test it. Maybe she'd made it a little too strong, the taste of the rum was overpowering, but she went ahead and took a big swig, anyway. Her throat burned, but then the warmth she felt was quite nice.

She relaxed into Harrison's embrace as Ally won the hand with a pair of Aces. Heather played with Harrison's poker chips as Sebastian dealt the next hand, and Harrison reached forward to grab his cards. He lifted them up, and she saw the two and seven of clubs. She could feel Harrison's frustration as he dropped them down again.

"But they're suited..." she whispered into his ear before dropping her head to kiss his neck, right where she could feel his pulse with her lips, and he laughed.

"You're a cruel wench," he said as he threw his cards in before cupping her chin with his hand and pulling her face toward his for another kiss.

She could feel that he was erect beneath her, and she was wet, too. Heather wondered if the others would even care if they went to their room now. She looked around the table and caught Sebastian's eye.

As though reading her thoughts, he announced with a wicked grin, "There's a ten-thousand-dollar fine if you leave the table first."

"That can't be a thing." She rolled her eyes.

"Oh, it really is." Hayden laughed.

"Well, what is 'leaving the table,' anyway? Harrison came over to see me, does that count?"

"It doesn't," Harrison said and then winked at her, "but I'd have done it even if it did. It's only if you leave the game."

"Why have I never heard of this rule before?" she grumbled.

"We made it up last week," Sebastian gave her finger guns and a wink as well, "some asshole wanted to leave the game."

"It was four in the morning, and I was tired!" Gabriel protested.

"Hang on, so I'm in Chicago, all on my own and in desperate need of a fiancé to fuck, all because you guys are up here playing poker all night instead of making an album like you're meant to be doing?" She poked her tongue out at them and took another big sip of her drink.

Ally shuffled the cards and dealt out the next hand as the conversation continued. Harrison was slowly stroking her outer thigh with one hand as he looked at his cards; this time, he had a pair of red queens and called the bet.

"Yup, that's pretty much right. Sucks to be you, Heather!" Hayden laughed.

"Apparently so. How is the album going?"

Gabriel and Sebastian both folded their cards this time, while Ally and Hayden stayed in the hand. She put three cards on the table, the five of diamonds, king of clubs and two of hearts.

"It's awesome," Gabriel said, "we'll play it for you tomorrow."

"Is it finished then?" She turned and looked at Harrison with excitement, "You're coming home?"

As the next round of betting finished, Ally put another card on the table, and it was the queen of spades. Hayden didn't bet initially, so Harrison made a fairly big bet, and Ally folded, but Hayden called.

"Sorry, angel, not quite. We think it'll be another week here. We've got the cancer charity event next Saturday while you're in New York, and then we'll both be back in Chicago on Sunday. If the album isn't done by then, the guys will just have to finish it without any bass."

He shrugged as if he was serious while Ally put down the river card; it was the five of hearts. Hayden bet big, and Harrison called him. Hayden showed his cards, he had a king in his hand, and he groaned as Harrison showed his cards, with Harrison's full house beating Hayden's two pair of kings and fives.

"Well, shit. We could've done the whole album without bass," Sebastian said dryly, "as long as you've got lead guitar, who gives a crap about bass?"

"Yes, darling, we're all aware that you're *the* most important person in the entire world, and the band couldn't possibly exist without you." She blew him a kiss.

"As long as you're aware, that's all I care about, lover." He winked at her.

"You didn't tell me how crazy these fuckers were, Heather," Ally laughed as she said it.

"And *you* didn't tell me that you were fucking my friend. A little heads-up text so I don't have to hear it from Mr. Knight next time would be nice!" Heather smirked across the table at her.

Ally grinned at her wickedly and pulled out her phone. It wasn't long until Heather's phone lit up on the table in front of her.

Hayden is fucking epic in bed.

Heather almost spat rum all over Sebastian's poker table as she burst out laughing.

Did not need to know that. Thanks.

Ally was grinning at her like the cat that got the cream.

You're welcome! I had to try out some of that crazy hot sex that you recommended so highly.

As a connoisseur of crazy hot sex, I'm glad to hear that you've decided to join the club.

Heather finished off her drink and got off Harrison's lap to go and pour herself another one. She poured herself the same, just as strong as the first, then walked back to the table but chose to walk around behind Ally so she could give her a hug.

"I'm glad you're here, darling."

"Me, too!"

"Hey, where's *my* hug, lover?" Sebastian pouted at her as Heather gave Hayden a hug, as well, wishing him happy birthday once again.

Heather laughed, then put her drink down next to Harrison's, walked around the table, and gave Sebastian and Gabriel each a hug.

"Sorry, I would've greeted everybody properly, but somebody distracted me when I arrived," Heather sat back down on Harrison's lap as she said it, and he laughed.

"Deal me out, guys," Harrison said, waving the cards away as Gabriel attempted to deal him some.

"Are you sure?" Gabriel raised an eyebrow at him, "Have you forgotten the fine?"

"Fuck the fine." Harrison laughed. "As soon as Heather finishes this drink, I'm going to go and have a ten-thousand-dollar screw."

Everyone laughed, as Gabriel skipped Harrison and dealt his card to Sebastian instead. Harrison had given up any pretense of watching the game, now. His hand had reached under her skirt to stroke her inner thigh, and her breath caught every time he got slightly too close to the place she was aching for him to touch.

"Are you okay, there, angel?" Harrison whispered into her ear, and she nodded. "Are you sure?"

His fingers reached the edge of her underwear, and she thought that her heart might stop beating any second, now, as she shook her head. She was decidedly *not* okay right now.

"Finish your drink, angel." He smirked at her.

Heather picked up her drink and drank it as quickly as she could, leading her to have a coughing fit as she finished it.

"Wow, Heather," Sebastian said, "you sure seem thirsty."

Everyone laughed, and Heather flipped him the bird as she jumped up off Harrison's lap, grabbing his hand and dragging him toward the door as she announced to the group.

"This thirsty bitch is going to get a drink. Night, guys! You'd better treat the birthday boy right, Ally!" Heather winked at her.

"Oh, I fully intend to." Ally laughed and kissed Hayden.

They left them playing poker and retreated to their bedroom for a repeat of the previous two weekends' events. Harrison seemed to want to spend as much time with her body during these weekends together, as he would've if they'd been together all week. He loved to drive her wild with lust and wouldn't fuck her until she was begging him to do it.

♥

It was a good weekend, hanging out with the guys and Ally. The band had performed on Saturday Night Live before, so they gave her some tips and helped calm her down. Ally promised to come along to the show and support her, so she'd have someone there with her, after all.

When the time came for Heather to leave on Monday morning, Gabriel found her as she was walking to the garage to put her bag in the car before she left.

"Hey, Heather."

"Hi, Gabriel. How are you this morning?" She smiled at him.

"I'm good." He looked serious. "Look, Ariana asked me to give you this."

He handed her an envelope. It had her name written on the front of it in neat writing that Heather recognized as Ariana's, and Heather frowned.

"What is this?" she asked, Gabriel, even though it was kind of obvious.

"It's a letter for you, from Ariana." He confirmed.

Heather flipped the envelope over and prepared to rip it open when Gabriel said, "No, don't open it here."

"What? Why not?"

"It's not short." He laughed. "Also…" he trailed off.

"Also, what?" she asked him.

Gabriel looked uncharacteristically nervous. "I don't know, Heather. Just, please remember what I said. Hear her out, okay? Don't read the letter if you're not ready to forgive her yet. Promise me?"

Heather smiled at him. "I promise."

She gave him a hug; he would always be one of her favorite people on the face of the planet. Heather tucked the letter carefully away in the front pocket of her bag; she would read it when she got back to Chicago. Maybe she and Ariana could catch up sometime this week before she flew to New York.

Chapter 12

LIVE FROM NEW YORK...

Heather thought she had experienced nerves when she did Fashion Week, but this was a thousand times worse. Knowing that she was going to be on live TV in only a few hours made her feel sick to her stomach.

"You have to eat something, Heather." Ally smiled at her.

They were sitting at a restaurant in Rockefeller Plaza, having an early dinner before Heather had to go head to Studio 8H to get ready for the dress rehearsal.

"If I eat something, it had better be tasty, because I'll be experiencing it twice." She grimaced.

"You're going to be fine. You were just as nervous as this before your show, and that was amazing."

"No way, I was nowhere near this nervous!" Heather took a perfunctory mouthful of the salad she'd ordered.

Ally laughed at her, "Yeah, you were. Remember when I told you Nicole Spencer had turned up? I thought you were going to hit me!"

"That's totally different; this is *live* television. I'm going to fuck everything up. I should never have agreed to this; I could be in Los Angeles with Harrison right now." Heather sighed.

"Nope, no pity parties, woman. I wouldn't let you have one over Nicole, and I'm not letting you have one now. The sketch is hilarious, and people are going to love you. How can you equally be the most self-assured and confident woman I know, while also being a nervous wreck?" Ally frowned as she speared some of her penne pesto pasta on the fork she was holding and put it in her mouth.

Heather laughed. "Ah, see, that's because you're getting to know the real me, darling. I think it comes from being with Harrison for the whole ride. I learned very early on that perception is everything, and I work very hard to ensure that what people perceive from me is a certain thing."

Ally reflected on what Heather had told her. "That must be exhausting. I shall feel honored that you like me enough to freak the fuck out in front of me, then," she said this with a grin.

"You should. You're in very elite company; you're in with people like your epic-in-bed crazy-hot-sex man." Heather laughed. "How is that going, by the way?"

"He's the best, Heather. So relaxed and chill, not at all like other guys I've dated. Men in New York tend to be"—she searched for the right word—"uptight. To say the least."

Talking about Ally's love life was a good distraction from her nerves. She was so grateful to have such a wonderful person in her life; she hadn't chatted with a friend like this since Ariana had left the tour two years ago; it was comforting. Heather was reminded of the letter that was sitting in her bedside drawer at home.

She had intended to read it when she'd gotten back to Chicago, but she'd had to go straight to her workspace to handle a production issue that had arisen. Then, she'd been so tense and worked up about this trip to do Saturday Night Live that she had wanted to honor what Gabriel had asked of her and decided to wait until after she got back to read it.

Once she got SNL over, she could hopefully relax. She was

ready now to hear what Ariana had to tell her, but she didn't want her nerves to temper whatever reaction she might have to what was written in the letter.

"Heather?" Ally asked her, and she realized that she'd zoned out and hadn't responded to what Ally had said.

"Sorry, got distracted. I'm so nervous! But yeah, Hayden's always been like that. He goes with the flow and doesn't get worked up about shit. I mean, given the choice you had, Hayden is a much wiser choice than Sebastian." Heather winked at Ally, and she laughed back at her.

"You say that like I even had a shot with Sebastian." Ally rolled her eyes. "I'm pretty sure he was fucking one of the models backstage as soon as she was off the runway."

"I wouldn't be surprised if he was. Now that I think about it, I wonder how he's coping being out at Galena with no women around."

"The skin on his palm is probably red raw." Ally smirked at her, and Heather laughed.

"He'll get his blue balls attended to at the Halloween event tonight, no doubt!" She pulled out her phone to send a text to Sebastian.

Hey there, darling. Ally and I know you've been sans ladies out at Galena, just a reminder to use protection tonight, don't forget it just because you're a horny fucker. STDs aren't hot.

The charity event they were going to in Los Angeles tonight was a big deal. They were at a table with Cooper and his team for the dinner. It was a very high-profile event that initially Heather was going to attend, but she'd pulled out when SNL had come up.

"Okay, so I haven't asked Hayden this, but I'm curious," Ally said after Heather had told her what she'd texted Sebastian. "Does he *really* sleep with as many women as people make out that he does?"

"More," Heather confirmed, "a lot more. I'm surprised the media doesn't hear about all of them. Then again, if I'd slept with Sebastian Fox, I certainly wouldn't be shouting it to the world." She clapped her hands over her mouth. "Oh my god, I'm a terrible friend!"

Ally laughed. "No, you're right. I'd be embarrassed to be a notch on that man's bedpost, that's for sure."

On cue, Sebastian's reply to her text pinged through, and they both read it on her phone screen as it lit up.

Don't you worry about me, lover. I never trust the bitch with the contraception. I ALWAYS use my own condoms. So I won't give you anything the next time we fuck.

"Ugh. So goddamn gross." Ally faked a gag.

"Yeah, welcome to my life. I love Seb, I do, but he's just so…awful to the women he sleeps with," she said as she wrote a reply to his text.

Charming. With sweet talk like that, I can see why women are lining up to be with you.

"I kind of get why he is the way he is, though. Women have always just thrown themselves at him, so he doesn't see them as having any value. Even before he was famous, he was always with some girl or other. He hasn't had an actual girlfriend since we were teens, though. He just sleeps with whoever he wants and moves right along to the next person in the queue."

"Tell me Hayden isn't like that!" Ally looked horrified.

"Nope, not at all." She smiled back at her.

"Good. I can't lie; I was worried. Because of the whole Cruise Control reputation, I had vowed to stay away from you guys and keep our relationship purely professional when you hired me. Why are you so damn nice?"

Heather was surprised by this. She didn't know exactly when she and Ally had ended up becoming friends, but it wasn't just because she was with Hayden now. Sometime before her fashion show, during all of the craziness and tension, she supposed. They'd started sending random, funny texts to one another to lighten the mood. Ally getting together with Hayden had just helped them get closer, and it was nice to have a friend.

"I know some people who wouldn't call me nice." Heather cringed.

"Ariana?" Ally asked her.

"Oh, no, I didn't actually mean her! To be honest, despite everything, I think she still wants to be friends with me." Heather shrugged.

"But you don't want to be friends with her?"

"No, I do. She's really nice." Heather pondered exactly what her problem was. "It's just a case of once bitten, twice shy, I guess."

"Do you want my advice?" Ally looked solemn.

"As long as it's not fluffy bullshit."

She grinned at Heather's comment, "Okay, well, your world is fucking crazy. Hayden told me a bit about what happened with her, and I might have done similar if I'd been in her position at her age. There's a reason I've been going out to Galena, not just because that's where they are right now. I don't particularly want the insanity of being 'with' Hayden."

"If you and Hayden ever break up, can we still be friends?" Heather was saddened by what Ally was telling her; it was painfully reminiscent of the sort of things Ariana had said to her back in the day.

"Oh, Heather, you were my friend first! Look, Hayden and I have talked about it. We're just having fun; it's nothing serious. I can't see him relocating to New York, and I'm so busy here, I couldn't move there. I'm literally not looking to settle down any time soon; my focus is on my business right now. Basically, I'm just here for the crazy hot sex!" Ally winked at her.

"You say that now, but if it does go sour, just don't ditch me without a word of warning, please?"

"I want to make a sarcastic comment," Ally told her with a smile, "but you seem pretty sensitive about this, so I'll just promise that I wouldn't do that."

"Thanks, I appreciate it. Fuck, what's the time?"

Ally checked her watch, "Yeah, we should go"—she looked at Heather's practically full plate—"you really should've eaten more. They'll probably have some snacks there if you feel like it later, I guess."

Callum met them at the entrance of the restaurant and joined them for the short trip through the building to the Saturday Night Live studio and disappeared when Heather went into hair and makeup, but she knew he'd be nearby.

"April!" Heather said when she saw her friend backstage.

"It's so good to see you, Heather."

They exchanged hugs and talked for a few minutes before Heather continued on to hair and makeup. She was sitting in the chair, having her makeup done when her phone buzzed, and Harrison's name was on the screen. She answered it and put it on speaker so she could talk while her makeup artist continued working on her.

"Hi, honey, how's it going?"

"Good, angel. Are you nervous?" His voice was soothing, and she smiled.

"Not as much now that I'm talking to you. What time are you guys leaving for the event?"

"It starts at seven, and it's just downstairs, so we're all chilling and waiting to head down."

"Hi, lover! You're going to be the sexiest cameo that SNL has ever had!" Sebastian's voice came from somewhere in the background, and Heather laughed as she saw her makeup artist's eyebrows raise at his comment.

"Am I on speaker?" she asked Harrison.

"No, do you want to be?"

"Yeah, go on," she waited until he confirmed she was on speaker, "thanks, Seb. Who else is there?"

Hayden, Gabriel, and Ariana confirmed they were there, and suddenly Heather's nerves were back. She wanted to tell Ariana that she would read her letter soon and organize a time to catch up, but it wasn't an appropriate time. They were on speaker, and her makeup artist had already made it obvious that she was listening.

"Have a great time tonight, guys. I wish I was there with you instead of being here!"

"No, you don't," Gabriel said, "you're going to be amazing, and you'll have fun, trust me. Charity events are a dime a dozen, Saturday Night Live is a rare occurrence."

"Gabe's right," Ariana's voice was soft and kind, "try not to be nervous. Can you tell us about the sketch?"

"Thanks, Ariana." Ally caught Heather's eye in the mirror, and Ally smiled and gave her a thumbs-up. "Oh god, you're going to die, Sebastian. So, it's Harrison and me getting married, but then you stop the wedding and tell me you're in love with me, and we run away together!"

Everyone on the other end of the line burst into laughter when she told them this, and Sebastian's voice came through after a minute, when he'd managed to control his laughter.

"Just how much input did you have into that sketch, lover?"

"Not much, actually," she said seriously, then only just managed to finish the rest of her sentence without laughing, "but one of the writers got a hold of my diary and read all my secret fantasies. The rest is history."

This caused another outburst of laughter from the other end of the phone before Harrison spoke up this time.

"I love you, angel. I can't wait to see you tomorrow, and we can watch the show together."

"Love you too, honey. I can't wait to see you, either. I'll call you after the dress rehearsal and let you know how it went."

She said goodbye to the rest of them, and they gave her another round of good wishes and luck for the show before she hung up the call.

"That went well," Ally said.

She caught Heather's meaningful glance at her makeup artist in the mirror as she rummaged around in a cart full of makeup for the right mascara to use. Ally nodded, understanding not to say any more until they were alone again.

They didn't get any time alone, however. Before her makeup artist had finished, the hairstylist arrived to do Heather's hair, and then the costume designer entered to assist her with getting changed before she was directed out in front of the live crowd to do her part in the eight o'clock dress rehearsal.

It went really well, and Heather was pleased. One of the other sketches fell flat and was cut in favor of extending the wedding sketch, which got massive amounts of laughter from the crowd. They decided to make it the last sketch of the evening, as well, instead of being mid-show.

She was back with Ally in the green room afterward, and she called Harrison while she had the chance.

"Hi, honey," she said when he answered the phone.

"Hello, angel." His voice was soft and seductive, and she longed to be with him.

"God, I miss you so much," she said.

Ally turned away to give her some privacy, even though she'd still be able to hear every word that was said.

"I miss you, too. Less than twenty-four hours, and I'll be home," he said.

"Not a moment too soon, I'm going to fuck your brains out the minute I see you."

"Is that a promise?" he asked with a laugh.

"You bet your sweet, fucking ass it is."

"How did the rehearsal go?" She could hear the unspoken lust in his voice as he changed the topic.

"It went really well; I'm feeling much less nervous now."

"I'm glad. I have to go, angel. I'll talk to you later. Love you so much."

"I love you too, honey."

She hung up the call, made her way over to a table at the side of the room, and grabbed a selection of food from it. She got a couple of sandwich quarters, some fruit and cheese, then went and sat down on the sofa.

"You two are so disgustingly cute," Ally said with a grin as she sat down next to her, then indicated to the plate Heather was holding. "I'm glad to see you're eating some food, too!"

"Thanks, I think? Harrison is my world; I love that man to death…and the crazy, hot sex is definitely an added bonus." She smirked at her friend.

"I can imagine. Okay, another thing I've been dying to ask—"

"Oh, I see how it is, you're just friends with me so you can find out all the secrets of the inner workings of Cruise Control!" Heather interrupted her and feigned indignation.

Ally laughed as she continued "—well, kind of. Like, what the fuck is up with you and Sebastian? You're literally about to imply to the world that you would call off your wedding to run away with him, and Harrison is fine with that? I know you had a huge hand in making that sketch as funny as it is, so what the hell is the deal?"

"Okay, so Seb's just been like that for as long as I can remember. He used to make similar jokes to Ariana, and he's just flirty as hell but not serious about it. I wouldn't be surprised if he starts on you, soon.

"Ever since people started this rumor that we're having an affair, we've just leaned into that because if you don't laugh about the dumb shit people say, you'll cry. As for Harrison being fine with that," Heather smirked, "trust me when I say that Harrison has *nothing* to be concerned about, which is why he isn't. That man can practically make me come with one look, no way I'd ever trade that in for Sebastian Fox."

Heather twisted her engagement ring around on her finger as she was explaining this. She wished more than ever that Harrison were here with her. Her world was always off-kilter when they were apart.

Ally laughed at what she'd said. "I get that vibe from Harrison. He's normally so quiet and reserved, but when he was drunk, and we were playing poker, I was kind of shocked by the way he practically molested you in front of us!"

"See? You are making your way into the inner circle. That's pretty much spot-on for what Harrison is like. Once he's comfortable with you, you'll see a totally different side of him. We like you, darling." Heather winked at her.

One of the assistants came to get Heather. Telling her that it was ten minutes until showtime, and they needed her on set. She put her plate down on the table, took a sip of one of the glasses of water there, and both women followed him back out in front of the audience.

The show went off without a hitch, Heather hit all her cues, and the wedding sketch got even more laughs than it did the first time with the changes they'd made to it. When the show ended, Heather was on a massive high; she understood why the guys were always so amped when they came offstage. There was adrenalin pumping through her body, and she had so much energy that she didn't know what to do with it all.

Ally and April both gave her a massive hug, and so did a lot of the cast and crew. They were headed out to a club for the after-party, soon. She expected that the charity event the guys were at should be either over or finishing soon, so she sent Harrison a text.

OMG honey, it was AMAZING! I loved it so much! Call me!

The rest of the night passed in a blur. They got completely drunk and had a blast with the cast of Saturday Night Live, she checked her phone and noticed that Harrison hadn't replied to her text, so she called him, but it went to voicemail and she left him a message.

"Honeeeeeeey! I miss you! I want to fuck you! I want to scream your name while I come light a freight train…wait, *like* a freight train," she said, while both Ally and April laughed next to her, listening in, "anyway. Call me!"

She also sent a text to Sebastian.

Seb yoou sexy fucker. I bet your fucking some chick's brains out right now! I hopeb you're using a confom!!!!!!!!!!

Heather left the party sometime around three in the morning amidst people begging her to stay.

"I can't," she laughed, "I have a flight back to Chicago at nine. As it is, I'm going to be wrecked!"

She gave Ally a hug, promising to see her soon, and told April to call her so they could organize to catch up some time back home in Chicago. Then, Callum appeared, ready to escort her back to her hotel.

"You're like a ninja, the way you appear and disappear out of nowhere," she laughed as they headed toward the exit of the club.

"That's my job, Miss York!" He smiled at her.

She stumbled slightly, walking up the stairs to the exit, and Callum grabbed her arm quickly to steady her.

"You might need to wake me up in the morning." Now that she was moving, she noticed that she was drunker than she'd thought she was. She was very unsteady on her feet and was slurring her words slightly, "Somehow, I don't think I'm going to want to get up in less than three hours' time to make my flight." She cringed at the thought.

"I've got your back." He grinned.

She checked her phone and noticed that neither Harrison or

Sebastian had replied to her messages, so she texted both again, then put her phone away as they made their way outside and through The Gauntlet, with Callum guiding her directly into a waiting limousine. This man was worth his weight in gold, she thought as they headed back to her hotel.

It had been an epic night, but tomorrow's flight back to Chicago would be hell. Oh well, she'd be home, and with Harrison, before she knew it and Gabriel was right, she had no regrets about coming to do Saturday Night Live instead of going to the event with them.

~NOVEMBER~

CRUISE CONTROL CHEATING SCANDAL!

We can NOT believe what we are seeing! We considered, carefully, whether or not we should run this story, but we have verified the authenticity of this picture, and it is legitimate. Harrison Fletcher in bed with an unknown brunette woman that is clearly NOT his fiancée, Heather York!

There have been rumors for some time now that there was trouble in paradise between Harrison and Heather, but we assumed all was well even though they haven't been seen in public together since September.

Cruise Control was at the Cancer Society charity event in Beverly Hills last night, also their first appearance in public together since September. Heather was noticeably absent, due to the fact that she was hosting Saturday Night Live last night.

She was spotted going wild at the after-party, and we thought she was just celebrating the show being a huge success, but maybe that sketch about leaving Harrison at the altar had more basis in truth than we thought? Have they broken up? Who cheated first?

More to come.

Chapter 13

A PICTURE IS WORTH A THOUSAND WORDS

Heather's head was absolutely pounding as Callum knocked on her bedroom door. She felt like she was going to puke, and she couldn't figure out what was going on. He knocked again, and she rolled onto her back, throwing her arm over her eyes as she did so. It was too bright; she hadn't closed the curtains when she collapsed into her bed last night. She was still wearing the outfit she'd worn to the club.

"Come in," she groaned with a croaky voice.

"Sorry for the intrusion, Miss York," Callum said with hesitation, "I had to use my key to get in. I tried calling you, but you didn't answer. It's already six-thirty, and I was fairly certain that you wouldn't have packed your bags last night when we got back to the hotel."

"Ah, fuck. You're right."

Why the hell had she thought this would be a good idea. Harrison was in Los Angeles and wouldn't be getting back to Chicago until early this evening; there was absolutely no need for her to fly home this early. She reminded herself that arriving in Chicago at eleven in the morning meant that Callum could take her home and at least get a portion of the weekend to himself.

It was this thought that caused her to force herself to a sitting position with another groan. She should've stopped drinking about three drinks before she did last night.

"I brought you these." Callum handed her a glass of water and some Aspirin.

"God, you're a fucking lifesaver. Thank you!"

She swallowed the pills and prayed they would kick in quickly as she fought off a wave of nausea that was caused just by getting out of the bed. Callum kindly offered to do her packing for her.

"You don't have to do that!" she protested.

"I think I kind of do." He gave her a wry grin.

"You're going above and beyond the call of duty. I think I love you." She relaxed back on the pillows and drank some more of the water as she directed him to all the places that she'd put her things in the large room.

When she finished the glass, she took an outfit and some underwear into the bathroom, showered quickly while fighting off the urge to puke everywhere, and got dressed, coming out of the bathroom to find Callum putting one her lace thongs into her suitcase along with the rest of her clothing.

Heather felt so sick right now that she could barely muster up the energy to be embarrassed by his handling of her unmentionables. She would have to talk to Harrison about paying him some kind of bonus. This really was well out of the realm of his job description.

Room service arrived about twenty minutes after Callum had, and he told her that he'd taken the liberty of ordering her breakfast, as well. She couldn't be more grateful as she ate the greasy bacon and fried eggs. The painkillers were kicking in now, and her head was pounding slightly less than it had been before. Her stomach was still roiling, but the food was good.

By the time that Callum was doing a final check of the room to make sure that nothing had been left behind, she felt a little closer to human. They made their way downstairs and checked out of the hotel; there were only two reporters here in time to catch her departure.

She told them how happy she was with the Saturday Night Live performance but was glad she had her dark glasses on so their pictures wouldn't show just how awful she looked right now. They got into a limousine that was waiting for them and headed to JFK airport. When they got to O'Hare, they'd take the black SUV to get home.

Heather pulled out her phone and frowned at it; she still didn't have any reply to her texts from last night. It was only four in the morning in Los Angeles, but she would've expected some kind of contact overnight. She sent Harrison a text.

Hi honey. Everything okay? Call me ASAP. I'm worried!

It wasn't like Sebastian to not reply to her, either. So, she sent him a text as well, cringing at the obviously drunken text she'd sent him last night.

Hi, darling. No reply from you or Harrison? That's unusual. Just how fucked up did you get last night?

She tried to push her concerns aside, sure they'd never failed to respond to her texts or calls before, but they were all together, nothing bad could have happened. If anything *really* bad had happened, those reporters surely would've told her about it. They'd love to get her in person reaction to the news of some kind of Cruise Control drama.

All the same, she was worried, "Cal, have you heard anything from Harrison?"

"Sorry, Miss York, no. Why?"

"He hasn't contacted me since last night. That's not normal. I'm sure it's fine, though," she shrugged.

That nagging feeling wouldn't go away; it followed her through another set of reporters that were waiting at JFK. She was fairly certain they just hung out there twenty-four hours a day to catch any celebrities that were coming or going. Once again, Callum was a lifesaver and kept them away. They checked in and made their way to the first-class lounge, killing time there in the quiet luxury until their flight was ready to board.

There was still no word from any of the band, so Heather called Harrison, but it went to voicemail.

"Harrison, I'm getting *really* worried now. I'm about to get on the plane, so I guess I'll call you when I land in Chicago. Please send me a text or something, though. I'm freaking out. I love you."

On a whim, she called Sarah, on the off chance that she'd been in contact with Harrison.

"Hi Sarah, has Harrison called you today?" she asked her as soon as she answered.

"Heather? What? No, Harry hasn't called me. Isn't he in Los Angeles?"

"It's probably nothing; I just haven't heard from him since yesterday." Heather tried to keep the panic out of her voice; there was no sense in Sarah being worried as well.

"No. I haven't heard from Harry, sorry, love."

"Okay, no worries," she lied, since she was definitely very worried, "it's okay. I'm sure he'll call me by the time I land in Chicago. Bye, Sarah."

Harrison's mom said goodbye, and they hung up the call as Heather's plane was called for boarding.

"I'm sure Mister Fletcher is fine," Callum said reassuringly, but Heather thought that even he looked a little nervous.

Heather opened the browser on her phone and searched for 'Harrison Fletcher' filtering for news. Nothing. Just pictures and articles from the charity event last night. Well, that was something of a relief. She tried again for 'Cruise Control', and it was the same. Okay, she still didn't know why the fuck no one was contacting her, but nothing bad had happened. The worst-case scenarios in her head of some horrendous car accident or jail time would definitely have been reported on.

They made use of the priority boarding and took their seats near the front of the plane. Heather checked the screen of her phone one last time before she switched it off—it was still blank. She didn't know if it was her nerves or her hangover, but she had to use the barf bag during the plane's take-off, and Callum was sympathetic.

Heather tried to relax during the flight, but they were some of the toughest hours of her life. She was definitely going to have a word with Harrison about how he could've eased her stress with a simple text. The air hostesses were wonderful; they brought her plenty of water, and she ate a second breakfast of bacon and eggs on the plane.

By the time they landed in Chicago, she was feeling much better, but she still couldn't wait to hear from Harrison. Callum grabbed her overhead luggage for them, and they got off the plane quickly. Heather switched on her phone as they were walking up the air bridge into the airport at O'Hare. She saw the logo light up, just as she heard someone call her name.

Looking up, she saw a group of people waiting at the gate and frowned. Paparazzi. A *lot* of paparazzi. She glanced over at Callum, and she could see that his entire body was on alert. This was unusual, to say the least.

"Do you mind taking this?" he asked her as she nodded and took over wheeling her carry-on instead of him doing it for her.

The paparazzi didn't usually bother coming through security to meet people at the gate. It required a ticket purchase for them to do so. In fact, she didn't recall anything like this since the whole "Ariel" thing after the Grammys. That was the last time the paparazzi had made this kind of effort to get to any of them; they'd followed the band around for weeks like this. Heather felt completely sick as she walked toward them. Her phone finally switched on, but she didn't unlock it, just put it back in her pocket and steeled herself for what was to come.

"Heather! What do you have to say about Harrison cheating on you?"

It was the first question that she managed to discern as she was about ten yards away from them. Heather managed to refrain from rolling her eyes, but only just. She kept her calm and kept walking.

"Heather, have you seen the photo?"

They'd reached them now, and she was so thankful that Callum had no carry-on luggage—his hands were free to push back the paparazzi and clear a path for her. Heather realized that, of course, this wasn't a coincidence. He was very good at what he did.

"What is your comment on Harrison cheating?"

"I have no comment." She kept her tone cool and calm.

Inside, she was seething. She had no idea what had prompted this kind of bullshit, but whatever it was, she wanted to punch them. Of course, there had been dumb rumors like this before, but nothing that had ever caused the paparazzi to come at her like this.

"So, you've seen the photo, then?" another person asked her.

"I have no comment," she replied.

They had made their way through the group, now, and were walking away, but the paparazzi were following them, repeating their questions about Harrison cheating on her.

"Do you want to see the photo, Heather?"

What fucking photo? She wondered but didn't answer. Whatever the hell this was about, it had clearly happened within the last three hours because there was nothing like this in New York. She desperately wanted to pull out her phone and see if Harrison had called her, but she didn't dare.

They made their way to baggage claim, and for the first time in her life, Heather wished she hadn't been in first class. Getting off the plane early was great, but there was always a wait for baggage. The group of reporters crowded around her again, but Callum forced them to keep a distance. They were still asking all the same questions about Harrison cheating and some photo.

She kept her face neutral but dared a glance at Callum. Their eyes met, and she tried to convey how worried she was, without giving anything away. Heather doubted she was successful, it's not like Callum was a mind reader, but he did shout at the group to give her some space, repeating to them that she'd already told them she had no comment to make.

The people around them were looking on with interest, and eventually, the baggage carousel started up. Heather had no idea how they were going to get their luggage; she didn't want Callum to leave her side, and the group was between them and the carousel. She was pondering this when one reporter sneered and turned his phone to her.

"Just tell us what you think of this picture, Heather."

Heather's heart stopped. It was Harrison, her Harrison. Wonderful, sexy Harrison in bed with another woman. The woman was brunette, and it would be clear to anyone looking at this picture that it was not Heather. Harrison was topless, probably naked, given the state of the woman with him. The bedsheets were rumpled and low enough across her body as she lay on him to make it obvious that she was naked too. They were both asleep.

The sickness and worry that Heather had been feeling before hit her again with full force, but she managed to keep her face free from expression. It couldn't be real. It couldn't. But why hadn't she heard from anyone yet? What reason was there for that? It couldn't be true; it could not be that Harrison hadn't called her because he was busy fucking someone else.

Heather managed a casual laugh and looked at the reporter who had shown her the photo, the sheer delight in being the person to show her this was reflected in his face.

"You'll have to come at me with something better than a shitty Photoshop if you want a reaction from me. Excuse me, but I think my luggage might be here."

She shrugged and tossed her hair behind her before striding confidently through the group to get to the baggage carousel.

"It's not Photoshopped!" She heard someone yell from behind her.

"The authenticity of the photo has been verified! What do you say to that, Miss York?" cried the voice of the man who had shown her the picture.

She said nothing, ignoring them and the very interested looks she was getting from the airport goers around her. Her phone was buzzing in her pocket, and she pulled it out to see the name she'd wanted to see all morning on the screen—Harrison Fletcher.

Heather sent his call to voicemail; she couldn't answer right now. Her mind was whirling as she saw her suitcase appear and was grateful that Callum's was only a few suitcases behind it on the carousel. The reporters were still calling out questions, getting more and more disgusting with what they were asking, obviously trying to get a reaction from her.

"Are you okay, Miss York?" Callum asked her quietly.

Heather nodded stiffly. She wasn't okay, though. The picture couldn't be real, but at the same time, she felt like it very well could be. Everything was slotting into place for her, especially Harrison's lack of contact this morning. Was he fucking some other woman while Heather was leaving a voicemail for him about how much she was missing him last night? Who took this picture? Clearly, it had been leaked before Harrison was even awake, and while she was on the plane.

She needed to talk to him. She needed to know his explanation. She needed to be sick. Callum was getting their suitcases, and she wheeled both hers and her carry-on so he would still have a hand free to deal with the paparazzi. It felt like everyone in the airport was watching her now; the other passengers all seemed curious about what was going on. Some were looking at their own phones, then staring up at Heather.

She worked to keep her face completely expressionless as they made their way through the airport to the area where Callum had parked the SUV in short-term parking. It wasn't too far, but it was, quite possibly, the longest walk of Heather's life. She needed to fall apart. She needed to search the internet and look at that photo again. She *really* needed to be sick.

By the time Callum opened the SUV's door to allow her to climb into the sanctity of its interior, she felt like she might break into pieces. He closed the door behind her, and she heard the people continuing to scream questions at her as he opened the trunk and put their luggage inside. He climbed into the driver's seat and turned on the car.

"Here, Miss York. I got this for you in case your hangover was still bothering you, but I think you might need it for another reason now."

He handed her one of the barf bags from the plane, and she took it, grateful for his forethought. He started driving away, and she managed to hold off until the group of paparazzi was well behind them before opening it and depositing her breakfast into it. Her phone was buzzing again, and Harrison's name was on the screen, but she didn't get to it in time before it was diverted to voicemail.

She unlocked her phone, seeing that she had multiple missed calls and text messages. Instead of looking at them, she opened her browser. The search result from earlier was still up and the page refreshed, this time it was full of headlines like "Cruise Control cheating scandal!" and every picture was the one of Harrison and the other woman.

Heather clicked on it and felt like she might puke for the third time today as she recognized who it was—Madeline Turner, Cooper's assistant. It felt like the world was spinning around her as she realized with complete certainty that this picture was real. She'd felt like it was before, but there was simply no way that this could have been Photoshopped this believably.

Harrison had cheated on her last night. She finally gave way to the tears that she'd managed to hold back for the last half hour. Her phone was buzzing again, this time it was Sebastian's name on the screen, but she couldn't answer it. She needed to talk to someone, anyone, to find out what the fuck had happened, but she was sobbing so loudly that there was no point answering right now.

Callum drove in complete silence. Normally, they would chat away as he drove her around, but it was nice that he was respecting her need to lose herself. She worked so hard in life to make sure that people saw this cool, calm, and collected persona from her, but she was human like anyone else. Her phone lit up again, but this time it was Ally's name on the screen, and she didn't give a shit that she was crying as she answered her friend's call.

"Heather? Oh, honey, I'm so sorry. Is it true, then?" The concern was evident in Ally's voice.

"Yes," Heather managed between sobs.

"I've been trying to talk to Hayden, but he hasn't replied to my texts, and I figured you were on the plane. I just saw pics of you at the airport, those assholes."

Heather tried to reply, but couldn't; she just kept sobbing uncontrollably.

"I'm here for you, hun. If you need me, any time, day or night. Just call me," she paused but continued when it became apparent that Heather wasn't going to say anything, "I'm going to let you go now. Stay strong."

Her phone was beeping in her ear that another call was coming through, right as Ally hung up. It was Harrison, calling her again. She answered his call, unsure what he could possibly say to explain what he'd done.

"Angel?" his voice was breaking her heart; it had the same effect on her senses as usual, which killed her.

"Why?" It was all she could get out as she continued to cry.

"I'm sorry, Angel," she could hear that he was devastated, too, "they think we were drugged. I'm at the hospital getting tested."

He had been drugged? What the hell? How? She couldn't stop the tears from flowing, and even through her concern at what he'd just told her, Heather's brain kept throwing up the image of him and Maddy in bed together.

"There's a picture," she managed to get out.

"I know, angel. I'm sorry. I can't even explain how bad I feel. I love you so much."

"You fucked Madeline, though."

Heather didn't hear his reply to that, as she dropped the phone, grabbed the barf bag that she'd carefully set aside before and vomited into it, again. She kept going until her stomach was empty, and even then, she couldn't stop retching into it. After she'd finally finished, she grabbed a tissue and wiped her mouth before putting it in the bag as well. She closed it and put it aside again, then grabbed a bottle of water that Callum helpfully handed to her and took a swig.

Their call was still connected, and Heather picked up the phone and put it to her ear, "Harrison?"

"Are you okay?"

"No, I'm fucking *not* okay. What the fuck kind of question is that?" Her anger at everything that had happened had finally reached boiling point.

"I deserved that. I'm sorry."

"Stop saying you're fucking sorry, Harrison. I get it." She was being mean; she inhaled a deep breath through her nose and let it out through her mouth, "Tell me what happened."

"We were at the dinner, next thing I remember, I woke up in bed…" he trailed off.

"With Maddy." She retched but didn't bother with the vomit bag now—there was nothing left to puke up.

"Yes. We're all at the hospital. Cooper had a seizure, and he's in intensive care. They think it was MDMA."

"Ecstasy?" Heather gasped, "Who else?"

"Everyone at our table. They don't think it was anyone else at the event, just us. They're guessing it was in the wine that we got served."

As far as reasons for cheating went, it was a good one. Her feelings of betrayal mixed with her love and concern for Harrison and her friends.

"Is everyone okay?"

"Aside from Cooper, yes. From what I know, Hayden made it up to his room alone and passed out, Sebastian fucked at least four different women, while Ariana and Gabriel had an epic night together."

"And you fucked Maddy," she couldn't stop herself from adding in.

"I'm sor—" he started to say, then cut himself off, "The rest of Cooper's team, I'm not sure about. I haven't really spoken to them."

"Just Maddy," she added again, knowing she was being a bitch.

There was silence on the other end of the line; Heather's heart felt like it was shattering into a million tiny pieces. She didn't know if she could forgive him for this. She didn't know that she *couldn't* forgive him for this, though. If he'd been drugged, then he was as much a victim in the whole thing as anyone, but it didn't change the fact that he'd slept with someone else. Someone she knew. He'd been fucking Maddy while Heather was wishing she was with him. It made her feel sick to think about, but she couldn't turn off the movie reel of them together that was playing in her head.

"I love you, Harrison," she said eventually, "when will you be home? We'll need to talk."

"I'm not sure," he replied carefully, "I'll call you and let you know."

"Can you text instead?" she asked him, "I think it's probably better if we stick to those until you get home."

"Sure, angel." He sounded broken.

She hung up the call without saying anything else and gave way to further sobs. Her phone lit up again, this time with Sebastian's name, but she sent him to voicemail. She couldn't summon the energy for another phone call. Instead, she sent him a text.

Hey Seb. Can't talk. Feeling like fucking shit. Harrison cheated on me. I can't even.

His reply was almost instantaneous.

We were drugged. We're all in shock. Harrison is a mess.

Heather went back to her browser and saved the picture, then sent it through to Sebastian.

Yes, he looks it. Are you feeling okay, though?

It wasn't fair to send the picture; she knew Sebastian had probably already seen it, but she couldn't get it out of her head. How lovely, she thought, to have this permanent reminder of the time her fiancé fucked another woman.

Ouch. I'm sorry, Heather. If I'd been sober, I could've stopped him.

It's not your fault. Fuck, it's probably not even his fault. FML.

They were finally pulling in to the garage underneath her apartment building, and Heather couldn't be more relieved. She put her phone in her pocket, and Callum helped her take her luggage upstairs. Once they'd gotten up there, he hovered near the doorway, looking uneasy.

"Will you be okay, Miss York?" he asked her, the concern evident on his face.

"Probably not," she gave a hollow laugh, "but you can go, anyway."

"I'm sorry, but I can't leave if I'm not certain of your safety," he grimaced.

Fuck, he thought she might actually hurt herself, today, "I'm not suicidal, Cal. I'm not okay, but I'm not going to kill myself because my fucking fiancé stuck his dick in another woman."

"Talking that way isn't helping," he frowned at her, "there are plenty of ways to be unsafe that don't go that far."

"I don't need a nanny, just a bodyguard. Go. Home." She glared at him.

"I'm sorry, Miss York. I will give you your space, but I can't leave when you're like this. I wouldn't be doing my job." He shrugged casually.

"Then you're fucking fired. Leave." She was angry; she wanted space to fall apart in private.

"You didn't hire me, Heather. I'm sorry, but I can't leave unless my employer tells me to."

On some level, she was grateful for this. She liked Callum, and she recognized that she was lashing out right now. She didn't really want him fired, just gone from the apartment for now. She pulled out her phone and texted Harrison.

Tell Cal to go home. Now.

Her phone rang, and it was Harrison's name on the screen. She didn't want to talk to him. It was clear from her interaction with Callum that she couldn't trust what came out of her mouth at the moment, so she rejected the call.

I said to fucking text. Tell him to leave me the fuck alone.

It didn't take long for Callum's phone to start ringing, and he picked it up and answered it.

"I understand," he said, then paused before replying, "I don't feel comfortable doing that."

There was another pause as Harrison obviously said something to him, or asked a question.

"I am concerned about what Miss York may do if she's left on her own. I don't intend on intruding in her space, but unless someone else is here, I wouldn't feel right leaving. Unless you're planning on firing me, I'll stay here. If you'd like to organize for a friend or family member to take my place here, that's fine as well."

Another pause, before Callum replied again to Harrison, "Understood, sir. I'll see you when you get here."

Heather glared at him, seething at the fact that he'd convinced Harrison that she needed a babysitter. At the same time, she understood that from a professional standpoint, he was doing the right thing. Why did they have to hire the best of the best? They should've gotten some shitty sub-par bodyguard who toddled off and left her alone.

"I'm sorry, Miss York." He shrugged, then went and sat on a chair near the hallway, an obvious attempt to give her some semblance of privacy.

"I'm fucking sick to death of hearing people tell me they're god damn sorry!" she yelled at him.

Heather headed to the kitchen, grabbed a tub of ice cream out of the freezer and a spoon from a drawer, then sat down at the kitchen table.

"Alexa, play songs about cheating on Spotify," Heather called out to the room.

"Playing songs about cheating on Spotify," Alexa answered back.

"Sorry" by Beyoncé started playing throughout the apartment from speakers that were wired into each room as Heather opened the tub of salted caramel Haagen-Dazs and began to eat it.

Chapter 14

CONTRA CONSILIUM MEDICINAE

It was a long and awful day. Heather had never given a second thought to the shitty news stories that had ever been printed about her, Harrison, or the band. Not even during the 'Ariel' saga, which had definitely been the most intense news cycle for them. Perhaps she'd just had the luxury of it not being about her. More importantly, the luxury of it not being true the times that it was.

She was deep down the rabbit hole now, though. She'd read nearly every news article about Harrison cheating, even though they were all pretty much a variation of the same theme. He'd cheated, but did he do it because she was having an affair with Sebastian? Who was the other woman? Was the wedding off?

The last question was the one that made her feel the worst because she didn't have an answer to that one. She wouldn't know herself until she saw and spoke to Harrison. He'd texted her to say that he would be back about six o'clock tonight, and she felt nervous and sick whenever she thought about the conversation that she needed to have with him.

Then there were the comments. It seemed as though everyone in the world had an opinion on her relationship with Harrison, and they all thought the internet was the best place to express it. Sometimes she would see a particularly nasty one about her, how she had almost certainly cheated on Harrison first, and Heather would go to the person's profile and see what she could find out about them. Then she'd make her own personal assessment of *their* lives in her head.

Heather was aware that what she was doing wasn't healthy, it was probably the kind of self-destructive behavior that Callum had been worried that she would indulge in, but he was leaving her to it. It was certainly the kind of thing she had told Ariana not to do when they'd been on tour together, and Ariana had seen stories about herself online.

She was reminded of the letter that she still hadn't read, how she'd decided to wait until she returned to Chicago to read it because she was supposed to be happy now. Fuck. Wasn't that a nice thought that she'd had. If only it had turned out that way. She could've been here, high on the success of Saturday Night Live and repairing her friendship with Ariana instead of waiting for her cheating scumbag fiancé to return home.

That wasn't fair, though. He wasn't a scumbag. They'd received the results of the drug test from the hospital. Harrison hadn't texted her; it had been Gabriel who had let her know that the doctors' suspicions were correct, and they all had MDMA in their system. Cooper had come out of ICU and been moved to the Special Care Unit. The police had met them at the hospital, taken all of their statements, and an investigation was underway.

Heather wished that knowledge could change something within her. It didn't, though. She hated more than anything that she couldn't simply be worried about Harrison, that she couldn't just support him through what was almost certainly a traumatic event in his life. She couldn't do that because, while he was under the influence, he had fucked someone else.

In their entire ten-year relationship, she had never once

doubted his love for her. She had sent him off on the *Heart Wide Open* tour alone and with zero doubt in her mind that he would remain faithful to her. Their love had seen her through some of the toughest times in her life; when her dad had died of cancer, he had been there to see her through. Was their love strong enough to survive this? Or was it tainted by what he'd done?

They'd both had relationships before getting together and been sexually active but had never actually gone the whole way and slept with anyone else. The thought of him having sex with Madeline made her feel physically ill, even now. Knowing that he got pleasure from someone else's body last night when all she'd wanted was to be with him.

Hayden had managed to make it back to his room safely. Why couldn't Harrison have done the same? Fuck, given their relationship status, Ally might not even have had too much of an issue with that if it had been the other way around. Heather gave way to tears for what felt like the thousandth time today. She was exhausted, and Harrison wouldn't be back for hours, so she headed to their bedroom to rest. She opened the door, saw the bed, and felt sick. Instead of going inside, she turned and made her way to one of their spare rooms and collapsed on the bed there, before falling asleep.

She woke hours later as Harrison called her name from the open doorway where light was streaming into the room. It was dark outside, and, glancing at the clock, she saw that it was nearly six-thirty in the evening.

Just seeing him was enough to send her into a fresh round of tears immediately. Everything in her ached to go to him and find the place she called home, but she was hurting too much to do it. He was heartbreakingly beautiful, standing there with the light behind him. He was wearing jeans and a T-shirt, his hair was a mess, as though he had spent many hours running his hands through it, which was something he usually did when he was stressed. He came over to the bed, leaving the door open to continue to let the light into the room and sat down next to her, but didn't touch her.

"I know you don't want to hear it," his voice was strained, "but I have to say it. I'm sorry, angel. If I could take it back, I would."

Heather sat up, wiping the tears from her face and taking shaky breaths of air.

"I know, Harrison. I know."

She wanted to ask him how he was feeling. She wanted to know that he was okay after being drugged. She loved him more than anything, but her brain wouldn't stop throwing the image of him in bed with Maddy at her.

"The picture…" she trailed off, unable to say more.

"I wish there wasn't a picture," he said, an angry tone to his voice.

"Why? So you could've kept it a secret?" She glared at him.

"No, angel," he sighed, "I would've told you. I just wish that you didn't have that image in your head. I wish that *I* could have told you, not some piece of shit who ambushed you at the airport the second you got off a plane."

Heather wondered, for a second, if she would have found what he'd done any less devastating if she'd had the chance to hear it directly from him first, instead of finding out by some sleazy asshole showing her the picture. She didn't think it would've made it any better, though she did agree that not having that image in her head would have been nice.

They sat there in silence for a long time, he seemed to be waiting for her to say something, but she didn't know where to start. She couldn't find the words to start the conversation that they needed to have. Instead, she decided to go with facts, beginning with the cause of all of this.

"Gabriel told me that the hospital confirmed that it was definitely MDMA," Heather couldn't look him in the eyes, choosing to fiddle with her engagement ring instead, spinning it around her finger repeatedly.

"Yeah, it was. The police came; they're looking into it. Look at me, angel."

Even though she knew that her heart couldn't possibly take any more of a beating today, she couldn't resist looking at him now. It felt as though there was a massive chasm between them, and that feeling broke her apart.

"Where do we stand, Heather? Is this…does what happened mean the end of us?" He looked as completely and utterly wretched as she felt about this idea, but she knew that she had to answer him honestly.

"I don't know, Harrison. I can't answer. I need time."

"You can take as much time as you need, angel. The fact that it's not an immediate 'yes,' is something." He gave her a wan smile.

Heather sighed, "I can't promise that it isn't a 'yes,' though, Harrison. All I can say is that I need time. That I understand that you were drugged, that you're a victim in this as well. I know that on any given day of the week, you would never cheat on me. Knowing all of that doesn't change the fact that you *did* cheat on me, though. It doesn't change the fact that every time I close my eyes, I see you fucking her. It doesn't change the fact that I feel physically ill whenever that happens."

Harrison looked completely miserable as she told him this, she felt the urge to touch him, and this time, she gave in. She moved over to him and put her arms around his waist, and he pulled her into a hug. It felt like it always did, as though she was coming home.

For a second, she thought that she could get past all of this until her brain helpfully supplied an image of Harrison and Maddy in the exact same position in the hotel room from last night, and she couldn't stop herself from tensing up entirely. Harrison must have noticed, as he dropped his arms from around her, and she followed suit, then moved back away from him again.

"I'm assuming that you didn't want to sleep in our bedroom, then?" He was the one who wouldn't look at her now.

"I think that for the time being, I'd prefer being in here."

Harrison looked defeated as he rose from where he'd been sitting on the bed, "Okay, angel. I still love you."

"I know. I still love you, too, Harrison. I don't know if I can get past this, but please know that I intend on trying."

He caught her gaze, then. She could see the guilt, fear, and longing written across his face. Heather hated that she felt completely and utterly hollow. Something inside of her had broken today, and everything that was important to her had seeped out. There was nothing left.

She slept fitfully that night; her dreams were nothing but a constant movie of Harrison fucking Maddy in a hotel room. In them, he wasn't drugged, though. He was enjoying it; he was telling Madeline that she was better in bed than Heather was, and the other woman was relishing in it.

Heather woke feeling horrendous, the nauseated feeling was back, and she had no idea how she was supposed to carry on with her life. It was Monday, and she was supposed to go to work today; the ladies had probably organized some kind of celebration for her performance on Saturday Night Live. Louise was an excellent baker and rarely needed much of an excuse to bring some of her delicious treats in.

She couldn't face leaving the apartment today, though. Heather got her phone and sent a message to the group chat she had with the ladies, telling them that she wasn't feeling well and wouldn't be in today. She didn't know if they would go into work. She didn't care if they did. She couldn't bring herself to care about anything right now. The hollow feeling was still there.

Heather made her way into the kitchen and put some bread in the toaster, deciding that toast was the safest breakfast for her uneasy stomach and knowing that she'd eaten and subsequently kept down so little yesterday that she needed to get some kind of food into her system today. While she waited for the bread to toast, she set about getting herself a glass of orange juice to go with it.

As she moved around the kitchen, Harrison appeared from the direction of their bedroom. He was only wearing a pair of old sweatpants that were riding low on his hips. His muscular chest was bare, and he looked incredibly masculine and sexy. Despite herself, Heather felt an ache between her thighs, she wanted desperately to take him back into their bedroom and ride him, but she was also feeling too raw. The knowledge that barely twenty-four hours ago, Madeline was riding him like that, was too cutting for her to follow through with her desire.

"Morning, angel." He gave her a tight smile.

"Good morning, Harrison." She was grateful for the distraction of her toast popping up, so she could turn away from him to deal with it.

"Are you doing that on purpose to hurt me?" he asked her softly.

"What? Eating toast?" She glanced over her shoulder at him, and he looked incredulous at her response.

"No, angel. Calling me 'Harrison' all the time."

She hadn't even realized that she'd been doing it, "It's not intentional. I'm sorry."

"I think that might make it worse," he sighed deeply and sat down at the kitchen bench as she turned with her plate of toast, took it, and her glass of juice with her to sit next to him.

"I don't know what to say, Harrison"—he flinched—"I guess it doesn't feel right calling you 'honey' at the moment. My 'honey' is someone who would never do what you did, drugged or not. I'm coming to terms with what happened and as shitty as it all is, my faith in you, which was previously completely and utterly unshakeable, has been shaken."

He dropped his head to his hands as she took a bite of her toast. Harrison looked so broken; she wished she could go back to two days ago. Heather wished she'd never gone to New York; if she'd been with him, this wouldn't have happened. They would've been together instead of him fucking someone else because she wasn't there.

"Did you wear a condom, Harrison?" Heather sighed, as she asked the question she needed to ask.

"I'm not sure," he said, then looked away from her. "I don't really remember anything."

There was a heavy silence between them. Heather felt as though he must remember more than he was telling her, but didn't want to push him on this, right now. What happened was awful, and she knew it wasn't his fault, but for the first time in their relationship, she felt as though he wasn't being completely honest with her.

"How are you feeling?" she asked him, then clarified, "I mean, physically. What did the doctors say?"

"I feel like shit. The doctors wanted me to stay in the hospital like everyone else," he confessed, "because they didn't know what dosage we'd been given or how pure the drug was. They wanted us all to stay for monitoring for at least a day. I need to call the others and find out how they're doing, actually."

Heather was confused by what he was telling her, "Wait, if they wanted you to stay, how are you here?"

The look that he gave her was full of pity and love, "You can't guess, angel?"

She shook her head at him; if they'd wanted him to stay so that he could be monitored, she didn't understand how he had convinced them to let him fly back to Chicago.

"I discharged myself against medical advice. Had to sign the world's longest waiver, they tried very hard to convince me to stay, I'm pretty sure they didn't want the death of a member of Cruise Control on their hands," he smiled ruefully at her, "but I needed to come home to you. Callum was worried about you, which worried me."

"Harrison Fletcher!" She glared at him, "How fucking dare you do that? Sleeping with someone else while drugged is bad enough, but how the fuck do you think I would've survived if you'd died from some kind of fucking complication mid-flight?"

Despite the fact that she was cursing at him, he looked pleased with her response and smiled at her, "Ah, angel. You do care."

Heather felt a surge of fury flow through her; she wanted to smash something. She inhaled deeply and blew out the breath of air slowly, trying to get a hold of her anger as she narrowed her eyes at him.

"Don't you fucking dare do anything like that again, Harrison. Put your health at risk again, even if it's to come and see me, and we're definitely through."

"Noted. I promise not to put my health at risk, again, angel. S—" he managed to cut off the word before it slipped out, "—o, what are you doing today?"

Even Heather managed a smile at his pivot away from the word 'sorry,' to the word 'so,' instead.

"Nice catch. I'm not going to work today," she found as she said it, that she didn't want to stay here in the apartment all day with Harrison either, "I thought I might go see my mom."

She'd said it as an excuse, but as she did so, she realized how much she needed to see her mother. Her mom had tried calling her yesterday, one of many calls that Heather hadn't answered, but it would be good to see her.

"Oh, lovely; tell her I said hello." Heather raised an eyebrow at him, and he grimaced, "Actually, probably not a good idea, I guess. I'll call Cal and tell him your plans; I wasn't sure what you were doing today, so I told him to wait until he heard from us."

"Thanks, I appreciate that."

Heather finished the last of her toast, stood up, and rinsed her plate and glass before putting them in the dishwasher; she hesitated next to Harrison on her way out of the room, then kissed him on the cheek.

"I do still love you, Harrison, and I'm glad you didn't die on the flight back here. Please see a doctor today and get checked up."

"Also noted," he smiled at her, "and I will."

Heather left him sitting there and realized that she would need to go into their bedroom to get fresh clothes. She was stung by a pang of hurt as she made her way into their room, the last time she'd been in here was right before she'd left for New York. She'd been on the phone to Harrison, and they'd had phone sex after he'd insisted that an orgasm was the perfect way for her to calm her nerves about performing on live TV.

She grabbed some clothes, and took them with her to the spare room, not wanting to use their bathroom to get ready. Heather showered in the guest room's bathroom instead. Once she was dressed, she called her mom.

"Heather, are you okay?" Her mom seemed worried.

"Yeah, I am. Can I come and see you today?"

"Of course, sweetheart. What time were you thinking?"

"As soon as possible," Heather breathed a sigh of relief; she didn't know where she would've gone if her mom hadn't been free.

"Okay, I'll see you then."

Heather pulled out her phone while she waited for Callum to arrive. Her screen was full of social media notifications; every platform was blowing up, of course. She didn't want to wallow anymore, though. The internet could keep its god damn opinions to itself, as far as she was concerned.

She opened up a text to Sebastian.

Hey, lover. MDMA all out of your system? Docs letting

you come home to me anytime soon?

It felt forced, even to her. The ignorance of the strained and weird situation they were in right now. She just wanted some tiny semblance of normality.

Yeah, they're letting us go sometime today. I'll be home soon.

I'm glad you're okay. I miss you.

She really was; a wave of anger rushed over her toward whatever asshole had done this to her family.

Me, too. Are you okay, lover? I've been worried about you.

Heather wondered how much Harrison had told him about how tense it was between them right now. It was nice that Sebastian was concerned for her, though.

You know me. I'll survive. Always have, always will.

Never anything like this, though. I hope you know I'm here if you need to talk. I do love you.

Heather smiled and sent back a text, thanking him. Despite his flaws, which were many and varied, Sebastian Fox really was one of her favorite people in the world, and she counted herself as blessed to be one of the few people who were granted his love.

She sighed as she heard Callum's voice coming from the living area. It was time to go, and she had a hell of an apology to give him for her behavior yesterday.

~DECEMBER~

HARRISON AND HEATHER ARE OVER!

Rumors abound that Harrison Fletcher and Heather York have officially called off their May wedding. Harrison was caught in bed with a woman named Madeline Turner last month, and he hasn't been seen in public with Heather since.

A close friend of the band tells us that they have broken up and canceled the wedding, but they have yet to make an official announcement. Heather was rumored to be having an affair with Cruise Control's lead guitarist and international playboy, Sebastian Fox, which many people think was what caused Harrison to cheat.

We've caught wind that the band has already recorded a new album that is due for release in March, but if Sebastian and Heather are together now, how will this affect the release of the new album? Can Harrison work with Sebastian now that he's stolen his girl?

Chapter 15

A THOUSAND WORDS

Heather sat on the sofa at their therapist's office, with Harrison beside her. It was Saturday; they'd both agreed to do relationship counseling and spent the start of their weekends in Brendan's office. The last month had been rough; they were essentially living separate lives now, having strained conversations when they crossed paths in the common areas of their apartment.

She did want to mend their relationship, which was why she'd agreed to do counseling with him, but she didn't know how they could ever come back from this. Heather sat in silence and played with the engagement ring on her finger, as Harrison was discussing with Brendan, once again, what had happened when he cheated.

"So, you were drugged when it happened. Do you feel like it would have happened if you weren't drugged?" Brendan asked him.

"No."

"You mean, of course, that he was drugged when he fucked someone that wasn't me, maybe without a condom. Who would know? Because, apparently, he doesn't fucking remember anything even though everyone else does." Heather raised an eyebrow, and Harrison looked upset.

"That's quite an aggressive way of phrasing it," Brendan looked at her over the top of his glasses, "why do you choose to say it that way?"

Ugh. Fucking psychobabble. She was actually a big proponent of therapy, but she was still feeling so incredibly raw, and she found these sessions very frustrating. It was practically the only time she talked to Harrison these days, and they just ran through him cheating over and over again.

"Because it's what happened." She shrugged.

"Yes, but did you see Harrison's reaction to what you said?"

Heather glanced over at Harrison and saw him watching her. "Well, yeah. I did," she confessed.

"How did it make you feel when Heather phrased it that way, Harrison?" Brendan asked him.

"Hurt. It feels like Heather is purposely saying things to hurt me a lot, lately," the sadness was evident on his face.

"Hang on, so Harrison fucks Madeline, and I'm trying to hurt him by pointing that out?" Heather frowned.

"Are you trying to hurt him, Heather?" Brendan tilted his head to the side as he asked this question.

She actually stopped and thought about it, then blew out a deep breath before admitting, "Yes."

"Why is that?"

Heather hated the tears that were coming to her eyes now; she wanted to be strong, damn it, "Because he hurt me. I want him to hurt, too."

Brendan handed her a box of tissues as she broke down into tears. The unfairness of their situation really struck her. It wasn't Harrison's fault he'd cheated, not really. By the same token, it also wasn't her fault that she was struggling to get past it.

"What do you think that you might achieve by hurting Harrison?" Brendan sat back in his chair and crossed one leg over the other as he did so.

"I don't know," she paused for a moment and tried to figure it out but couldn't come up with an answer, "I really don't."

"Hmmm. Harrison, what do you think?"

"I think that Heather is scared to forgive me. She'd rather drive me away," she frowned at him, as he said it, "it's like she's trying her hardest to get me to leave."

"Interesting. Is splitting up something that you think might happen?"

"I don't want it," Harrison told him, "but Heather will barely speak to me, so I have no clue what she wants."

"What I want is for you to go back in time and not sleep with Madeline. Can you fucking do that for me, Harrison?" she crossed her arms over her chest, knowing that she was probably doing exactly what he said she was doing.

The idea of forgiving him was terrifying; it meant trusting that he wouldn't do this again. She knew the chances of him being drugged again were minuscule, the security around the band was tighter than ever, and everyone had their own personal bodyguard now. She probably could forgive him if it weren't for the fact that she still could not get rid of that image in her head of Harrison having sex with Maddy.

She'd looked at the pictures in the series of their night together more times than was healthy. There were pictures of them sitting next to each other at the charity dinner, obviously flirting. Another one was of them kissing in the hotel lobby. Shots of them leaving the hotel together the next morning with Gabriel and Ariana, all of them looking the worse for wear. One of the pictures she'd come across was a wider one of the hotel room; it showed Maddy's bra and thong lying on the floor in a pile on top of Harrison's own clothes. It really helped to get a true mental image of exactly how he had cheated on her. Clearly, Harrison stripped first, then had Maddy get naked afterward.

Did Maddy give him head before she fucked him? Did he grab

her hair and look at her the way he did to Heather? It didn't matter if he had or not because Heather could still see it happening, anyway—Maddy on her knees in that pink, lacy underwear set with Harrison's cock in her mouth.

Heather's nights were filled with dreams of the two of them together. She'd barely slept all month, spending her days at Serenity, designing new clothes, and taking business meetings to try and keep her mind occupied. Pretending to the world that everything was fucking dandy.

The paparazzi were camped out the front of their building day and night. They'd already figured out Maddy's identity, and she was suffering an inferno of criticism online. Cooper had been going to fire her for sleeping with a client until Heather called him and told him not to. She'd said that she didn't want Maddy working with her or Harrison anymore, but at the end of the day, she was drugged as well. It wasn't Maddy's fault, either, and Heather didn't want her to lose her job for it.

It was the only kind action that she could bring herself to take, knowing that it was the right thing to do. Maddy had given her resignation to Cooper, anyway, but at least Heather knew that she hadn't been fired on their behalf.

The remainder of their hour dragged on; Heather did her best to keep her bitchy remarks to a minimum, but really felt, once again, like she'd wasted everyone's time by attempting this when she clearly wasn't ready to forgive Harrison and may never be ready.

"I'll see you next week," Brendan told them as they all stood from their seats when the session was over.

"Can't wait. Stoked. It'll be great!" Heather muttered under her breath as she made her way to the door.

Harrison glared at her, but Brendan didn't comment. No doubt, he would make approximately a thousand notes about her shitty attitude as soon as they'd left the room. She followed

Harrison out into the waiting area. Callum and Michael Pearce both joined them, as soon as they exited Brendan's office. Michael was Harrison's new bodyguard. She stood next to them as Harrison paid for their session, then the two men followed behind as she and Harrison walked in tense silence to the elevators that headed down to an underground garage.

Brendan's office was in a building full of many disciplines of private practice; it was part of why they'd chosen him. They could come and go in relative peace, hopefully without the media figuring out they were doing counseling.

"Are you going back to the apartment?" Harrison asked her as the elevator doors opened.

"Yes. You?"

"I might go to Hayden's or something." He shrugged.

"Cool. Have fun."

She walked away without another word; it felt odd to be almost strangers with Harrison. This was the man she loved more than anyone else in the world, but it was as though there was a massive chasm between them all of a sudden. She was on one side; he was on the other, and there was no bridge for either of them to cross.

Callum opened the door of her SUV at roughly the same time that Michael opened the door for Harrison's. She glanced over at him and thought she might physically break into pieces. It all felt so fucking wrong. Being apart from him, not getting into the same car, not going to the same place. For roughly the millionth time since that day, she wished that she had gone to that stupid charity event instead of to New York for Saturday Night Live. She would take being drugged and not doing SNL over this awful nightmare that she was living, any day.

Heather got in the car and pulled out her phone as Callum started driving them home. She had a text from Gabriel.

Hi, H. I know this is a shitty thing to ask, but did you read Ari's letter? I know you're going through a rough time,

and I think she could be a good friend for you right now.

What the fuck? She'd practically forgotten the letter existed. Was this really the same man that begged her to wait until the right time to read it? What kind of dumbass was he, that he would think that *now* was the right time?

Are you fucking for real, dude? Fuck off.

Oh, she really was in fine form today—F-bombs galore for all of the people she loved the most.

Please read it. Trust me. I know you're hurting, and I wouldn't ask you to read it if I didn't think it would be good for you.

Heather thought about it for a second; her life was in ruins right now, there was nothing Ariana could say to make it worse. She'd practically forgiven her already anyway, especially after she found out about that horrible experience Ariana had with the reporter. Truthfully, at this point, everything that was outside of her relationship with Harrison felt unimportant, anyway. She might as well read the damn letter and see what Ariana had said.

Fine. I'll read it when I get home. Gabriel knows best.

Yes, he does. Thanks, H.

She was walking into her apartment and was about to head to hers and Harrison's bedroom when her phone pinged with another text. To Heather's surprise, it was from Ariana.

DO NOT READ THE LETTER!

Well, now, that was interesting. She quickly replied.

Why not?

Now is NOT the time. Trust me.

Ariana replied almost immediately, and for the first time all week, a smile came to Heather's face. Why the hell would Ariana give her a letter to read and suddenly not want her to read it? It made her laugh because this whole thing was crazy.

Okay, now I'm definitely reading it. No time like the present, darling!

Damn. She'd shown her hand by slipping into the usage of that nickname without thinking. Her phone started buzzing, and Ariana's name was on the screen now. Oh, hell, no. She was reading this damn letter right now. She dropped her phone on the kitchen bench and continued to the bedroom.

Heather rushed to her bedside table, pulled out the envelope that was still sitting there, and opened it. The letter was written by hand, on thick, cream paper, and in purple ink that had a silver sheen to it.

Dear Heather,

I barely even know where to start. There are no words that will ever be enough to make up for what I did to you. Please read this letter in full. If you read it all and still want nothing to do with me, then I'll completely understand.

Heather smiled; already, she could tell that Ariana had put a great deal of effort into writing this letter. Her previous concerns about not meaning anything to her seemed unfounded.

It goes without saying that I had no right to leave without saying goodbye. I can't tell you how much I regret that. How many times I beat myself up for the fact that the last words I said to you were that I would come and see you, but I didn't follow through with that.

In the early days, Heather had well and truly dwelled on that fact. It was a sticking point for a long time that Ariana had lied to her on that phone call, saying that she would come to see her when she really went to pack her things to leave them all.

Obviously, I know now that leaving was probably not the right thing to do. Even though Gabriel and I are happier together now than we ever were before, I still feel so much guilt over the time we lost. He's forgiven me, though, so I need to try and forgive myself as well.

I never really explained to you why I was so scared of the life we lead. My uncle is Darius Thompson.

Her uncle was *Darius Thompson*?! Surely not *the* Darius Thompson. Mega A-list movie star? Heather suddenly remembered Gabriel and Ariana chatting to Darius and his wife at Harrison's birthday party. It made *so* much sense, but what the hell, how did she not know this?

Yes, THE Darius Thompson, I know you just said that out loud. Everyone does.

Heather laughed at the fact that Ariana could so accurately predict her reaction. She supposed that it was similar to the reaction people would give her about Harrison if there was actually anybody in the world that didn't know she was with him.

I've spent a lot of my life watching the terrible, awful things that the paparazzi did to my family.

Ah, fuck. Darius Thompson. Cheating scumbag of the highest order.

Don't get me wrong. My uncle played his part in all of that. If he had never cheated on my aunt, then maybe all of the bullshit they go through wouldn't have happened.

Okay, yup. This is probably why Ariana thought it was a bad idea for her to read it. Just what she needed right now, to read about men being cheating cheaters who cheat.

It's likely it still would have, though, in some form or another. The things they put us through are no different; hell, those dumbasses have even printed bullshit rumors about Harrison cheating on you before.

Ouch.

They don't care that it's not true. They don't care that we're human beings with feelings. They just care about eyeballs on their papers or their magazines or their websites.

Double ouch. Nope, *that* was why Ariana thought she shouldn't read it. She'd written it at a time when Harrison cheating on her was something that everyone thought could never, ever be an actual thing that would happen.

My aunt and uncle have been happy together for years, but the stories just keep coming, and every time they print a new one, it's painful for my aunt.

Great. She'd been subjected to these types of stories in the past, as well. So that's what she had to look forward to if she did work things out with Harrison, she guessed. Frequent, painful reminders of him fucking Maddy. Lucky for her, she'd get to revisit the picture every time as well, no doubt.

My cousins are awesome, but they got teased all the time at school about it. Can you imagine constantly seeing stories about your dad cheating on your mom?

And, yes, if she and Harrison got married and had children, they too could see a picture of their father in bed with another woman. Delightful!

For me, I grew up seeing all of this. By the time I met Gabriel, I already hated fame and celebrity.

Right now, Heather kind of hated fame and celebrity, too. She hadn't felt like Ariana had actually hated fame when she'd known her, though. More feared it. It made a bit more sense now she knew why that was, of course.

Sebastian practically groping me the first time I met him probably didn't help,

Ugh. Heather had heard that story. Sebastian and Gabriel were both drunk as fuck, and Sebastian had actually tried to hit on Ariana, with zero success, of course.

but Gabriel was different. I loved him from that first night, Heather. I loved him, and it scared the fucking shit out of me.

He is the single, most amazing human being on the face of the planet, and I desperately wanted to not love him.

Given what Ariana was telling her, Heather started to understand. From the first day she'd met Ariana, it had been obvious that she was in love with Gabriel. Heather had been shocked when she saw them together; she'd never seen Gabriel so happy before. He'd had other girlfriends, but there was something about his relationship with Ariana that just made him seem so…whole.

Our world is one that I never wanted to be a part of, but Gabriel came to me packaged with fame, and I wasn't ready to deal with it back then.

'Our world,' it pleased Heather to see Ariana write it like that. It was obvious that she had finally come to truly be a part of their world. Previously, she'd hidden in the shadows, but now she was in the light with the rest of them, bearing the brunt of the intensity that light brought to your life.

It's hard to explain the way I used to think. Deep down, I just felt worthless. I couldn't accept that Gabriel could love me and that I could ever be enough for him.

Poor Ariana. Heather had sensed this about her at the time, from the way she spoke about herself. The panic attacks that she had when the media were nearby, it was all starting to make a lot more sense now.

In my experience, men (particularly famous men) cheated on their partners as soon as the opportunity arose.

Ouch. Hello, Harrison Fletcher.

The more that Gabriel tried to show me that he loved me and was in it for the long haul, the more that my brain looked for signs that it was all just a show. I was so fucking insecure that I literally blew up our relationship to prevent, you know, our relationship from blowing up.

Heather laughed out loud at this; Ariana's phrasing was amusing. She could practically hear her saying it.

It was dumb. Stupid. Most idiotic thing I've ever done or will hopefully ever do!

Yeah, it had been pretty fucking dumb, that's for sure. She couldn't wait to rip on Ariana for that. If it weren't for the fact that she was really getting into this letter and finding out all the things that Ariana had written to her, she'd call her right now to agree with her about how dumb it had been.

Your friendship during that time was so invaluable to me,

though, Heather. I know that you tried to talk sense into me repeatedly, and for that, I'm grateful.

It was nice to feel appreciated. At the time, Heather had often felt like she was talking to a brick wall, so it was good to know that at least some of what she'd said at the time had sunk in. Of course, given Ariana's family history, Heather had actually had no clue what she was talking about.

I've missed you. So fucking much.

This brought a smile to Heather's face, and she actually wiped a tear away from her eye. She'd missed Ariana, too, if she was being honest with herself.

You were my best friend, but when I left, I just thought that cutting everyone off completely would be the easiest thing for everyone. I worried that I would come back if I spoke to anyone, and at the time, to me, that would've been terrible.

Man, she really was fucked in the head when she left. Heather would definitely have to talk to her further about this, to try and understand just how she had come to the conclusion that leaving the way she did was the right way to go.

I had completely and utterly convinced myself that I was ruining Gabriel's life, and I didn't want that for him. Again, it was dumb, and I know now that, of course, it wasn't true.

None of them would ever have thought that about Ariana. All of them had loved her deeply and could see just how good she was for him. The flip side of that, of course, had been the way he'd reacted when she left.

I want to reassure you that I will never do anything like that again.

Good.

There is nothing that could be worse than not having Gabe in my life again. Those were the worst two years of my life.

A tiny part of Heather was glad to hear that Ariana had suffered in their absence. They'd all gone through hell, so it wouldn't have been fair if Ariana hadn't at least been in purgatory.

Not just not having him, but all of you as well. You accepted me, you welcomed me into your lives, and I didn't treat that gift with the care it deserved, for that, I am truly sorry.

Heather stood up, went to the bathroom, and grabbed a box of tissues before coming back to pick the letter up again. She got a tissue and wiped the tears from her eyes. Ariana had always had a way with words, but this description to sum up how she'd hurt them was such an apt one that it stung.

If you can ever forgive me for what I did, I would love to be friends again.

Of course, she wanted to be friends again. Gabriel was right. She needed a fucking friend right now, and reading this letter *was* good for her.

I had been hoping that we could catch up out here at Galena, I would much rather tell you all of this in person.

Heather had been wondering when she'd written it. Obviously sometime in October, then.

Unfortunately, with work, I can only be here during the week, and Harrison said you're busy with Serenity and can only come out on weekends. It sucks; I really want to see you, even if you think I'm Yoko Ono and breaking the band apart!

Heather laughed out loud again. Wow, she and Sebastian had been pretty fucking mean to Ariana that night. Harrison had said it at the time, but she did owe Ariana an apology for that. Just thinking about Harrison brought a pang of hurt to Heather, she'd forgotten about him and everything that was happening for a minute or two, there.

If you're still reading this, Heather, thank you for giving me a chance to say my piece. If you can't forgive me, I will do my best to stay out of your way. I won't come between your friendship with Gabriel, and I certainly don't want to be the cause of any kind of drama with the guys.

Ariana had always been sweet. The way she'd behaved since returning to their lives was equally no different to the way she'd been before, whilst also being completely different from the way she'd been before. She was still the same, lovely and thoughtful Ariana. She just also braved paparazzi bullshit now, too.

I also want to say that I'm so proud of you and of Serenity. Your fashion show was amazing, I wish that I could've been there, but I watched the video, and it was brilliant.

Heather felt a glow of pride as she read this. It was nice to get this feedback from someone whose opinion she valued so highly.

If you can ever see your way to having a friendship with me, again, I am open to it. I hope that you are, too.

With all my love and affection,

Ariana

Heather put down the letter, grabbed a tissue, and blew her nose. She was glad she'd read it. She was even kind of glad that she'd waited to read it until now. Reading this letter was exactly what she needed today. She headed back out to the kitchen, picked up her phone, and saw five missed calls from Ariana and multiple texts.

PLEASE don't read it.

There's stuff in there that you don't need to read right now.

I want you to read it, just not today.

Heather? Are you reading it?

Heather laughed; poor Ariana. She must've been so stressed at her lack of replies. She found that she really wanted to see her and talk.

You silly cow. Are you free? Can you come over?

It was about thirty seconds before Ariana's reply popped up on her screen.

Absolutely. See you soon.

Chapter 16

AFTER TEN A.M.

Heather went back into the bedroom, retrieved the letter, and read it again while she waited for Ariana to get there. It really was, without a doubt, the loveliest letter she'd ever read. Heather was looking forward to getting a chance to clear the air with Ariana.

It wasn't long at all before Callum was showing Ariana into her living room. She looked nervous, and there was a tall man who looked to be in his early forties trailing behind her. He looked around the room, seeming to assess the situation, and Heather assumed that this must be Ariana's bodyguard.

She saw Heather, followed her gaze, and smiled, "Heather, this is Ross Weber, my bodyguard."

"Nice to meet you, Ross," he nodded at her, "you guys met Callum?"

Ariana nodded, and both men disappeared into the hallway. Heather had felt odd when Callum first started working for her and would spend hours just sitting near the door, but she'd gotten used to it. He would sporadically do checks of the apartment, both inside and out, and liaise with the doormen and security downstairs in regard to any comings or goings in the building.

"Did you want a coffee or something?" Heather asked Ariana.

"How about something stronger?"

"It's a bit early in the day for alcohol, isn't it?" Heather raised an eyebrow at her.

"Hey, I believe it was you who once told me that cocktails were fine as long as it was after ten in the morning," Ariana shrugged at her, and Heather grinned.

She went to the kitchen and grabbed the orange juice out of the fridge, got two big glasses, and went to the bar, coming back with a bottle of vodka. Ariana smiled when she saw what she had in her hands.

"You haven't forgotten."

"It's practically the only thing you ever drink," Heather grinned and poured them each a vodka and orange before putting the orange juice back in the fridge, "here."

Ariana took the drink from her. They made their way to the sofa, sitting down and facing each other, and there was silence for a few moments.

"So, where do you want to begin?" Ariana took a big swig of her drink.

Heather laughed, "Am I that scary that you need Dutch courage to have a conversation with me?"

"If you'd asked me the night we were at Sebastian's house, yes," Ariana grinned at her as she said it, though.

"I'm sorry for that night, Ariana. I was a major bitch to you. I…" she paused, trying to collect her thoughts and remember how she'd been feeling at the time, "…well, to be honest, I was tired and stressed and still really fucking hurt by the fact you left the way you did."

"I get it, Heather. I wish I hadn't left the way I did. I can't change it, but if I could go back, I would definitely do it differently."

"Ugh," Heather said, involuntarily, then continued as Ariana looked mildly offended, "sorry, not you. It's just that it's not the first time today that I've wished someone could go back in time and change some stuff."

"Harrison, I'm guessing?" Heather grimaced and nodded, as Ariana hit the nail on the head, "How are things with you guys?"

"Terrible. Truly awful. We've been going to counseling every Saturday, and I was a major bitch to him today, too. Apparently, it's just my go-to move." Heather sighed.

"I've seen Harrison," Ariana said quietly, "he's come to our place a couple of times. He seems so unhappy."

"Your place?" Heather raised an eyebrow, even as her heart ached at the confirmation that Harrison was as miserable as she was.

"Yeah, Gabriel and I moved in together when he got back from Galena." Ariana smiled.

"I'm so happy for you guys."

"Do you care, Heather?" Ariana asked with a wicked grin.

"Oof! Okay, I deserved that. All right, you wanted to talk that night, and I should have. There's something in your letter that I wanted to ask you about"—Heather got up and grabbed the letter from the kitchen bench so she could refer to it—"okay, why the hell did you think that you should leave without saying goodbye to anyone? I don't think anyone's ever hurt me as badly as that…well, until now," Heather corrected herself, and a feeling of sorrow washed over her.

"That whole thing with the news stories happened, and I was reading the shit online, and all of my insecurities just hit me at once, it was a perfect storm. I had already been feeling like I wasn't strong enough to lead this life, and suddenly everyone knew about me.

"I knew that they didn't have my real name. I thought if I could just leave, Gabriel could find someone who was stronger than I was, and I could go back to the real world. I stupidly thought that I was doing the right thing, even though I obviously wasn't.

"I knew that if I spoke to anyone, I'd crack and come back. I missed you guys all so damn much. I listened to everyone's voicemails over and over again," she confessed, "whenever I missed you, I'd listen to your voicemails just to hear your voices. In some ways, it was masochistic, though. It killed me every time I did it, but I don't think I was in a healthy place, mentally, at all."

Heather thought about what Ariana was saying. Some of it was painfully relevant to herself right now. Was some of this any different than her dwelling on the picture of Harrison and Maddy? She was guilty of letting the stories online about Harrison cheating on her get to her, as well.

"Gabriel was right," Heather said.

"Right about what?" Ariana smiled, just at hearing his name.

"You're different. Like, you're still you, but you just seem…different."

"God, Heather, if I weren't different now, I'd literally want to slap myself. Even when I saw Gabriel at the meet and greet, I ran away from him. I'm still dumb sometimes, but yeah, I did a lot of growing up and even some therapy in the last two years. It's helped me a lot, I think. At the end of the day, I've lived through the worst thing imaginable. If Gabriel ever leaves me, at least I won't have the knowledge of it being my own fault to torment me," she shrugged.

It was an interesting take on it and, oddly enough, very close to what Harrison had said to her about accepting Ariana back into their lives.

"I like New Ariana," Heather grinned.

"Me, too. I'm so glad you're being nice to me again. I think being back with Gabriel and not getting to just be friends with you again was probably worse than being away from you." Ariana cringed.

"This is nice. I'm sorry I was a bitch, and fucking hell do I need all the friends I can get right now." Heather finished her drink off and raised her empty glass to Ariana, "Do you want another?"

Ariana finished her own drink quickly and nodded. Heather got them a second round, possibly putting a little too much vodka into the drinks.

"Here's the thing," Heather said as she handed Ariana her drink and sat down on the sofa again, "the things that you're saying are very close to home. I know that I should forgive Harrison; it's not his fault that he cheated on me."

"But you're not going to forgive him?" Ariana asked her.

"I really and truly don't know. Everyone keeps asking me that. I want to, so badly. I want everything to go back to the way it was, hashtag couple goals," Heather rolled her eyes, "but I keep having nightmares about him sleeping with her. The rare occasions where he's touched me, I feel sick knowing that he touched someone else. I don't know how your aunt has done it."

"I was wondering when we'd get around to the topic of Uncle Darry," Ariana smiled, but it didn't reach her eyes, she was obviously concerned about what Heather was saying to her.

"Oh yes, that helped everything to make a *lot* more sense. Why didn't you just tell me before? We talked about this shit so often; it would've helped me to understand."

"They're not my secrets to tell," Ariana said, "you're the only person I've ever told all of that to, other than Gabriel."

"So he knew? When?" Heather's mouth dropped into an 'O' of surprise.

"Before the tour. I don't know if you remember, there was a night that a picture of us was taken, at April Conway's birthday party."

"Holy shit, yes, I remember! So, he knew all along?"

Heather finally understood why Gabriel had always been so patient with Ariana and her fear of celebrity. He'd been firm in them making accommodations for her and, privately, she knew that at least Harrison and Sebastian had wondered why but they'd never really questioned it and had just done what was asked of them. She'd loved Ariana and tried to talk her around, but ultimately gone with the flow, herself.

"Yeah, he did. Heather, can I ask you something?" Ariana bit her lip and looked nervous.

"Sure, what?"

"How bad was it when I left?"

Heather's heart dropped; she didn't want to be the one to have this conversation. She understood now why Harrison had balked at her asking the question of him the night of their engagement party. Heather pushed away the feeling of hurt that she got from remember that night and sighed before answering.

"Really bad, Ariana. About as bad as it could ever get. I don't want you to dwell on it, and I don't particularly want to relive it, myself, with everything that's going on with me at the moment," it was a bit of a cop-out, but at least there was some upside to this shitty situation, "I guess if you really want the honest truth, with no holds barred, you know who you should ask."

"Sebastian," Ariana cringed, "do you think he'll ever forgive me?"

"Honestly?"

"Yes, it's something I'm freaked out about."

"Then, yes. I do think he will. He said that Hell would freeze over first," Heather laughed, "but it must be cold down there right now because I think he will if I know him as well as I think I do."

"Why do you think that?" Ariana looked at her with curiosity apparent on her face.

"Because, darling, you've got me on your side now. If you hadn't been able to convince me, you wouldn't have been able to convince him. Plus, you're different now, like you said. After we heard what that reporter did to you, I think both of us softened toward you. Seb might take a little longer, but he'll get there."

"Well, I've got all the time in the world for him to come around. I'm not going anywhere." Ariana grinned.

"I'm glad about that, can I ask you something now?" Heather was unsure if she actually wanted to ask her question.

"Sure," Ariana had no idea what she was walking into right now.

"The night you guys were drugged, what do you remember?"

Ariana sighed heavily, "Are you sure you want to know?"

Heather took a moment to think about it, while she sipped some more of her drink. Yes, she wanted to know as much about that night as she could find out, so she confirmed this to Ariana.

"Okay, what exactly do you want to know?" Ariana squeezed her eyes tight and seemed to be bracing herself to have this conversation.

"Everything that happened from the time you guys got off the phone to me," Heather said it so quickly, she hadn't realized how much she wanted to ask this.

"Well, we just hung out until it was time to go downstairs. We went to the ballroom and found our table and sat down. Cooper's team was already there with him at the table when we arrived." Ariana wrinkled her nose.

"Harrison was sitting next to Maddy, wasn't he?" Heather interrupted Ariana to ask this.

"Yes, he was sitting in between Gabriel and Madeline. Cooper brought her to fill your seat," Ariana looked sad. Like she didn't want to be the one to tell Heather any of this and confirmed it when she asked, "Are you really sure you want to know?"

Heather nodded, so Ariana continued, "We were all having a good time. Nothing was strange with the first few bottles of wine. We had our entrées; there were some speeches and a charity auction. Harrison was *not* flirting with Madeline at that point. They think it was in the bottles we were served during the main course.

"About, I dunno, half an hour or thereabouts after we ate, I started to feel weird. It was like everything in the world was perfect. Gabriel literally glowed to me. I think that was when I noticed Harrison flirting with Madeline."

Heather felt a familiar wave of nausea hit her. She could practically see everything that Ariana was telling her.

"They were giggling and being really handsy with each other. Part of me thought that it wasn't okay, but a huge part of me thought that it was perfect and everyone should love everyone," Ariana's eyes were downcast and she looked like she felt guilty for not stopping them.

"It's not your fault," Heather said, "what happened then?"

"I can't remember the timeline exactly after that. Sebastian went to the dance floor and started basically fucking some chick. Hayden said he wasn't feeling well and went to his room. Harrison and Madeline disappeared together," Ariana cringed, and Heather wanted to cry.

"Do you have any idea what time that was?" Heather asked her.

"Not a clue; I'm really sorry. I wasn't with it. Gabriel and I left after that before Cooper even had his seizure. They think he had an extra glass of wine and ingested too much of the drug. Luckily, Helen had only had one glass, and they were still at the event when it happened, so she was with it enough to get help, which was basically right there.

"The amount of the drug that was in our bodies when they tested was incredibly high. We're lucky that nobody else ended up in the ICU, to be honest. Gabriel and I didn't figure it out until the morning; we had all these calls from Helen asking us to get to the hospital. Once they figured out that both she and Cooper had been drugged, they wanted us all to get tested."

Having these details filled in for her was bittersweet for Heather. Finding out exactly how everything had happened was incredibly painful; it mixed with the feelings of regret that she hadn't just been there with them.

"When did you find out about Harrison? I saw pictures of you guys leaving the hotel, together with Maddy."

Ariana looked incredibly uncomfortable now like she didn't want to answer this question.

"Tell me, Ariana." Heather caught her gaze, and Ariana sighed again.

"We couldn't get on to him, so we went to see if he was there and take him with us to the hospital. He wasn't answering his phone, and we couldn't get in, so Gabriel went down and convinced the hotel manager to open his room."

"You saw him in bed with Maddy." Heather felt tears spring to her eyes, as Ariana nodded her confirmation.

"Whoever took the picture had already been and gone. We woke Harrison..." she trailed off, looking distant.

"How did he react?"

"I've never seen someone so heartbroken. It was like watching him break in half right in front of our eyes as he realized what he'd done. Madeline was just as horrified. We could barely get Harrison to stop crying long enough to get out of the hotel and into the car. Not that it would've mattered—there was nothing to hide. The paparazzi were out the front of the hotel to ask us all questions and showed us the picture.

"Harrison kept trying to call you and send you texts, but he also knew that you were on the plane. He just kept calling, over and over. He didn't want you to find out the way you did. When we all saw the pictures of you at the airport, he was devastated. He knew that they had told you, and he was terrified that you wouldn't forgive him."

What Ariana was telling her was awful. Knowing that Harrison had experienced that level of pain, she felt guilty that she still couldn't find a path to forgiveness within herself right now.

She was looking for it, hearing how terrible he'd felt about cheating should have illuminated it for her, but she still just felt broken and empty.

"He said that he discharged himself against medical advice. He's lucky Cooper was in intensive care; he'd have lost his mind, otherwise!" Heather gave Ariana a wry grin.

"Yeah, oh my god, it was a massive drama. They called in the head of the hospital to try and talk him out of it, then literally had a lawyer come in to oversee him signing the discharge papers. We tried to get him to stay, but he said that Callum had told him you were going to hurt yourself, and he had to get back to you."

"Okay, that's not exactly what Cal said. He was just concerned that I'd do something stupid. I told him that I wasn't going to commit suicide because Harrison stuck his dick in another woman, and his exact response was 'talking that way isn't helping, there are plenty of ways to be unsafe that don't go that far,'" Heather rolled her eyes, "then I told him to leave, tried to fire him, and he told me that Harrison was his boss. So I texted Harrison to make him leave, and he called him, and Callum told him that he was 'concerned about what Miss York might do if she's left alone' and that he'd only leave if he was fired or a friend or family member took his place."

"Did he have good reason to be concerned, though, Heather?" Ariana asked her gently.

"Well, yeah. I mean, I wasn't going to hurt myself, but I might very well have set my world on fire, metaphorically."

"Okay, I have to ask," Ariana said, "what was the worst thing you considered doing that day?"

"The worst? Revenge sex. One hundred percent. I thought about just getting trashed, finding some random guy and fucking him," she admitted quietly.

Heather sighed, as a wave of guilt crashed over her for even having thought of doing something like that. What Harrison had done was a terrible mistake, but for her to do that on purpose would have been unconscionable.

"I'm sure as shit glad I didn't. It just hurts so badly to know that Harrison had sex with someone else."

"You guys were with other people before, weren't you?" Ariana asked.

"Not really; I think he got head from some chick, might have fingered a couple of girls, but I was his first. Same for me; I gave my high school boyfriend head…while pretending it was Harrison, I might add!"

"High school Heather had the hots for him that badly?" Ariana actually laughed.

"I really did, he's always been the man of my dreams. The first night we actually hooked up was one of the best nights of my life, and it's only been better since," Heather said wistfully.

"So, why are you letting this terrible one-off mistake come between you?"

"I wish that I could explain it, Ariana. Even hearing all of this from you, it doesn't make it better for me. Harrison has been mine for so long, I have never doubted his love for me. I don't even doubt it now. It's the fact that he took pleasure from someone else; it hurts me so much to think about. Some of the stuff you said in your letter about your aunt was cutting as well, like, if we get married and have kids, those pictures will always be there."

Ariana cringed, "Yeah, I definitely regretted some of the stuff I wrote in that letter. When Gabriel told me that he'd convinced you to read it, I was horrified."

"I bet he was proud of himself, too!" Heather laughed.

"He really was," Ariana laughed as well, "he was, like 'hey, Ari! I told Heather to read your letter, and she's going to do it!' with this big, dumb grin on his face, and I'm just, like, 'noooooooooooo!' He couldn't understand, but I had never told him exactly what was in it."

"I'm glad I read it, though. Look, some of the stuff was hard to read, but a lot of stuff right now is hard for me. Getting to hear your side of the story and why you did some of the shitty, stupid things you did," Heather poked her tongue out at Ariana, then continued, "was actually really good. It explained a lot, and I accept your apology, and in case you hadn't guessed, of course, I want to be your friend again."

Ariana drank the last of her drink, put the glass down on the table, then moved over to give Heather a massive hug.

"I really missed you so much, Heather!"

"I missed you, too, darling. Gabriel is one of my favorite people ever, and you make him happy. I have to trust that you won't leave him again, but from everything you've told me, I'm a lot less scared now that you will."

Heather finished her drink as well, grabbed Ariana's glass, and headed to the kitchen to pour them another. They spent the next few hours talking, drinking, and catching up on the last two years.

Heather was sad to hear that Ariana had stopped writing when she'd left the tour. "Oh, I really enjoyed reading what you were writing, darling. Why did you stop?"

"Because it was pretty much all about Gabriel, and I was trying to forget him," Ariana laughed.

"Well, you should start writing again," Heather told her with a wink, "you can write all about how he was so in love with you that he ditched Elena as soon as you were back in the picture."

"Sorry about that, I know you guys were close to her," Ariana said.

"What the fuck?" Heather was confused, "did Gabriel tell you that?"

"No," Ariana cringed, "I read it online the day he told me he was dating someone."

Heather rolled her eyes, "Do you believe everything you read online?"

"Well, no, I know I shouldn't. Now that I think about it, I can't believe I still thought that, actually. It said she'd met his family, and they were planning to get married," Ariana laughed.

"As far as I know, she never met his family," Heather said while shaking her head, "and they definitely weren't engaged. You know how news articles are, though. Mostly bullshit and half-truths."

They were still sitting there when Harrison walked in about thirty minutes later, with Michael trailing behind him.

Immediately, the air in the room became thick with tension. Harrison looked as beautiful as ever; he was wearing his regular jeans and T-shirt, and Heather longed to be in his arms.

"Hello, Ariana." Harrison smiled politely at her.

"Hi, Harrison."

He looked at Heather, then back at Ariana, "It's good to see you here."

"It's great to be here," she said to him, "Heather and I have been catching up."

"That's wonderful," he smiled a genuine smile at her, then looked at Heather, "Hi, angel."

"Hello, Harrison."

The smile fell from his face immediately. She really wasn't doing it intentionally, but she still couldn't bring herself to call him 'honey' anymore. It killed her to know that she was hurting him; she could see how it tore him up whenever she used his name, and she wished that everything could be different.

"I'll leave you to it," he said, then walked away in the direction of their bedroom.

Ariana let out a breath of air, once he was out of earshot, "Fuuuuuck, you could cut the tension with a knife. Is that what it's like all the time?"

"Pretty much," Heather cringed.

"How do you stand it?" Ariana grimaced.

"I barely can. We hardly ever spend any time in the same room anymore. I miss him." Heather felt like she might cry with the admission.

"As someone who blew up her life and wasted two years that I could have spent with Gabriel, I feel like I should warn you that you might be heading down the same path."

Heather glared at her, "This is *not* the same thing, Ariana. Gabriel never cheated on you; you were just stupid."

"I'm going to let that slide because I know you're hurting," Ariana raised an eyebrow at her, "I know it's different, Heather. I'm just saying that, well, remember you telling me time and again that I needed to get over my fear of celebrity? You need to get over this Madeline thing, or you're going to blow up your life."

"Let's not forget that 'this Madeline thing' is Harrison fucking another woman!" Heather yelled.

Ariana smiled sadly at her, "I haven't forgotten. I'm not saying you need to get over it today, or even any time soon. Just that if you don't, it's going to fester and become infected and poison your relationship. Ask me how I know."

Heather didn't say anything to this; she knew that Ariana was right. All of the tension seeped out of her body at once, and she flopped back on the sofa, looking in the direction of the bedroom where Harrison had disappeared to.

"I really don't think I can." Heather's eyes were downcast. "I've been trying to finish off my wedding dress, but it's too painful to even look at, Ariana."

Ariana gave her a hug and left not long after that, with a promise that she would see her again soon. She sent Heather a text shortly after she left, and they continued to text back and forth as Heather made herself dinner. Harrison didn't come out of his room all evening.

It had been an emotional day, but it was nice to have Ariana back. Even when she was yelling at Ariana for daring to give her some home truths, having her back in her life was a relief for Heather. How cruel it was that she got Ariana back just as she was sure that she was losing Harrison.

~JANUARY~

NEW CRUISE CONTROL SINGLE GOES OFF!

We are not the only ones rocking out to Cruise Control's new single, 'Rules to Break'! The band dropped the song over the weekend, and the video quickly became the most viewed new video of all time on YouTube with more than 100 million views within 24 hours of it going live.

Rumor has it that the video was only recorded last month, and is it just us, or does there seem to have been tension between Harrison Fletcher and Sebastian Fox on the set? The band released a behind the scenes 'making of' video which we loved, but Harrison and Sebastian definitely seemed frosty with one another.

There has still been no official word on whether or not Harrison's May wedding to his fiancée, Heather York, is still on or not. The lead-up to their wedding has been rife with rumors of Heather cheating and proof that Harrison definitely did. We don't know what to believe anymore. I guess we'll see what happens come May…

Chapter 17

DEATH BY A THOUSAND CUTS

Heather was sitting in the comfy armchair at a late-night show in New York. It was Friday night, and she was being interviewed about Serenity's official release in department stores. Somehow, despite the insanity of the last two months, Heather had managed to keep everything on track with her business. This was something of a miracle, given that there were times that she didn't care if everything fell in a hole. Without her amazing staff, it wouldn't have been successful. Heather no longer really cared about anything but went through the motions for something to do.

"How are things with you and Harrison?" the host asked her with a cheeky smile near the end of their interview, and Heather wanted to slap him, this had been on the list of 'do not ask' questions that her PR firm had given them.

She bit her tongue, wanting desperately to answer with 'absolutely fucking brilliant, remember that time he fucked another woman? Wasn't that fun!' It would make for a great headline tomorrow if she did.

"Great," she smiled widely, hating the lie.

"Is the wedding still on for May?" he pressed her.

"Sure is," as if she'd tell him if it wasn't, "unless you know something I don't know?"

"Well, we all know what happened…" he trailed off and had the grace to look embarrassed.

"Do we? Why don't you fill me in on the finer details?" She smiled at him, put her elbows on his desk, and rested her chin in her hands, apparently waiting for an answer, and the audience all laughed.

"Okay, I see your point," he laughed as well, and she sat back in her chair, "but I had to ask," he shrugged.

"Well, I'm not running away with Sebastian, if that's what you were wondering," she smirked at him.

"Are you sure? We all saw Saturday Night Live." He raised an eyebrow.

"Ah, yes, a well-known source of truth if ever I came across one," she quipped, and the audience laughed again.

"Well, all the best for the wedding. Heather York's clothing line, Serenity, is available in all major department stores from Monday. Heather York, everybody!"

The audience applauded, Heather shook his hand and left the set. Hayden and Ally met her backstage, with grinning faces.

"Way to put him in his place, bitch," Ally laughed.

"Thanks, he was out of fucking line. Cooper will be pissed. They weren't supposed to ask about Harrison."

"I like the way he waited until the end of the interview, so if you stormed off, he'd still filled out the slot," Hayden rolled his eyes.

"Classic move. Okay, let's get the fuck out of here and go dancing," Heather grinned.

Callum escorted them all out of the building along with Hayden's bodyguard, Jesse Howell. The got into a waiting limousine, and it headed to a trendy nightclub in Chelsea. On the way, Heather got a text from Sebastian.

You looked good tonight, lover. You won't reconsider running away with me?

She laughed and told Ally and Hayden about the message.

"You guys still joke around like that?" Ally asked her, "Even with everything that's going on between you and Harrison?"

"Yeah, why would the shit with Harrison make a difference?" Heather asked.

"Well, I mean…" Ally trailed off and looked at Hayden.

"You mean, what?" Heather raised an eyebrow at her as she texted Sebastian back.

I was just saying that for the cameras. Of course I'll run away with you.

"Your relationship with Sebastian is bordering on inappropriate at the best of times. I would've thought that Harrison would have a real problem with it, now that everything's so shit with you two."

Heather gave a hollow laugh, "Harrison fucked somebody else. He literally wouldn't dare step to me about my friendship with Sebastian. Besides, I've told you, it doesn't *mean* anything. Right, Hayden?" Hayden nodded his confirmation, "We're just taking the piss."

"What the hell does that mean?" Ally looked confused.

Hayden laughed, "Kip Soundly taught it to us when we were first in Australia, it means they're just joking."

Heather laughed, remembering their very drunken night with the Australian pop star when Cruise Control was over there for the Australian version of the Grammys.

"My point is," Heather said, "you've seen us in person; surely you can see that there's nothing there?"

"What I've seen is you two saying wildly inappropriate things to one another that nobody ever calls you out on, it's completely bizarre to watch, to be honest," Ally shrugged.

Heather smirked at her, "Just wait until the next time you're around us. I'll show you how 'wildly inappropriate,' I can get!"

Ally laughed, "Oh god, what have I done?"

"You're going to regret this, Ally!" Hayden laughed, as well.

The limousine pulled up outside the club. They entered amidst camera flashes and questions from reporters. They all went to the bar and got drinks before hitting the dance floor. It was a great night; Heather hadn't realized how tense her life in Chicago had gotten until she was here in New York and able to let loose.

She realized, with sadness, as she was lying alone in her hotel room later that evening, that it was the first time in her life that she'd been glad to be away from Harrison. When she was at home with him, now, it was tense and awkward. They still weren't making any progress in their therapy sessions. Brendan kept trying to guide her to the path of forgiveness, but she couldn't get there.

Heather had started seeing her own therapist separately. Her goal there was purely to stop the nightmares that she was still having daily, but she wasn't having any more luck with Zoe than she was having in her joint sessions with Harrison and Brendan. She'd managed to cut down on the amount of time she spent actively dwelling on what had happened, but couldn't control the things that her subconscious threw at her when she slept.

It made her resentful and, most of all, tired. When she woke in the middle of the night from these nightmares, she struggled to get back to sleep. The nightmares frequently removed the being drugged aspect of Harrison cheating, and she was subjected to dreams about him and Maddy in pure, sober lust with each other.

It was the times that she woke from these dreams, that she would fall back into the nasty habit of looking at the pictures and stories online again. She ached to have Harrison in bed with her and had considered going to his room many nights, but she never did. Aside from a few brief hugs here and there, he hadn't touched her since she'd been out at Galena with him for Hayden's birthday, and she didn't want him to, despite the all-consuming desire that she still felt for him, frequently.

The next morning, Heather packed her things and made her way to Hayden and Ally's room. They had room service breakfast, deciding to stay well away from the hotel's restaurant and maximize the peace they had before braving the paparazzi to get to the airport.

"Okay, who wants to put money on Harrison having cheated on me while I was here?" Heather said grimly.

"That's not funny." Hayden shook his head.

"Hey, I wouldn't have bet on it last time I was in New York, but now there's a precedent for it, the odds are better that it'll have happened," she shrugged nonchalantly.

"Come on, Heather, you know he won't have cheated on you this time," Ally said.

"I actually don't know that at all, maybe he's taken to fucking Madeline on the regular to satisfy his needs; god knows he's not getting any from me," she grimaced.

"Stop it, Heather. You know that Harrison isn't cheating on you, so why the fuck are you saying this stupid shit?" Hayden glared at her.

Heather met his angry gaze with her own for a second, before she lost the ability to keep up her high and mighty attitude, and tears began to well in her eyes.

"Because I'm scared, Hayden. The idea of making the trip back to Chicago is harder than I thought it would be, and I keep remembering the last time I made the trip back from here. It's been so bad between Harrison and me since it happened. I don't think I can continue doing it anymore."

Ally stood up from where she was sitting and came around to give Heather a hug, but Hayden wouldn't look away from her. He understood exactly what it was that she was telling him.

"You're going to end it." He looked sad, and Ally gasped as Heather nodded her head.

"No, you're not!" Ally looked at her, open-mouthed.

"Being here, it's made me realize just how terrible it's been back home, lately. Harrison and I are meant to be getting married in, what? Four months' time? We're supposed to be happy; we're supposed to be excited. I don't want to start a marriage this way. With us barely talking outside of counseling sessions. With me feeling sick every time he touches me. It's not the way it's meant to be."

"Harrison is going to be devastated," Hayden said softly, the sadness for his friend evident in his tone.

"I know. I wish it could be different." Heather wiped away the tears that were falling freely from her eyes now.

"Why can't it be different?" Ally asked her.

Heather gave her a small smile, "Because Hayden made it back up to his room, alone, and Harrison fucked Maddy"—she caught the look on Hayden's face as he started to protest—"that's the thing, it's not anyone's fault. Everyone reacts differently to drugs, but you didn't fuck anyone. Meanwhile, Gabriel and Ariana apparently had a fucking amazing night together, Seb told me that the sex he had was beyond anything he'd ever experienced and Harrison…" her voice cracked, and she couldn't finish her sentence.

She couldn't voice out loud that he'd had high sex with someone else. They hadn't asked for the experience or wanted it at all, but the others had told her how good the sex was while they were under the influence. When they'd told her about their own experiences, she didn't think they'd realized what exactly it meant for what she was thinking about Harrison.

Heather also questioned Harrison's re-telling of the night's events. Maybe, he'd been trying to spare her feelings, but everyone else seemed to be able to recall a shitload more than he would tell her, even in their counseling sessions. He remembered something, anything, more than just being at dinner and then waking up, she was sure of it.

The mood in their group was somber as Hayden and Heather said their goodbyes to Ally. She wished Heather luck for the conversation she was going to have when she got back to Chicago and told her to text, or call, any time of the day or night. Then they made their way through the large group of paparazzi that was out the front of the hotel and into a limousine, with the help of Callum and Jesse.

The media were still hounding Heather about the cheating scandal, but Cruise Control had also released their new single, "Rules To Break", recently, so there was even more attention on her this trip since she was traveling with Hayden. They had chosen to go with the song they'd recorded the day she was out at Galena with them as the first single off the album, which they'd named, *Games We Play*, and it was bittersweet for Heather. Every time she heard it, she remembered the day it was recorded and the hours she'd spent with Harrison afterward.

Heather felt completely numb as they boarded their flight to O'Hare. Hayden took his seat next to her on the plane. Callum and Jesse were in the row behind them. As soon as they had sat down, Heather turned her head to the window and began to cry. It had been hard getting through the paparazzi without giving anything away, trying not to let anyone know that her heart was shattering into tiny pieces knowing that she was about to go and call off her wedding.

"Are you sure about this, Heather?" Hayden asked her gently, while passing her a tissue.

"No, I'm really not. I don't want to do this. You know that, right?" She blew her nose and put the tissue aside.

"So, don't do it. Just...postpone the wedding, instead," he pleaded.

"For how long, Hayden? Indefinitely? Because things sure as shit aren't getting any better between us, right now. I am dying in that apartment, and Harrison is, too. Maybe a break is what we need," she shrugged.

"A break? Or are you ending it? A break, I can understand, but ending it…you'll kill him, Heather."

"Why am I expected to forgive and forget? I've been trying and I can't, I already feel like a fucking failure of a human being for that. We all know that he was the victim of something awful, and I hate the fucker that did this to you guys, to me. Ariana told me how terrible Harrison felt when they woke him up, and he realized what he'd done. I feel awful for not being able to forgive him, but I can't stand the nightmares and the tension of being around him every day anymore."

Hayden put his arm around her shoulders, and she cried into his chest for a lot of the flight. When they were about forty-five minutes away from Chicago, she went to the bathroom, washed her face, then re-did her makeup. It wouldn't necessarily hide her red eyes, but she would put her sunglasses on before leaving the plane just in case the paparazzi met them at the gate again.

She didn't have to worry, though; they hadn't made the effort, and their group was able to at least make it to the baggage claim and get their luggage in relative peace. They were swarmed from there, though, but Callum and Jesse kept them safe until they reached the black SUV. She and Hayden had traveled from her apartment to the airport together, so they'd be going back in the same car, as well.

Heather found herself feeling similar to the way she had the day of her fashion show. Now that she'd made the decision to call off the wedding, it was like she had a list of tasks to check off before reaching the final one, 'break up with Harrison.' In the same way as that day, it stopped her from focusing on what she had to do if she just focused on each task in and of itself. When they reached her apartment building, Heather felt sick, knowing what she was about to do.

"Do you want me to come upstairs, Heather?" Hayden asked her, looking concerned.

"Can you give us a minute?" Heather managed to ask Callum as he opened the door for them to get out of the car, and he nodded before closing it. She was barely holding it together right now, "Please don't, Hayden. I can't handle small talk right now. I just need to get this over with."

"I know you've decided already, but I have to beg you again to rethink this, I wouldn't be a good friend if I let you just go ahead without telling you that I think this is a bad idea."

Heather smiled at him, "You're a good friend, Hayden. One of the best. I love you."

She gave him a final hug, then opened the door of the SUV and got out. The familiar feeling of emptiness washed over her as she gave Hayden a sad wave goodbye. She and Harrison were supposed to be having a session with Brendan this afternoon, but instead, she was going to end their engagement. Callum followed her to the elevator, he looked concerned, and she knew that he'd overheard a lot today.

They entered the apartment; Michael was sitting near the entrance, and Heather nodded as she passed him. Callum hung back and didn't follow her as she made her way further into the apartment. She heard him say something in a low undertone to Michael and was sure he was telling him that they needed privacy right now.

Harrison was sitting on the sofa in front of the TV, an action movie was playing, and he was drinking from a tumbler of amber liquid. Heather frowned; it was too early in the day for him to be drinking. She had joked with Ariana that any time after ten was okay, but sitting alone and drinking before noon seemed wrong.

He looked so beautiful; his hair was a mess, but it always was lately, because he was as stressed as she was. He was wearing a pair of sweatpants and a T-shirt. Heather wondered if he'd even gotten dressed today, or if he was still wearing what he wore to bed last night. She just stood there watching him for the longest time, she drank in the sight of him, knowing that this might be the last time she saw him for an indeterminate amount of time.

Heather didn't know how long she stood there, exactly. It wasn't until Harrison paused the movie to go and refill his glass that he noticed her. As usual, his expression softened the instant that he saw her, but these days, his initial reaction was always met by an immediate increase in tension in the room. There was no putting it off any longer.

"We need to talk, Harrison."

He smiled grimly and held up his empty glass, "Why do I get the feeling that I'll need another one of these soon, angel?"

Heather walked toward him. As she did, he put his empty glass back down on a coaster on the coffee table and turned the television off as she sat down, facing him on the sofa.

"I don't even know where to begin," she admitted.

"Just rip the Band-Aid off, please." He looked completely miserable.

"This isn't working, Harrison. I've tried so hard to get past it, but I can't."

He nodded but didn't say anything, so she continued.

"I can't stop the nightmares. It's awful in this apartment together, the way it is between us, I'm going to suffocate from the tension that's always there. It's too much, and I can't handle it."

"I've been expecting this." He picked up his phone, unlocked it, and showed her the screen. On it was a picture of her, Ally, and Hayden dancing in New York last night. Heather hadn't even known that it had been taken, but she looked so relaxed in the photo, and was obviously having fun, "I haven't seen you like that in so long, angel."

She couldn't stop the tears that had started to fall, and she wiped them away as she told him, "I will always love you, Harrison."

"I know, because I will always love you as well, my angel."

They sat in silence for a few minutes, and Heather realized

that he was crying as well. It broke her. She put her head in her hands and began to cry harder than she had been. How the hell was she supposed to exist in a world where Harrison wasn't a part of her life? She realized, painfully, that she had been existing in such a world, already. He hadn't really been a part of her life these last two months. At least this way, she wouldn't have to suffer having him so close to her physically, but so far away emotionally.

Heather finally raised her tear-streaked face to meet his eyes, and a fresh wave of sobs overtook her before she managed to ask, "Where do we go from here?"

"You can stay here. I'll find somewhere to go." He seemed resigned to this conclusion.

"Are you sure, Harrison?"

He winced, as he usually did when she used his name. "Yes, angel. Like I said, I've been expecting this. I've just been waiting for you to tell me. I've had a lot of time to think about what we would do when the time came."

"I don't think I can survive without you," she choked out as she continued to cry, "but I can't keep living like this, either."

She realized that she was playing with her engagement ring. It was something that she did so often and had become such a habit that it wasn't a conscious thing, but she had the horrendous realization that she needed to give it back to Harrison now.

As if in slow motion, she pulled it off her finger. Her body was wracked with sobs as she held it out to him in the palm of her hand. She couldn't look at him; she closed her eyes and continued to cry.

"Angel, no…" he sounded wounded.

"Please, just take it, Harrison," she begged him, still unable to look at him.

His fingers were warm against the palm of her hand as he grasped the ring. It felt so wrong, she was flooded with a million different memories of his touch, and as soon as she felt him take the ring from her, she dropped her head to her hands and sobbed hysterically.

Chapter 18

CHAPTER NEVER REVISITED

Heather lay where she was on the sofa, long after Harrison had collected up a few things and told her, quietly, that he was leaving. She knew that they would need to talk at some point and sort out the logistics of their split, but neither of them was in the mental state to do that right now.

She sat up at the sound of insistent knocking on the door. She wiped away the tears from her eyes as she did. Whoever it was clearly wanted her attention badly. As she walked toward the door, her phone started buzzing and lit up on the coffee table where she had been sitting.

She glanced over at it and saw Sebastian's name on the screen. Opening the door, she saw Sebastian himself standing on the doorstep, his phone up to his ear as he was calling her.

"Oh, Heather." His face was full of sympathy, and she could barely stand it.

"Please don't, Sebastian." Heather felt the tears start to fall afresh, and she couldn't stop them if she tried.

Sebastian swept into the room, closing the door behind himself and put his arms around her, hugging her tightly to his chest.

"Are you okay?" he asked her quietly.

"No, but that doesn't change anything." Heather sighed, breaking their embrace and heading back to the sofa.

"I don't like seeing you cry, Heather."

Sebastian sat down next to her and put his arm around her shoulders, pulling her toward him so that her head was resting on his chest. She could hear his heart beating, and it was oddly soothing. She continued to cry, and he simply held her while she did.

"It wasn't his fault, Seb. I think that's what makes this so hard," she told him once she'd finally managed to pull herself together.

"I get that he was drugged, but he knew you weren't there. He knew it wasn't you. I don't understand how he could ever have mistaken that slut for you, no matter how high he was." Sebastian's words were full of venom.

"He's sorry, and Maddy's not a slut. He's apologized to me repeatedly. I just can't get that image out of my head, though, Seb. I see him touching her. I see him kissing her. When I sleep, it's like watching a movie that picks up right when that picture was taken. They wake up in bed together and fuck, and I just see it all."

Sebastian put his other arm around her now to hug her tighter as she started to cry again.

"I'll kill him," he said, whispering it into her hair.

"No, you won't," she said through her tears. "You love him as much as I do."

"Yes, but I love you, too," he said candidly, "plus, he's in the wrong."

For most women, having Sebastian Fox tell them that he loved them would be a dream come true. For her, it was just sweet. She knew it wasn't a romantic love that he had for her any more than he had for Harrison. They were closer than siblings.

"I don't even know what I'm going to do now, Seb."

"Have you canceled the wedding yet?"

"Shit, Sebastian," she sat up and glared at him, "give me five seconds. We literally broke up two hours ago."

"Sorry, I didn't mean that to sound like I was pressuring you. I'm just trying to figure out what needs to be done," he put his hands up in a conciliatory gesture.

She appreciated his concern, but she couldn't even face the reality of the fact that her wedding that was supposed to be taking place in less than four months, wouldn't be happening now.

"Where's Harrison?" he asked her.

"He didn't say where he was going. Robert and Sarah's, or Hayden's, maybe? He told me that I could stay here and he'll rent an apartment. How can I stay here, though, Seb? Everything here reminds me of him. It's just so full of *us*."

The tears were threatening to fall again as she pondered the problem of her living arrangement.

"Come out to Galena with me," Sebastian said to her.

"What?"

He stood up from the sofa, grabbed hold of her hand and pulled her up to standing before hugging her again.

"We'll go out to Galena. Nobody will bother us there. No paparazzi, no drama. We'll tell the others where we are, but we can switch our phones off if you don't want to talk to anyone. We can do whatever you want, get drunk, go swimming, play pool. None of the bullshit that you'll get if you stay here," he offered.

Heather was very tempted. The picture he was painting was an attractive one. Sebastian's property would be the perfect place for her to heal and lick her wounds.

"Are you sure?" she asked him.

"Positive," he replied with a smile. "Pack your bags, lover. We'll go now."

She laughed at his use of the stupid nickname, and it made her feel like everything was normal, even though it very much wasn't. Heather didn't know how much to pack. She decided to bring a weekend bag with casual clothes, along with some swimming costumes and underwear. She needed to be back in Chicago on Monday, anyway.

Before she knew it, she'd told Callum that he was free to go home and that she'd call him out to Galena if she needed him. Luckily, he followed her instructions; she couldn't bear to have any kind of contact with Harrison right now. It was an awful reminder that their lives were so entangled that it would take a lot of effort to disentangle them.

They approached Sebastian's powerful, red Ferrari, "Wait; you drove yourself here?"

"Yeah, I told Daryl to stay home, I figured I'd be parking under here and always planned to offer for you to come out to Galena."

As the gate to the underground parking garage opened, and Sebastian edged the car out and waited for traffic. The group of paparazzi that had been waiting nearby took pictures of them driving away together.

"Oh, great," Heather drawled, "I can just see the headlines, 'Sebastian Fox and Heather York's love affair continues!'"

Sebastian was surprisingly serious as he replied, "Yeah, I'm sorry about that. I know it's not what either of you two needs right now."

The reality of the situation hit her as they were speeding away from Chicago. She relaxed into the buttery leather as the distance between them and the city increased, but it was the distance that she was putting between her and Harrison that broke her. Ten years she'd been together with him. She'd thought that nothing could ever break them, but all it had taken was some asshole spiking his drink and one monumentally stupid mistake on his part.

Heather began to cry again, frustrated with herself, and Sebastian reached his right hand over to hold her hand in his.

"You'll be okay, Heather," he assured her. "It'll take time, but you'll survive this, I promise."

He squeezed her hand supportively, then let it go and pulled a pack of tissues out of the center console, "Here, I thought you might need these."

As she continued to cry, he called ahead to his maid and groundskeeper, letting them know that he would be visiting from today. He asked them to ensure the place was ready and then to please give them some space. Heather was glad that she would be given the opportunity to grieve the ending of her relationship in private.

"Running away like this, it's not going to solve anything," she sighed deeply.

"Maybe not, but you'll be safe, Heather. Galena is perfect for that."

"I'm worried about Harrison," she said between tears.

"Me too. Hayden's going to look out for him, though." Sebastian gave her a grim smile.

"And you're on 'Heather Duty,' then, I'm guessing."

"Awwww, lover, spending time with you is never a chore…but yeah, I'm on 'Heather Duty,'" he reached over and squeezed her hand again.

She sighed and looked out the window at the world that was passing them by. Heather couldn't believe that she'd actually done it. It still seemed unfathomable that she'd handed back her engagement ring to Harrison. She rubbed the place on her finger where it should be sitting. It felt wrong, the bare skin there.

The worst part, really, was the sense of relief that she felt, knowing that she wouldn't have to spend time with Harrison anymore. It made her feel like a traitor. She loved that man more than anything or anyone else in the world; it was wrong of her to feel this way. She felt sick, thinking about what the future held for her.

At least for now, it seemed like her friends weren't choosing sides. She knew from yesterday that even though Hayden was with Harrison now, he was just as much her friend as Harrison's. They would obviously just have to catch up, separately. Would there ever be a time that she could maybe have a friendship with Harrison, as well? Was there some future where she had a different partner, where Harrison did, too? A group catch-up with Gabriel and Ariana, Hayden and Ally, and their respective partners that weren't each other?

The thought of a future like that made Heather unbearably sad. She didn't want another boyfriend, fiancé, or husband. She wanted Harrison. Every fiber of her being ached for him. Belonged to him. How did everything go so horrendously wrong? This wasn't fair.

Her phone pinged, and she saw a text from Ariana.

Where are you and Sebastian going?

"Harrison?" Sebastian asked her.

"No, Ariana," she replied.

Obviously the pictures of them had already hit the internet.

We're going to Galena. I broke up with Harrison.

Heather knew that Ariana would already have been told, but she would have wanted her to hear it directly, as well. It felt terrible just writing those words.

I know. I'm sorry, Heather.

Heather sent back a GIF of an explosion with a dark laugh that caused Sebastian to look over at her.

"I know it's not what's important right now, but I see you're no longer Team Sebastian," he laughed.

Heather laughed as well; it was nice to actually find something funny, "Sorry, Seb. I'm a traitor of the highest order. Ariana is the best. I don't know how I would've survived the last month without her support."

"I suppose she told you to end it with Harrison?" he asked.

"No, she thinks I'm blowing up my life the way she did with Gabriel and that I'll regret it." Heather grimaced.

"At least she has *some* sense," Sebastian said.

Heather rolled her eyes at him, "You're going to end up friends with her again, Seb."

"What makes you say that?"

Heather grinned wickedly at him, then pulled a sad face, "Because I'm *really* upset right now, Sebastian Fox. I just broke up with Harrison after ten years, and it would make me just a tiny bit happier if you forgave Ariana."

"Ooh, the emotional blackmail is strong with this one," Sebastian laughed, "you know you're one of the few people in the world who might actually be successful with a tactic like that."

"Wait? You're telling me that all I have to do is break up with my fiancé to get you to do things for me? I'll keep this in mind for the future; the tradeoff seems worthwhile," she gave a hollow laugh.

They made the rest of the journey in relative silence. The pervasive feeling of emptiness that Heather had these days was all-consuming. She still didn't know how she would survive without Harrison, and the knowledge that she needed to call all of the vendors on Monday and cancel their wedding was killing her.

When they reached Sebastian's place, he parked in the garage and carried her suitcase inside for her. They went upstairs, and for an awful second, Heather thought that Sebastian was going to take her to the room she'd shared with Harrison on her previous visits, she hadn't thought about where she would sleep while she was here.

Thankfully, he turned in the opposite direction, instead, and opened a door some way down the hall. He stood aside and allowed her to walk in before him.

"My room is right next door if you need anything," he smiled at her.

"Noted for our late-night fuckfest," Heather said with grim amusement.

It felt like a lifetime ago that Harrison had made that joke to her in New York City the day before her fashion show. She'd give anything to go back to that time and be with him again.

Sebastian went and sat on an armchair near the window as Heather started emptying her suitcase and grinned at her, "I stocked up on condoms, so we're all good."

They went back downstairs, and Sebastian got them both some drinks. He also grabbed some snacks that they took with them into his theater. Heather sat back in one of the reclining chairs as he put a comedy on for them to watch. When the movie finished, he chose another one, and Heather was grateful to just zone out, while Sebastian ensured her drink was refilled each time it was empty.

About twenty minutes into the second film, her phone lit up with a text from Hayden.

Hey, Heather. Harrison wants to go clubbing. I've told him I don't think it's a good idea, but he's pretty insistent.

"Read this," Heather said, handing her phone over to Sebastian as he paused the film.

He frowned as he read it and handed her phone back to her, "That's not good."

"I know, but it's not like it's my place to stop him."

The knowledge that she had no right to have any input in Harrison's movements now was so painful that she felt like she was being torn into pieces. Sebastian got his own phone, sent a text, and then showed her the screen. He'd texted Harrison.

Dude, don't go to a club. The press will have a field day.

As she was reading it, Harrison's reply came through, and Heather was able to read it before Sebastian had a chance to turn the phone away.

What do I fucking care? Nothing matters anymore. I'm

going to get fucked up.

He'd punctuated it with the shrugging emoji. Heather was worried, she'd known that Harrison would be hurting tonight, but she was actually concerned that he might hurt himself.

"Surely, Michael wouldn't let him go?" She bit her lip, "I mean, Cal wouldn't let me out the day I found out about Maddy."

"Yeah, but you're not Callum's boss. He could fire Michael if he tries to stop him from going, like you tried with Callum."

She'd told Sebastian the story of the day she'd come back from New York and found out about Harrison. Heather sighed and sent a text back to Hayden.

Thanks for the heads up. Please keep him safe, Hayden.

Heather saw a notification that she had a DM on Instagram from @meggggzy2005. Only people that she followed could message her, and she wondered what Megan had said.

Hi Heather. You might not read this but I just wanted you to know I don't believe you cheated on Harrison. If its true you guys have broken up, thats so sad. I love you guys so much!

She didn't really want to reply and give her any information, but Megan was so sweet that she didn't want to leave her on 'read', either.

Thanks. I didn't cheat. It's nice to know someone believes that. I appreciate the support, Megan. :)

Heather closed the app without waiting for a reply and turned to Sebastian, "Shall we finish watching this movie, and can I get another drink?"

"Sure, are you going to eat anything, though?" he indicated to the snacks and looked concerned as she shook her head, but took her glass and refilled it before turning the movie back on.

By the time the movie had finished, Heather was very drunk, and Sebastian refused to refill her glass this time, "You've had more than enough, lover."

"But Seeeeeeeb, I'm saaaaaad!" she whined at him, and he

laughed.

"Nope, the emotional blackmail thing doesn't work when what you want is bad for you."

"You suck," she sulked.

"Come with me; you need to eat something. How about I heat up a frozen pizza?" he offered.

Heather was actually hungry now, so she nodded and stood up to follow him to the kitchen. As soon as she was upright, she swayed on her feet, and Sebastian laughed as he took hold of her arm and steadied her.

"I told you that you'd drunk too much, lover. Maybe you should have some coffee with that pizza?"

He helped her up the stairs and led her to the kitchen. She sat on a stool at the kitchen bench as he turned on the oven to heat up. Heather grabbed her phone and searched for 'Harrison Fletcher.' She was rewarded with a page of articles about him, and sure enough, there were pictures of him and Hayden entering a club about an hour ago.

"God, I hope he's okay." She dropped her phone onto the kitchen bench and spun it around so that Sebastian, who was standing across from her, could see it.

"Hayden's with him, he'll be okay."

"Why do you sound so unsure, then, Sebastian?" She raised an eyebrow at him.

He didn't answer her question, just grabbed a frozen pizza from the freezer and opened the box, put the pizza on a tray, then slid it into the oven.

Heather couldn't resist asking Sebastian, "What's the worst that you think he could do?"

"Come on, Heather," she knew he was serious, he had used her real name, "you don't want me to answer that."

"No, I do. I broke up with him today, and all day, I've been running through worst-case scenarios in my head. An overdose would be pretty fucking bad, I've decided. Having sex with someone else again, though, that would possibly be worse for me. Which I know is unfair, considering he's technically free to screw whoever he wants now."

Heather felt utterly miserable at the idea of Harrison in bed with someone else and had to wipe away the tears that had sprung to her eyes as she said it. It was the basis of every one of her daily nightmares, and now he could theoretically go ahead with it.

"He's not going to do either of those things," Sebastian said confidently.

"You sound so sure of yourself, considering we're talking about a man who specifically told you he's going to get 'fucked up,' tonight."

"Damn, I was hoping you didn't have time to read that," Sebastian said, and grimaced at her.

"Sorry. I didn't mean to, it just popped up, and I couldn't stop myself. I want to call him, Seb. I want to tell him to come here and be with me and never leave. I hate myself because I won't do it."

"Don't hate yourself. I understand why you did it," he shrugged casually.

"Really? You're the only one if that's the case. Okay," she corrected herself, "one of the only two people, since Harrison was unsurprised. But Hayden, Ally, and Ariana all tried to talk me out of it. So why is it that Sebastian Fox, Mr. Commitment-phobe himself, gets it?" She gave him a wry grin.

"Because I'm scared for him, now, but I was scared for you before."

Heather frowned, "What do you mean? Explain."

"I've watched you become a shell of your former self for the last two months, Heather. I even talked to Harrison about it a couple of weeks ago. He had noticed, too. The only time I've seen you like that before was when Ariana left, but this was different;

worse.

"When she left, you were clearly upset. You weren't eating, and we could all tell that you were devastated. These last two months"—he paused and seemed to search for the right words to describe it—"you've seemed empty. Like you don't have any feelings at all. The light's gone out from behind your eyes, and it's terrifying to see.

"It was more like Gabriel was back then. I chose 'Heather Duty,' because I know what Harrison is going to be like, now, and I can't stand it. I trust that Hayden will keep him safe, but I can't be the one to do it. Not again."

Sebastian turned away from her as he finished his explanation, and Heather thought that she saw tears in his eyes. He busied himself with making them both coffees, and she thought about what he'd said. For someone who hated relationships, he was surprisingly insightful about them. He was the only person, aside from Harrison, who had noticed how empty she was feeling.

"I'm broken, Seb," she said quietly, "I'm broken, and I don't know how I can fix myself. Two months of therapy with two different therapists, and I'm still fucking broken. I'm having nightmares every fucking time I sleep. How am I supposed to get better? What Harrison said to you in his text? I feel that, too. Nothing fucking matters anymore. Nothing matters because some asshole spiked your drinks, and Harrison slept with someone else."

"I've been thinking about that…" Sebastian turned to her, brought their coffees over to the counter, and slid hers in front of her before turning back to get the pizza out of the oven.

"Yeah, me too," she said darkly.

"No, not the cheating," he clarified, as he grabbed a pizza cutter from a drawer and started to serve them up a couple of slices of pizza each, "the drugging. How much money do you think those pictures of Harrison were worth?"

Heather was horrified, "What? No. You think someone did it

on purpose to get pictures like that?"

"In case you were wondering, the answer would be 'a motherfucking fortune.' I'm going to talk to Cooper this week about it. He's been liaising with the police on the investigation, but I don't think they've found anything, yet."

"I just assumed the picture was taken by some maid or someone who came into the room in the morning," Heather frowned, "but if what you're suggesting is right, fuck. That *would* make sense."

Heather took a bite of a slice of pizza. It was tasty, and she felt better now that she was eating something. Sebastian's theory was awful, but it would also explain a lot. Otherwise, there was no real reason for their table to have been targeted with the drugged wine.

"How could they be sure that they'd get something good, though? I mean, they sure are lucky that Harrison cheated on me."

"I don't know; it's just a theory. Like I said, I'm going to talk to Cooper and see what he says. Maybe it's nothing, but it could give the police something to go on, I guess." He shrugged.

Heather didn't know how to feel about this idea. She'd known all along that Harrison was a victim of being drugged, but the idea that it had been so that somebody could take advantage of him was even worse.

"If you're right, Seb," she said slowly, "then that's like what happened with Ariana and that reporter, but about a million times worse. The fact that someone did that to Ariana makes me think that, fuck, there's at least a possibility that you could be right."

"Yeah, it's scary. I hope that I'm wrong," Sebastian replied as the coffee that Heather was drinking plus the topic they were discussing sobered her up a lot.

She picked up her phone and searched Harrison's name again. This time, there were pictures of Harrison and Hayden leaving the club, bodyguards keeping the paparazzi at bay. Michael seemed to be helping Harrison to walk in a similar fashion to the way

Sebastian had helped Heather, earlier.

He looked too beautiful to be allowed, even in this state. She started to cry as memories of the life they'd shared together flooded over her. She missed him with every fiber of her being. It was strange to believe that it was only this morning that she'd seen him last. It had been a long, and very draining, day.

She clicked on one of the articles to read it and found that, of course, it was speculating on their possible breakup. The pictures of her and Sebastian leaving the apartment together were here, and it was noted that, of course, she wasn't out with Harrison tonight. They were putting two and two together and coming up with five. Yes, they were right that she and Harrison had broken up, but she was as likely to sleep with Sebastian tonight as Harrison was to sleep with anyone else.

Sebastian looked over at her as she finished her food and saw what was on her screen, "Don't read that shit, Heather."

"What? You don't want to go upstairs and fuck, then? I was just about to offer…" She raised her eyebrows at him, and he laughed.

"Well, I mean, of *course,* I want to go upstairs and fuck," he looked at the phone again, "I'm glad he's out of there and on his way home."

"Looks like he had a few too many drinks," she cringed.

"As if you can talk, lover!" Sebastian laughed. "Are you ready for bed?"

Heather nodded, and he took their plates and cups, then put them in the sink before coming back to hug her. They went upstairs, and as Heather was lying alone in her bed, the reality of her situation hit her once again. She'd gone to bed alone every night for over two months, but this time, there was no Harrison in a nearby room. Heather hadn't realized how much comfort she had drawn from that fact.

When she woke later that night from yet another nightmare,

she couldn't stop herself from crying hysterically. In her dream, Harrison had gotten into the black SUV after leaving the club, and Maddy had met him at their apartment, where they'd had sex. Heather knew it wasn't what would've happened tonight, but the dream had been so very real that she actually felt sick.

There was a knock on the door of her bedroom, and she tried to call out to Sebastian to come in, but couldn't manage any words. He opened the door anyway and came into the room, holding a glass of cold water, which he set down on her bedside table before sitting on the bed next to her.

He didn't try to force her to talk or explain what was going on, just sat there to be with her. Eventually, she calmed down and was able to sit up and drink some of the water he'd brought for her.

"Thank you," she said.

"You're welcome," he replied with a warm smile, "go back to sleep, Heather. You look like you need it."

She moved over to him and gave him a hug, then lay back down and went back to a thankfully dreamless sleep.

Chapter 19

TRUTH HURTS

Heather was alone in the bed when she woke up the next morning. Her head was pounding, and she had no idea what time it was or even where she was for a second, but it must have been late because the sun was well and truly streaming in through the windows.

She got up, looked around the room vaguely, and realized that she was out at Galena. Then it all came rushing back to her, and she suddenly felt sick. She had broken up with Harrison yesterday. Heather dashed to the adjoining bathroom and promptly vomited in the toilet there. Last night's pizza and alcohol made their way out of her body, and when she was finished, she flushed the toilet and went back into the room to grab her toiletries bag.

Heather brushed her teeth and had a shower, feeling a lot more human after she did. She got dressed and went and knocked on Sebastian's door, but there was no answer. She made her way downstairs, and when she reached the bottom of the staircase, she heard familiar voices coming from the sitting room nearby.

When she reached it, she grinned massively as she saw Gabriel and Ariana sitting on the sofa, talking to Sebastian.

"Oh my god, what are you guys doing here?" Heather rushed

over to give each of them a hug, then sat down in between Ariana and Sebastian.

"Seb called us last night and asked if we would come up today," Gabriel told her.

"Did you?" Heather asked Sebastian, and he nodded.

"We've just been catching up," Ariana said with a smile.

"See?" Heather laughed, "I told you that it was getting frosty down in Hell."

"Yeah, positively freezing, I heard," Ariana smirked.

"Oh, please, as if I could stay angry at you when this one"—he indicated to Heather—"was all 'Seb, I'm saaaaaad, and the only thing that could possibly make me feel better is if you forgave Ariana!'" he rolled his eyes and laughed.

"Did you really say that, Heather?" Ariana laughed as well.

"Of course, what's the point in calling off your wedding if you can't use it to your advantage. In fact, you guys can expect to hear that a lot, now"—Heather flipped her hair—"'I'm sad, can you get me a drink?', 'I'm sad, can we watch something I like, instead?', 'I'm sad, can you let me beat you at pool, Sebastian?'"

Everyone laughed as Sebastian said, "Not fucking likely. I love you, Heather, but not *that* much."

Heather was so grateful to Sebastian for inviting Gabriel and Ariana to come to Galena. Their presence was soothing after having such a rough time the night before. She was lucky to have people in her life who loved and supported her as much as they did. She sent a text to Hayden.

Hi, Hayden. Did everything go okay last night?

"Who are you texting?" Ariana asked her.

"Hayden. I just wanted to make sure Harrison got home safely," Heather frowned as she said it, not knowing exactly where he was staying right now.

Maybe, if he knew she was out at Galena, he might've gone home to their apartment. Heather knew, though, that Harrison was a man of his word. If he'd told her that he wasn't going to stay there, he wouldn't have stayed there even if he knew she wasn't there.

"So, you blew up your life, even after I told you not to, huh?" Ariana gave her a sad smile.

"Yeah, look, I considered not doing it, but then I just backed up a truckload of TNT and went to town, instead."

"I'm really sorry, Heather," Gabriel's voice was quiet, "I can tell that you've been trying to get past it, the last couple of months. I know you haven't done this on a whim."

"Not like *some* people, who just walk away without thinking," Sebastian said, directing this at Ariana.

She grimaced, "You've got me. I'm the first to admit that I fucked up, Sebastian." Ariana looked at Heather, "Are you okay if I ask Sebastian that thing we talked about, or would you rather not be here when I do?"

"No, go ahead," she looked at Sebastian now, "I'm fine to hear it, so feel free, to be honest."

Gabriel looked tense, and Heather felt like Ariana had probably warned him about the conversation that she was wanted to have with Sebastian, who looked curious.

"What was it like when I left?"

Sebastian cringed, Heather knew that there was certainly a time that he would've relished in giving Ariana a blow-by-blow rundown of that terrible time, knowing that it would be painful for her. The current circumstances, with Heather's breakup with Harrison being so fresh, definitely made this harder for everyone, though.

"Are you sure you want to know?" His reply reminded Heather of the way Ariana had responded to her own question regarding the night of the charity event. Ariana nodded, and Sebastian looked at Gabriel, "And you want me to answer this?"

"Go ahead, Seb. Ariana is back now, what happened is in the

past and can't hurt us, anymore," he put his arms around Ariana and hugged her to him, tightly.

"Well, you walked out on me, and I was left in your shitty hotel room. I was so fucking angry at you, I considered running after you and forcing you to come back upstairs and face Gabriel, but I didn't. I felt so guilty for letting you go.

"I went back upstairs and had to tell everyone what you'd done. We were all just sitting around Gabriel's suite in total shock. When I told them all that you'd walked out, taking all your things with you and had told me you had a plane to catch, I watched Gabriel break into pieces in front of my eyes."

He looked at Gabriel, who had his eyes downcast, and Heather felt her heart throb painfully; it reminded her of what she'd done to Harrison yesterday. Ariana looked terrible as well, and Sebastian was clearly not enjoying this.

"Are you sure you want me to continue?" he asked Ariana, and she nodded, "Okay, well we'd just won the Grammys, and that stupid fucking Ariel story was blowing up thanks to the skank I'd brought with me, sorry she was such a bitch, by the way. Anyway, we had to do about a thousand interviews.

"Gabriel was pretty much catatonic, so Hayden and I would answer questions on his behalf. Harrison was constantly stressed because Heather was almost as bad as Gabriel."

Heather whimpered at the sound of Harrison's name and what she'd inadvertently put him through, even though it was nothing like what she knew she was putting him through now.

"Cooper was lording it the fuck over everyone, saying that he knew all along that you were going to do something like this. I got into a massive fight with him and almost punched him."

Gabriel looked as shocked as Heather felt at hearing this and said, "I don't remember that."

"You weren't there," Sebastian smiled, "anyway, basically, it was all fucking shit."

"The last message you left me," Ariana asked, "what made you leave it?"

Sebastian looked away from her and didn't answer the question.

"Sebastian?"

He gave a heavy sigh, then looked Ariana in the eyes and continued, "It got pretty dark. For a long time, I was scared to leave Gabriel alone. He said some things to me that hinted that he was pretty depressed, but that day, he outright told me that he was going to get a bottle of pills and take them all.

"I refused to leave his side after that. I think that my reaction shook him out of it a bit, because that night when we were out to dinner, he admitted that he needed to let go of you. He called you and told you he was letting you go. I followed him when he left the table, of course. Leaving that message was the second-worst day for him, I think," Sebastian looked at Gabriel, then, who gave a small nod.

"I babysat him for at least two weeks, sat in a chair next to the bed while he slept, would barely even let him shit in peace," Sebastian gave a half-laugh, "he got really fucking annoyed about it, and I told him that I'd let him have some freedom if he agreed to do some sort of counseling.

"We were on tour, so we found a therapist who would do Skype sessions, and finally, he started to come around."

This was all new information to Heather; she hadn't realized how bad Gabriel had actually gotten. She looked over at Ariana and saw her openly crying at this news. Gabriel had her pulled toward him so that her back was against his chest and was hugging her tightly.

"I'm sorry I put you through that," she whispered, "all of you. I didn't know. I was so stupid; I thought I was doing the right thing, but it almost caused Gabe to…" she trailed off.

Sebastian got up from where he was sitting, walked over to the couple, and put his arms around both of them. After a few seconds, he returned to his seat.

"I accept your apology, Ariana. I'm also sorry for being such an asshole to you when you two got back together. I was just scared that you'd do the same thing again. It was pretty obvious from the outset that you'd changed a lot, though. Walking The Gauntlet, being subjected to bullshit from paparazzi, being subject to bullshit from us…" he indicated to himself and Heather, causing everyone to laugh, and it lightened the mood slightly.

There was silence in the room for a few minutes as everyone reflected on what had just been revealed. Finally, Heather gave a big sigh and said, "Too bad we didn't have this conversation six months ago when we could all be happy. Why are you such a stubborn fucker, Seb?"

"Just me, lover?" He laughed. "If I recall correctly, there was someone else who only just got over their shit enough to forgive, Ariana."

"Who? Me? You must be remembering incorrectly, *I* was completely magnanimous and absolutely lovely to Ariana always and forever," Heather raised her eyebrows at Sebastian.

"Oh, my bad. Yes, I completely remember it that way, now that I think about it. Right, Gabriel?"

Gabriel was still holding Ariana facing away from him, so he couldn't see her face as he laughed, "Yes, of course. Heather was the nicest and sweetest person to Ariana ever since we got back together. It was just you being a dick, Seb."

"I'm surprised that any of you have forgiven me," Ariana said quietly, and the look on her face betrayed the inner torment that she was suffering right now.

Gabriel let go of her and moved around so that he was in front of her, "Oh, Ari. Nothing from the past can hurt us now. Look at me?" she raised her eyes to meet his, "Heather and I are fine, and we're here with you. We can't change the past, you've worked hard to become a different person, don't fall back there, sweetheart."

He kissed her, and Heather looked away from them. Seeing Gabriel and Ariana so in love was painful. They had been through so much and come out the other side, why couldn't she have done the same with Harrison? Gabriel had forgiven Ariana for leaving, even when he'd become suicidal after she left. All Harrison had done was sleep with someone else.

Maybe there was a chance that they might come out the other side of this together, too. Heather knew that it was what she wanted more than anything else in the world, but she also knew that she just couldn't do it until these nightmares stopped. Her next session with Zoe was on Wednesday; she'd have to talk to her about some kind of technique or something to force her subconscious into submission. It was clear that she couldn't continue living like this.

A small part of her had hoped that calling off the wedding and leaving Chicago would flip the 'off switch' in her brain for the nightmares. It had been so disappointing to have another one last night as if she hadn't gone to the effort of blowing up her life to try and stop it. The reality of her situation came rushing back to her, and she sighed deeply.

"What am I going to do when I go back to Chicago tomorrow, guys?"

She rubbed the bare skin on her ring finger where her engagement ring should be sitting as she said it, staring across the room and out the window showing the view of the green fields of Sebastian's property.

Ariana moved closer to her and gave her a hug, "You'll survive. One day at a time. Do you have to go back tomorrow?"

"Yeah, I do," Heather gave her a tight smile, "in my infinite wisdom, I blew up my life two days before my fashion line launches in department stores. I have press events booked solid. In fact, I'll probably need to leave stupidly early. Sorry, Seb."

"Hey, I don't care. We do whatever you need to do when we're on 'Heather Duty,' lover." He smiled at her.

"We have to go back tomorrow, as well," Gabriel said, "Ross drove us here, so you can come back with us if you want to."

"Oh, that would be great." Heather appreciated the offer. "In all honesty, I actually don't give a shit about Serenity right now. If it weren't for the women that I have working for me, I'd close up shop tomorrow, hole myself up in a room and drink alcohol while eating ice cream for the rest of my life."

"Thank fuck for those women, then," Ariana said with a grimace.

"Okay, enough doom and gloom," Sebastian announced, "we have a whole day ahead of us. What does anyone say to going for a swim?"

"Swimming in January?" Ariana asked him, "Hard pass, thanks!"

"My dear, Ariana, what kind of rock star would I be if I didn't have an indoor heated swimming pool for just such an occasion?" He raised an eyebrow at her.

"Umm, you'd be the kind of rock star that any of the other three I know are like?" She laughed, and he smiled as well.

"You know what, I've missed you, Ariana Chamberlain!" he announced to them all.

"I'm glad to hear it," Gabriel told him.

"Sorry to say, Seb, I didn't think we'd be swimming today, so I didn't bring anything to swim in." Ariana shrugged.

"Hey, I don't think that's ever stopped you before!" Gabriel laughed, then dropped his head to hers and kissed her again.

When they finished their kiss, Heather told Ariana, "I brought more than one swimsuit, you can borrow one of mine."

"You brought more than one swimsuit for a two-day trip to Galena?" Ariana laughed.

"Correct. Do you even know me?"

Ariana followed her upstairs to the room that she was staying in, and they came back down in their swimsuits. Heather saw the pure, unadulterated lust in Gabriel's eyes when he saw Ariana and felt the pain of Harrison's absence. She knew that he would look at her like that if he were here, too.

Once the guys had gone upstairs and changed, with Gabriel borrowing some swimming trunks from Sebastian, they came down all tanned skin and bulging muscles.

"Woo! Sexy!" Heather couldn't resist yelling at them with a laugh.

"Thanks, lover, you don't look too bad, yourself!" Sebastian gave her an obvious wink, and both Gabriel and Ariana laughed at them.

They made their way through the house to a room at the back of it. When Sebastian pushed open the door, Heather was amazed to find an absolutely stunning pool tucked away behind it. It was lit around the edges with underwater lights, and when Sebastian flicked a switch, and the overhead lights came on to light up the room, she actually gasped.

The whole area was tiled, and behind a glass wall on the other side of the room, she could see there was a gym with state-of-the-art equipment that overlooked the pool. It was a concrete pool, taking up almost all of the vast room; he'd even gone to the effort of having someone tile the Cruise Control symbol into the middle of it. Over near one side of the room was a raised spa that could be accessed from some steps within the pool.

Above them, the dropped ceiling contained hundreds of tiny lights dotted over a dark blue backdrop and was eerily like looking at a starry, night sky. To the other side of the room were massive, glass French doors leading to the outside grounds and big windows with the same dark, wooden framing that allowed for a spectacular view. Next to those was a tiled, open shower. The rest of the spare area was taken up with cushioned loungers for people to relax on, and there was an open cupboard with towels next to a rack of bathrobes.

"Holy shit," Ariana was the first one to speak.

"It's pretty nice, isn't it?" Sebastian sounded pleased with himself.

"The Four Seasons called, they want their indoor pool area back, Seb!" Ariana laughed.

"Ahem," he faked a cough, "I think you can clearly see that this is a *Cruise Control* pool. Not a Four Seasons pool!" He indicated to the logo.

"Yes, we see that," Heather laughed, "heaven forbid you own anything without that damn logo on it."

She walked casually over to him, as though she was going to just look at the symbol, but shoved him hard as soon as she was close enough. Sebastian grabbed her arm as he fell, and they both toppled into the pool.

They came up for air, laughing as Gabriel jumped in after them, and Ariana lowered herself carefully into the pool. The next two hours were spent chilling out in the pool area. Sebastian did go and get them drinks, and they sat in the spa, talking and drinking for a while. It was relaxing, and Heather was able to unwind, enjoying this time with her friends.

When they got out of the pool, they took turns rinsing off in the shower before grabbing robes to put on over their swim clothes and heading upstairs to change. As she was pulling on a fresh outfit, her phone lit up, and she saw that not only had Hayden replied to her text from earlier, but she had a text from Harrison, as well. Her heart leaped to her throat as she read it.

I love you, angel.

Heather dropped onto the bed and gave way to tears. She was dying inside; this thing between them was raw and painful. She didn't even know how to respond to his text. What could she say? She loved him, too, but he knew that. What would she gain from sending him that? Her endless amounts of love for him meant nothing when she couldn't get past what he'd done.

She was committed, with everything that was within her, to try to get past it. Heather did not want to give him hope that it would happen, though. Until she could sleep peacefully, she couldn't make any commitment to Harrison Fletcher. She backed out of his chat and checked Hayden's instead.

It was okay. He got really drunk. I stopped him from telling everyone you've broken up on the way out.

Thanks, Hayden. I'm sorry.

I'm not the one that's hurting, Heather. You don't need to apologize to me.

Ouch. It was the very painful truth.

Apologizing to him won't change anything.

I know. I'm not angry at you. He wants to go out again tonight. Just be prepared. I don't know how long it'll be until he spills everything, especially if he gets wasted again.

Damn, Harrison Fletcher. She wanted to text him and tell him to stay safe at home with Hayden, but that wasn't her place anymore. A part of Heather knew that he would probably do it if she asked him to, though.

I need him more than I need to breathe, Hayden. Just…keep him safe. Please. Do that for me.

Always, Heather. That's what I'm here for.

She hadn't intended to reply to Harrison's text, but now Heather wondered if she should. She needed to say something, but she wanted to be careful. There was a real concern that she might say something that could tip him over the edge and cause him to do something stupid, but not replying might equally do the same.

Heather looked at his text for five full minutes. Typing and deleting, then typing again, a reply to him multiple times before she finally sent one.

I love you, too. Please be safe. I need you to be safe.

She'd refrained from using his name; it might be the thing that tipped him over the edge if she did. It must have been less than ten seconds before he replied to her.

I will. I know you're out at Galena, when are you coming back?

Tomorrow. I have a shitload of press to do for Serenity.

What will you tell them about us?

Fuck. She hadn't thought about that. They would ask, was there any point in lying now? Especially when she would be calling vendors in between interviews to cancel their wedding.

What do you want me to say?

I don't know.

I don't think I could say 'the wedding is off' without losing my shit completely right now, anyway.

Even typing it made her feel nauseated. Combining that with the familiarity of sending texts to Harrison was making her want to cry. It took longer for his reply to come through this time, and Heather wondered what he was doing. She'd just about given up on waiting for him to reply and was going to go downstairs to find the others when it finally appeared on her screen.

Don't say that, angel. I know it's off. They don't need to know. Not yet.

She closed her eyes to block out the sight in front of her; his pain was evident in his text, and she couldn't look at it any longer. Heather inhaled deeply and slowly, counting to ten as she released the breath. She opened her eyes and wrote a reply.

"I'm not comfortable talking about that right now." ← Is that okay?

It held the promise of the truth, while also not committing to anything. Heather also didn't want to deal with the drama down the track of having lied when it inevitably came out that they *had* already broken up when she did these interviews.

Yes. I wish the answer was "we're blissfully happy and

we're getting married in May".

Me too. Also, "and we had crazy hot sex last night".

Shit. Heather had replied without thinking. She wanted to climb into her phone and claw the text back through their connection. There was too much hope in it. She wasn't meant to be giving him that.

I keep thinking about you out at Galena. What we did the last time you were there.

Fuck. Fucking fuckity fuck. This is exactly how phone sex happened between them. Heather needed to put her phone down right now and walk away from this conversation. Tonight, she would go to sleep and be treated with a nightmare of Harrison having sex with another woman. Until that stopped, she couldn't indulge in this. It would give him hope that she was somewhere near forgiveness.

I can't think about it, Harrison. Please don't make me. It hurts too much.

She was on edge, waiting for his reply this time. Unsure of how he would respond to what she'd said.

Okay, angel. I'll stop. I love you. We will need to talk sometime this week.

I know. Remember what I said. Be safe for me. For everyone that loves you.

What Sebastian had told them, earlier, about how dark Gabriel had gotten when Ariana had left him had really scared her. She didn't want Harrison ever to get there, but she also didn't know how she could possibly stop him if she couldn't somehow forgive him and stop these fucking nightly nightmares from happening.

Heather gave way to a fresh set of tears. Eventually, when she had managed to calm down, she made her way downstairs and found the others in the games room, playing pool.

"Hey there, lover. Just in time to see me kick Ariana's ass as punishment for ditching us. Clearly, she didn't think she was ever going to come back as she has *not* been practicing."

Ariana laughed and pointed her pool cue at Sebastian, "Yes, but now I have the rest of my life to try and beat you, so there's that."

"Thirteen years of friendship, and I'm still trying, so good luck with that, darling!" Heather laughed.

When their game of pool finished with a resounding victory from Sebastian, they all moved into the kitchen, where Ariana made a pasta dish for their dinner. Gabriel helped her by making a salad, while Heather and Sebastian sat on the stools at the bench watching them.

"I like the new staff that you've hired for the place," Heather said casually to Sebastian.

"Yeah, they're okay. The price is right, too; they work for free."

"Really? Did you use a company to find them, you must let me know how you stumbled upon such a deal, darling. They're both so pretty, too. I always wish for attractive help. Nice to look at, you know!" Heather looked shocked.

"Oh, yes. All my staff must be able to go straight from the kitchen to the runway, and they're actually not through an agency at all. I literally just sent one text to a special number, and they appeared the next morning like magic."

"My word, how fascinating! Does this work all the time?" she asked him.

"I must be honest; it's the first time I've tried it. I'll let you know if it happens again."

"Please do!"

Ariana laughed at them, "Yes, yes, Gabe and I are suckers to come here and make you guys dinner. Can one of you go ask Ross if he wants to eat with us? I feel bad that he's been wandering around on his own, all day."

Sebastian saluted Ariana, then disappeared out the back of the house to some unknown area of the property to find Ross.

"I did wonder where he was. For real, it's so weird having 'staff,' don't you guys think?" Heather cringed.

"Yes!" Ariana said immediately as she began to serve up plates of pasta. "I don't like it. I feel like a bitch when he's sitting around for hours doing nothing while I do whatever I've got to do. I know it's his job, but it's so odd."

"Sebastian's got no problem with it, of course. He's got a maid and a groundskeeper for this place," Heather rolled her eyes, "of course, look at the place. He'd never manage it without help. Can you see him going around here with a vacuum cleaner?"

They were all laughing when Sebastian walked into the room about ten seconds later with Ross following him, "I heard that, Heather York, and I'll have you know that I am perfectly capable of using a vacuum cleaner. Just because I can, doesn't mean I will."

"I'll believe it if I ever see it," she grinned at him.

"Unlikely. This way, I get to give someone gainful employment, *and* I don't have to go around this place with a vacuum cleaner. The way I see it, everybody wins!"

"Did you want to eat with us, Ross?" Ariana asked him with a kind smile.

"No thank you, Miss Chamberlain, I don't want to intrude on your time with your friends. If it's all right, can I take a plate with me, though? Your cooking is the best!"

Ariana thanked him for the compliment, dished him up a plate of pasta, and put some of Gabriel's salad on it before handing it to him along with some cutlery that he took off to wherever it was that he was staying on the property.

They took their food to the dining room table, and Sebastian got everyone drinks. As they were eating, Ariana cleared her throat to say something.

"So, Heather, we've all been talking," Ariana looked nervously around the table, "well, you've said to all of us that you aren't feeling okay about going back to your apartment."

"Yeah, just the thought of being there makes me feel sick," Heather sighed as she said it.

"Well, we were thinking that I could help you find a rental. Just a short-term lease, in case…things change."

"What? No, you don't need to do that. Besides, Harrison and I need to talk about money. I mean, technically, I don't have any other than what I get from Serenity, and Serenity owes a shitload of money to Harrison."

Shit. She'd actually forgotten about that fact until just this minute. What the hell *was* she going to do about money? It had been a long time since it had even factored in to any of her thoughts, outside of the loan from Harrison to Serenity. She wasn't even taking a salary from Serenity—she didn't need to—and she wanted it to be profitable, so her not taking a salary accelerated when that would be.

"Heather," Gabriel smiled at her, "nobody is going to see you out on the bare bones of your ass, least of all, Harrison. I mean, if you want to get technical, you've been with him so long that you're almost certainly entitled to some sort of money. I'd fucking hope that you guys never reach the lawyer stage anyway."

Lawyers? Her and Harrison? Another thought that hadn't occurred to her until now. He'd be able to afford the best lawyers in Chicago if he wanted them. Ones that would push her around and ensure she got as little as possible. Despite what Gabriel was saying, she had done nothing to earn the money that Harrison had. Yes, she'd been by his side, but she also hadn't worked since Cruise Control became famous, not until she had started Serenity.

Sebastian saw her face and glared at Gabriel, "You're freaking her out, Gabriel! There aren't going to be any lawyers, and you don't need to worry about money. I'd literally go and write you a check for a million dollars right now if you needed it, lover. Do not stress about money."

Heather stared numbly at Sebastian as he said this. It was such a casual comment, yet the fact that it was true was plain for everyone to see. He really would hand over that much cash to her if she needed it, and realistically, it wouldn't make much of a dent in his bank account if he did.

"Now you're freaking Heather out," Ariana frowned at Sebastian, "the point is not to do with lawyers or stupid amounts of cash, the point is that we're here for you, Heather. We will find you a place to stay, and if it makes you feel better, we'll keep a tally of any money that we outlay for you, and you can pay us back whenever, okay?"

Heather couldn't stop tears from springing to her eyes, and Ariana got out of her seat, came around to Heather, and gave her a hug.

"We're here for you," she said to her softly. "We're clearly all *very* over the top," she rolled her eyes at the two men, "but we're here for you."

The rest of their dinner was a lot more relaxed. They ended up watching a movie in the theater room that night. Heather drank quite a bit, and ended up crying when she saw pictures of Harrison and Hayden going to a club again. She had gone to bed before any pictures of them leaving were posted online, she just had to trust that Hayden would keep him safe.

In the middle of the night, she woke from a nightmare where Harrison was having sex with Maddy, while Heather stood at the side of the room with a lawyer who was telling her that she had to give him all of the money she had. She was showing him her empty purse and crying, telling him that she didn't have any.

Heather hadn't realized how loudly she'd been crying until Ariana appeared in the doorway, "Do you want some company?"

Heather nodded, and Ariana entered the room. She gave Heather a hug, then lay down next to her in the bed.

"I'm dying without him, Ariana, but I can't stop what happens in my head after I go to sleep."

"I know, Heather. I don't think there's anything I can say that will fix this, but I know you're trying."

Once again, with a friend by her side, she sank into a dreamless sleep.

~FEBRUARY~

WHERE IS HEATHER'S ENGAGEMENT RING?

As we all know, the rumors just won't stop coming surrounding the wedding of Cruise Control bass guitarist Harrison Fletcher and his fiancée, Heather York. The pair were meant to be getting married in May, but amidst one cheating scandal after another, the couple appears to have split.

Heather's clothing line, Serenity, launched in high-end department stores last month, and eagle-eyed fans noticed that Heather was not wearing her engagement ring during any of her interviews for the launch. That beautiful piece of bling has been a permanent fixture for Heather since Harrison proposed at his thirtieth birthday party last June.

Surely, this is the confirmation that we have all been waiting for that the wedding is off, right?

Chapter 20

ONE MILLION DOLLARS

Zoe frowned at Heather as she sat on the sofa opposite her, with her legs tucked up underneath her. Her therapist was young, and they got on better than Heather did with Brendan. She was a calm presence in Heather's life, with her soft, quiet voice and thoughtful questions about what was happening each week.

"So, you're still having the nightmares?"

"Yes," Heather cringed, "I've done all the things we talked about. I'm focusing on work as much as I can. I've stopped looking at the pictures and articles, even when I wake up from my nightmares. Harrison and I have talked; I even went to another bloody joint counseling session with him last Saturday, despite the fact that we've broken up now. Nothing will stop them."

"I can see that this is really frustrating for you," Zoe frowned.

"Not to mention, tiring as fuck," Heather said with a sigh.

"How did the conversation and counseling session with Harrison go?" Zoe asked her.

"Well, the conversation was kind of just to organize the counseling session. I'm really worried about Harrison, though," Heather admitted, "he looks terrible. He's still going out and getting drunk *all* the time. It's very concerning."

"Do you think that concern for him is playing into why the nightmares haven't stopped?"

Heather considered this for a moment or two before replying, "No. The nightmares have been constant since he cheated. They haven't gotten any worse or better since Harrison started partying on a daily basis."

"You've moved out of the apartment now, haven't you?" Zoe wrote a note down on her notepad.

"Yes, but so has he," Heather gave a hollow laugh, "it's sitting there empty. We need to do something about it, but neither of us seems to be the one who wants to pull the trigger."

The issue of their shared apartment was one of those things that just sat at the edges of her consciousness. She was brought to the brink of tears if she dared to think about getting rid of it. At the same time, she couldn't bear the thought of actually going back there. Sebastian and Hayden had kindly gone there and gotten all of her things to take to the apartment that Ariana had found for her.

Heather's new apartment felt transient. It was on a month-by-month lease and came fully furnished. It felt like living in a hotel. If she was being honest with herself, nothing there was hers. It wasn't home for her by any stretch of the imagination.

Harrison had moved in with Hayden, and Heather couldn't be more grateful for this fact. She'd had more text conversations with Hayden than she could count; he kept her up to date with what Harrison was up to. Sometimes Heather wondered if this was good for her mental health. She'd been meaning to mention it to Zoe, actually.

"Hayden basically gives me a blow-by-blow account of what Harrison does every day. Is this healthy?"

"Did you ask him to do this?" Zoe raised her eyebrows.

"Well, not really. I mean, kind of. I just need to know that Harrison is okay, you know?"

Zoe wrote some more notes on her pad, "How would you feel if Hayden didn't give you these updates?"

"I don't know. Stressed, I guess. I've spent every day of the last decade knowing where Harrison is and what he's doing. The idea of not knowing freaks me out."

"But you told me that he went on that tour without you? Did he keep you constantly updated while he was away?" Zoe looked surprised.

"Well, no. Not then." Heather pursed her lips.

"Okay, so what I'm hearing is that your need to know what Harrison is doing every day is a recent development?"

"Yeah…maybe since he got drugged and slept with someone else?" Heather shrugged with a wry grin.

"Maybe." Zoe wrote more notes, "How are you feeling now that you've officially canceled the wedding?"

"Shit. I don't even care about the money we lost on deposits, it just felt so final to make those calls, though," Heather grabbed a tissue and wiped some tears away from her eyes.

"Did you consider having Harrison make the calls instead of you? Or have someone else do it for you?" Zoe looked at her with curiosity.

"I could never make Harrison do that; it would kill him. I don't know, I never thought of asking someone else to do it. I guess it felt a bit like it was my punishment for calling off the wedding."

"Hmmm, I see," Zoe said and wrote some notes again, "do you feel that you should be punished for doing that?"

"Not really. I don't know. I feel guilty that I couldn't get past what happened for both of our sakes," Heather sighed.

"What happened to Harrison was terrible, but your feelings are valid, Heather. You're entitled to feel whatever you feel about it," Zoe smiled at her, "you're still working, right?"

"Yes, the one fucking thing in my life that is going right is Serenity. Even though I couldn't give less fucks about it."

"You've said this before, why do you not care about your business?"

"Because," Heather gave her a forced smile, "nothing matters if I don't have Harrison."

"So, you put no value on having a successful business if your relationship isn't successful as well?"

Ouch. That was a painful way to put it. Heather was ashamed of the way she no longer cared about Serenity. It made her feel awful that this thing that she had dreamed about for years and worked incredibly hard for meant so little to her now.

"It's not quite like that," Heather frowned and tried to find the right words to describe it, "I've never had to give a shit about having a successful relationship because I had it. What's the saying? 'You don't know what you've got till it's gone,'? Everything I've done, it's been while secure in the knowledge that Harrison was there with me, by my side through thick and thin. No matter what happened, it was us against the world."

"Okay, so now it's you against the world, but you said that your friends have been very supportive?"

Heather smiled a genuine smile, "Yeah, they've all been great. So supportive. Sebastian even offered me a million dollars."

"I'm sorry, he offered you *what*?!" Zoe's eyebrows shot up so high that Heather thought they might fly off her face entirely.

"Hah!" She smirked. "I never thought I'd manage to surprise you with something."

"I'll admit, that is something that I haven't had a client say before," Zoe smiled at her, "was he serious?"

"Deadly. I was worried about money because all of the money we have is Harrison's, and I haven't been taking a salary from Serenity, which is the only work that I've done in years."

"Did you take him up on this offer?"

"Of course not!" Heather was mildly offended.

"Were there strings attached to it?" Zoe asked her.

"No. What? Why would there be strings attached to that?" Heather frowned.

"Because it's a million dollars, what did Sebastian want from you in return?" Zoe seemed confused.

"Nothing. For me to be happy and not stressed, I guess?" Heather shrugged. Zoe was writing rapidly in her notepad now, and Heather laughed, "Oh god, you're about to tell me that my friendship with Seb is 'wildly inappropriate,' I can just feel it."

"That's interesting phrasing that you've used, do *you* think it's wildly inappropriate?" Zoe tilted her head to the side, and Heather wondered if this was just a standard therapist move, since Brendan had done it several times, as well.

"No, but someone else said it to me, and it's stuck in my mind since," Heather laughed, Sebastian hadn't really come up much in these sessions before now.

"I'm aware of the rumors about you two," Zoe admitted, which surprised Heather since she was the consummate professional. She had never given a hint to any further insight into Heather's life than what she had been told by Heather herself, "From our discussions, I understand that they are not true, of course, but I find it interesting that someone has said that to you."

"Well, those rumors are a part of it. He has me in his phone as 'My Lover,' and his nickname for me is 'lover' now, as well. It's just a joke, though." Heather shrugged again.

Zoe was writing once more; she looked up and met Heather's eyes, "And he offered to give you a million dollars?"

Heather wrinkled her nose, now that she was saying it out loud, she could see how it would seem strange, "Yes, but that's nothing to Seb, and it doesn't matter because I didn't take the money, anyway."

"How does Harrison feel about your friendship with Sebastian?" Zoe asked her, then amended, "Before you split up, of course."

Heather shook her head and laughed, "You're not going to believe me, but he was fine with it. He was fine with it before we split up, he was fine with it while we were splitting up, and even now, he's still fine with it. Nothing's changed between Sebastian and me during that time; my friendship with him is separate from my relationship with Harrison. One of those is sexual, one is platonic, and I can tell you now that I did *not* spend ten years being celibate!"

"Okay, we might circle around to this again in the future," Zoe warned her.

Heather rolled her eyes but laughed again, knowing that she did not have Zoe convinced that her friendship with Sebastian was not sexual, and she hadn't even told her half the shit they said and did.

"What did you do, financially, if you didn't take Sebastian up on his *very* generous offer?"

"Harrison and I talked about it; he's still suffering from major guilt, so he took exactly half of his available cash and put it in a bank account in my name."

"I see," Zoe was writing again, "how did that make you feel?"

Heather sighed, "Like shit. I didn't want it. It's a stupid amount of money, so I haven't touched it. I opened a second new account in my own name and started drawing a salary from Serenity, instead."

There were very few things of value that Heather had taken away from her relationship with Harrison. She took all of her clothing, of course, but anything that was a joint item had been left behind. She'd taken her Tesla as well; it was about the only valuable thing that she'd kept other than jewelry.

"So, we've somehow managed to circle back to your business. Do you see how it's valuable to you right now, then?" Zoe looked at her with curiosity.

"You're right. I do care about it, and it is important, at the very least, because part of my goal with it was always to give people a job who needed one. I just never imagined that I'd be one of the people who needed a job!" Heather smiled.

At the end of her session, Heather thanked Zoe and headed out to the waiting room where Callum met her and hovered behind her while she paid for her session. She confirmed her booking for the next week, and they made their way down to the black SUV.

"Where are we off to, Miss York?"

"Back to the office, Cal. Thanks!"

He drove her to Serenity's office. They'd had to scale up production again, now that they were officially producing clothing on a larger scale to meet the demand of the stores that were stocking her.

Heather's office was near the back of the building, and she stopped in on the production floor to have a look at the designs that were being hand-sewn by the women there before she made her way to her office.

Her hour with Zoe had given her a lot to think about. Serenity did mean more to her than she realized. Heather had been sinking so far down into the darkness of Harrison not being in her life anymore, that she had lost sight of what was important. She had worked really hard on her company—she employed other women, gave them a livelihood.

It was unfair of her to have neglected it the way she had been. She vowed to herself to make more of an effort with the company. In the meantime, she would pay everyone a bonus this week, and a bigger one for the women who had been with her from the beginning and had stepped up in her mental absence.

Serenity was doing well, and if it took her longer to pay back Harrison, it would just have to take a bit longer. If he decided to call in the debt at any point, she would have to pay him back from the money he'd given her. In her mind, it was his money, anyway, and she had sworn to herself that she wouldn't touch it.

Her wedding dress sat in the corner of her office. It was hanging on a mannequin, covered over with a sheet so it couldn't be seen. This wasn't to keep it a secret; it was because it hurt heather too much to look at it. Every now and again, she would lift the sheet and just stare at the dress. Heather sighed, and even though she knew it wasn't healthy, she sent a message to hayden.

How is he today?

She pulled out a fresh drawing book and, for the first time in two months, started to sketch some ideas for new designs. At first, they were clunky and forced, but soon she got into a rhythm, and it wasn't until she heard someone cough at the doorway to her office two hours later that she realized how much time had passed.

"Hi, Gabriel. This is a nice surprise!" She smiled at him, got up from her desk, and walked over to him for a hug.

"Hey, Heather. Sorry, I didn't want to bother you at work, but I wanted your advice about something, and now that I'm here, I'm thinking this was a bad idea," he looked incredibly nervous; it was very sweet.

"Well, now you've got my curiosity piqued!" she laughed as she led him over to a sofa at the side of her office, and they sat down. "What on earth could Mr. Gabriel Knight want my advice on that warrants a visit to my office?"

"It's about Ariana…" he trailed off.

"Gabriel, if you're going to break up with her, I will slap you." Heather was horrified at the thought. They'd only just gotten back together.

"No, no, pretty much the opposite. I wanted your advice on how…" he trailed off again, paused, then tried another attempt at telling her what he was trying to say, "…as soon as I saw you, I knew it wasn't fair to ask you."

Heather realized what he wanted to ask her with a mixture of horror and delight. He wanted her input on how to propose to

Ariana. She'd given him advice like this in the past, back when he'd first wanted to tell Ariana that he was in love with her. She was reminded of what she'd said to Zoe this morning.

"I've never had to give a shit about having a successful relationship because I had it."

When she'd helped him to plan out his elaborate 'I love you,' she'd had the luxury of being in a secure place with Harrison. She had reveled in helping Gabriel to do it, so pleased that he got to be happy like she had been for so many years. At the same time, she was still happy for them now. They had been through the wringer; they deserved every moment of happiness that they could get.

"You want to ask her to marry you," Heather said with a small smile.

"Yeah, I do. I wanted your help with planning how to do it, but, as I said, it's not fair to ask you. I'm sorry, Heather."

It felt like someone was physically taking a knife to her heart with how much it hurt. She could imagine Harrison back when he had been planning to propose to herself the day of his party. How sweet and nervous he must have been about it, even though there had never been any doubt about what her answer would be.

So many things had changed in the last nine months. If she could go back to that day, would she still say yes? Of course, she would. There was only one night in her life that she would change if she could. Now that she thought about it, would Serenity be as successful as it was now if she hadn't done Saturday Night Live?

It was hard to say because, at the end of the day, she *had* done it. Harrison had gone off to California for that charity event, and Heather had gone to New York for SNL, and everything had changed. She'd certainly experienced a great deal of exposure after doing Saturday Night Live, just not necessarily for the right reason.

Nothing of her situation had a bearing on what Gabriel was asking of her, though. That was why she gave him a kind smile and said, "Don't be silly, darling, of course I'll help you. What were you thinking?"

"I'm not sure," he gave her a wry smile, "it has to be perfect, though. I thought about skywriting and hot air balloons and big, grand gestures, but Ari would hate all of those things."

"Thank god you came to me if that's the best you've managed!" Heather laughed.

"I know, right," he laughed as well, but stopped quickly, "I also have an appointment with a jeweler in two hours' time, but I completely get it if you don't want to come with me."

Heather rubbed her ring finger, right where her engagement ring should be sitting. She did this a lot, almost as much as she used to play with the ring itself. It was a constant reminder to her of the broken connection between herself and Harrison.

"I'll see how I feel when it's time for you to leave," she smiled at him, "I won't promise anything, but I love you two, and I'm honored that you're even asking me."

Gabriel gave her a grin, seeming relieved, "So, I thought about maybe taking her away somewhere to do it. She's got next weekend off work, and I told her that I was planning a romantic weekend away for the two of us."

"If I know anything about Ariana, I know that she isn't like you and me, Gabriel. She won't want a spectacle," she smirked at him, "so no skywriting!"

"I could write her a song…" he considered.

"Meh." She rolled her eyes dramatically.

"There are plenty of women who would die to have a Cruise Control song written about them, you know!"

"Yeah, and you wrote an entire fucking album about Ariana, already. She's in the strange position where you writing a song about her *isn't* something special." Heather poked her tongue out at him.

"Oh, I'd forgotten that."

Heather burst out laughing, "You're useless, Gabriel Knight! Okay, so you're going to take her away somewhere. Any idea where, yet?"

"I don't know. Paris, maybe?" He looked thoughtful.

"Oh. My. God." Heather gasped, and her mouth dropped open as the answer was illuminated to her, as clear as day.

"What's wrong with Paris?" he asked, obviously confused by her reaction.

"What's wrong with Paris is that it's not Washington, DC," Heather told him.

"Washington isn't roma—" his mouth dropped open as well, to match her surprise, "—it's fucking perfect, Heather."

"Do you think that you could get the same room?" Heather asked him, "You *need* to get the same room."

It was in Washington, DC, that Gabriel had first told Ariana that he loved her. He'd written a song about her, the first one he wrote for *Heart Wide Open*, and performed it at a concert that night. Afterward, Heather had kept Ariana distracted while he went up to their room so he could meet her there.

They'd worked with the hotel staff to set up the room. Everything was covered with red rose petals and lit candles. From the door to the suite had been a path of white rose petals that led to the bedroom, which was set up in the same way. On the bed had been the words 'I LOVE YOU' spelled out with white rose petals.

Gabriel had sent her pictures when he got there, and it had looked amazing. They had both been ecstatic with the end result of their planning, and of course, Ariana had completely and utterly loved it.

"Room 1403. I'll never forget it. Best night of my life," he had a massive grin on his face, "oh god, if we can pull this off, it's going to be incredible."

Heather felt a rush of excitement; she was pleased that he'd come to her for this. A part of her was sad, but also thrilled to get to plan this surprise for her friend. They set to work, calling the hotel from her office at once to see if the room was available. It wasn't, but Gabriel offered to pay the difference for the people who were booked into it to stay in the penthouse, instead.

At first, they were speaking to just the normal hotel worker, but they soon put them on to the manager, after taking a deposit for the room from Gabriel's card to ensure they weren't being pranked. This manager wasn't the one they'd dealt with in the past, who had since moved on from the hotel, but they had heard the story of the 'I LOVE YOU.' Apparently, it had become an urban legend amongst the hotel staff, and the manager was delighted to get to be a part of the sequel.

After that, they booked a private plane to fly Ariana and Gabriel to Washington next Saturday and a limousine service to take them to the airfield. Once that was all done, it was time for Gabriel's appointment with the jeweler.

"Are you sure you want to come?" he asked her.

"You've got to be shitting me. In for a penny, in for a pound. I've worked too hard on the proposal itself, now. Don't think I'm going to miss out on helping you to pick out the ring!" She laughed.

Heather told Callum that he was free to take the black SUV to her apartment building, and they would go with Ethan Jackson, Gabriel's bodyguard, to the jeweler. Once they were in Gabriel's SUV, Heather pulled out her phone and saw a text from Hayden. She'd practically forgotten that she'd texted him many hours ago.

He's coping. We've got a meeting with Cooper today about Games We Play.

She looked up at Gabriel, "You saw Harrison today?"

"Yeah, we had a meeting about the release for *Games We Play.*"

"How is he?" She bit her lip.

"Honestly?" She nodded. "He's pretty bad, Heather. I think today's one of the few times I've seen him sober since…" He didn't finish his sentence.

"He's drinking that much?" Heather was concerned.

"Possibly more, I can only speak for when I've seen him."

"I've seen the pics, I was kind of hoping that it wasn't as bad as they make it seem," she sighed. It hurt to hear that Harrison was struggling as badly as she suspected he was.

"Have you read any of the stories?" Gabriel asked her.

"Not really, Zoe thinks it's bad for me. I just search his name sometimes to look at the pictures of him," she admitted.

"They're going hard on this thing about you and Sebastian having an affair; I assume they're still going at you about it?" he asked her.

"Yeah, all the time. Although they like to ask me more about Maddy, whatever they think will get a reaction, I guess," she rolled her eyes.

"Okay, well, they go fucking hard on him about you cheating on him. They say the most disgusting things about you and Seb. I'm worried that he's going to snap soon. Michael has had to physically restrain him a couple of times when he's been drunk."

"God, I hate this"—Heather dropped her head to her hands and shook her head—"it's the worst."

He put an arm around her shoulders and gave her a hug, "Hey, I know it's really bad right now, but don't lose hope that you guys might be able to work through this."

She sighed deeply, then lifted her head to look at him, "You're right. I'm sorry, I don't mean to be a downer. This is an exciting day!"

"Don't fake it for me, Heather," Gabriel smiled kindly at her, "you can be sad. I know you're still happy for us."

Heather was grateful that Ethan pulled the car into a parking bay in front of a row of elegant stores, one of which was the jeweler they were going to visit, so she didn't need to respond to his comment.

"Thank god, there's no paparazzi. I was worried someone would see us going in and ruin the surprise," Gabriel said.

"Hey, just because I'm fucking Seb doesn't mean I'm not free to become your fiancée. I'm sure Ariana will be fine with that!" Heather laughed.

"She just might be, you could take some of the heat off her by being my intended, instead of her," he grinned.

"Why not, then all I'd need to do is just blow Hayden in the middle of Grant Park or something to complete the Cruise Control set. You know…make sure that I catch 'em all!"

They were both laughing as Ethan opened the door to the car, and they got out. There was a security guard at the entrance to the jewelers, and he swiped a card to open the doors for them. This was the type of place that could only be visited by appointment.

Once inside, they were seated at a desk. There was a couple at another desk, talking through the design they were looking at getting made. The woman who'd shown them to the desk offered them tea or coffee. Heather asked for a coffee, but Gabriel, who looked incredibly nervous now, declined.

After a few minutes, she came back with Heather's coffee, escorted by a man who introduced himself as Julian.

"I'm one of the head jewelers here, and I'm honored that you would choose us to create your engagement ring, Mr. Knight," he said with a smile.

"You come very highly recommended. I have to ask, is there any chance of getting the ring by, say, Thursday next week?"

Julian frowned but replied, "Well, if you're happy to pick one of the diamonds that we have in stock, we can certainly accommodate your request, depending on the design. There will be an additional fee for the quick turnaround."

"Not a problem," Gabriel smiled, "as long as we can get the ring by Thursday, that would be amazing."

Julian asked Gabriel a few questions about what type of design and diamond he was looking for. After taking some notes, he walked away before coming back with two large, wooden boxes of rings, one sitting on top of the other. Each box had cushioned velvet lining, and between each cushion, a selection of rings had been placed. He sat the boxes side by side and allowed Heather and Gabriel to look through them.

There must have been around sixty rings all told, each completely unique in design and stone. Eventually, Gabriel came across the one he was looking for.

"It's perfect," he looked up at Heather, the delight evident in his face.

"Yes, darling, it really is."

The ring was fairly simple; it was set with a large, round, brilliant-cut diamond in the center. Down the sides of the band was a twisting pattern with smaller diamonds dotted either side of it. Unlike the engagement ring that Harrison had chosen for Heather, it was understated but very much suited Ariana.

"This one has a matching wedding ring if you'd like to see that?" Julian asked him, and Gabriel nodded.

Julian came back with a wedding band that sat perfectly against the engagement ring. It had the same twisting pattern, with diamonds dotted either side of the twists.

"It's glorious!" Heather gasped.

"We can also make a matching eternity band, should you feel the need for one," Julian assured Gabriel.

"Yes. This is it. Both the engagement ring and the wedding ring, please."

"Not a problem, sir. I'll take these away and bring a selection of diamonds for your choosing." He took both boxes away, leaving the chosen engagement and wedding ring in front of them on a piece of velvet material.

Gabriel couldn't stop staring at them. He was picking them up, placing them together, and then spinning them around to look at every facet of them.

"So, you're getting the wedding ring as well, huh?" Heather

smirked at him, "What if she says 'no'?"

Gabriel snapped his head around to her, looking suddenly panicked, "Oh my god, what if she does?"

Heather laughed, "Don't be stupid, Gabriel. She's not going to say no. I'm just teasing you."

"You're right. Fuck, Heather. I didn't think I'd be this scared to ask her," he cringed.

"Surely you saw Harrison sweating like a motherfucker when he asked me? Just because you know she's going to say 'yes,' doesn't mean it's any less scary."

Again, the painful reminder of the night that the only man she'd ever loved had proposed to her. Still, she was here to support Gabriel, not dwell on the past. Julian returned with another wooden box, this one was also lined with velvet and contained roughly twenty diamonds for Gabriel to choose from.

Each diamond had a matching Gemological Institute of America certificate that gave information about the cut, color, clarity, and carat. They had narrowed it down to a choice between two diamonds. Each was quite large, but the slightly smaller one was better quality overall.

Heather looked at the GIA certificate for the smaller diamond and laughed, "Hey, this one is dated the fifteenth of June. Wasn't that the date you guys first went out?"

Gabriel looked at the certificate and went completely pale, "2018. This was literally certified on the day of our first date."

"Gabriel, you have to get it!" Heather gasped.

"Yes. This one, please," he indicated to their choice, "it has to be *this* diamond."

"Very good, sir. I completely understand. What a crazy, random happenstance!" Julian grinned as he took the diamonds away again.

Gabriel handled the rest of what was required of him. He paid an exorbitant sum for the ring that made Heather wonder, vaguely, just how much Harrison had paid for hers, considering it was so much more extravagant, and they headed back to the SUV.

Once they were on their way to Heather's apartment, Gabriel turned to her, "I can't thank you enough for helping me today, Heather."

"You're one of my favorite people in the world, darling. I'm just honored that I got to be a part of it."

It really was the truth.

Chapter 21

AARON, AARON HAMILTON

As she walked out of the bathroom, toweling her hair dry, Heather noticed that her phone was buzzing on the bedside table, just as it fell silent. It was Thursday morning, and she was about to head to Serenity—the new designs she'd started a few weeks ago were coming along nicely. She and Rachel had started making a few prototypes. Heather was surprised to see the name 'Cooper Powell' on the screen as her missed caller.

She didn't have any press events going on at the moment; it was odd for him to be calling her. Heather finished getting dressed, headed down to the parking garage with Callum, and called Cooper back as they were on their way to Serenity.

"Hi, Cooper, I missed your call. What's up?" Heather greeted him when he answered the phone.

"Heather, I need you to come to my office at two today," he said in his usual terse manner.

She rolled her eyes at the way he ordered her around; it was almost like she was his client and not the other way around, "That's not going to work for me. I'm busy today, and you need to give me some advance warning if you want me to come to your office."

"If I'd had advance warning, myself, I'd have given it to you.

Harrison suggested that you might want to come, but I suppose you don't have to be there. We're being given a briefing on the state of the investigation into what happened." He sounded very tense as he said it.

Heather felt shocked, "Have they found out who did it?"

"I don't have details, but I believe an arrest has been made. Are you coming or not?"

Cooper Powell, all business.

"Yes, holy shit, yes. Of course, I'll be there."

They hung up swiftly after that, and Heather realized that she hadn't even had a chance to ask him who else would be at the meeting. She sighed, knowing that Harrison would almost certainly be there, and rightly so, of course. With a horrendous, sinking feeling, she wondered if Maddy would be at the meeting, as well.

Heather thought that she might be sick. Before all of this had happened, she'd like Maddy well enough. They hadn't had massive amounts to do with each other, but she'd always been polite and friendly. It was strange. Because of her daily nightmares, now, Heather felt as though she knew Maddy so much more. Even though she understood that, of course, the woman in her dreams was not the woman in reality.

She picked up her phone again and dialed Zoe's office.

"Hello, it's Heather York calling. I was wondering if there is any possibility of speaking to Zoe at all?" she asked when the receptionist answered her call.

"I'm sorry, Miss York, Zoe is with a client at the moment. I can get her to give you a call back if you'd like?"

"Yes, please," Heather sighed, disappointed even though she had known that this outcome was likely, "if it could possibly be before two o'clock, that would be great. Please tell her that it's important."

"Of course, Miss York."

No doubt, Zoe's receptionist got calls like this frequently. It must be tough dealing with people who were stressed and anxious all the time. Heather decided to send a text to Sebastian.

Hi, darling. Did you hear from Cooper?

She'd be shocked if he hadn't, since Cooper had obviously told Harrison. Sebastian's reply came through.

Yeah. Are you coming?

At least she'd have Sebastian for support, and Ariana would be there, too, hopefully. She cringed as she replied to his text, not wanting to ask but needing to know the answer to the question that was running through her brain.

I am. I'm sure Harrison will be there. Any idea about Maddy?

She held her breath while waiting for his response. The dots on her screen told her that he was typing, and after a tense thirty seconds, she got her answer.

Yes to Harrison. Yes to Madeline. I asked.

Damn it. Fuck, Sebastian was amazing. It was nice that he'd thought to find out on her behalf.

I didn't think to ask. Thanks. Good to know.

Her phone started ringing, and she laughed as she saw that it was Sebastian.

"Hey," she answered him.

"Are you okay, lover?" He sounded worried.

"Yeah, I'll be fine. I mean, I'm not looking forward to it, but I need to know what they've found out, and you guys will all be there," she bit her lip, though. This was an incredibly stressful proposition for her.

"Let me talk to the others. Are you going to Serenity today?"

"Yeah, we're almost there. I didn't call Cooper until I was already on the way, although the distraction will be nice, I guess," she sighed loudly.

"Okay, well, we'll pick you up from there. You don't have to go alone. You'll have us."

"God, I love you, Sebastian Fox." She smiled, even though she actually felt like crying from the relief of knowing that she would have company on the way to Cooper's office.

"Most women do," he laughed.

They ended their call as the car was only a minute or two away from Serenity. Heather opened the browser on her phone and did an image search for 'Harrison Fletcher'. She didn't do this often, now, because it was still incredibly painful when she did, and Zoe told her off for it in every one of their sessions when she had to admit that she hadn't stopped.

There he was, her ex-fiancé, looking tragically beautiful in the pictures of him. These pictures seemed to be from last weekend, and he was leaving yet another nightclub. Hayden was dutifully by his side, and he was being escorted out by Michael. He looked wasted, as usual. Heather didn't think she'd seen a single picture of him lately where he didn't look drunk. Not even on the pictures of him entering the clubs. It was clear to her in those pictures, even if it was perhaps not obvious to anyone else, that he had been drinking before he'd arrived.

It was this kind of knowledge that killed her. The fact that she knew him so well, it made it obvious to her that he needed her in his life as much as she needed him. Perhaps, if she had managed a single full night's sleep in almost four months, she could give them both what they needed.

Heather made her way into Serenity, met up with Rachel, and they set to work. It was an excellent distraction, and she really dove into what they were doing to keep her mind busy—cutting fabrics, pinning them, sewing the designs.

Sometime mid-morning, her phone rang, and Zoe's name was on the screen. Heather answered, walking swiftly away from where they'd been working and closing the door to her office behind her as she entered it.

"Hi, Zoe, thanks for calling me back," Heather didn't want to waste Zoe's time with pleasantries, knowing that she was interrupting her workday with an unscheduled call request, "Cooper rang me this morning. There's a meeting this afternoon at his office. They've arrested someone for the drugging. Harrison and Maddy are both going to be there."

There was silence on the other end of the line for a few seconds before Zoe replied, "I see. You must be feeling quite a lot right now."

"Yeah, I am. It's the first time I'll be seeing Maddy…" she didn't know what else to say.

"Have you thought about what you might say to her?" Zoe asked.

"What? No. I don't want to talk to her at all," Heather frowned; she hadn't thought about talking to Maddy. She'd assumed that she'd just stay as far away from her as possible during the meeting.

"Do you think that it might be beneficial, at all, to talk to her?"

"No. I don't want to talk to her. I have nothing to say," Heather pursed her lips.

"Okay. Well, what about Harrison?" Zoe was calm in the face of Heather's tense tone.

"I'm not sure that I'll talk to him that much, either. I don't really want to go, but I need to know what they've found out," Heather cringed at the impossible situation she was in.

"Of course, that makes sense. Well, I would suggest using grounding techniques if you find yourself becoming overwhelmed. Focus on your breathing. Have something to drink. I'm assuming this meeting isn't just you, Harrison, and Maddy with Cooper?" Zoe asked.

"No, it's everyone that was affected, I think. Sebastian, Ariana, and Gabriel are picking me up, and we're going together."

"That's a good choice; having support will be very beneficial. Does Harrison have support as well?" Heather could practically see Zoe's head tilting to the side as she said it.

"Yes, he does," Heather replied, somewhat defensively, "Hayden's taking him. I would never want him to have no support while I had all the support!"

"Very sensible. I know you care about him very much," Zoe's tone was calming, "unfortunately I need to go as I have a client due in a few minutes. I'm pleased that you called me to discuss this, though. I know that the nightmares haven't stopped, but you *are* making progress, Heather."

It was nice to have that validation. Heather thanked Zoe and hung up the call. After that, she dove right back into her work. Simply focusing on each cut, each stitch she needed to make, and seeing the clothes come to life in front of her eyes allowed her to pass the time until her phone buzzed at a quarter past one with a text from Ariana.

We're here.

Heather hadn't realized how late it had gotten. It took her a few minutes to clear up, and Rachel offered to finish up for her as she shot a text back letting Ariana know that she would be out soon. Thanking Rachel profusely for her help, she made her way to the entrance where Callum met her and escorted her to the waiting SUV.

There were no paparazzi here, today. Heather was amused by that fact, knowing that she was about to get into a car with Gabriel, Ariana, and Sebastian in it. They would've been salivating over the idea of catching them all together.

After she'd gotten inside, Callum got in the passenger side of the car to sit next to Daryl Kelly, Sebastian's bodyguard, as he drove them to Cooper's office. Because there were so many of them together today, it had been decided that Callum would come along as well.

Heather did wonder if the choice to have her own bodyguard come instead of Gabriel or Ariana's was a purposeful one to allow her to be slightly more comfortable at the meeting. If it was, she was grateful. Callum had become one of her favorite people—he was good at his job, and she always felt safer when he was around.

The danger that she was going to face today wasn't a physical one, though. It wasn't something that Callum could ever protect her from. This danger was one that she had prepared to face with Zoe in her counseling sessions, and now was the time to find out if the things she'd learned would keep her safe today.

"Hi, darlings," she greeted them as she buckled her seat belt, and Ariana gave her a hug.

The mood in the car was a somber one, and as Ariana ended their hug, she asked, "Are you ready for this?"

"Are any of us ready for this?" Heather asked with a hollow laugh.

"We're here with you, lover," Sebastian said with a kind smile in her direction, "no matter what we find out, we'll all be with you."

"Thanks, Seb. I can't thank"—she stopped as she choked on her words, took a second, and then continued—"I don't know how I could ever have survived all of this without you guys. I know you've been…helping Harrison as well. Keeping him safe, as much as he'll let you. That's almost more important to me than what you've been doing for me. Thank you, guys."

Heather felt the tears starting to flow, then, as Ariana put her arm around her and hugged her close once more. Gabriel grabbed a tissue from a packet that was next to him and handed it to Heather. Sebastian kicked her leg gently to get her attention as she wiped the tears from her eyes, and she looked up at him.

"We all love you, Heather," he said gently.

"Thanks, I know this must be hard for you guys, too. You've all been through so much. I really appreciate you all making so much effort just to support me."

The trip to Cooper's office didn't take long, and when they arrived, Heather was horrified to see that there was a group of paparazzi collected at the entrance. She wondered how they had gotten wind of this meeting. Had they seen Harrison and Hayden entering the building before them? Oh, god, had Maddy arrived as well? Or were they the first to arrive?

Callum and Daryl got out of the car, came around and opened the curbside door for them to exit. Sebastian was the first to leave the car, followed by Gabriel, then Ariana, and, finally, Heather herself. They stood there for a second, before the paparazzi noted the entire group and descended as Daryl closed the car's door.

The questions she'd had about whether or not they were the first to arrive were answered swiftly as the first person called out a question to her, even though she was at the back of their group.

"Hey, Heather! Harrison is here with Madeline Turner! Is he marrying her in May instead, then?"

It seemed to be the cue for the other reporters to add their questions to the fray. Ariana held Heather's hand as they made their way slowly through the throng.

"Gabriel! How did you propose?" Somebody else called out.

"Show us your ring, Ariana!" Heather squeezed Ariana's hand for comfort, her ring safely hidden between them.

There were already pictures on the internet of Ariana wearing her engagement ring, but Heather had little doubt that today wasn't the day that her friend would want to do a show and tell with the media. They had almost reached the building when one reporter called Sebastian's name to try and get his attention.

"Sebastian! How does it feel to finally be free to be with Harrison's girl? It's what you've always wanted, right?"

It was rare for Seb to lose his cool with the press, but he rolled his eyes, spun around, and strode over to the man as he snarled "Get fucked. You piece of shit."

Daryl reacted almost instantaneously once Sebastian had moved. He stepped in between the two men as the reporter's eyes gleamed with joy at the reaction he'd succeeded in getting, "Ooh, did I touch a sensitive spot, Sebastian? You and Heather *are* screwing, then!"

"I am *not* screwing Heather, and even if I was, it would be none of your god damn business. Just leave her the fuck alone, you miserable failure of a human being."

Callum and Daryl took hold of one of Sebastian's arms each and forced him away from the man, then back over to their group, and they finally made it inside. As soon as he was inside, Sebastian kicked a chair that was sitting near the door, and it went flying across the room.

"Fuck!" he yelled loudly.

Cooper's receptionist, Stephanie Jennings, stared at them in complete shock, "Um, hello. Can I help you?"

There was silence within their group for a second, before Gabriel spoke up, "Hi, Stephanie, it's good to see you, again. We're here to see Cooper."

Stephanie nodded and left the room, presumably to get Cooper.

"Are you okay, Seb?" Gabriel asked him, going over to him and putting a hand on his shoulder.

"No. Fuck. I shouldn't have done that"—he turned back to face them all—"I'm sorry, guys. They were just being such assholes, and I'm over it."

"It's okay, Seb," Ariana said, "we're all stressed, and it's like they know exactly what buttons to push when they want a reaction."

Sebastian looked at Heather, "Are you okay? I probably just made it worse for you, I'm sorry."

They were all on edge, she realized. Every one of them had probably been as stressed as she had been since Cooper had contacted them all this morning and told them about the meeting today. Sebastian's reaction just now was the culmination of not just one day of stress, but almost four months of it since they were drugged. That reporter had caught him at precisely the right moment to be able to get him to snap.

"Hey, what woman doesn't want Sebastian Fox as her overprotective lover?" She grinned at him, trying to lighten the mood, even just a tiny bit.

He blew out a breath of air, "Man, I thought you were going to be pissed at me."

She walked over to him and gave him a hug, "No, but you should apologize to Stephanie. I think you might've scared the living daylights out of her!"

Sebastian looked over at the chair, laying on its side in the middle of the room and cringed. He walked over to it, picked it up and placed it back where it had been before he'd kicked it, just before Stephanie and Cooper walked into the room from a hallway at the back.

"Sebastian, what the fuck is your damage?" Cooper glared at him, obviously infuriated.

"My 'damage' is getting harassed by shitheads when all I want to do is get in the fucking building," Sebastian said though gritted teeth.

Gabriel walked over to stand next to Sebastian, crossed his arms over his chest, and said coolly to Cooper, "Get better security, Cooper, or at least let us know if there's a horde of paparazzi at your front door."

"I was too busy dealing with the police chief sitting in my conference room that's flown to Chicago just to give us a debrief. I didn't realize that Sebastian was going to have a temper tantrum because he had to deal with a few fucking photographers," Cooper seemed to be fired up.

Heather realized that he, too, was clearly stressed out. She had almost forgotten that he was a victim in the drugging, as well. Hell, he'd suffered the worst of them that night, physically, at least.

She was standing next to Sebastian and Gabriel. Heather stepped forward toward Cooper and kept her tone calm and soothing as she said, "Okay, we're obviously all stressed. Shall we go do what we came to do?"

The tension in the room eased a little bit, and Heather was pleased with herself. She'd been learning a lot from Zoe, besides missing the head-tilt thing, that was straight out of her therapist's playbook. Hopefully, she could deal with the rest of what was to come just as well.

Cooper nodded and turned without another word to walk back down the hallway. As they passed Stephanie, Heather heard Sebastian mumble an apology to her for scaring her. It was the opposite to the way they'd gotten out of the car—Heather was leading the way behind Cooper now, with Ariana just behind her, while Gabriel and Sebastian brought up the rear.

Callum and Daryl followed at a distance, and Heather knew that they would stand guard at the door to the conference room. Sure enough, Michael was standing there already and nodded at Heather as she approached him. Her heart leaped right into her throat when she saw him. The paparazzi had been right, then, Harrison was already here.

As soon as they reached the glass wall to the conference room and she could see inside the room, Harrison was the first person she saw. It was like her body knew instantly that he was in the room; she yearned to walk over to him and kiss him. Every fiber of her being was aching to be in his arms, to find her way to the place that she had always called home.

Harrison looked up and caught her gaze as she walked into the room. It was as though time had stopped. As though they were talking without words. She could feel his love for her, his guilt over what he had done, his desire to be with her. He looked as beautiful as he always had, even though he looked like a wreck. He was completely gaunt, unshaven, and had slight bags under his eyes.

It broke her to see him this way. He might be feeling guilty for his one night's mistake, but she felt guilty for all the nights since. Heather hated herself for the nightmares she was still having. A part of her had started to hope, after Cooper had called her this morning, that maybe *this* was the thing she needed to get over them. Some sort of resolution from the police case and an arrest.

With that thought, Heather looked around the room as she took a seat on the opposite side of the table to Harrison. A part of her had thought that she should sit somewhere else, but her inner masochist wanted to be able to watch him. Helen Powell was sitting to Harrison's right, and Cooper sat down next to her.

Hayden was sitting on the other side of Harrison, and as Heather caught his eye, he gave her a tight smile, "Hi, Heather."

"Hey, Hayden." She smiled back at him.

There was a spare seat next to Hayden, but in the one next to that sat Maddy. Heather couldn't bear to even look at her; the other two members of Cooper's team were beside Maddy. Again, Heather had forgotten amongst everything, that other people had been drugged as well.

Heather was sitting in between Ariana and Sebastian, while Gabriel sat on the other side of Ariana. At the front of the room, a man in a very fancy police uniform with a lot of badges on it was standing and talking to a man that was next to him and wearing a suit.

"Now that we're all here," Cooper said, "we can probably begin, Aaron."

The man in the police uniform nodded and shook the hand of the man in the suit, who went to sit next to Cooper.

"My name is Aaron Hamilton. I'm the Chief of the Los Angeles Police Department. Firstly, I want to express my sincere regret that any of you had to go through what you went through.

You were guests in our city, and it's awful that this happened to you.

"We've had a task force on this since the day it happened, and we made arrests on Monday morning with charges being filed on Tuesday afternoon. We've already received one full confession, and we may receive more information, but that was enough to build a very firm case.

"I'm here to debrief you, and I'm going to assume that you will probably have some questions. If you can hold them until the end, I may cover them during the debrief. We suspected from the outset that someone from the hotel must have been involved. It could have been the catering company, and we did investigate that angle heavily, but ultimately came to the conclusion that no one from the company was involved."

This made sense to Heather—someone working for the hotel would have access to both the wine, as well as the room to take a picture of Harrison and Maddy. She glanced across the table and saw that Harrison wasn't looking at the police chief, he was looking at her, with a look of such pure love on his face that she caught her breath.

Heather stared back at him, losing track of what was being told to them and was unable to look away until Harrison broke their gaze. She closed her eyes and took a slow breath, god, she missed him so much. It hurt like hell to be sitting across from him and to not get to be with him. She realized that she was so distracted that she was missing out on the very reason she'd come to this place today.

"...it definitely caused us some issues because we couldn't check the security footage. We were suspicious about that; it was too convenient, so we started digging around for possible financial motivations."

"It's always about fucking money," Sebastian said quietly under his breath next to her, and Heather gave a single nod of her head.

"The photo of Harrison and Madeline," Heather put her hand against her heart and closed her eyes, as though putting pressure on her chest might somehow make hearing this hurt any less, "sold for over a million dollars for the initial licenses to print. That was just for the rights to print it in the United States. Tallying up the total cost of ongoing royalties for the photograph worldwide came to a *very* large sum of money.

"I do want to acknowledge that we did receive the news of your theory, Mr. Fox," he nodded to Sebastian, "and it was a good one, pretty much spot on. We had already begun working the theory by that point and had started to interview all staff that had been working in the hotel at all over the course of the weekend. Eventually, we were able to convince a maid, who was driving around in a brand-new Mercedes, to give a confession.

"In short, there was a group of hotel staff involved, the head of the operation was the hotel manager—" This elicited a gasp from several people around the table.

"He was so nice and sympathetic to us!" Ariana said out loud.

The police chief gave her a compassionate smile, "Yes, hiding in plain sight is, unfortunately, a common tactic for criminals. He was very helpful to us at the beginning of our investigation, as well. Once we started asking more questions about the missing security footage, he skipped town.

"We put a warrant out for his arrest, and a bounty hunter tracked him down in Nebraska. As soon as we could, we arrested and charged him, which is where we stand at the moment. Now, as I said, I'm sure you have questions?"

Sebastian was the first to speak up, "How did they manage to drug the wine if no one at the catering company was involved?"

"The catering company supplied the food and beverages, but it was all served by hotel staff. This was by design; it allowed them to ensure that it was only your table who received the drugged wine."

"What are they being charged with?" Cooper was the one to ask this.

"They're being charged with ten counts of felony Willfully Poisoning someone; each count carries a maximum of five years in prison. We will also seek the extra three years of jail time for the count of your poisoning as you ended up in the Intensive Care Unit, which we believe falls under 'great bodily injury.'"

"Did they say why they waited to drug us until the main course?" one of Cooper's team asked.

Heather looked over at the man and saw that he looked like he was horrified by this whole thing; so many people had been harmed by this.

"They wanted to make sure that you'd all had enough alcohol to not notice or be suspicious about the MDMA. I'm sure the doctors told you that it's very dangerous to take MDMA with alcohol, so this is part of what makes this crime more atrocious."

"How have the media not caught wind of this?" Hayden asked, more as a rhetorical question, but Aaron Hamilton answered anyway.

"We've had a tight lid on it. We didn't want any interference in the investigation. There will be a press conference tomorrow that Cooper will be attending with me. We do not expect any of the rest of you to attend that," he told them.

"I suggest you all lie low after the announcement tomorrow. I expect that it will get hectic," Cooper said.

There was silence then for a few moments before Heather finally found her voice.

"What I don't understand," she began as everyone in the room turned to look at her but she stared firmly at Aaron Hamilton as she voiced the question that had been running through her mind for a while, "is how they knew that Harrison would cheat on me with Maddy."

She felt, more than heard, the low groan from Harrison and

knew that this conversation and the reminder of what he'd done, was hurting him.

"They didn't," was the reply that she received.

Heather frowned, "What? You said they did it for the money. Well, they're pretty fucking lucky that Harrison couldn't keep it in his pants, aren't they?" She raised an eyebrow, while instantly feeling a rush of shame at the fact that she had stooped so low with her phrasing.

The air in the room got tense as people started to see Heather's point, though, and Aaron Hamilton had begun to look decidedly uncomfortable. She was sure that there was some information that he was withholding from them.

"So, Mr. Hamilton, how did they know?"

Everyone turned to look at him as they all waited for his explanation.

He sighed, then answered her, "As I said, they didn't. From what we know, they took key cards and searched all the rooms as soon as it was confirmed that you were all in attendance at the function. They were looking for anything that might be scandalous and worth money. The drug they chose to use wasn't a coincidence. Once they saw Mr. Fletcher leaving with Miss Turner, they waited until they could capture a series of photos to sell. The ones from earlier in the night were all sold by the same source."

Heather was horrified and spoke up again, "This sounds…intentional. Very well planned out. Basically, what you're saying is that it could've been any one of the band members for any number of reasons, but it just happened to be Harrison?"

"From what we know, they began planning this from very early on once Cruise Control was confirmed to be attending the event."

Harrison stood quickly from his seat and only just made it to the trash can in time before he vomited into it. Heather wondered if it was just the information he was being given or if he'd been day drinking again. She longed to go over and comfort him but knew she couldn't; she wasn't strong enough. She gave a panic-stricken look to Ariana, who grabbed a bottle of water off the table in front of them, rose from her seat, and went over to Harrison to comfort him for her.

Heather was reminded, terribly, of the conversation she'd had with Ariana about the lengths that people would go to in order to get to celebrities. They had thought that they'd experienced the worst of it when Ariana had been targeted the way she had been, but this was so much worse. Their health had been put at risk, and Cooper had ended up in the Intensive Care Unit, he could have died. All because a group of people had dollar signs in their eyes when they'd realized that they would have access to Cruise Control.

"Who took the photo?" a quiet voice asked Aaron Hamilton.

Heather dared to look over at Maddy; the other woman was looking at the police chief as he continued answering questions. It was strange being here with her. Heather had expected to feel more badly toward her, but she didn't. This was the woman that she still dreamed about every night, but she looked as broken and devastated as everyone else around this table, did.

Aaron Hamilton sighed. "From what we know, they had plenty of photos from during the event the night before, no doubt you've seen some of those. They would have sold them for quite a sum, anyway. However, in the early hours of the morning, they sent one of the maids into the room to see if she could get a picture of you in bed together. If she'd been caught, she was going to say that she was just there to clean the room."

It was more awful than Heather could have imagined. The way they had taken advantage of Harrison and Maddy made her feel sick. Knowing that someone had come into their room as they slept was terrible. She looked at Harrison and longed to be with him more than ever.

When the meeting wrapped up, Cooper's team were the first ones out of the room, along with Cooper, Helen, and the man in the suit, who it turned out was his lawyer. The police chief left with them, and Gabriel asked Cooper as he was leaving if the band could use the conference room for a few minutes, which he agreed to.

Heather couldn't recall off the top of her head, the last time that they had all been in a room together. Quite possibly, it hadn't been since their engagement party last August. She would give anything to go back to that night, to a time when her biggest concern was preparing for Fashion Week and being a bitch to Ariana.

"Are you okay, Harrison?" Sebastian's voice was full of concern.

"Yeah," his voice sounded hoarse as he replied, before taking a sip from the bottle of water that Ariana had given him.

"This is insane," Hayden sighed, "I can't help wondering if it would've been me if I hadn't just gone upstairs and passed out."

"I *wish* it had been me," Sebastian said.

"A Sebastian Fox four-way is nowhere near as marketable as 'Harrison Fletcher cheats on Heather York while she hosts Saturday Night Live,'" Heather said in a monotone voice. She saw Harrison flinch and felt bad, "Sorry, I didn't actually say that to try and hurt you, Harrison. I mean that of all the available options, they must have felt like they'd hit the fucking jackpot when they saw you leaving with her."

"What do we do?" Hayden asked.

"Nothing. We do nothing. The police are handling it, and Cooper is doing the press conference," it was Ariana who replied.

Heather remembered that, of course, Ariana knew a lot more about this kind of thing than the other guys realized. She had seen her family go through this, maybe it hadn't been a crime like they'd experienced, but the Thompsons had certainly weathered their fair share of media storms over the years.

Ariana continued what she was saying, "We all have security now, and we make sure that none of us are exposed like that again. We definitely don't go around calling the press 'miserable failures of human beings', even though some of them definitely are," she gave Sebastian a wry smile.

"You didn't, Seb!" Hayden actually laughed.

"Check your phone, dude. There's probably a video online by now."

After a few more minutes, they all stood up from the table and started to say their goodbyes. As they were leaving the room, Harrison grabbed Heather's wrist to stop her from walking away. She knew before she'd even turned to look that it was him, the feeling of his hand on her skin was so familiar to her.

The others seemed to notice but continued walking, anyway, and it was only a few moments before she was alone with Harrison for the first time in what felt like forever. Now that he had her alone, she got the distinct feeling that he didn't know what to say to her and hadn't thought this through.

"What, Harrison?" Heather asked him softly.

"I don't know. I just needed to be near you, angel."

Every time she thought that her heart had taken as much of a beating as it possibly could before it gave up working altogether, it would be forced to take yet another one, like the one it was suffering as she looked at Harrison right now.

He looked so in love with her and in so much pain from her absence in his life that she could barely stand it. She dared to reach her palm up and rest it on his cheek as she said the same words that she had told him the day after it had happened, so many months ago now, "I do still love you, Harrison."

He turned his face and pressed his lips to the palm of her hand. His kiss burned her skin, and she felt all of her nerve endings come alive, as though the entire world was suddenly aglow. She couldn't resist—she stepped forward, wound her arms around his neck, and kissed him. He kissed her back with all the passion and love that she knew he held for her.

For a moment, everything was right with the world again, but then she remembered. What the hell was she doing right now? This was supremely unfair to Harrison. She needed to know that finding out who had done this to them had been enough to stop her nightmares before she ever attempted some kind of reconciliation with him.

Heather broke their kiss, even though her entire body was telling her that she was doing the wrong thing. It was the first even slightly sexual thing they'd done since that day, and she was surprised by how she'd reacted to it. Heather had expected to be deluged with visions of him and Maddy like she had in the beginning, but she wasn't. Maybe the sessions with Zoe were actually working.

They stood there for a few more moments. Harrison's gaze burning into hers as they both tried to catch their breath, then Heather turned and walked out of the room. God, she really hoped that tonight would be nightmare free.

~MARCH~

CRUISE CONTROL'S DRUG DRAMA!

The drama never ends for our favorite rock band, Cruise Control! The last year has seen them embroiled in multiple affair scandals, a broken engagement, and heated run-ins with the paparazzi.

Now, more information has come to light about the night that Harrison Fletcher cheated on his ex-fiancée, Heather York. According to a joint press conference given last Friday by the Chief of the Los Angeles Police Department, Aaron Hamilton, and Cruise Control's manager, Cooper Powell, the band was the target of 'Willful Poisoning' at the event.

While they were sketchy on the details of what exactly that entails, a source close to the band tells us that they were all slipped a party drug that night. Is that really why Harrison cheated, or was it just because Heather had been having an affair with his best friend?

We don't know for sure, but we do know that Gabriel Knight's 30th birthday party this month sure will be interesting!

Chapter 22

DIRTY THIRTY

Heather was sitting in a chair in Gabriel and Ariana's apartment. Jessica was doing her makeup, and Tristan was working on Ariana's hair. It was Gabriel's thirtieth birthday today, and they were going to his birthday party tonight. It promised to be as big an affair as Harrison's had been.

She had thought she had been nervous before that night, knowing that Ariana would be in attendance, but it paled in comparison to how she felt right now. So many things had changed in Heather's life since that day—here she sat next to Ariana, who was once again one of her closest friends. Not only that but her other close friend, Ally, would be accompanying Hayden to the party tonight.

Would she swap these two friendships in exchange for having Harrison back? If she were being honest with herself, she would. As much as she loved these two women, the hole that Harrison had left in her life was brutally painful to try and brick up, and as much as she enjoyed her new friendship with Ally and the rekindling of her friendship with Ariana, her entire world was askew without the balance that Harrison lent to it.

The nightmares had continued after they'd had the debriefing a month ago at Cooper's office. Heather had woken that very night from a dream about Harrison and Maddy. It was maybe worse because in her dreams now, Maddy wore that terrible guilty look that she'd had during the meeting. Not even the Harrison and Maddy in her dreams were enjoying themselves now. Everybody was miserable.

That night, Heather had cried harder than she had since the day she'd found out what had happened. It felt like she would never get past this. Every step she tried to take had failed for her, and she was feeling completely out of options. Now, she had to go to Gabriel's birthday party tonight and see Harrison, knowing that she had failed them both.

While her nights were filled with nightmares of him cheating on her, her days were filled with memories of their last kiss. She replayed it over and over again in her head. Her reaction to his touch was the hope she clung to that they might get through this and come out the other side of it the way that Gabriel and Ariana had.

"Thank you so much for your help; it was lovely to see you again!" Ariana said to Tristan and Jessica as she escorted them out of the apartment. She came back to Heather and smiled at her, "Man, they're so nice, and they do such a good job!"

"They really do," Heather said, "you look amazing, darling."

Ariana looked stunning, as usual. Her brown hair was pulled back on one side with a loose braid that led down to the nape of her neck, and the rest of her hair was down in flowing waves. Jessica had done a great job on her makeup as well, really highlighting Ariana's beautiful emerald green eyes.

Heather had made them both dresses to wear tonight, the same way she had for the Grammys years ago. She was excited to get Ariana's reaction as she pulled down the zipper on the garment bag that she'd brought her dress in, and was rewarded with a stunned gasp from her friend.

"Heather, it's gorgeous!"

The dress that she'd made for Ariana was blush pink. The dress itself was a sheath, strapless dress. It was knee-length and had a cutout back that dropped low to the waist. Over that, there was a sheer layer of slightly stiff tulle fabric, almost seeming like a separate dress as it provided sleeves, then came around and gave some modesty across the exposed back. From the waist at the front, it came down a good foot lower than the dress and dropped to being floor-length at the back.

Heather's dress was a lot less intricate than the one she'd made for Ariana. It was a simple, red cocktail dress with an off-the-shoulder sweetheart neckline. Her blonde hair was in a half-updo with the part that was up having intricate braids running around the crown of her head while the rest flowed down her back, and Jessica had accentuated her lips with a fierce, red lipstick that matched her dress.

She went into their spare bedroom to get into her dress and came out to find both Gabriel and Ariana ready to leave.

"Looking good, Gabriel," Heather said approvingly.

"You don't look too bad yourself," he smiled at her.

"Are we ready to party until the break of dawn, old man?" She couldn't resist teasing him.

"Excuse me, if I recall correctly, you're turning thirty-one next month, aren't you?" He laughed.

"You're both old," Ariana announced with a wicked grin and then dashed over toward Heather, laughing, as Gabriel tried to chase after her, "Stop, Gabe! I'll fall in these heels and break an ankle. If we end up in the A&E instead of going to your party, it'll be all your fault!"

She stopped running, and he caught her to him, put his arms around her and held her close. Heather tried not to overhear, but Gabriel wasn't quiet enough when he said, "I'm not too old to fuck you stupid later."

"God damn, you two," Heather figured there was no point pretending she hadn't heard and fanned herself for effect, "I haven't had sex in far too long. It's not fair to show off like that!"

Gabriel dropped his arms from around Ariana's waist at once, and she stepped away from him.

"Shit, guys, it was just a joke," Heather laughed at their reaction, "it's not like I'm unaware that you two fuck like bunnies. That being said, shouldn't the car be here soon?"

When their limousine arrived at the venue for Gabriel's birthday, there was a huge number of paparazzi there. It was being held in the ballroom of a five-star hotel in downtown Chicago. There were barriers at the sides of the steps leading into the hotel lobby, and there were policemen ensuring that none of the people who weren't guests of the party or the hotel were allowed past the barriers.

They posed for a few photos together on the way in, then Heather posed for some on her own and answered a few questions from the media. She tried her hardest to ignore the ones about Harrison or Sebastian and even managed to refrain from rolling her eyes.

"Heather, Sebastian brought another girl with him tonight, are you jealous?"

She couldn't stop herself from laughing, though, and she smirked at the woman who had asked the question, "Pigs will fly before I get jealous of Sebastian's many, many girlfriends. We're just friends."

"What about the girl that Harrison brought with him?" Someone else asked her.

Heather's head whipped around at once, "I'm sorry, what?"

The reporter had gotten both Gabriel and Ariana's attention as well, and he seemed very pleased with himself as he repeated, "Yeah, Harrison brought a girl tonight. What do you think about that?"

Heather felt sick. Harrison had brought a girl with him? Who? Surely not Maddy. He wouldn't. No, they would've known who she was, and they *definitely* would have told her. They wanted a reaction; she'd already given them one, but she wouldn't indulge this further. She needed to get inside and find out what the fuck was going on.

"Obviously," she said, giving him her most condescending smile, "I've only just arrived, so I have no idea what happened before I got here. I hope you have a wonderful night."

With that, she turned and strode as casually as she could through the doors and into the hotel lobby. She didn't stop once she was inside, she didn't even wait to see if Gabriel and Ariana were behind her, just followed the signs toward the birthday party. She made her way across the lobby and to a hallway that apparently led to the ballroom.

"Heather, stop!" Ariana called out and jogged a little bit to catch up with her and Gabriel trailed behind.

Ariana grabbed her arm to pull her to a stop, and Heather spun to look at her. "He brought someone with him tonight, Ariana."

She thought that she might split into a thousand pieces just from saying it. The betrayal was worse than the one she'd experienced when he'd cheated on her. Her brain told her that, in fairness, they were broken up. How long could he reasonably be expected to wait for her to get over her shit enough for them to be together again? At the same time, how could he possibly be moving on so soon?

"Heather," Gabriel said quietly, "they could just have been trying to get a reaction from you. It might not even be true. Harrison wouldn't do that."

Heather looked at him; what he was saying made sense. It was far more likely that she'd been lied to than that Harrison had brought someone else with him tonight. She was shaken, though. The possibility of Harrison moving on and being with someone else was absolutely terrifying, but she was still having those fucking nightmares.

She took a deep breath and released it slowly, then nodded, "Okay, you're right. Let's go. Super Fun Happy Party Time?"

"Something like that," Gabriel smiled and put an arm around her shoulders, "but also if you want to have Shitty Depressed Sit And Drink Time, that's okay, too."

Heather winced, "I'm afraid that Harrison's been doing that enough for the both of us, lately."

Neither Gabriel nor Ariana replied to that, and they continued on to the ballroom for the party. As the doors opened and Gabriel walked into the room, everyone in there cheered, and they were greeted by a whole host of people.

Heather searched the room to find Harrison, terrified that she might see him with someone else, as unlikely as she knew that was. A group of people moved slightly on the dance floor, and she saw him. He was sitting at the bar on the other side of the room, drinking from a tumbler of whisky. Heather felt an immense sense of relief when she saw that he was alone.

Still, she needed to talk to him, needed to know that he hadn't done what he'd been accused of doing. Heather strode across the room with purpose, brushing off the people who were welcoming her as she did so. Even Sebastian tried to get her attention as she passed him dancing with a blonde woman she vaguely recognized from some TV drama, but she just shook her head at him and kept walking.

Harrison noticed her when she was still about twenty feet away from him. He looked worse than she'd ever seen him look. It was clear that he was several drinks into the evening's festivities.

"Hi, angel. Why don't you pull up a stool and drink away your sorrows with me?" He gave her a wry grin, then turned to the bartender, "Can you get a rum and Coke for the most beautiful woman in the world?"

The bartender nodded and started making her drink. Heather frowned, unlike Ariana, she didn't have a go-to drink, so it took her a moment to realize why he'd chosen this one. Her expression cleared as she realized why he'd chosen it for her.

"Yes, angel, it's what you were drinking the weekend we last had sex," he told her, not appearing to care about the bartender hearing as he handed Heather the drink, "I can't pretend that I don't hope that it'll happen again, tonight."

"So, you didn't bring someone else with you, then?" she asked him, taking a sip of the drink she'd been given.

"What the fuck?" He looked surprised, "No, I wouldn't. Why would you think that?"

Heather was unsurprised by how relieved his confirmation made her. She should have known that it was a load of bull, but it had touched something deep inside her when she'd been faced with the idea of it.

"The reporters outside told me that Seb had brought someone with him and asked if I was jealous. When I told them that pigs would fly before I'd get jealous over a girl with Sebastian, somebody else said that you'd brought a girl with you, too."

Harrison frowned for a second, then laughed, "Ally. I came with Hayden and Ally, she mostly avoided The Gauntlet, and it wouldn't have been obvious that she was with him, not me."

"Oh, and it's a much better story if she's here with you instead of him, too. The guy seemed very pleased to be able to tell me you'd brought someone with you," she rolled her eyes.

"How did that make you feel, angel?" He raised an eyebrow at her.

She laughed, "What are you, Harrison? My therapist?"

"No, just your curious ex-fiancé who is desperately hoping that you still care," he gave her a sad smile.

"Yes, Harrison," she sighed before admitting, "I felt more jealous than I've ever felt in my life. I thought I might literally die if you were here with someone else."

Heather felt bad because she knew that this conversation was giving Harrison hope, she knew that because it was giving her hope, too.

"Heather York, you are the only woman I want. You are the only woman I will ever want."

Harrison stood up from his stool and took the single step needed to bring him close enough to her that she could see the golden flecks in his irises as she looked up at him from where she sat. He reached his hand out and softly brushed her bottom lip with his thumb. Her breath caught in her throat, and she felt the ache between her thighs that she hadn't felt for so long.

He lowered his head to hers slowly, giving her time to respond. She knew that she should stop this, but she didn't want to. It was exhausting to fight against the desire to be with him just because it was the right thing to do.

So, she let him continue on his path until his lips met hers. He tasted of whisky and something that she just attributed to him in her brain. His scent was intoxicating, more so than the alcohol she had been drinking.

His hand made its way to the back of her head, and he held her hair, tilting her head up to gain better access to her mouth. She parted her lips, allowing his tongue to slip inside. Heather had missed this so much; she stood up while they kissed and slipped her arms around him, underneath his tuxedo's jacket.

His hands dropped to her waist, and he pulled her hard against him. It had happened, she was finally home. Heather could feel his growing erection pressing against her and longed to have it in her mouth. She had missed him so much. Finally, their kiss ended, and he put his forehead against hers, breathing as heavily as she was.

"I've missed you, angel," he said, pulling his head back to look into her eyes.

Every single one of her senses was on fire, being here and in his arms, "I've missed you, too, Harrison."

Heather felt his entire body tense, and he closed his eyes before turning his head away. She had almost forgotten why she had called off their wedding. It was a reminder of how tense it had been living with him for those months after the drugging.

Harrison started to pull away from her, but she held her arms around him tighter; she needed this, to be in his arms right now. So, she begged him, "Please don't."

"What do you want from me, angel?" he asked her.

"I want to be here. With you. Right now. Just…stay here."

The tension eased out of his body as he put his arms back around her and kissed the top of her head softly. Heather didn't know how long they stood there, just being with one another. It felt as though her heart was having a soothing balm applied to it. Being home was simply the most wonderful feeling, and she was exultant in it.

"We should be social." Heather wanted to stay there all night but knew that they couldn't, and she sighed.

"Being social is the worst," he said with a laugh as he dropped his arms from around her waist. She pulled her own arms out from under his jacket and stepped back from him.

"We still need to talk, Harrison," she warned him.

"I know," he gave her a warm smile, "but it's a start. Finish your drink, angel."

"Evil man," she said with a laugh as she picked up the drink and took another sip.

Harrison grabbed his own drink, then reached his free hand out toward hers. She joined hands with him, and they turned to face the room together. The party appeared to be in full swing, and their interlude seemed to have gone all but unnoticed by anyone else here; however, she spotted Ally and Hayden standing on the other side of the room and looking at them. Ally was smiling at her, and Heather smiled back.

They made their way over to their friends, and by the time they'd reached them, Sebastian had appeared next to them.

"Hi, darling," Heather smiled at Ally. Normally she would give her a hug, but she didn't want to let go of Harrison's hand.

"Hey, lady. You seem like you're having a good time," Ally smiled back at her.

Heather glanced up at Harrison before looking back at her friend, "Better than I expected to have."

"I get the feeling that our love affair might be over," Sebastian said with a dramatic sigh, and everyone laughed.

"Sorry, Seb," Harrison told him, "but I really hope so."

"Ah, well, we'll always have Galena," he told Heather, giving her a wink.

"It was fun while it lasted, darling," she grinned at him.

They talked for a while before Harrison asked Heather if she wanted to dance. They spent the next few hours dancing and talking with their friends. It felt so familiar and strangely as though nothing had changed between them.

At the back of her brain, she knew that their relationship wasn't magically fixed, but she also felt so good right now that she didn't care. They cheered for Gabriel together as speeches were made celebrating him. Heather drank too much, but it was all around one of the best nights of her life.

As the party was winding down, Harrison was standing behind her, his arms around her and his head resting on hers as they watched the partygoers beginning to leave the ballroom. Heather didn't think that there had been a time at all this night that he hadn't been touching her somehow.

"Where to, now?" he asked her in a husky voice.

It was a good question. Heather knew that she wanted him in bed with her tonight. She needed it, but which bed? She didn't want to go back to Hayden's with him, and for some reason, she also didn't want him to come to the temporary living arrangement that she called home right now. Their apartment was an option, but she didn't feel emotionally ready to return there.

The answer was fairly obvious, "Well, I mean, we are in a hotel…" she trailed off.

That was all Harrison needed to hear. He dropped his arms from around her, took her hand in his, and led her over to Gabriel and Ariana.

"We're leaving," he informed them. "Happy birthday, Gabriel. The party has been awesome!"

"It certainly seems like you've been having a good time," Gabriel smirked at him.

Heather stepped forward and put her free arm around Gabriel to give him a hug, "Happy thirtieth birthday, darling."

"Thanks, Heather. It's nice to see you two together."

Heather cringed slightly, "There's still a lot to work out, but," she looked up at Harrison and smiled at him as she repeated his words from earlier, "it's a start."

They left the ballroom and headed to the lobby of the hotel, where Harrison booked them into the fanciest room that was available. Once the elevator arrived on their floor, they followed the signs to their room, and Harrison opened the door, walking into the room with Heather following behind him.

The air in the room crackled with tension as Harrison walked to the middle of a living area, then turned to face Heather, "Shall we talk now, angel?"

She shook her head. They needed to have a conversation, but not now. Now, she needed him inside of her.

"Come here, then."

Heather walked over to him; it was a path that she had walked a thousand times before. The path from any given place that led her to Harrison. When she was standing in front of him, he put his arms around her and claimed her lips with his, then took her hand once again and let her to the bedroom.

"On the bed, angel," he said, the lust he was feeling, evident in his tone of his voice.

Heather obliged, climbing on to the bed and lying with her head on the pillows. Harrison stared at her for what felt like hours, and she could feel herself getting wet. She'd been on edge all evening from his nearness, and she hadn't had this for so many months.

Eventually, while still looking at her, he removed his tuxedo jacket, folded it neatly, and placed it on a dresser nearby. Then, he undid the buttons of his shirt, removed that, and placed it carefully on top of the jacket. Heather groaned as she saw his muscled chest in the flesh; she longed to touch him.

He removed his shoes and socks, placing them next to the dresser, and Heather bit her lip as he turned back to her, caught her gaze again, and unbuttoned his pants. This strip show that he was giving her was driving her crazy. She wanted him now.

Harrison swiftly pulled off both his pants and underwear, placing them with the rest of his clothes. The reality of Harrison standing naked in front of her, with his cock on display was enough to make Heather lick her lips in delight.

He climbed onto the bed and placed himself near her lips, "Is this what you want, angel?"

She nodded with a moan as she took him in her mouth. Holy fuck, she had missed this so much. He thrust his hips back and forth as she sucked him, and she reveled in the feeling of giving him a blow job, again.

All too soon, he pulled his erection out her mouth, and she pouted, "I won't last very long if you keep doing that, angel," he said with a laugh.

Harrison pushed her dress up over her hips and ever so slowly pulled her red, lace panties down and slid them off over her ankles. He pushed her knees apart, and she was exposed for his viewing pleasure.

He traced her innermost part with one finger and groaned, "I can't wait to taste you. I've missed you so fucking much."

Then he put his head between her legs and traced the same line with his tongue before setting to work on her clit. Heather thought that she might explode, and it wasn't long until she was coming under his ministrations.

Normally, Harrison would take his time and spend as long as he could teasing her, but there was nothing normal about this night. They had been apart for too long—the need to be joined together in the most sacred way possible was too urgent. He held himself over her for only long enough to tell her, "I love you, angel," before he gave them the thing that they had both needed all night by pressing himself into her.

When they were finished, Heather was tired from the drink and the sex. She felt satiated and drifted off to sleep in Harrison's arms. It was many hours later that she woke, crying, from a nightmare of him having sex with Maddy.

"Angel, what's wrong?" he pulled her tighter to him as she cried, and she took some shaky breaths to try and calm herself down.

Heather had become so used to this nightly ritual of waking from her nightmares, that it was odd to have him with her for comfort. She rolled over to face him, barely able to see his face in the dark bedroom with only the moonlight coming through the window to brighten the room.

"I had a nightmare," she told him.

"About what?" he asked her, though she felt he probably already knew.

Heather just shook her head at him.

"About what, angel?" he asked again, rubbing her back with one of his hands.

"About you and Maddy," she cringed as she said it, knowing that this would hurt him.

"How often do you have nightmares like this?"

"Every night," she confessed.

"Oh, angel…" he didn't say anything more, just pulled her tighter to him and kissed her.

Chapter 23

THE FINAL HURDLE

Heather was sitting on Zoe's sofa, her legs tucked underneath her the way she usually did and was rubbing the skin on her ring finger as they talked.

"So, you've been having sex again?" Zoe asked her.

"Yes, we have," Heather confirmed.

They'd seen each other twice since Gabriel's birthday party, and each time, they had spent a good portion of those visits in bed together.

"What was it that prompted you to take that step?"

"I think it was just realizing how terrifying the idea of him being with someone else really was to me. This journalist asked me how I felt about Harrison taking another woman to Gabriel's birthday party, and I thought I would die," Zoe smiled at Heather's dramatics, "I realized that all of my reasons for splitting up were still there, but my desire to be with him was stronger than those reasons."

"How has it felt being with him again, physically?"

"Absolutely perfect," Heather smiled, "I was worried that I would be tormented with images of him and Maddy together if we tried having sex, but I've never been able to focus on anything but

Harrison when we're in bed together, anyway."

"Have the nightmares decreased or stopped?" Zoe asked her.

"No," Heather's eyes were downcast as she admitted it, "I'm still having them every night. Harrison's been great about it."

"So, he's been with you when you've had them?"

"Yeah, they're still happening nightly, so every night we've been together, I've had one. I'm going crazy, Zoe. Harrison's so understanding and wonderful, but it's been months of this shit, now. I'm tired, physically, and emotionally, of dealing with this night after night," Heather sighed.

Zoe wrote something in her notepad, then put both it and her pen down on the table next to her chair.

"I'm going to suggest something, Heather," Zoe looked thoughtful, "have you considered talking to Maddy about what happened?"

"No."

Heather was partially answering the question, but also partially resisting the idea.

"Hear me out. You've said several times to me that you believe Harrison remembers more than he says he does. For whatever reason, he doesn't seem able to tell you any more than he has. This whole time, you've had the pictures in your head and told yourself stories about what exactly happened that night.

"Maddy is another source of truth that you could seek out. If finding that out is what you need to truly get past this and stop the nightmares, would it not be worth having the conversation with her?"

Heather frowned as she thought about what Zoe was suggesting. On the one hand, it did make sense; on the other hand, she was absolutely terrified about what Maddy might tell her.

"I'm scared," Heather admitted, "what if she tells me something that makes me stop loving Harrison?"

The thought of being told something that could break her love for Harrison was almost too much for Heather to bear. She realized that the unknown element of the truth of what happened that night was the monster under her bed that had been scaring her for months.

"Do you really think there is something she could tell you that might cause that to happen?" Zoe asked.

"No. I'm still scared, though."

Zoe smiled at her, "Most people would be. The unknown is scary. Is it worse than what you know right now, though? The daily nightmares don't seem to be easing off; I'm just suggesting that this might be something that is worth a try."

"I'll think about it," Heather told her.

Zoe picked up her pad and pen, now, and wrote something down, "That's very good. So, what do you feel is the progression for this new relationship with Harrison?"

"What do you mean?" Heather was confused.

"Okay, well, when you broke up, you were engaged to be married. Do you see yourself back in that position? I see you're not wearing your engagement ring."

"Whoa, slow down," Heather raised her hands in a 'stop' signal, "we've fucked a few times, that's it. We've talked about it, and we're not really putting a name on it right now."

"That's exactly what I mean, is there some path toward a full reconciliation that you can see? What would that look like to you?" Zoe did the head-tilting thing.

Heather thought about it. What did the path to reconciliation look like? She'd been in the dark on this aspect for months, but now she could kind of see what she needed to get there.

"Okay, well, I don't think I'm ready to be engaged again. I know within myself that until the nightmares stop or even decrease dramatically, I can't marry Harrison. I just don't want to start our marriage that way. I do know that my days are better when he is in them, the two times we've seen each other, it's just been less painful to exist.

"We haven't talked about moving in together again, yet. I'm pretty sure that Harrison is taking my lead on that, and I'm not ready for it. I'm still wary about going back to our apartment. I keep reminding myself that we have so many more good memories there than we have bad memories, but I'm scared.

"What we have at the moment feels fragile right now, it's so precious to me that I'm scared of doing anything that might shatter it. I don't think either of us would survive another breakup."

"Do you consider yourselves to be 'together,' then?" Zoe asked when Heather had been silent for a few seconds.

"Like I said, we haven't really put a name on it," Heather shrugged.

"Sorry, that's not what I meant to ask, do *you* consider yourself to be 'together' with him?" Zoe raised an eyebrow at her.

"Oh…" she trailed off and thought about it, "yes, I do. I would never be with anyone else, and now that we've started having sex again, it feels like getting back together is an inevitability."

Zoe nodded, writing something down on her pad and said, "Well, it seems like you're going well. It's natural to be hesitant, given what happened, but you're in a much better place mentally than you were back in December when you first saw me."

"I've been trying really hard," Heather smiled.

Zoe smiled back at her, "That's been very obvious. I feel like you know what the next step to take is, but you need to be sure that you're in the right place to take that step. When you're ready, I really think that might be the thing that helps with the nightmares."

"You've almost got me convinced," Heather laughed and then sighed, "I don't like the idea at all, but I'm committed to beating these shitty dreams, and if I don't do it, then I can't be honest with myself that I've tried everything within my power to do that."

"You'll be surprised at what good can come from getting some truth and hopefully some more understanding of the topic."

Their session finished soon after that, and Heather thanked Zoe as she left her office. She had a lot to think about. She was seeing Harrison again on Friday, but she knew that the idea of talking to Maddy wasn't something that she wanted to discuss with him.

That conversation would be too painful for both of them, especially if she didn't know if she was actually going to do it. She felt like she probably was going to, though. Zoe was right; it would give her the answers to questions that had been at the back of her mind for months.

Was this why she was still having the nightmares? Was it because in the absence of the whole truth, her brain had to fill in the gaps with the ideas it had about how it had all gone down?

♥

After meeting up with him on Friday, Heather spent the entire weekend with Harrison at her apartment. Cruise Control was gearing up for the release of *Games We Play,* and it was his last free weekend for a while. They were lying in bed together on Sunday evening after having sex, and he had his arms around her; she was so at peace with the world right now.

"So, you have to tell me the truth," she began, with a serious look on her face, "who chose the release date for the album?"

He grinned at her, "You want to know if I was so tragically desperate for you that I insisted we release our next album on your birthday?"

"Pretty much," she laughed.

"I can't lie, I did suggest the date on a whim, but everyone agreed to it, and it worked with the schedule for the release. I think everyone just felt sorry for me and gave me what I wanted."

"Well, I mean, it's not as good as having an entire album dedicated to you like Ariana got, but I guess I'll take what I can get," she winked at him.

He laughed, then dropped his head to give her a kiss, "Cheeky wench!"

They still hadn't given what they were doing any official label. Heather didn't need to have a discussion with Harrison to know that he wouldn't be sleeping with anyone else, and it was the same for him. She'd been thinking about her last session with Zoe and what steps she needed to take in order to make this reconciliation official.

Heather had decided to call Cooper tomorrow and ask him for Maddy's contact details. The whole idea of talking to her was utterly terrifying, but it was something that Heather needed to do in order to move forward. Once she'd had that conversation, she would talk to Harrison about the possibility of some kind of trial living together again to see how it went.

This weekend had been something of a low-key trial for Heather to see if there was still that awful tension between them, and she was pleased that it wasn't there. When she'd woken from her nightmares each night, he simply held her until she calmed down. Last night, she'd initiated sex afterward, and it had easily burned the memory of her nightmare away from her brain.

♥

On Monday, she sat in her office at Serenity, and she was sweating. Her heart was racing, and she had to take several deep breaths to try and calm down. It was just a phone call; she just needed to speak to Cooper and ask for Maddy's contact details. Fuck, if she felt like this now, how was she going to feel when she needed to call Maddy.

She stared at her phone, with Cooper's name on the screen. One thing at a time, that's all she needed to do, and she would hopefully end up back with Harrison. Step one, call Cooper. She pressed his name on her phone's screen and waited as it rang in her ear.

"Heather. How can I help you?" he answered in his usual curt tone.

"Hi, Cooper, how are you doing today?" Heather asked him.

Occasionally she liked to play this game where she forced him into pleasantries, just to make him act like a normal human being, today she was just putting off what she'd called to ask, though.

"I'm fine. What can I do for you?" Heather felt some grim humor at his response.

"I'd like Madeline Turner's contact details if you have them, please?"

"I don't think that's a good idea, Heather." He sounded stern.

"Okay, well, it doesn't matter what you think is a good idea. I need those contact details." She'd thought that he might have this reaction.

"Except that I don't have to give them to you, Heather. Nor, do I think I should."

"Cooper, you're just the easiest way to get them. I can find her details using other methods if I have to," she sighed and pulled out her ace card, "my therapist thinks that it's a good idea. Hopefully, it will really help me with Harrison, and I know you'd like him to be more focused on the album release."

Step two, find the bottom line, present Cooper with it. It was the truth, though. If this helped, then it really would help things to be a lot smoother between her and Harrison, which would undoubtedly be good for his mindset during promos for the album. Especially since reporters would almost certainly ask him about her.

"I hope you know what you're doing, Heather. I don't know that she'll want to talk to you, but I'll give her your number and ask her to call." Cooper sounded concerned.

"Thanks, Cooper, and one last thing, can you not tell Harrison about this?" she asked him.

"I thought you were doing this to try and help him?" Cooper sounded surprised.

"Yes, but I think it's best if he doesn't know I'm planning to talk to her. I think he will stress about it, and there will be more pressure on me for it to go well," she decided to be honest with him.

"I understand."

He hung up, and Heather sat there, feeling numb. Would Maddy even call her? There was nothing that she could do now but wait. She distracted herself with work. The new designs were coming along really well, and Heather was excited for the direction that Serenity's next collection was taking.

A few hours later, Heather was distracted from her work when her phone started buzzing on the table nearby. She looked at the screen and saw a number on the display that she didn't recognize.

"Hello?" Heather felt her nerves reach boiling point as she answered the phone.

"Hi, is this Heather?" the person asked.

"Yes, is this Maddy?"

"It is." Heather heard a deep sigh from the other end of the line. "Cooper asked me to call you."

"Thanks for calling me." Heather hesitated, unsure of how to ask the question she needed to ask, and realizing that there was no point in beating around the bush. "I was wondering if you would be willing to meet up and talk to me?"

"I'm not really sure…" Maddy trailed off.

"I know that it's uncomfortable, trust me, I'm not enamored with the idea, but it would mean a lot to me to get some answers to questions that I have about that night," Maddy didn't answer immediately, "please, Maddy?"

"Okay, I guess. Where do you want to meet?"

Heather let out a breath that she hadn't realized that she'd been holding, "I know that I'm asking a lot, but would you mind coming to my apartment? I can give you a code to get into the underground garage. It'll mean that we can meet up, and there won't be any paparazzi bullshit about it."

"Will Harrison be there?" Maddy asked, sounding concerned.

"No, he won't." Heather laughed. "As if I want you two in a room together again. Sorry, that was bitchy." She immediately corrected herself. "I apologize. No, he won't be there. We don't live together at the moment. He doesn't even know that I'm planning to talk to you."

"I see. When do you want to meet?"

"When are you free?" Heather asked her, and they organized to meet the next day at seven in the evening.

♥

Heather was incredibly stressed for the next twenty-four hours. Harrison sent her a text on Tuesday afternoon, and when she saw his name on her screen, she thought for a second that Cooper must have told him about Maddy.

Hey angel. Want to catch up tonight? I'd love to see you before my flight.

All of Cruise Control was flying to Los Angeles the next day for press events to promote *Games We Play*.

I can't. God, I wish I could. Maybe you could call me?

Spending the evening in bed with Harrison was a much better proposition than what she was actually going to do. Heather knew that she needed to get this conversation over and done with. She would see how tonight went for sleep before she could see him again. By tomorrow, Heather would know within herself where exactly she was mentally, and they could move forward from there.

Of course I can, angel. I'll look forward to it. Can I book you in for next Monday after I fly back?

She grinned, the knowledge that he wanted to see her as soon as he was back in the city was pleasing.

Yes. I think I can pencil you in. I love you, Harrison.

I love you too, angel. Always and forever.

By the time seven rolled around that evening, Heather was wound tighter than a spring. She was incredibly tense and jumped when she heard a knock at her door. Oh, god, this was happening. She walked to the door, feeling as though she was walking toward the gallows, and couldn't help thinking that having her head chopped off would probably be better than this.

Heather opened the door to see an incredibly nervous-looking Maddy on the other side. She looked so young and completely vulnerable that Heather felt bad for her and a wave of gratefulness that she'd even come tonight, washed over her.

"Hi, Maddy. Please come in," she stood aside, holding the door open for Maddy to enter the room. "Do you want something to drink?"

"I haven't drunk anything since…" she trailed off.

Heather nodded, feeling bad for Maddy. She'd obviously been scarred by what had happened, and Heather wondered if she'd been having any kind of therapy. It wasn't her place to recommend it, but Heather hoped that she was.

"Would you like coffee or tea or juice or something?" Heather asked.

"A coffee would be nice," Maddy said.

Heather made them both coffees, then they walked over to the dining table and sat down opposite one another. Heather took a deep breath and looked at Maddy. This was the woman she'd dreamed about every night for the last five months; she'd seen her perform hundreds of different sex acts with Harrison in her brain. She'd resented her for a lot of that time, but now that she was here in front of her, Maddy was nowhere near as scary as she'd imagined. She just looked broken.

"How are you coping?" Heather surprised herself with her first question; she hadn't expected to ask it.

Maddy gave a hollow laugh that Heather recognized from when people used to ask her how she was doing, "Oh, just brilliant.

The entire world knows me as 'the slut who fucked Harrison Fletcher.' It's been so much fun."

"I can imagine that's been really hard for you," Heather grimaced.

She recognized the use of the coarse language as a defensive mechanism that, again, she had used herself plenty of times over the last five months.

"You have no idea," Maddy caught her eye and actually laughed this time, "Okay, you probably do. I'm so sorry, Heather. I don't think I'll ever be able to apologize to you enough. I know that you told Cooper not to fire me. Thank you for that, you didn't have to do it."

"I was very angry at you," Heather told her, "but you were a victim as well. I couldn't let Cooper do that; it wouldn't have been right."

"Thanks. I couldn't keep working for him, though. Everyone knew what happened; I felt so ashamed. Of course, I've started a new job where everyone knows what happened, anyway," she cringed, "but at least they weren't there and watching it happen that night, you know?"

In all of the run-throughs that Heather had done in her head of this conversation since Zoe had suggested this, she'd never imagined herself to be sympathetic in any way, shape, or form to Maddy. She'd imagined a lot of shitty outcomes from tonight, but it was clear that Maddy had suffered as badly as she and Harrison had since it happened.

"That's exactly what I wanted to talk to you about, Maddy," Heather said gently, "I know that this will probably be hard for you and I'm sorry about that, but I need to know everything that happened that night."

Maddy shook her head, "No, Heather. I'm sorry, but I don't think you really do."

"You'll be surprised, but my therapist thinks that I apparently do. I have nightmares every night about you and Harrison in bed together, did you know that?" Maddy looked horrified. "Yup, that's the reaction I was looking for. Every night since I found out, my brain has treated me to a sex show of you and my ex-fiancé in bed together. I just want a full night's sleep, and Zoe thinks that if I find out what happened, my brain might chill the fuck out on filling in the blanks for me."

"Heather, I'm so, so sorry."

Maddy wiped a tear away from her eye, and Heather walked over to the kitchen, grabbed a box of tissues and came back as she handed one to Maddy, "I think we might both end up needing these."

"Okay," Maddy swallowed heavily, "what do you want to know?"

"Tell me everything that you remember, please, from the time Harrison sat down next to you until the time you last saw him."

"I was so stoked when Cooper told me I could go to the event in your place. I don't normally get to go to the cool stuff. It all started out normally—they arrived a little bit later than us, and everyone was in a good mood. I met Ariana for the first time, and she was really nice to me.

"During the entrées and stuff, Harrison and I were just chatting. He talked about you a lot," Maddy laughed, "like, a *lot*. He was telling me all about Saturday Night Live and how proud he was of you. Oh, he mentioned the sketch about you leaving him at the altar, and I thought it was super weird that he was okay with it because he was clearly mad about you.

"I actually said that to him, and he said 'it's funny because nothing could ever break us apart, though,'" Heather grabbed a tissue as the tears began to flow for her, too; neither she nor Harrison would ever have predicted what had happened that night, "Are you really sure that you want me to continue?"

Heather nodded, "Yes, I know I'm crying, and I'm going to

do that a lot, I'm sure. I appreciate you being so honest with me, please don't hold anything back."

"Well, then the main course came out, and we were eating it. Harrison was being really nice and asking me about what my career plans were. I remember thinking that maybe if I impressed him, Cooper might promote me and put me on the Cruise Control account," Maddy said bitterly.

"I'm sorry, Maddy." Heather was sad.

"Not your fault," Maddy gave her a wry smile, "anyway, a bit after that, everything started to feel really weird. Sorry to have to say it, but Harrison is fucking hot, and I hadn't really been interested in him before that, suddenly it was like I couldn't think about anything except how hot he was."

"I'm aware that he's sexy as fuck," Heather laughed, even though this was painful to hear, and she wanted to clarify, "but I'm glad to hear that you hadn't been interested in him when you were sober!"

"Then he was flirting with me, telling me I was beautiful. I mentioned you because I did think about you and he went on a long rant about how wonderful you were and how much he loved you. I was so in love with you from what he was telling me. It was completely and utterly strange.

"We were still eating, and we were talking about how *amazing* the food was. We had a second glass of wine, each and after that, we started talking about sex and the idea of leaving to go have it. He said, 'Heather loves sex, and she'd want me to have sex tonight,'" Maddy rolled her eyes, "like, now it's obvious that of course that wasn't the case but at the time it felt like the truest fact I'd ever known."

"I have to ask, was there any part of you that wanted this, or was it only the drugs?"

Maddy shook her head, "I would never have slept with him, otherwise. I won't lie, I've certainly bragged to my friends about getting to be around Cruise Control, and they're all gorgeous, but I'm trying to have a career in talent management. Sleeping with clients is one of the biggest no-nos."

"Okay, continue, then," Heather smiled reassuringly at her.

"We left the dinner, and he kissed me when we were in the lobby, while we were waiting for the elevator, then we went upstairs to his hotel room and had sex, then—"

"No. I need more information than that, Maddy," Heather said, "I need to know exactly what you did."

"I'm not comfortable telling you every gory detail," she cringed.

"I understand that, and I appreciate what you're doing for me tonight. You didn't have to do this, and as I said, I know it's difficult for you. If I'm going to try and stop these nightmares, I need to know as many details as you remember."

Madeline sighed, "Okay, well, we went into the hotel room, and he got naked, and I thought he was a god. Like, an actual god. My brain thought that he was a god sent to earth to have sex with me for some reason. I gave him head for a bit," Heather cringed as she heard this, and Maddy looked down at her coffee as she continued, "sorry. Then he got on the bed, and I got naked, too. I was on top for a bit, then he did it from behind."

Heather grabbed another tissue and handed it to Maddy, who was crying again. Somehow, this wasn't as bad for Heather as she'd thought that it would be, maybe because she wasn't hearing anything that she hadn't imagined or seen in her dreams, anyway. She felt bad that she was putting Maddy through this, though.

"I had a shower to wash off, and he came and joined me. We didn't have sex in there, just kissed a lot. Then we went back to the bed, and he was talking about you and how amazing you were, and I thought that I wanted to have sex with you, as well. He was describing the sex you guys had the last time he saw you, and he got hard again, and so I got on top of him, and we had sex again."

"Did he use a condom?" Heather asked, almost certain of the answer to this question.

"I'm sorry, no he didn't," Maddy shook her head, looking ashamed, "I was given the morning-after pill at the hospital, and as you can see, I'm not pregnant," she gave Heather a grim smile, "I've also got a clean bill of health. They tested us at the hospital, I've had the follow-up test done, as well."

"That's reassuring," Heather said, "what happened then?"

"I think we were starting to come down. We both got *really* tired, and the next thing I remember is being woken up by Gabriel and Ariana. I was really confused at first. I was naked, and Harrison was naked, and I could feel he was hard, and I felt sick. As soon as I put it together, I started getting flashbacks of what had happened.

"I felt like a piece of shit but not as bad as Harrison did. He started crying immediately. He felt guilty as fuck, he wanted to call you straight away and tell you, but Gabriel and Ariana told him that we needed to leave straight away for the hospital.

"I had to put on the clothes I'd been wearing the night before, then we all went to my bedroom so I could get changed into a fresh outfit. The whole time, Harrison was crying, and I think that was the first time he tried to call you. He checked your flight time, and you'd already left New York.

"He kept apologizing to me, too. Saying he was so sorry, he shouldn't have done it. I kept apologizing to him, as well, for the same reason," Maddy gave a small laugh. "It was pretty pathetic. I thought that was the absolute worst I would ever feel. Then we went outside. There were thousands of people waiting for us, I'll never forget the moment I saw that photo," she cringed and squeezed her eyes shut tight. "It was fucked up. I felt violated. I had felt terrible for having slept with Harrison, but that photo made me feel completely sick.

"We got into a limousine, and Harrison just kept trying to get on to you, but he couldn't. He kept saying 'they're going to show her the picture,', 'they're going to show her the picture,' and I searched on the internet and saw it. Someone had been in the fucking room with us while we were sleeping. It was the worst feeling."

"Oh, Maddy," Heather sighed; she could only imagine how horrible that must have felt, "I'm so, so sorry."

Maddy nodded her thanks and was silent for a minute or so before continuing, "Once we got to the hospital, I was taken to a separate room, and I didn't see Harrison again until that day at Cooper's office. Is there anything else that you want to know?"

"Has it gotten any better for you since it became public that you guys were drugged?" Heather asked her.

"Not, really. I've shut down all of my social media accounts. The hate online was just too much. I was super stoked to have hashtag Madeline is a slut trending worldwide. That was just wonderful. I'd been drugged, slept with a man who was engaged, had some asshole come in, and take a picture of me naked that was shown to the world, and I was the bad guy in everything. The woman who broke up the world's favorite couple."

"Hashtag couple goals," Heather said with a roll of her eyes, and Maddy laughed, "I appreciate your honesty with me, Maddy. I'm glad to finally know the truth."

"I'm assuming that Harrison gave you a watered-down version?" Maddy smiled.

"That's the understatement of the year. All he remembers is being at the table and eating dinner, then waking up the next morning. Hey, maybe it's true," she shrugged.

"I doubt it," Maddy said and cringed, "but I also don't blame him. This has to be up there as one of the worst conversations I've had in my life. How are you two going? I heard that you broke off the engagement."

"Yeah, we've actually just kind of started seeing each other again. That's part of why I wanted to talk to you. I'm trying to get past this, and, like I said, my therapist thought that this might be the key. Fuck knows I've tried everything else I can think of." She pursed her lips.

"Well, I really hope that you do, Heather. I'm sorry for the part that I played in all of this."

"I forgive you, Maddy," as she said it, Heather realized that it was true, she held no ill will toward the woman sitting in front of her, "I really do. I hope that you can get past this, as well. I have never blamed you for any of this; I knew that you were a victim as well. I hope those assholes rot in prison for what they did."

"Me, too. Thanks for asking me to do this, Heather. I didn't realize how much I needed to talk about it; it's actually been good. I feel…relieved."

"I'm glad," Heather said and hesitated before adding, "look, it's not my place, but I've been having weekly therapy sessions, and if you haven't talked to someone, I'd really recommend it. What happened to you was awful and traumatic, and it's okay if you need help to get over it."

"Thanks for the advice. I'll think about it."

Heather stood up from the table, and Maddy took this as her cue to rise, also. They hugged one another as they said goodbye. Heather was fairly certain that she'd never see Maddy again, but it was a relief to clear the air.

Later in the evening, Harrison called her. She thought about telling him she'd seen Maddy but decided not to. They had phone sex, though; it felt so familiar, and it was reassuring to Heather that her conversation with Maddy hadn't changed her feelings toward Harrison, at all.

"I love you, angel," He said as he wished her goodbye.

"I love you, too, Harrison. More than I thought I could ever love someone. When you get back from Los Angeles, maybe we can talk about what we want to do moving forward?" she asked him.

"That would mean so much to me," she could hear the smile in his voice, "I look forward to it."

She went to bed that night, exhausted from the emotional toll that the day had taken on her, but with a strange feeling of peace coming over her. The truth had been nowhere near as terrifying or hurtful as she had expected it to be. Zoe was a damn good therapist.

Chapter 24

SWEET DREAMS

Sunlight was streaming into the bedroom in her apartment, and Heather blinked her eyes in confusion. It was morning; that was odd. She realized that it was strange because she'd grown accustomed to waking in the middle of the night, and she didn't remember anything after going to bed.

Heather realized with a smile that she hadn't had a nightmare last night. For the first time in months, she had slept through the night. She had the urge to call Harrison but decided not to; it might have been a fluke. She'd tell him what had happened if it was all still going well when he came back to Chicago on Monday.

She'd tell Zoe at their session today, though. Oh, she couldn't wait to let her know how it had gone and get her thoughts on it. This felt massive to Heather. Not just that she hadn't had a nightmare last night, but her feelings this morning, as well. It was like there was a part of her soul that had been restored through her conversation last night and the peace she'd finally come to.

Heather set about her day, took a shower, and got dressed ready to go to Serenity. She looked at her phone and saw a text message that Harrison had sent her an hour ago.

On my way to the airport. Can't wait to see you when I

get back. I'll call you when I can.

This man, she loved him so much. The weekend had been amazing, if the lack of nightmares became an ongoing thing, she would happily move back in with him soon. She needed him; she wanted to go to bed with him by her side and wake up next to him every day. She sent him a text back.

You're probably on the plane by now. I love you, honey.

Heather debated internally for a second, whether she should send it, but it felt right. Heather was whole again, and it finally felt okay to call him that. He'd see the message when he got off the plane, and she got shivers thinking about him reading it. She knew that it would make him happy.

She saw that she had a text from Sebastian as well.

Is Harrison with you?

Heather frowned, that was fucking weird. He'd sent it about thirty minutes ago, right when they should've been getting on the plane. Her phone rang as she was typing out a reply and it was Ariana calling her.

"Heather, is Harrison with you?" Ariana asked her when Heather answered the phone; she sounded concerned.

"No. Why? He sent me a text that he was going to the airport an hour ago. What's happening?" Heather had a growing knot of fear in her stomach.

"He missed the flight to Los Angeles; the guys had to fly without him because they couldn't get on to him. They thought he might be with you, so I said I'd try and get on to you."

Heather felt sick; the last time she hadn't been able to get on to Harrison was the night he'd cheated on her, "Did you try Michael?"

"Yes, he's not answering, either. I'm really worried, Heather."

"Fuck. Is Cooper on the plane, too?"

"Yes. I don't know what to do. I'm at work; what do I do?" Ariana sounded fretful.

"Okay, I'll keep trying Harrison. Everything is probably fine," Heather didn't feel so sure of that, Harrison had never missed a flight in his life, "but you keep trying Michael."

Heather had tried calling Harrison five times in a row when her phone rang with a number she didn't recognize. Her heart skipped a beat. Was it Harrison calling her back from a different phone?

"Hello?"

"Could I speak to Heather York, please?" the person asked.

"Speaking. How can I help you?"

"Miss York, my name is Doctor Davies from Chicago Hospital. I'm calling you because you're listed as the in case of emergency contact in Harrison Fletcher's phone," his tone was even and calm.

Heather fought the urge to be sick, "What's happened to Harrison?"

"He's been involved in a car accident, and he's in surgery at the moment. Can you come to the hospital immediately?" he asked.

"Yes, of course."

Harrison. She wanted to lose herself in worry and despair, but she couldn't. She needed to be where he was.

"Cal!" she called out, and he appeared almost instantly.

"Yes, Heather?" His face dropped when he saw her, "What's wrong?"

"Harrison's been in an accident, can you take me to Chicago Hospital?"

He nodded, "Of course, let's go now."

As soon as they were in the car and on their way to the hospital, Heather called Ariana.

"Hi, Heather. Did you get on to Harrison?"

"No. A doctor called me; he's been in an accident. He's in surgery. I'm on my way to Chicago Hospital," as she said it,

Heather finally gave in to tears.

"Oh my god, Heather," Ariana gasped, "I'll meet you there."

Heather wanted to tell her not to; it was her instinct to try and assure Ariana that she would be fine, but she wanted her there, "Thank you."

After they hung up, Heather knew that she needed to call Sarah and Robert to let them know, as well. She hadn't spoken to them since she'd had a very awkward call with Sarah shortly after the night Harrison had cheated on her.

"Heather?" Sarah sounded pleased as she answered her call, "It's so lovely to hear from you. How are you, dear?"

Heather choked back a sob as she tried to say something, but couldn't.

"Heather? Are you okay?"

"Harrison. He's been in an accident," Heather struggled to say through her tears.

"No!" The pain was evident in Sarah's voice.

"He's in surgery," Heather managed.

She needed to say this. It made it clear that he was still alive…for now. That thought broke Heather, and she sobbed loudly. They'd only just started to make things right again. If he died today, she knew that she would not survive it.

"What hospital?" Sarah asked her.

Heather gave up and put the call on speaker, leaning forward to drop it in the passenger seat, before sitting back to continue crying.

"Hi," Callum said, "I'm not sure who I'm talking to."

"I'm Sarah, Harrison's mother, who is this?" She sounded confused and terrified.

"My name is Callum Archer. I'm Heather's bodyguard. I'm driving her to Chicago Hospital where Harrison is in surgery."

"We will meet you there," Sarah informed him.

Sarah hung up the call, and Callum drove Heather the rest of the way to the hospital in silence. When they arrived, he parked as close as he could to the entrance, assessing the situation as he drove past it. There was a throng of media near the entrance, and Heather felt sick.

She was insanely nervous right now; the last thing she wanted was to deal with paparazzi. If that was what she had to do in order to get to Harrison, though, she would do it. Heather would walk on hot coals to get to him right now.

Sure enough, as soon as the paparazzi spotted them, they were swarmed. Heather said nothing. Tears were still rolling down her face, and she couldn't stop them if she tried. She just needed Harrison to be okay.

Once they got inside, they were directed to a waiting room where other stressed family members and friends sat, waiting for news about their own loved ones. Heather sat in one of the chairs next to the wall, and Callum sat next to her.

Heather pulled out her phone and searched for 'Harrison Fletcher.' The top news stories were about the accident. Apparently, their SUV had been t-boned by someone who had blown through a red light. There were pictures of the carnage, and Heather felt sick. Where had Harrison been sitting? Surely, he must have been behind Michael, or he would almost certainly have been killed instantly.

Heather wondered if Michael had survived; was he in surgery, too? She looked around the waiting room but couldn't discern if anyone else here was someone that Michael knew. She had actually met Callum's wife, Ellen, a couple of times, but she'd barely been around Michael because of her split with Harrison.

They'd been sitting there for about half an hour when Ariana arrived with Ross Weber behind her. She made her way directly to Heather, gave her a massive hug, and sat down on the other side of her. Callum moved over to stand next to Ross near the door. Both of them seemed to be on alert.

"He'll be okay, Heather," Ariana said.

"He has to be, Ariana. I can't live in a world where he doesn't exist," just the thought of it was too painful to bear.

Living their lives separately had been hard enough to deal with. The universe wouldn't be so cruel as to take him away from her now. The man that she loved more than anything, the man that she had finally figured out how to forgive. He could not leave her now.

"I've let the guys know. There's a couple of interviews that they can't cancel contractually, so they're doing those and then coming back immediately."

Heather nodded, thankful that she wouldn't have to have those conversations. She put her head in her hands and cried quietly as Ariana rubbed her back, which was soothing to Heather. Eventually, Robert and Sarah joined them. No words were exchanged; Heather didn't have the strength to talk at all. Every time a doctor came into the room, Heather's heart leaped to her throat, but they never came to her, just sought out some other patients' loved ones to update them.

After what felt like forever, a doctor entered the room, looked around it, and spotted her. He made his way over to her, and she couldn't tell by looking at his face if the news was good or bad. The image of the scene of the crash flashed through her brain.

"Miss York, my name is Doctor Davies, we spoke on the phone"—she shook his outstretched hand, feeling completely numb as she did so—"I have good news. Harrison is out of surgery and is in recovery now."

Heather felt a fresh round of tears come upon her as the relief she felt flooded her emotions, "Oh my god, thank you!"

"What happened?" Robert asked.

"Harrison was in an accident, he arrived unconscious, but our main concern was tension pneumothorax, a quite bad presentation of a collapsed lung," he answered the unasked question about the medical term. "Once he was in surgery, we were able to relieve the pressure but discovered some internal bleeding that we were able to stop as well."

"But he's going to be okay?" Heather asked.

"He'll need to remain in hospital for the next week or so, but there's no reason that we wouldn't expect a full recovery. He does also have broken ribs, so he'll need to take care while they are healing," Doctor Davies told them.

"Thank you so much." The relief she was still feeling was immense.

"You're welcome. If you'd like to come with me, Miss York, we like to have someone in recovery for when the patient wakes up."

Heather quickly gave hugs to Ariana and Harrison's parents, promising to give Harrison their love, then followed the doctor through the hospital until she was brought to a room with the door closed. As he opened it for her to walk through, Heather saw Harrison lying on the bed, asleep. He looked so unbelievably beautiful, and he was breathing. That was all she needed from him. To keep breathing.

The doctor pulled a comfy armchair over to the bed for her to sit in, and Heather asked, "How long until he wakes up?"

"It could be many hours; it's very hard to say," Heather nodded as he said this and sat down in the chair.

Harrison had been tucked into the bed with his arms resting at his sides on top of the blankets; she took his hand and held it in hers. His skin was warm, and she remembered him holding her hand in his all night at Gabriel's birthday party. She desperately needed him to be okay.

Heather considered getting her phone out and looking at it. No doubt, she would have missed calls or messages, but she didn't do it. The only person in the world that she cared about right now was lying in front of her. She knew that Ariana would be letting the others know the news, but until Harrison woke up, there was no conversation that she wanted to have more than the one where she would tell him how much she loved him and needed him in her life.

Time passed slowly, but Heather didn't mind. She counted Harrison's breaths, loving the sound of him breathing more than she had ever thought that she would. She watched the rise and fall of his chest. Heather only let go of his hand when the nurses came in to do their observations.

Her phone rang occasionally, but she didn't answer it. She did take time to send a text to Ariana, though.

He's still asleep. He's stable.

She didn't bother waiting for a reply and just locked her phone again, then went back to watching Harrison. Sometime later, as the sun was getting low in the sky, Harrison groaned.

Heather stood up swiftly and said, "Harrison?"

He groaned again, then, after another few moments, opened his eyes and looked at her, then around the room, "Heather? Where am I?"

"Oh my god, honey. You're in the hospital. You were in an accident, don't you remember?"

He shook his head, and she pressed the button to call for the nurse.

"Is Michael okay?" he asked her, sounding concerned.

"I'm sorry, I don't know. They haven't said anything," she cringed.

As they were waiting for the nurse, he said softly, "Angel? Did you just call me 'honey'?"

She smiled down at him, wanting more than anything to just kiss him, but also needing to be gentle with him because she was worried that she would hurt him.

"Yes, honey, I did. You didn't have to go and get yourself almost killed to convince me to do it, either. We have a lot to talk about."

Heather stopped talking as the nurse came into the room. They checked Harrison over and got the doctor to come and talk to them both. After that, Heather made some calls to Ariana and Sarah, to let them know that Harrison had woken up and would be free to have visitors tomorrow. Ariana told her that the band had arrived on a plane back from LA an hour ago and were itching to see Harrison. Then, finally, they had some moments to themselves in which they could talk.

"So, all I needed to do was get myself crashed into and end up in surgery to get you to forgive me?" he asked her with a wry smile. "If I'd known that, I'd have done it months ago!"

"No. You promised me that you wouldn't put your health in danger, so that definitely wouldn't have worked," she laughed, "actually, it wasn't your accident that did the trick."

"Really? What happened, then, angel?"

"I saw Maddy last night," she said, as casually as she could manage.

"I'm sorry, you what?" He looked shocked.

She took his hand in hers and held it tight as she continued, "I asked Cooper to get her to call me. Zoe gave me the idea, she said that it might help me to get past it if I had the truth about that night, so my brain didn't keep filling in the blanks. She agreed to meet me; that was why I wasn't free for you to come over."

A horrible thought occurred to her. If he'd been at her place, he might not have been in the car accident. She took a deep breath, exhaled, and pushed away the dark thought. It didn't matter; he was here, and he was safe.

"I made her tell me everything," Harrison winced, "I don't know how much you really remember, and now isn't the time for that discussion, but, honestly, it wasn't any worse than what had been in my dreams. Heck, most of it was actually much better than I expected.

"Maddy has had a *really* tough time since it happened. I feel terrible for her. Anyway, by the time she'd left, I'd made my peace with her and what happened. When you and I spoke, I almost asked you to come around, but I didn't because I wanted to see if I would have another nightmare last night."

"Did you?" he asked, looking wary.

"Nope. I slept like a baby," she grinned at him, "first full night's sleep for me since October."

"Oh, angel," he smiled at her.

"Then, I was so happy. I was planning to tell you about it when you got back from LA, but then Ariana called me and told me you'd missed your plane, I found out you were here and that you were in surgery, I sat here all day, and you woke up, and I started telling you this story," she finished in a rush, and he laughed.

"I want to kiss you," he said.

She walked over to him and carefully placed her lips on his to kiss him. He lifted one of his hands to hold the back of her head and explored her mouth with his tongue. Heather could feel the arousal rising within her, she longed to be with him but knew that she couldn't right now.

"Harrison Fletcher," she told him with a breathless voice, "if I wouldn't literally break you doing it, I would climb on top of you right now and ride you until the break of dawn."

He laughed; the sound of it was smooth and seductive and did things to her insides, "I think I might take that trade-off with the way I'm feeling right now, angel."

"Well, lucky for you, I am completely sensible and rational and not ruled at *all* by my emotions. Therapy has been good for me!" She flipped her hair and gave him the haughtiest look she could manage before smiling at him as she sat back down in her chair.

"So, where does this leave us?" he asked her.

"Well, it leaves me hating that fucking apartment I've been

staying in and not wanting to spend another night away from you ever again," it was true, she wanted to be home again, in his arms and in their bed, "I don't know about you?"

"Look, I love Hayden, and I appreciate him giving me a place to stay, but I'm ready to leave."

"It's been a long five months, honey," she took hold of his hand again and kissed it.

"The worst five months of my life, angel," he confirmed.

"I was really worried about you," Heather said quietly, "you were drinking a lot."

He looked ashamed, "Yeah, I was. I wasn't coping, and I knew that I'd promised you that I wouldn't put my health at risk, but I also couldn't handle reality when I was sober."

"That's really concerning, Harrison," she said with a frown, "like, *really* concerning."

"I know, angel. Hayden cut me off many days. I owe him a lot for keeping me from hurting myself. I'll speak to Brendan about it, and if it's still a problem now, I promise to get treatment," he smiled at her.

"You still see Brendan?" Heather asked, unable to resist rolling her eyes.

Harrison laughed, "Yes. You two really did not get along, did you? He's actually been really good, and he's probably another reason I didn't hurt myself."

They were quiet for a few minutes, and Heather had two questions that she knew she needed to ask Harrison. She'd had a lot of time to think today. There were two things she knew for certain, she wanted to marry this man, and she had to do her part to right some wrongs. Might as well start with the scariest one first.

"Honey, I need to ask you something. I have an idea, we'd need to run it past Cooper, but I really think it's a good idea," Heather bit her lip, nervous about his reaction.

"What is it, angel?" he raised an eyebrow at her.

"I want to give an interview. You and me, Maddy as well if she's willing. I want to tell the world what happened."

Harrison looked shocked, "Why would you want to do that?"

"Speaking to Maddy last night, it highlighted so many things to me. The press conference that Aaron Hamilton and Cooper gave, it didn't really clear much up for anyone. She has suffered badly, Harrison. You were both drugged, and, officially, you were poisoned. That's a lot.

"I don't believe for a second that she would have slept with you if she hadn't been, and I know you wouldn't have slept with her. In her lowest moment, having woken up and figured out what she had done, she was then confronted with the picture and found out that someone had been in the room and taken a picture of her, naked, while you were sleeping. 'Violated' was the word she used to describe how it felt.

"After all of that, the world turned on her. You know how the fans can be—they're very protective of you, of us. In their eyes, she was the horrible person who broke us up. Maddy said that even after the press conference announcing the drugging, it hasn't gotten any better.

"I feel like if we gave an interview, told the truth. Hearing it from our mouths and seeing that we have come through this, well, if it can make her life even a tiny bit easier, then we should do it. Maddy didn't ask for any of this; I know that we didn't, either, but she just got caught up in our world. She was a visitor, and she got burned by the light we bear every day. Now she has to try and live a normal life wearing a permanent red 'A' on her reputation."

Harrison didn't speak for some time, as he appeared to process what she was asking of him. Heather was still holding his hand, and she squeezed it for comfort. If they didn't do this, it wouldn't hurt them at all, but if they did it, it could be so beneficial to Maddy.

"I love you, angel. I can't lie; I'm scared by the idea of reliving that in an interview, but your reasoning is sound. I feel terrible for Maddy; I've definitely seen the shit online," he smiled at the look on Heather's face, "you're not the only one who sank into the depths of reading internet articles about what happened. Part of my guilt was definitely around the way she was being treated, also feeling guilty to you for feeling guilty to her, if that makes sense."

Heather laughed, "Believe it or not, it does."

"Anyway, we should talk to Cooper and see if he's open to the idea. We'll almost certainly need legal advice and probably information from the LAPD about what we can and can't reveal. Once we've done that, we can approach Maddy…or have Cooper approach her, maybe. See if she wants to be involved or, at the very least, give her the heads up that it's happening if she doesn't."

He was such a beautiful man. She'd missed him so much; he was so thoughtful and caring, which was why she wanted to ask him the other thing.

"Okay, that sounds like a plan. So, there's something else that I wanted to ask you," she smiled at him, "you've been by my side for almost eleven years now, and I couldn't ask for a better person to be my life partner. I can't imagine my life without you in it."

She'd been rehearsing this in her head for hours now, practicing it to make sure she got it right. She dropped to one knee beside his hospital bed, still holding his hand in hers.

"Most importantly, I don't *want* to imagine my life without you in it. Harrison James Fletcher, will you marry me?"

~APRIL~

THE COUNTDOWN IS ON!

Only ten days to go until the release of 'Games We Play', the latest album for our favorite rock band, Cruise Control. No, this is not an April Fool's Day joke! We've been rocking out to 'Rules To Break' since January, and if the rest of the album is anywhere near as good, it's bound to be a smash hit!

The band recently canceled some promotional appearances in California when Harrison Fletcher was involved in a car accident. He spent a week in hospital, and our sources tell us that he's well and truly on the mend. Hopefully, he'll be fine by the time they're ready to tour!

Speaking of Harrison, it also seems that his on-again, off-again wedding to longtime girlfriend and fashion designer, Heather York, might be on-again? Heather was spotted at lunch with Gabriel Knight's fiancé, Ariana Chamberlain, this week, and we spotted a very familiar rock on her finger.

Will they be making a wedding announcement during the prime-time TV interview they're giving on Friday? It's been promised to be a shocking insight into their world, but many are wondering if the timing isn't a little too convenient, given how close it is to the release of 'Games We Play'. Still, we'll be watching…

Chapter 25

THE PRIMEST OF TIMES

Heather looked around their apartment, though it didn't really look like their apartment, right now. Crew members had been here for the past twenty-four hours moving furniture around, taking down almost all of their own decorations and putting up different ones. There was now some very convenient framed photos of her and Harrison, along with other members of the band all within easy viewing of the camera.

The living room was full of people, cameras, and lighting. Their theater room had been taken over as a makeshift makeup studio for them to have their hair and makeup done away from the chaos.

It was Wednesday, and she was missing her appointment with Zoe again this week to do this interview, which would be airing on Friday night. She'd been in the hospital with Harrison last week and had completely missed her session. She'd talked to Zoe on the phone on Thursday and told her everything that had happened. Zoe was definitely on board for the idea of this interview, though, which had resolved any doubts about it that might have been in Heather's head.

The rights for their exclusive interview had been sold for a very hefty price to a prime-time television show. Heather and Harrison had fought hard to ensure they only received twenty percent of the fee, which they would be donating to a charity that helped people rehabilitate from using drugs. Maddy would receive the remaining eighty percent.

Part of these negotiations had included the show's insistence on holding the interview in their private domain. Heather had been reticent about this, but she wanted to do the interview, and now that it was happening, she was comforted to be in her own surroundings. Her concern was more for Maddy and how coming to this place would make her feel.

Heather's cynical side was telling her that the show's producers insisting on this so hard had been partially for that reason. They wanted her and Harrison to be at ease, while 'the other woman' was uncomfortable. The entire process had felt a little bit as though they were at war with the show. Perhaps, it was just Heather's intense dislike for the media coming through, after what she'd been put through over the last year, though.

Luckily, the host of the show, Carol Sampson, was kind and very well respected for doing these types of interviews. She had put Heather at ease, almost immediately, once they had met and helped Heather to feel better about it.

Heather sat down in a chair to have her hair and makeup done. She'd been there for roughly ten minutes when one of the show's producers brought Maddy over to sit in another chair. It was the first time she'd seen her since the night she had come to Heather's old apartment.

"Hey, Heather," Maddy said, giving her a grim smile.

"Hi, Maddy. Are you feeling okay?"

"If you define 'okay' as 'needing to puke,' sure." Maddy rolled her eyes.

Heather laughed, "Sounds pretty okay, to me!"

"I wanted to say thank you," Maddy said in response, "I know that this whole thing was your idea."

Heather smiled at her, "No worries. I did a lot of thinking after we talked, and I really hope that this actually improves your quality of life a bit."

"It sure as shit can't make it worse!" Maddy cringed.

It wasn't long before Heather was sitting on their sofa, her hand held in Harrison's as they talked to the host. The plan was that they would be interviewed first, then Maddy would join them later.

"Thank you for doing this interview, I'm honored you chose me," Carol said with a smile.

"You're welcome," Harrison replied, "would you believe me if I told you that you were the only person who wanted to interview us?"

Carol gave a good-natured laugh, "No, I really wouldn't, Harrison. Heather, I suppose we should start with the most obvious question here. We can all see that you're wearing your engagement ring again, is the wedding back on?"

"Yes, it is." Heather smiled and couldn't resist looking up at Harrison.

It had been a stressful week, but they'd been relieved to find out that Michael had only sustained minor injuries, and he was back on duty now. Harrison had been discharged from the hospital on Monday, and they'd even had very careful sex yesterday. Both of them had been horny as hell, but Heather was terrified of damaging his healing ribs.

"Was it ever really off?" Carol asked.

"I have a ton of lost deposits that say yes," Heather told her with a wry grin.

"What about the rumors of an affair between yourself and Sebastian Fox?"

Carol had discussed this with them prior to filming. They'd agreed that this was the time to address the rumors that were still raging about Sebastian.

"Sebastian and I are just really good friends. We've been friends for thirteen years; he is absolutely one of my favorite people on the face of the planet, but we've never been anything more than that. Harrison has only ever been the one for me," he squeezed her hand as she said it.

"So, America's favorite couple called it quits. You've been together for a long time, how was that for you, Harrison?" Carol looked at him as she asked the question.

"Terrible," his face fell as he said it, "Heather is the only woman I've ever loved. I'd made a terrible mistake, something I would never have done, normally, and we did try to get through it, but it was too hard to get past at the time."

"Let's talk about what happened," she sounded curious, "there's been a lot of speculation about that night, from the time it happened, through to the press conference that was given by the Chief of the Los Angeles Police Department, Aaron Hamilton, and your manager, Cooper Powell. Even now, it seems as though we don't have the full story. What can you tell us about that, Harrison?"

They'd had a two-hour-long meeting with lawyers at Cooper's office yesterday, and Aaron Hamilton had dialed in from California. They couldn't specify who had drugged the group, for what reason, or how they'd done it, but they could give the general details surrounding what had happened. Heather assumed that Maddy had been briefed to the same effect.

"Obviously," Harrison began, "there is a current criminal case regarding this, so we can't be quite as open as we'd like. What I can say is that Cruise Control was specifically targeted at the Cancer Society event. We were given MDMA—a drug that is commonly referred to as ecstasy."

"So, this was the Willful Poisoning charge that has been made?" She looked thoughtful.

"Yes, that's correct."

"And it was everyone who was sitting at your table, correct?" Carol asked, and Harrison nodded his confirmation, "I see. So, that would have included Miss Turner?"

"That's right," Heather replied, "Maddy was as much a victim as anyone else at that table."

Carol looked at her with interest as Heather spoke up, "You seem quite defensive of a woman who slept with your fiancé, Heather."

"I'm not going to lie, I was very angry in the beginning, but I always knew that Maddy was a victim," Heather looked up at Harrison and immediately, any tension she was feeling seeped away, she looked back at Carol as she continued "I am the lucky woman whose fiancé cheated on her but also had a *very* good excuse for it. It was tough because I still had all of those feelings associated with being cheated on, but at the same time, how do you get to be angry at someone who has been the victim of a crime that caused them to do it?"

The interview continued on, with Carol running through their time apart and Harrison answering a lot of questions about how much he'd been drinking. Then they got Maddy out to sit on the sofa with Heather and Harrison.

"Madeline, thank you for joining us," Carol said kindly, "you've been painted by a lot of people as the scarlet woman—the person who broke up the golden couple, how has that been for you?"

She could feel Maddy bristling next to her as she said, "Well, it hasn't been great, Carol!" and Heather had to stifle a laugh.

"No, I suppose it wouldn't have been. Heather has been very defensive of you throughout our interview"—Maddy looked at Heather and gave her an appreciative smile—"what are your feelings toward her now?

"I don't think we're ever going to be best friends, but I'd like to think that there are no hard feelings between us."

"That's correct. Maddy and I sat down and talked things through one night, and I don't think I'll ever be able to thank her enough for being willing to do that. Hearing from her how it felt to be drugged and then do something you would never do while sober, only to face the violation of someone spreading your naked picture all over the internet…how could you hate a woman who had suffered all of that? Even if she did sleep with your fiancé!" Heather shrugged.

"Let's talk about that," Carol looked directly at Maddy, "in your words, Madeline, what was that night like for you?"

They proceeded to run through the events of the night from Maddy's perspective, with a lot less detail than she'd given Heather when they talked it through. Eventually, they neared the end of the interview, and Carol turned to Harrison.

"Harrison, your fans have been very protective of you during all of this, do you have a message for them?"

"Yes," he smiled down at Heather, and she felt her heart race as she looked in his eyes. He looked back up at Carol before replying, "I guess, if I were to tell them anything, it would be that I'm okay. Heather and I are okay. That Maddy is not to blame for anything that happened and, honestly? That even if I had cheated in the traditional sense, it still wouldn't have been Maddy's fault.

"I would ask them to please let Maddy live her life in peace. Please don't attack her on my behalf. I don't want that, and Heather doesn't want that. Save your anger for the people who did this to all of us," he looked over at Maddy and smiled at her, as well, "I'm sorry that you've had to go through this, Maddy."

"Thank you, Harrison, that means a lot to me," she smiled back.

"Well, thank you all for coming today and being so open and honest with me. I really appreciate it. What you've all been through must have been incredibly tough. Let this be a reminder to us all that things aren't always the way that they appear on face value.

Best of luck with your wedding, Harrison and Heather; I'm sure it will be absolutely beautiful, and we look forward to hearing *Games We Play* when it's released next week, Harrison."

Then, the interview was over. They'd been warned in advance that the cameras would stay rolling to capture some behind the scenes after the interview footage as Carol thanked them profusely. Heather told her how pleased she was with how delicately she'd handled their interview, and that it was a massive relief to know that the world would soon know the truth because they got to speak it themselves.

The crew was still working in their apartment to set it back to normal, matching everything against pictures that had been taken prior to changing anything, so they knew where everything needed to be put in order to go back to where it had been.

"Would you like to join us for a coffee out on the balcony, Maddy?" Heather asked her.

"Sure, that would be nice."

Harrison made them all coffees, and they headed out onto the balcony together, sitting down at a table and chairs out there.

"That wasn't too bad," Maddy was the first one to speak.

"It really wasn't," Heather agreed, "I do hope that it has a positive effect on your life, Maddy."

"Even if it doesn't, the money will make up for it," she gave a dry laugh, "I can't believe that you guys did that for me."

"It's the least that we could do," Harrison said gently, "I really am sorry for what happened, Maddy."

"Don't be. It happened, and none of us can change that. If I could go back in time and not drink that wine, I would. I've spent so long dwelling on that, but since I talked to Heather, I've realized that there's no point in doing that. I'll just end up bitter as hell if I do. I have a therapy session booked for next week," she smiled at Heather.

"I'm glad to hear it."

They each finished up their coffees, hugged Maddy, and she left their apartment. It took a few hours for the crew to reset the place to normal, but eventually, they went as well, and it was finally just Heather and Harrison, alone at last.

"Come here, angel," he said to her as she closed the door behind the last of the crew leaving their apartment.

He was sitting carefully propped up on the chaise section of their sofa after taking another of his strong painkillers once their interview was over. The doctors had barred him from flying, so the rest of the guys had stepped up for promotional events for *Games We Play,* and Harrison didn't have any obligations until the release party on her birthday next Friday. This interview was the only press event he had until then.

Heather joined him on the chaise, careful not to put too much pressure on his chest, and wrapped her arms low around his waist to avoid his ribs. He closed his eyes and rested his head on hers. They sat together in silence for some time. Everything in their world was finally where it needed to be.

"Angel, I've been thinking…"

"Do I want to know?" she asked him with a laugh.

"I wanted to know if you still want to get married on the ninth of May?" he asked her.

They had picked that date because it was her father's birthday. She'd loved her dad so much, and this way, it felt like he would get to be a part of their special day.

Heather pulled back from him and looked up into his face, "Are you serious?" He nodded. "You want to get married next month?"

"I do, angel. I know what that date means to you, and I don't want to wait another year to call you my wife."

"Harrison James Fletcher, you dated me for ten years, and now you suddenly can't possibly wait another year to get married?" She raised an eyebrow at him.

He laughed at her outrage, "Well, yes, that was dumb. I should've proposed to you long before I did. I was happy just having you in my life; I didn't need a ring or a piece of paper to prove our love."

"For the record, neither did I!" she grinned.

"Then Gabriel got back together with Ariana. He was so happy, and it made me really assess what you and I had. It made me realize that I did want to be able to call you my wife, because having seen what Gabriel went through, I knew that I didn't want to spend a day of my life without you in it.

"I was so happy when you said yes. I couldn't wait to stand up in front of the world and swear to our love. Then all that other shit happened, and I did have to live my life without you in it. I just feel like we've been through so much since then and they already took five months from us, I don't want them to take our wedding date as well."

Heather looked into his eyes; they had suffered so much this year. Why would she want to put off their wedding for another one? They deserved the love and happiness that they had promised one another back when he proposed in June.

"We'll never get the wedding venue booking back," she said slowly, and he grinned.

"So, is that yes, then, angel?"

Heather smiled at him, "It's completely and utterly insane, but it's a yes. It's a yes, even though we will struggle to find vendors, and barely anybody will be able to make it, and we will probably have to get married at a bus stop because all the venues will be booked.

"It's a yes because I fucking love you, Harrison Fletcher and because the only thing that matters is that you're there with me, with the people we love when we say 'I do.'"

He looked like a kid on Christmas morning; such was the delight in his face as she agreed to his proposition. Harrison dropped his lips to hers and kissed her deeply. Their tongues intertwined, and she dropped her hand from his waist down to his crotch, where she could feel him starting to harden.

"Mmmm, angel. We'd better get as much engaged sex in as I can physically manage before we become a boring, old married couple," he grinned wickedly at her.

"Very good point, honey. We are time-limited, now, before our sex life suddenly becomes shit. I've heard that having a wedding ring on your finger decreases your ability to maintain an erection by seventy-three percent," she said.

"Seventy-three percent, you say?" Harrison asked, and Heather nodded seriously at him, "Well, that does sound problematic. Where did you hear about this?"

"Some study that I read online, I think," she made a thoughtful face.

"Was this study peer-reviewed, though?"

"Of course!" She feigned outrage, "I only *ever* pay attention to peer-reviewed studies."

"Well, in that case," he laughed and kissed her lips softly, "you'd better come with me quickly, angel. We're running out of time."

They made their way to their bedroom. Those days of Heather being unable to enter this place felt like long ago. She had been right when she'd told Zoe that there were far more good memories associated with this apartment than bad ones.

They were also making new good memories on a daily basis, like the way Harrison was looking at her right now. He walked over to stand next to the bed, turned to face her and unzipped his pants, then let them fall to his ankles.

"Come here, angel," he said, and she walked over to him, "on your knees."

She grinned at him and dropped to her knees. Heather pulled his underwear down to his ankles as well, taking his semi-erect penis in her mouth. She was exultant in the feeling of him getting harder as she did so, and it wasn't long before she was moving her mouth back and forth along his length.

Harrison placed his hand on the back of her head and looked down at her as Heather made an effort to touch her nose to his stomach and stay there for a moment before pulling her head back to get some oxygen.

"You're so fucking sexy, angel," he groaned down at her, "I will never tire of watching you do this for me."

Heather removed him from her mouth, ensuring that she licked him from base to tip as she did so, "And I will never tire of doing it for you. I would be a happy woman if I could spend the rest of my life on my knees in front of you."

"Now, now, angel. If you did that, then I would never be able to return the favor." He raised an eyebrow at her.

"Fair point," she laughed.

Heather placed her mouth around him again, working hard to make sure that she took him as far as she could, as often as she could. This was probably her favorite sex act, and he made it so enjoyable with his responses to her as she did.

"Enough, angel," he told her, eventually, "it's my turn."

"No, Harrison," she said to him, "you have to be careful because of your ribs."

He smiled at her, "Let me worry about my ribs. You just take your clothes off, angel."

She took her clothes off, and he stripped as well before he got her to sit at the end of the bed. He knelt in front of her and placed a hand on either one of her knees before spreading them apart. He proceeded to bring her to orgasm multiple times.

"Harrison," she panted after the second one, "I can't take anymore!"

"Yes, you can, and you will, angel," he gave her an evil grin, "I'm going to eat you until I'm finished, and I'm not finished yet."

Heather was dizzy and shaking by the time he stood from where he was and instructed her to get onto her hands and knees. He took her from behind, allowing him to stay standing and protect his ribs. She thought that she might collapse by the time he finished deep inside her.

They made their way to the shower where they cleaned off, together. Harrison washed Heather carefully from head to toe, then held her close to him and kissed her deeply as they stood under the spray. When they were finished, they went back to bed and fell into an exhausted sleep.

Chapter 26

SUPER FUN HAPPY PARTY TIME

"Why the hell did I think that I should plan a wedding in a *month*?" Heather moaned to Ariana and Ally, as she was pinning up their bridesmaid dresses in Serenity's office.

It was quiet here today because it was a Saturday, so they had the place to themselves. For the bridesmaid dresses, Heather had gone with a one-shoulder design, with the right shoulder exposed. To offset that, she'd done a thigh split on the left leg with the fabric ruched on the left-hand side of the waist.

Ariana had looked so good in the blush pink dress at Gabriel's birthday that Heather was going with a blush pink again, but with slightly more peach tones, and both women looked amazing in the dresses.

"Apparently, you've got a big thing about specific dates?" Ally asked, "Isn't that why Harrison insisted that Cruise Control needed to release an album on your birthday?"

Heather laughed, "You've got me."

This was the final fitting for the ladies' dresses. In the end, she had decided to only go with these two ladies in her bridal party. A part of her had wanted to add someone, maybe Chloe, or even

Nikki, as a bridesmaid, just to match the number of groomsmen. However, the wedding felt so special and important to her that, even though she loved her family, it had been these people who had seen her through her worst moments this year, and it was these people that she wanted by her side on the day.

"Sorry, Seb, you won't have a partner in the bridal party," Heather had told him when she'd come to the decision.

"Good. I don't want to be tied to one woman, unless it's you anyway, lover!" he'd replied with a wink.

They were all going to Sebastian's apartment tonight for a combined bachelor and bachelorette party. Sebastian had been pretty insistent that they should throw Harrison a "proper" bachelor party, but Harrison had stamped out that idea pretty quickly. Everyone had a fairly good idea what that would have meant, and Harrison told Sebastian that he'd had enough of drinking and clubs over the last five months to last him a lifetime.

The reminder of that awful time had been enough to make Sebastian change his position. Heather was pleased, there were quite a few people coming tonight, and it promised to be a good night.

"Okay, so we've got a surprising number of guests confirmed for the wedding," Ally said after taking her dress off and opening up her laptop.

"Are you planning to direct my wedding like it's a fashion show?" Heather laughed.

"No, but I don't think you'd pull this off without me," Ally grinned.

She wasn't wrong. Ally's skills, not to mention her contacts within different aspects of event coordination, had been invaluable for getting this together in the ludicrously short amount of time that they had. The venue they had originally chosen was long gone, and they hadn't been able to find anything anywhere near as suitable until Sebastian had offered up Galena.

It made perfect sense. There was more than enough room for a wedding, it would make a beautiful backdrop for photos, and most important of all, both she and Harrison loved it out there. It had fast become one of her favorite places in the world since she'd first visited in October.

Games We Play was sitting at the top of the charts, and Galena was full of amazing memories of their time recording it. Yes, she had also gone out there at her lowest point, but even then, the house had been full of love and music.

"Even though you'd called it off, it seems like everyone who's anyone still wants to come to your wedding."

"Of course they do," Ariana laughed, "after that interview you guys gave, you're even more 'hashtag couple goals' than ever. Who the hell would want to miss out on being a part of your special day?"

Heather grinned, "Well, all I care about is that you guys are there. My family and friends, that's what matters. Anyone else who comes to celebrate with us is an added bonus."

"Spoken exactly like the woman who isn't trying to organize catering," Ally rolled her eyes dramatically.

"Am I going to be the death of you, Ally Morrison?" Heather laughed.

"Yes, you really are. You're lucky I like you, Heather, but I should warn you that my fee for your next fashion show has tripled, now!"

"Still worth it." Heather blew her a kiss.

When they were finished running through the plans for the wedding, Heather showed them her wedding dress, which was close to being completed.

"Heather," Ariana gasped, "it's absolutely gorgeous! I've been meaning to ask you." She looked a little bit nervous. "Can I commission you to make my wedding dress for me? I'm happy to pay you, of course!"

Heather laughed, "Of course I will, darling, and if you try to pay me for it, I'll be insulted! It will be my gift to you for the wedding."

Ariana smiled, and they hugged each other tightly. Heather was so glad that she had this woman back in her life again.

They spent the rest of the day together, having lunch and getting their nails done, before heading back to Heather's where they would be getting ready together for the party that night. As soon as they walked in the door, Heather saw Harrison and ran over to him, coming to an abrupt stop in front of him.

"Hi, angel," he said with a smile and carefully wrapped his arms around her.

It had been four weeks since the accident, and they were hoping that he'd be recovered fully by their wedding in two weeks' time, but just in case, they'd decided to delay their honeymoon by a couple of weeks so Harrison could get the all-clear from the doctors before they left.

"Hey, honey," she said, turning her face up to his to kiss him.

Sparks of electricity shot through her body, and she desperately wanted to take him into their bedroom and have her way with him. Unfortunately, they had guests and had to be social.

"Hi, ladies," Harrison greeted Ariana and Ally, who smiled at him from the sofa where they had happily seated themselves, Ally choosing to sit next to Hayden, who was smiling at her.

"Oh, Hayden. I didn't see you there, sorry, darling!" Heather said, looking over at him.

"You did seem slightly distracted." Hayden laughed. "I'll forgive you, this time. They don't call me, Sebastian Fox. He'd never stand for you ignoring him like that, Heather!"

Harrison and Heather headed over to the sofa as Ally shook her head and said, "I *still* don't get the joke!"

"What don't you get, Ally?" Harrison asked as he eased himself down on to the chaise section.

"The jokes about Heather and Sebastian having an affair. The stuff they say to each other, it surprises me that you're comfortable with it." She looked confused.

"'Wildly inappropriate,' she called it, Harrison!" Heather stuck her tongue out at Ally from where she was sitting, Harrison's hand in hers.

"It is!" Ally protested.

Harrison thought about it for a moment. "You're right, Ally. It *is* 'wildly inappropriate,' I suppose, but maybe that's just what we all are. I'm comfortable with it because I'm certain of Heather, and I'm certain of Sebastian. I also know that if they thought for a second that I wasn't okay with it, the joke would die in an instant."

"If I were you, I wouldn't be certain of Sebastian Fox for a second." Ally rolled her eyes, and they all laughed.

It was Hayden who replied, "I'm surprised you haven't realized by now, Ally. Seb sleeps with other women—"

"A *lot* of women!" Ariana emphasized with a grin.

"Agreed." Hayden continued, "But the idea of him sleeping with Heather is hilarious because she's probably the one person he would never sleep with, well...one of the three women, he would never sleep with." He put his arm around Ally and gave her a wink as he nodded his head toward Ariana as well. "Seb's also probably the single, most loyal person I've ever met. He would die for any one of us."

"I suppose that makes sense," Ally said, kissing Hayden, and then when they broke their kiss, she added, "but I stand by my original assessment at Galena that you guys are crazy!"

Heather got everyone drinks, and they talked for a while before going to get ready for the party. Once they were all dressed, they had another round of drinks, and Ariana and Ally walked over to Heather with wicked grins on their faces.

"Heather, my dearest darling, you need to wear this!" Ariana put a gaudy, pink veil coming off a plastic tiara on her head, and everyone laughed at her horrified look.

Ally slipped a white, polyester sash over her head that had 'Bride-To-Be' emblazoned on it in gaudy, pink writing. "And this as well!"

"No, way. I hate you guys, so much!" Heather laughed. She didn't hate them, though. It was so tacky, but she also loved that they'd done this for her. "Just know this, Ariana, I shall not forget this when your bachelorette party arrives! You will rue the day that you *ever* put polyester anything on me!"

"You can't scare me with polyester," Ariana said as she poked her tongue out at Heather, "I'm not you."

"Oh, it's not the polyester that you should be scared of. Just you wait…" Heather trailed off ominously, and everyone laughed.

They had a final round of drinks while they waited for the limousine that was going to be taking them to Sebastian's place. When they arrived, the party seemed to have already started without them.

Most people had already arrived and were spread throughout the apartment, drinking, and talking. There was music playing from the speaker system, and Sebastian greeted them, his arm around her cousin's waist.

"Hi, Seb. Bye, Seb!" Ariana said with a laugh as she walked off to find Gabriel, who had been helping Sebastian to set up today.

"Hi, darlings." Heather smiled and gave each of them a hug. "Point me in the direction of the alcohol, Sebastian Fox. It's my bachelorette party, and it's time to get my drink on!"

He kissed Nikki's neck, and she giggled, then he dropped his arm from her waist to take Heather over to his bar, which was being tended by a hired bartender tonight.

"What would you like to drink tonight, lover?" he asked her.

"Rum and Coke. It's turning into my new favorite drink." She smirked, and the bartender nodded.

She turned to look at the room as she waited for the drink,

and her mouth dropped into an 'O' of horror. There were balloons everywhere that she hadn't noticed until now—balloons with her face on them.

"Holy shit! Your face..." Sebastian started laughing so hard that he had doubled over.

Harrison had joined them and high-fived Sebastian, also laughing at Heather's reaction.

"I hate you both!" Heather announced, taking her drink from the bartender and taking a massive swig of it before continuing, "I don't think there's enough alcohol in the world to make me forget these. Sebastian, you are no longer my lover, and Harrison, the wedding is off again!"

Harrison slipped his arms around her waist, bent his head and nipped her earlobe with his teeth, then said in her ear, "Is that so?"

She felt the arousal coming over her, but even still, she maintained her haughty demeanor and said, "Yes, that is exactly so. I can never get past this."

He pulled her tighter to him, lowered his head further, and kissed her neck before drawing his tongue up in a line back to her ear and saying, "Are you really sure?"

Heather smiled, turned around in his arms, and met his lips with hers to kiss him. When their kiss ended, she laughed. "Okay, I might *just* be able to forgive you, but *only* because you're a fucking sex god." She turned her head to smirk at Sebastian. "So, you're shit out of luck on the forgiveness front, Seb!"

"You know what, *lover*?" He emphasized the word, heavily, "That look on your face was worth it. I have no regrets."

"I see you're back with Nikki this evening?" Heather raised an eyebrow at him.

"Yeah. I do have a one-time-only policy, so she should be off the table, but I might have to make an exception for the York women, you know? We'll see what happens; there are a few options here tonight."

He grinned at Heather, and she frowned back at him. "Please don't be a dick to my family, darling. If you're not going to sleep with her, don't lead her on, at least."

"Why must you always ruin my fun?" He rolled his eyes at her.

"I thought I was your fun?" She laughed back at him.

Harrison ordered himself a whisky, and when he had it, they circulated the room. All of their closest family and friends were here tonight. They'd left their parents off the guest list, but everyone else had made it out tonight.

Heather took a selfie of herself with one of the balloons and posted on Instagram with the caption:

@sebastianfoxofficial can rot in hell for these! Life pro-tip, balloons with your face on them are never flattering! #partyhard #HarrisonandHeatherWedding #SebsHouseIsAboutToGetTrashed

A few minutes later, her phone pinged with a notification that she had a comment on her post from @megggzy2005, and she took a look.

Every picture of you is pretty @heatheryorkofficial! I can't wait to see your wedding dress!

Heather showed her phone to Harrison, who was standing next to her and told him, "She's the sweetest kid!"

He smiled at her; she'd told him about driving Megan home when it had happened but hadn't really mentioned about the message she'd sent Heather when they were split up.

"She's also completely right," he smiled at her, "every picture of you is perfect."

"You're biased," Heather stuck her tongue out at him, "would you be okay if I invited Megan to come to the wedding?"

"I'm fine with that, angel. As long as you are there saying 'I do,' it doesn't matter to me who else is in attendance." He kissed her, then, long and slow.

When their kiss ended, Heather sent Megan a direct message.

Hey, Megan. Thanks for the comment and being such a great fan. Do you want to come to the wedding? If you do, shoot me your address and I'll send you an invite. Your parents can come, too, of course.

Heather laughed when Megan's reply came through almost instantaneously.

Are you SERIOUS?!?!?!? OMG YES!!!!!

The next message contained the address for where to send Megan's invitation. It was the same place they'd dropped her off that day back in October.

Harrison took her to get another drink, and Heather realized she was starting to get quite drunk. She could barely keep her hands off Harrison but was trying to be mindful of the fact that there were a lot of people around them and made sure to be careful of his healing rib cage.

They made their way over to the pool table, where Sebastian was holding court as the reigning champion of the evening. Apparently, he'd beaten Jake on roughly the fourth game that anyone had played tonight and had beaten everyone else, since.

"You want to play with me, lover?" Sebastian asked with a wink, "And I don't mean pool, of course!"

Heather laughed, "Well, I am horny as fuck, right now! Let's go, then…" she paused for a second or two before continuing, "and I *do* mean pool, of course!"

Harrison chuckled, standing directly behind Heather and slipping his arms around her waist as Sebastian racked up the balls for their game.

"I think you might have paid Seb back for the balloons, angel," he smirked at Sebastian, "I think he just about had a heart attack, thinking that you were serious for a second."

"My brain doesn't work so well when it's fueled by Glenfiddich," Sebastian told them with a laugh, as he lined up to break.

Their game didn't take long. Drunk or not, Sebastian was still a skilled pool player, and Heather wasn't great at the best of times, much worse when she had reached what must be her seventh drink of the night.

She had fun, though; between each shot as she was waiting for Sebastian to take his turn, she was in Harrison's arms. He was teasing her and had been all night, she realized after a while. He would stroke her arm, or her thigh, or her neck, lightly with his fingers. Every now and then, he would kiss her on her lips or her neck. It was nothing that would look particularly erotic to anyone who saw it at the party unless you had watched him do it to her repeatedly for hours.

Heather was starting to get very worked up, and by the end of their match, she didn't give a crap about playing pool anymore. She just wanted to leave this party and have sex with her future husband. When Sebastian potted the black ball, she congratulated him and turned immediately to kiss Harrison passionately.

"Is something up, angel?" he asked her quietly.

"I certainly fucking hope so," she slipped her hand down to his crotch and squeezed him quickly before putting both arms around his neck to kiss him again.

"Tease," he said to her when they came up for air.

Heather laughed, "Like you can talk. Don't think that I don't know what you're doing, honey."

He dropped his head and kissed her neck before asking in her ear, "What am I doing, angel?"

"Driving me crazy, that's what," she shivered.

"Good, that's what I was hoping to do," he gave her a wicked grin.

Sebastian walked over to them and said casually, "You know, I've always imagined Heather in my bed; I just expected that it would be me in there with her. The room's free if you need it," he winked at them.

Harrison grinned at him, "I'm about ten seconds away from taking you up on that offer!"

"Okay, Seb, I get the point," Heather sighed dramatically and put a tiny bit of distance between herself and Harrison so they could be mildly less inappropriate in front of their guests.

Harrison kept Heather on edge for the rest of the night, though. Continuing his slow torment of assaulting her senses with his touches and kisses as the time went on. She didn't drink any more; she'd had enough, and she wanted to be with it enough when they got home to have sex.

Near the end of the night, there was a round of very drunk speeches from the people that were left at the party. They were far more inappropriate than the ones that had been given at their engagement party. Embarrassing stories that could never have been shared in front of their grandparents.

When they were leaving, she thanked Ariana, who had helped Sebastian organize the party, and who wanted to make it clear to Heather that she'd had nothing to do with the balloons. Heather laughed and asked her to pass her thanks on to Sebastian, who was in the corner of the room, making out with a brunette woman that definitely wasn't Nikki.

As she and Harrison made their way to the elevator to leave, Heather took great delight in popping a balloon and called out to the room, "That's what I think of that!"

~MAY~

HERE COMES THE BRIDE!

Rumors are running wild about the upcoming wedding of Harrison Fletcher from Cruise Control and fashion designer, Heather York. They're getting married on the 9th, and we can't wait to see the pictures!

Sources say that it's being held at an exclusive hotel in the center of Chicago. We're not sure exactly when the wedding was officially back on again, as confirmed in last month's interview with Carol Sampson, but this must have been put together quickly.

We're told that it's going to be a very romantic affair, and the couple has handwritten their own vows for the occasion. We can't help wondering if Harrison has written a special song for his love to celebrate their special day?

Chapter 27

THE WEDDING

Heather was sitting in a limousine, and they were about twenty minutes away from Galena. Ariana, Ally, and Jake were sitting with her. Her brother was walking her down the aisle today.

"I didn't think that I'd be nervous!" she announced to the car.

"It's pretty normal to be nervous, sis," Jake said to her, with a grin, "I was so worried that Chloe wouldn't show up on our wedding day!"

"That's dumb," Heather rolled her eyes at him, "she loves you. Of course, she was going to show up."

"Exactly," he smirked.

Ariana laughed, "You can all remind me of this when it's my turn!"

"I wonder how all of your celebrity friends took the news when they were told they had a three-hour-long drive to the wedding," Ally said.

"Oh god," Heather laughed, "I'm going to cop some major shade for that, no doubt! I wish I could look online and find out."

The others laughed because Heather had been subjected to a social media blackout, and Ariana was holding Heather's phone hostage this morning. Any of their guests who hadn't known in advance that the wedding was being held out at Sebastian's estate had been given the address of an upscale Chicago hotel as the venue. A lot of their guests had booked into the hotel, and everybody had been warned to plan for two nights in Chicago.

When their guests arrived for the apparent eleven o'clock wedding, they should have been directed to limousines that took everyone to Galena. Every limousine had been decked out with food and drinks for the trip.

After arriving at Galena, everyone was to be treated to cocktails before heading out to the area where the wedding ceremony was being held. Heather's breath caught as they pulled up to the gates. There it was, the fancy gold script on the gates always looked impressive to Heather.

Maison De L'amour Et De La Musique

The place that she would marry the love of her life. The man who was her heart's song.

They drove up the long driveway, and Heather felt her nerves rising. This day had been a long time coming. She had loved Harrison since she was a teenager; they had been through so much to get to this place today. Heather looked at her hands and realized that they were shaking.

"You're going to be fine," Ariana smiled at her kindly, as they pulled to a stop under the porte-cochère.

Callum opened the door to the limousine and poked his head inside, "It's time, Miss York."

"Which means that you're officially off the clock, Cal. Go find Ellen and sit down; I need all the guests there when I walk down the aisle," she smiled at him.

"Yes, ma'am!" He gave her a salute, and she laughed.

Heather stepped carefully out of the car; her dress was just as amazing as she'd always hoped that it would be. In the end, she'd ended up making it with an intricate lace-detailed bodice that had a plunging, V neckline, coming down to a tulle skirt that flared out with the lace detailing carried down the skirt. Underneath the tulle skirt, she'd gone with a baby blue fabric. The end result was absolutely gorgeous, and she couldn't be happier with it.

It was her 'something blue.' She had a pair of her grandmother's pearl earrings on, her tiara was a stunning one that had been loaned to her from an exclusive jewelry designer in New York City, and Harrison had promised to take care of her 'something new.'

Before he'd left for Galena last night, he had given her the most amazing, diamond, heart lock necklace. It was absolutely stunning in white gold, and the diamonds sparkled. Heather loved it, and Harrison told her as he helped her to put it on that he couldn't wait for her to become his wife today. She knew that she would never take it off; it was her favorite piece of jewelry, ever, after her engagement ring.

"Are you ready for this?" Ally asked her as they stood in a group, waiting for their cue to head down to the ceremony.

Heather grinned at her, despite her nerves, "I feel like I'm going to be sick, but I'm also more than ready for this. Thank you guys so much, not just for today, but for everything this year. I'm not sure what I would've done without your support."

Ally and Ariana both hugged her as one of the support staff that were assisting with the event arrived to tell them that it was time.

Heather could hear beautiful classical music playing as Ally started walking away from them. She didn't know who had pulled the strings required to hire people from the Chicago Philharmonic Orchestra to perform at their wedding, but the result was amazing. Ariana gave her a final hug and a wish of good luck before she started off.

"You'll be fine, sis," Jake assured her, as he held his elbow out to her for them to link arms.

Heather hooked her arm around his, then went back to gripping her pastel pink and blue bouquet in a death grip before replying with, "Thanks, Jake."

Then they were signaled to go. They walked through an archway near the garage that led down to the grounds. Sebastian had a gorgeous gazebo down by a beautiful lake that had made for the perfect place to hold their wedding ceremony. As it came into view for Heather, she could see that it had been decorated with tulle and flowers in keeping with the pastel theme.

The guests that had previously been seated on white, wooden chairs were all standing and looking at her now. There were a lot of them, more people than she ever could have expected. Jake's steadying arm was comforting as she continued walking the long, red carpet toward the ceremony, and the bridal march continued playing.

Her eyes flew to her goal—there in the gazebo, standing in front of their celebrant, was Harrison. The tension and nerves left her as she started to make her way through their guests toward him and caught his gaze. This familiar path was soothing, knowing that it would lead her to his arms. Once again, she was heading home. It didn't matter that this was the most important day of their lives; all that mattered was that she was going home.

Gabriel was standing next to Harrison as best man, Ariana opposite him as Maid of Honor. Hayden and Ally were opposite one another next to them. Sebastian stood next to Hayden. It was oddly fine with Heather that there was no partner for Sebastian, it felt strangely appropriate in her mind, and she grinned at him as she passed him.

Then she had arrived at her place, in the ceremony, and in life. She was standing next to Harrison. Everything in her longed to just run straight into his arms, but her brother stood between them for the archaic tradition of 'giving her away.'

Finally, Jake gave her a hug and took his place sitting down next to her mom in the front row. There was nothing and no one between her and Harrison now. As they moved closer, he held her hand in his, and she caught her breath.

"Hi, angel," he said quietly to her in an undertone that only she could hear.

"Hi, honey," she smiled back at him.

The celebrant had started talking again, about love and what it means. As if he could tell Heather anything that she didn't know. He was talking about love as a concept, but all she could think about was love in regards to her relationship with Harrison. Smiling up at him, their love felt all-consuming. She knew now that their love could withstand some of the toughest things that had ever tried to test it.

It wasn't long before the celebrant was asking Harrison to say his vows. He let go of her hand and pulled a sheet of paper out of the inside pocket of his tuxedo, unfolded it, and began to read.

"I've thought a lot about what to swear to you in my vows today, angel. Heather York, I promise to be the person who will love you more than anyone else in the world. I promise to be the person who will support your dreams, no matter what they are. I promise to spend every day of the rest of our lives proving to you that I am worthy of loving you. I promise to do my best to make you laugh and to try never to make you cry."

Heather already had tears starting to stream down her face as she was hit with the force of his love.

"I see that I'm off to a terrible start," he said, and their guests all laughed, along with Heather, who dabbed at her tears with a tissue that Ariana handed to her, "I can't promise that there won't be tough times. I can promise, though, that I will hold your hand through those times. I promise these things to you, Heather York, with every part of my heart and soul, which have always belonged to you."

Heather wanted nothing more than to kiss him, to be in his

arms right now. There were things that needed to be done before she could reach that point, though. Step one, swear her love to Harrison in front of everyone here, which was what the celebrant was asking her to do right now.

"Harrison Fletcher, you are my constant. When I'm with you, I'm home. I know that you will be everything that I need you to be. What I promise to you is to love you with everything that I am, to be by your side even when the world tries to tear us apart. I will never forget that you love me. I will rinse all dishes immediately and always use a coaster and only eat in my car sometimes but never, ever in yours," Harrison laughed at her.

"I will accept all of the love that you deign to give me. I will be the angel you desire and also the one that you need. I will do everything in my power to bring as much happiness and joy to your life as I possibly can, every day, for the rest of our lives."

Harrison seemed to be glowing. She vaguely wondered if this is what Ariana had meant about Gabriel the night they'd been drugged. The entire world was aglow, but nothing glowed brighter than Harrison, who she beamed at with pride.

The celebrant led them through exchanging their rings, and Heather loved the feeling of sliding Harrison's wedding ring on to his finger. Heather felt as though all of her love for him was bound in that ring, in the promises that she'd made to him today. That seal of her love would be worn on his finger for the rest of his days.

Once that was done, the celebrant said, "You have kissed a thousand times, maybe more. But today, the feeling is new. No longer simply partners and best friends, you have become husband and wife, and can now seal the agreement with a kiss."

Harrison's gaze locked with hers as he lifted her veil over her head. The world was clear now she didn't have the veil in front of her eyes, but Harrison still glowed, burning brighter as his lips pressed against hers. His arms made their way around her waist and pulled her to him, continuing to kiss her for another few seconds as their guests cheered before he let her go.

"Honored guests, if you could all please stand, I present to you, Mister and Missus Fletcher!"

Their guests all cheered as they made their way back down the aisle, hugging people here and there on the way. Eventually, they reached the back and began greeting friends and family before they were whisked away by their photographer to have photographs taken.

"Heather Fox, isn't it?" Sebastian grinned, as they were having bridal party photos taken.

"Wrong 'F' name, darling," Heather poked her tongue out at him.

Harrison put his lips close to her ear and whispered, "I've got an 'F' word that describes exactly what I'll be doing to you later, wife."

Heather shivered as she looked up at him; he was her husband now. He was still glowing; she loved this man so much, and they had truly come out the other side of what would hopefully be the worst thing they would ever experience.

Once the photos were all done with, they made their way to a massive marquee that had been set up on the expansive lawn area, where their guests were waiting for them. Heather was talking to Ariana, Ally, and Hayden, when a very excited and nervous-looking Megan came over to her, trailed by an older woman who Heather assumed must be her mother.

"Hi, Heather! Thank you *so* much for inviting me. The wedding was *gorgeous*!" she said with clear excitement in her voice.

"Thanks, darling. Is this your mom?" Heather asked.

"Yes! Mom, this is Heather York...wait, Fletcher!" Megan corrected herself, and Heather shook her mom's hand.

"Hi, Heather. It's lovely to meet you. Megan talks about you all the time. I'm Pamela."

"I'm flattered. Megan is a sweet girl; you should be very proud of her," Heather smiled at her.

"I am," Pamela said.

"Megan, this is Hayden, Ally, and Ariana," Heather introduced them, and Megan looked completely blown away, particularly at meeting Hayden.

"I'm *such* a huge fan!" she said to him repeatedly, and he laughed.

"Well, thanks," he smiled.

"Come on, Megan," Heather grinned, "how about I go take you to meet Sebastian, Gabriel, and Harrison."

Megan and Pamela followed Heather until she managed to find Gabriel and Sebastian over by the bar.

"Hi, guys," Heather said to them, "I wanted to introduce Megan and her mother, Pamela. Megan's a big fan of Cruise Control."

"It's great to meet you, Megan," Gabriel said, smiling at her.

"Can I give you a hug, Gabriel?" she asked him, looking more shy than Heather had ever seen her look.

"Sure." He was so kind, and Megan looked like all of her dreams had come true when he hugged her.

"Nice to meet you, Megan," Sebastian said to her.

"Thanks, Sebastian!" She grinned at him.

"Call me Seb," he said with a smile, and Heather and Pamela both laughed at the expression on Megan's face.

"I'm. Dead." Megan said, dramatically, to them both as they left Gabriel and Sebastian behind to go and find Harrison, "I am dead, and I've gone to heaven and Cruise Control are there!"

"I did try to tell her that celebrities were normal people," Heather said to Pamela, as they made their way across the marquee and through a bunch of people, toward Harrison, "I don't think it stuck."

Pamela laughed, "No, I don't think it has. Thank you again for inviting us. It's just Megan and me, so getting to attend an event like this is pretty exciting for us."

Heather hadn't realized before, but as she said this, some things clicked into place for her. Pamela was a single mother. They didn't live in a terrible area of Chicago, but Pamela obviously must have worked very hard to give Megan as much as she could.

They reached Harrison, and Megan was very excited, once again, to be meeting a member of Cruise Control.

"I love your music so much! 'If I Were You' is my favorite song, like, ever! You and Heather are my favorite people in the world, and I'm so glad you got back together. I'm so sorry you had that shitty thing happen to you guys, but I knew that you guys could work it out. I can't believe I got to be at your wedding! This is the best day ever!"

Megan finally finished, and Harrison laughed, "I agree, Megan, today *is* the best day ever! Also, you said that 'If I Were You' is your favorite Cruise Control song?" Megan nodded, "Well, I think there's a surprise later that you should look forward to," he winked at her.

When Megan and Pamela walked away to find their seats, Heather put her arms around Harrison, and he kissed her. He'd been given a clean bill of health at the hospital on Thursday, but she was still glad that he would have another two weeks until their honeymoon started. She wanted him as healthy as a horse for that.

"I love you, Mister Fletcher," she smiled at him.

"I love you, too, Missus Fletcher." It was so weird that she wasn't Heather York anymore.

They made their way to the bridal table and took their seats for the rest of the festivities. Later in the evening, Gabriel, Sebastian, and Hayden took places on a stage where their instruments were set up. One of the Cruise Control backup musicians was on bass, and they performed "If I Were You" while Heather and Harrison had their first dance.

All in all, it was an utterly perfect day, and sometime near midnight, as their tired guests were making their way to the line of limousines that would take them back to Chicago, Heather and Harrison headed inside the main house. Sebastian had kindly offered for them to spend the next three days here before they had to go back to Chicago for Heather to get some work done at Serenity to make sure everything was in place for their two-week honeymoon.

They were back in the room they'd stayed in when they were out at Galena back in October. It felt like forever ago. It felt like yesterday. Every day of her life had led up to this single, perfect day. The day where she finally got to marry the man she'd wake up to for the rest of her life. Harrison looked devastatingly handsome, standing in the middle of the room wearing his tuxedo, face aglow as he looked at her. She walked over to him, and he wrapped his arms around her.

She was home.

Epilogue

Heather was stretched out on a sun lounger under a parasol on their private beach. She and Harrison had been married for four weeks now and were having their honeymoon in the Seychelles. She watched Harrison from behind her sunglasses as he swam in the beautiful, aquamarine water in front of her.

It was his birthday, today, and their second last day here on the island. They probably hadn't spent as much time as they should have doing sightseeing while they were here, but they'd been completely preoccupied with having so many free hours in the day to explore each other's bodies.

Heather watched as Harrison made his way back to the beach, enjoying the view immensely as he walked toward her wearing nothing but swim trunks, with water dripping off his muscled body. She bit her lip as she felt a growing ache between her thighs.

He was looking at her in a way that reminded her of how Gabriel had looked at Ariana as they'd walked downstairs in their bikinis at Galena. She remembered thinking that Harrison would have looked at her that way if he had been there, and she had been right.

Heather could never have imagined that weekend that she would have ended up marrying Harrison exactly on schedule. That she would be here, with him in this beautiful place right now to celebrate their marriage.

"Having fun, angel?" Harrison asked her, as he dropped down on the sun lounger next to hers.

"Well, I'm certainly enjoying the view, that's for sure," she smirked at him as her eyes flickered to his crotch, "is there anything special that you'd like for your birthday, husband?"

Harrison laughed, and it was a laugh that was filled with sexual promises for Heather.

"Come here, angel."

Sneak Peek For The Baby

Lita Ciccone was busy coding a video game for her employer, Silicon Street. She'd come across a bug and was trying to find out how to fix it when her phone started buzzing on her desk. She frowned and answered it, vaguely recognizing it as being a Chicago phone number as she did so.

"Hello?"

"Hi, am I speaking to Miss Lolita Ciccone?" the woman on the other end of the phone asked.

"Yes, this is Lita."

"Oh, Miss Ciccone, excellent. My name is Stephanie Jennings, and I'm calling from the office of Cooper Powell," Lita's mouth dropped open in shock. Cooper Powell was the manager of her favorite band, Cruise Control, "I'm calling you to congratulate you on winning the competition you entered for a night out with the band!"

"Are you serious? Is this a joke?" Lita couldn't believe what she was hearing right now.

Stephanie laughed, "No, definitely not a joke! Now, the prize includes flights to Chicago as well as a hotel room for two people while you're here, inclusive of airport transfers. You will need to fly from Seattle on a Friday and out from Chicago on a Sunday.

"On Saturday night, you and your friend will be treated to a night out with Cruise Control. We have two available weekends to do this. One is the weekend of the twenty-sixth of June, and the other is the weekend of the third of July. You don't need to answer immediately, and I'll be putting all of this in an email to you. I just call because people tend to miss emails or think that they're a scam."

Suddenly, Lita was suspicious, "*Is* this a scam?"

"Feel free to hang up now, look up the phone number for Powell Management and call me back," Stephanie laughed.

"You sound very honest, but I think I will do that," Lita said, not caring that she sounded rude.

"No worries, talk to you soon!" Stephanie said.

Lita hung up the call and did exactly as Stephanie had asked. There was the number from the top of the search results, and sure enough, it was the one that had just called her. The excitement started to build in Lita; holy hell, she might actually be getting to meet Cruise Control!

She called the number, and it answered on the second ring, "Hello, Powell Management, how can I help you?"

"Hi, I'd like to speak to Stephanie, please?"

"Oh, yes, that's me! Is this Lita? I thought it might be you, but I couldn't be sure," Stephanie laughed.

"Yes, it is. Sorry I didn't believe you; it just sounded too good to be true."

"Completely understandable. Anyway, as I was saying, I'll be sending this all to you in an email. If you can reply back as quickly as possible with your chosen weekend and the name of the person you'll be traveling with, I can get it all booked for you,"

They ended their call shortly after that, and Lita sat back in her chair in complete shock. She remembered entering that competition on a whim. She'd been bored and had been looking at Cruise Control's website for more information about *Games We*

Play when she'd seen it.

She'd been a fan of theirs for years and had seen them in concert on both the *Cards Have Been Dealt* and *Heart Wide Open* tours. Lita had streamed *Games We Play* the minute it had been released on Spotify and knew all of the lyrics off by heart already. She had a real affinity for learning song lyrics and never felt like she could really enjoy a song properly until she could sing along word for word.

The first day, she'd listened repeatedly while reading the lyrics. Every song spoke to her in some way or another—that was what she loved about their music. It felt purposeful, not like it was just something random that had been thrown together.

It didn't hurt that every single member of the band was absolutely to die for, either. Harrison Fletcher had just gotten married to his longtime girlfriend, Heather York. Gabriel Knight had been with his fiancé, Ariana, for over a year now. So that left Sebastian Fox and Hayden Vega, and there were rumors amongst the fan base that Hayden was seeing someone on the down-low.

Not that Lita thought she had a shot in a million years with any of the members of Cruise Control, even knowing that she was going to get to meet them now, but she'd had the biggest crush on Hayden for the longest time. He seemed really sweet and lovely in interviews, and she wished there was a guy like that for her in real life.

Sebastian, meanwhile, was the kind of guy that she wouldn't touch with a ten-foot pole. Lita didn't think she'd ever seen a picture of him with the same woman twice. If the rumors were to be believed, he slept with an abhorrent number of women, particularly fans. A lot of who got a weird kind of glory in the fanbase for having done it.

It was insane that Lita was finally going to get to meet them. She pulled out her phone and texted her best friend, Becky.

Hey, what are you up to on the 26th of June?

Becky didn't take long to reply to her text.

Nothing planned. Why?

Want to come meet Cruise Control with me in Chicago?

Her phone immediately started ringing, to Lita's complete non-surprise, and she answered the phone with a laugh, "Yo, bitch. So, you coming to the mid-west with me or not?"

"Lolita Serafina Ciccone, you can *not* just ask me that as if it isn't the coolest and most insane thing ever! How the hell did you get this?" Becky sounded like she was as shocked as Lita had been when she'd been told.

"I entered a competition on their website last month and, apparently, I won! So, are you coming or not? Because I bet I could find someone else to go with me if you're not interested..." Lita trailed off ominously.

This threat was enough to spur Becky into action, "Yes! Oh my god, yes! A million times, yes!"

Lita hung up the phone and checked her email. Sure enough, there was a very official-looking email from Stephanie laying out the details of the possible weekends. She replied with haste, telling her that the weekend of the twenty-sixth of June would work best for her and thanking her again for her patience with Lita thinking it was a scam.

As she hit send on her email, Lita couldn't believe her luck. She was going to get to meet her favorite band. The twenty-sixth of June was going to be epic.

Sneak Peek For Harrison's Wedding

It's Sunday morning, and I'm stretched out on the chaise section of our sofa. I'm playing a race car game on the PlayStation. My girlfriend, Heather York, is lying on her back with her head in my lap, using it as a pillow. She's scrolling through Instagram on her phone. This is a pretty normal Sunday morning for us if we don't have anywhere to be.

My girlfriend is the most beautiful woman in the world, and I'm lucky as hell to have her. I finish the race and come in fourth, which is annoying because I needed to place in order to open the next track. I look down at Heather, but she's distracted with whatever the latest happenings are in her social media feed.

I smile at her and stroke her cheek gently before looking back at the TV. I can feel her smile when I do it.

"I love you, honey," she tells me and turns her face to kiss the palm of my hand.

"Love you, too, angel."

I pick up the controller to start another race when Heather gasps.

"What's wrong?"

"Elena was kissing some random at a club last night."

"What the hell?" I'm confused and also angry at the news.

Elena is the girlfriend of one of my best friends, Gabriel. He's the lead singer of the band I'm in, Cruise Control. They've been having some trouble lately, but I didn't think that she would cheat on him. Heather shows me the picture, and it's definitely Elena kissing a man that is absolutely not Gabriel.

I grab my phone and send a text to Gabriel.

Dude, we saw the pics of Elena. Are you okay?

My phone starts buzzing almost immediately, and I'm not surprised by the name displayed on it, 'Gabriel Knight.'

"Hey, there, Harrison Fletcher," Gabriel says dramatically when I answer his call.

"You don't sound like you're upset by the news. Have you seen the pics?" I ask him.

"Yeah, I have," his tone sobers, and he adds, "I feel bad about Elena."

I'm confused. "What do you mean, 'you feel bad about Elena.' Didn't she cheat on you?"

Heather has given up on her phone and is paying avid attention to our conversation, now. She's signaling to me to put him on speaker, and I shake my head at her.

"No, she didn't. Is Heather there?" Gabriel asks me.

"Yeah, she is."

"You might as well put me on speaker. I know you'll tell her everything, anyway." He laughs.

I mean…he's not wrong. I would tell Heather everything he said to me. I put him on speaker and tell him that I've done it.

"Hey, Heather. You having a good weekend?"

"Better than you, I would've thought," she tells him. "Why are you not crying into your Cheerios about those pictures, Gabriel Knight?"

Heather has narrowed her eyes, and I've realized what she's

thinking. Oh. This makes complete sense. Gabriel sounds happy. Happier than I've heard him sound in two years.

"Elena and I broke up a couple of days ago."

"Why didn't you tell us?" Heather asks him.

"Do you need to know everything that happens in my life, Heather?"

"Maybe. So, you're obviously completely and utterly heartbroken about it, I can tell."

I raise an eyebrow at her and give a small shake of my head. Her tone seems fine, but I can hear the bitchiness behind what she's saying.

Gabriel just laughs, though. "Okay, well yeah. I'm fine with it and with those pictures. Elena can kiss whoever she wants because Ariana and I are back together."

Heather hisses quietly under her breath, and I cough to cover it. There's silence for a moment, and I realize that I should say something.

"That's awesome, dude. I'm happy for you."

Heather's eyebrows raise, and I shrug at her. What am I meant to say? Okay, so he's back with the girl who broke his heart two years ago. I can't say that I didn't expect this to happen from the moment she showed up at our concert a few months ago.

"Thanks, Harrison. It's just..." he pauses for a few seconds, "...I'm just so fucking happy, guys. I can't believe she's back in my life. I'm kind of in shock, to be honest. But yeah. That's the deal. So, no, Elena didn't cheat, and to answer your text, Harrison, I'm more than okay. I feel like I'm fucking flying."

I smile and say, "I really am happy for you, Gabriel. Tell Ariana I said hi. We'll see you sometime soon, no doubt."

"Yeah, I was going to ask if you're okay with her coming to your birthday party."

"Of course. You didn't even need to ask. She's more than welcome to come."

"Thanks, dude. Well, I'll talk to you guys later. Have a great day!" Gabriel says, then he hangs up.

There is complete silence in our apartment after the call ends. I'm in shock, and I think that Heather is, too. I look down at her, and she looks up at me. I can remember, vividly, how terrible it was when Ariana and Gabriel broke up.

I can understand it; I wouldn't be able to handle it if Heather and I ever broke up. That concept is so foreign to me, and I frown. No. I don't ever want to be without Heather. She's still looking at me, and she's so beautiful, my angel.

Heather shakes her head. "He's making a mistake."

Okay, so she's feisty and troublesome and says the first thing that comes to her mind, but I love her more than anything or anyone that ever existed. I can't stop the smile that comes across my face.

"Why the hell are you smiling? This isn't funny, Harrison." She frowns.

I smile even wider and have to resist the urge to laugh. I'm going to ask Heather to marry me. We've been together for ten years, and I can't believe I haven't done it yet. If there's one thing that I've absolutely certain of, it's that I don't ever want to be without her.

ACKNOWLEDGMENTS

This book wouldn't be what it is if it weren't for the people that supported me along the way.

Mum – You get top billing this time. You are my number-one fan. You're the person who tells me that my books are a bit of all right. I know that you know I wrote those sexy scenes, and you know that I know that you read them. I love our long arguments, and discussions about my characters, and I'm sorry that I'm writing this acknowledgement to you instead of more of *The Baby*!

Ally – Oof! You rode this rollercoaster with me, hard. It was a wild ride and I'm glad that I had you with me. This one was definitely a rough ride, and I don't know if I would've survived it if I hadn't had you living through it and splooshing over Harrison and Sebastian with me.

Daena – I adore you and our writing discussions. I cannot thank you enough for being my sounding board in the middle of the night when all of the Aussies around me are sleeping. Thanks, my gorgeous, insomniac ex-pat, for being available nearly 24/7 for me to talk to.

Divia – Holy crap, you're amazing. One of the best people I've come across in this journey. The fact that you love and believe in my books as much as you do means so much to me. I don't think that I will ever be able to thank you enough for reaching out to me. I'm still amazed. You. Rock.

Kathy – My favourite one-star reviewer. Goodreads insisted that replying to your review was a bad idea, but I'm so glad that I did. I might have only turned *The Album's* review into three stars on its rewrite, but I'm glad you loved this enough to give it five because I don't think I could ever rewrite it (famous last words, probably!). Thanks for being awesome and a great cheerleader!

Maddy – The most voracious rock star romance reader that I know. I'm so stoked that you like my series. I defer to you for all things rock star romance, your knowledge is wide-ranging and sound.

All my advance readers – Thank you all for taking the time to read my work, give your feedback, and encouraging me to keep writing.

Dana Hopkins – I appreciate the time and effort that you put into editing this book. I might have cut next to nothing because I'm a terrible writer who can't kill her darlings, but your feedback was helpful in ways I'll never be able to explain.

Mark and Lorna Reid – I swear, *next* book is the one where you'll have oodles of time to do your thing. Thank you again, from the bottom of my heart for doing everything you can to make my book as wonderful as if it was your own. You two are the fricking best.

Damien – I always leave you 'til (second) last because you are the backbone of me being able to do this at all. Without you, this wouldn't be possible at all. Thank you for putting up with an absentee wife who spent five weeks in her own world while writing and only coming up for air to do the bedtime routine. You know I love you for it and, hopefully, the people mentioned below will send you some good wishes when they read this and realise what you sacrifice for their reading pleasure. ;)

My readers – If you're reading this, thank you. I hope that you enjoyed this book even a tiny bit as much as I enjoyed it. This one, it means so much to me, I was deeply and emotionally invested in it, and I hope that you were, too. I know, this book is a *lot.* I like to give people somewhere to escape to, but I'm not sure this book does that. It certainly gives you a place to…feel a lot of feelings that aren't your own? So there's that. You're the best. My readers are the best readers, and *that* is the hill that I will die on.

ABOUT THE AUTHOR

Siân Ceinwen lives in Western Australia with her husband and two sons. She grew up with a love of telling or writing stories for her friends to read and enjoy.

The Wedding is the follow-up to her debut novel, *The Album*, and is the second in four stories about the members of Cruise Control.

If you enjoyed this, please share it with your friends, and please write a review on Amazon or Goodreads.

It would really be appreciated, as this helps more people to discover the book. Reviews assist with the algorithms used by these platforms to display books, so every little bit helps indie authors to get noticed.

You can also join Siân on Facebook or Twitter for all the latest news on the Cruise Control series of novels.

Were you wondering what Gabriel was thinking and feeling the night that he met Ariana? If you're interested in receiving "The First Song", which is the first chapter of *The Album*, from Gabriel's point of view, you can get a copy of that by subscribing to Sian Ceinwen's newsletter here.

CPSIA information can be obtained
at www.ICGtesting.com
Printed in the USA
LVHW110950270720
661486LV00016BA/1933/J

9 780648 362197